Fire
of the Sun

R. B. Clague

Fire of the Sun

R.B. Clague

For Jakob, Sam, and Chrissy.

CHAPTER ONE

Rob Swift stood in front of the building. He recognised it in an instant as the police station he'd attended when he'd last been in Melbourne, almost two years ago. It was daytime, in the summer. He could feel the warmth in the air, hear the birds singing in the surrounding trees and looked on as people went about their business.

The birds with sudden abruptness stopped their cheerful chorus and a deep silence seemed to fill the air. He knew something was going to happen, although he had no clue as to what. He heard a rumbling, like the approach of thunder and as he watched, the building exploded in front of him. The roof seemed to shoot upwards and then fall back down, imploding in on itself and a huge, yellow fireball erupted from out of the front doors, spraying glass and metal fragments out into the street like missiles launched from the turret of a great gun. The sound was deafening. Rob shielded his face as debris from the explosion launched itself from the building and across the street, only to pass through him as though he was a ghost.

The shockwave from the explosion knocked over several telegraph poles, sending them careering into the passing traffic, smashing the roof of a truck and causing nearby cars to collide. High voltage cables whipped along the street and relieved several people of their lives in an instant.

Rob stood frozen, stunned. He'd never before witnessed a scene of such absolute destruction and it took him a few seconds to process it all. For a long moment, there was nothing but dead silence, interrupted only by the sound of the burning, collapsing building and the sizzle of the electrical cables, as they charred the flesh off the bodies they touched. As people began to come to their senses, the screaming and yelling for help began as those trapped in the wreckage of the vehicles and those who came face to face with the dead began to come to grips with the reality of their situation.

Rob moved towards the burning building, instinctively dodging between the cars and the gathering crowd, some who'd come as shocked spectators, and others who were already lending their assistance to those in need. He could hear the approaching sirens of the police, ambulance, and fire brigade in the distance and was glad help would be there soon. He hoped it was quick for those who'd died and they didn't feel any pain or the anguish of knowing they were about to lose their lives. He reached the outside stairs and went up towards the now non-existent sliding glass doors at the top. He could tell at a glance much of the building was unstable, or was burning away fast with the intense fires that seemed to be everywhere.

He walked inside, knowing he couldn't be hurt, but more than a little apprehensive about what he was going to find. He took the stairs to the first floor, passing several bodies on the way, who may have made it outside and lived had the explosion occurred only a couple of minutes later. The place was full of smoke and he could hear a number of voices close by, calling for help or just screaming in agony. He knew in his present form he couldn't help any of them, but what he could do was concentrate on the reasons he'd come inside in the first place. He saw Tony Green first. He was dead, lying on the floor, his lifeless eyes gazing at the ceiling, the back of his head crushed by a huge lump of concrete that had fallen from the ceiling as the explosion ripped through the building. Rob knelt down beside him and wished he could've closed his eyes. He was a good man and a person he considered a friend, who certainly didn't deserve to die like this.

Rob stood and looked over at Carbone's office on the other side of the room. He could see a shoeless foot sticking out of the doorway and knew it belonged to Clare before he even got there. Her death had been different from that of her colleague and she had a large shard of glass sticking out of the left hand side of her neck, severing her carotid artery. She would have bled out in a moments, in long spurts with each successive beat of her heart. Her blood coated a far wall of the office, like some bizarre, crimson abstract painting and made him feel sick to his stomach. Rob moved around to the detective's desk, hoping to find something that would give him a clue as to whether this was happening right now, or if it was a glimpse of the future. If this was the future, he might be able to warn Clare and Tony in time and save their lives, as well as the countless others who were also in the building.

Much to his amazement, he found Clare's computer was still operating. He looked at the bottom of the screen and saw the date as the 28th August 2010. 'Oh, shit, that's tomorrow, not counting the time difference. I'm gonna have to get to a phone and that's not going to be easy.'

Rob sat up in a cold sweat, fully awake, feeling the energy it sapped from his body every time he had a dream that encompassed some use of his psychic sight. He grabbed the jug of water from beside his cot and drank, hoping to wash away the sense of dread he felt in every part of his being, as though the water could make him clean inside, although he ultimately knew it wouldn't. He threw his legs over the side of his cot, liking the feel of the cool floor under his feet. He reached over to the dresser, removed a box of matches from the drawer, struck one, and set aflame a candle, bathing the room in a soft, amber glow. 'Jesus,' he said, 'I haven't got long.'

He jumped up and paced the floor, not knowing exactly what to do first. He put on his robe, which hung behind the door of the little room, grabbed his cigarettes and the candle, left the cell, and entered the hallway. He was careful to be quiet, lest his echoes woke those who slept in the nearby rooms. He continued walking until he came to a small bench, where he sat, removed his cigarettes and looked out to the east. He waited until the light began to appear and then blew out the candle, smiling as he watched the blue smoke dissipate into the wind. The cigarette tasted awful after a year of abstinence.

He watched on in awe as the bright sun of Tibet rose over the snow-capped mountaintops of the Himalayas and almost gasped at the beauty in front of him. He knew he had to go, to leave this place and he wouldn't be coming back for a very long time, if ever. There was so much more to learn, so many things to contemplate with regards to his psychic abilities and the development of them that leaving would almost seem to be cutting off his education whilst in kindergarten.

'You have to leave,' said a man's voice from behind, which was so familiar, it didn't even cause Rob to look up. 'Your destiny lies elsewhere.'

'You really think so? There's so much more I want to learn.'

'There's also a chance you may one day, return.'

'We both know that's not going to be the case. Once I've gone from here, I won't be coming back.'

The old man smiled and it seemed to Rob right then another sunrise had just occurred. 'Perhaps, Rob, you've already learned the lessons that will enable you to progress, to either reach the blissful place, or to become a more mature and wise man, if you're to return again in your next life.'

Rob laughed. 'Look, I know you guys believe in all that Nirvana, reincarnation and karma stuff, and if I was to remain here, I'd probably end up believing it, too, Mr. Betung, but I haven't been here that long and you haven't quite convinced me, yet.'

Betung hugged Rob, laughing. 'You cannot blame me, can you? The core of all religions and callings is to recruit others.'

'No, I guess not,' replied Rob moving the old man backwards, clutching his arms, to take a good look at him. 'I'm really going to miss you, Mr. Betung and the others who've assisted you to teach me.'

'I, too, will miss you, Robert. You have been a good and keen student and courageous, to say the least. We have put you through a lot over the past two years and you have excelled yourself. I think you have others things to do, other people to help. It is time to go. It is too bad the power is out, it may have made things easier, but that is just not how things are. You'd have gone anyway.'

'Yeah, I know. I need to help my friends. It's something I can't really avoid. I'll prepare to leave as soon as I've had breakfast and the sun is properly up.'

'Yes, it would be best,' said the old man smiling. 'It will take you a half day to reach the village on foot. I hope you can make it in time.'

'Do you already know about what's going to happen to Clare and Tony?'

'You are my student,' replied Betung, 'you are never out of my sight, even when you sleep. I saw the destruction of the police station in Australia. I am also aware of how helpful your next telephone call will be. I saw you would return there, to help find this man. You are ready.'

'Will I be successful? Will I get him?'

'I cannot see that far into the void,' answered the old man, 'so I cannot tell you. I know if anybody can, you can, Robert, or you will at least give it your best shot.'

'Thank you,' said Rob, rising and bowing to the old monk. 'I'll go and eat and will then prepare for the journey.'

The old monk rose from the bench, 'I'll come with you,' he said, 'I might never get a chance to break bread with you again and it will provide me with an extra memory of you when you are gone.'

The two men dressed in the orange robes of the order walked along one of the many hallways and entered a small dining room where a dozen of the monks were already enjoying their morning meal. Rob took some bread and fruit, as did the old monk. They sat at a table not far from the front and ate in silence, without uttering a word between them, although when Rob looked closely, he could see the subtle change in the expressions on their faces as they conversed with their minds. He surmised that if he could've heard the many voices actually talking in the room, he would've thought he was in a crowded, noisy place, instead of the quietness that prevailed.

Rob cleaned off his plate and placed his utensils in a pile to be washed at the end of the meal, by the monks and devotees who were rostered for the week to take care of such duties. He headed for the door, eager to begin the journey to the nearby village, where he could get access to a phone.

He returned to his room and found his former western clothes, which had been stored in a cupboard for over a year and had a slightly musty smell about them. He hoped that once he got out into the clean air, the odour would soon go away. He dressed in a pair of blue jeans, a thick long-sleeved t-shirt and a woollen pullover. It certainly felt strange to be back dressed in civilian clothes. Over this, he put on a thick, blue parka with a hood to fight off the cold. He also wore thick woollen socks and pair of sturdy Colorado hiking boots, which he remembered fitted him perfectly. He wanted little else aside from his credit card and money, which he'd left within the monastery's safe, along with his passport. He reflected on the fact that he'd survived without money for the past year. His only currency had been in how hard he'd trained. If he trained well, which he always did, he would receive a decent ration of food and freedom. If on the other hand, the masters felt as a student he was not living up to his potential, he would receive punishment in small, subtle ways, at first, such as receiving a not-so-generous ration of food at the dining table. This was to warn the student, that if their game did not pick up, they faced expulsion. Rob had witnessed about a dozen expulsions of this type throughout the last year and counted himself fortunate for not having been among them. He was sure for many of them it came a relief, realising they wouldn't have to live a life devoted to the practices of the order. It's a lot to ask of anyone to become a fully ordained monk, especially in this particular order, which is capable of penetrating the very essence of your mind and memories. No part of you lies untouched and not viewed by your master, and so everything about you is vulnerable to the one who teaches. Thus, you become more powerful, by confronting the painful memories of your past and using more of your mind to concentrate on your abilities, while testing the water, to perhaps, see and utilise other powers of which you are unaware. It requires arduous training and full concentration.

Rob was sad to be leaving after such a short time, but in truth wasn't sure he would've made it through another twelve months, if the current regime of training was to continue, or as expected, to increase. The emotional and physical toll of the training, while rewarding, had been excruciatingly exacting and he was in a way, glad to be able to be able to remove himself from it with the respect of his masters intact.

When he was packed, Rob went to the main entrance of the monastery and there he met Betung again, waiting patiently for his arrival. 'I've come to say one final goodbye, my dear friend. I hope all is well with you in the days to come and remember; your training will hold you in good stead in those times of need, or danger.'

'Thank you,' said Rob, hugging the old monk like a son hugs a father.

'There's one more thing I need to say to you.'

'What's that?'

'You are a powerful man now, Rob. More powerful in your mind than most you will ever encounter. Remember, this is a blessing and a gift and one you mustn't abuse, despite the temptation to do so.'

'Yeah, thanks, I'll try to remember that,' said Rob as he picked up his backpack and made ready to leave. 'I really wish I didn't have to go.'

'I know,' replied the old monk, 'but wishing for something else will not get you to where you want to be. Go now, save your friends and bring some justice to the world.'

'I'll try,' said Rob, stepping out of the monastery door and into the cold of the morning. 'Thirty miles through cold and snow, isn't that far, really.'

'No,' agreed Betung. 'It's not that far. Stay along the main road and you may get a lift with a farmer. They might only travel at walking pace, but at least you can rest and get out of a cart and move your muscles as you go. Getting out of the cart to walk, will also keep you warm.'

'Thanks,' replied Rob with a wave, as he began to depart the monastery, walking down a long cobblestone path to the tunnel and then over the bridge. Without further adieu, he disappeared into the thick forest of trees in the surrounding countryside. The old man looked on for a while, then turned and walked back into the monastery, closing the door behind him. 'Good luck,' he whispered.

Rob walked out onto the roadway. He looked both up and down, but didn't spy any vehicles to assist him to get to the village, He decided to set off to the village, placing one foot in front of the other and hurrying for all he was worth. Betung had been right about the physical exercise of walking keeping him warm, and Rob could feel the perspiration building up inside his parka and zipped it open for a while, enabling him to cool down. After about an hour, he stopped and thought about how far he'd come, which, he estimated, to have been about five kilometres. This left about twenty-five kilometres to go. He hoped someone would come along and pick him up, soon. Until then though, all he could do was continue to walk as briskly as he could. He'd get to the village one way or anther, even if he contracted a mild case of hypothermia on the way.

The snow began to fall harder, forcing Rob to hunker down into his parka and battle fierce winds that travelled up the road and buffeted against him. 'Oh, great,' he said with some sarcasm. Just when he was about to give up the notion he'd be picked up, the loud blare of a horn ripped through the air behind him, almost frightening him out of his wits, causing him to jump and turn in astonishment at the same time. In front of him, he saw a small, yellow van, with a single driver and no passengers, who waved at him to climb aboard. Rob ran though the almost blinding snow and found the passenger door open. He swung himself inside the cabin and smiled at the older, Tibetan fellow who drove the vehicle.

'Where you going to?' the driver asked.

'I'm headed into the village. I need to use a phone, it's very important.'

'Yeah, okay, I take you,' said the older fellow. 'I go to the village. The road to village is going to be hard. The snow makes driving dangerous. It will be good to have another strong man to help if I should slip off the road.'

'Yeah, no problem,' smiled Rob. 'If we get in the shit, I'll help you. You can count on me.'

'Okay,' said the old Tibetan fellow as he pulled his cap back down over his ears and put the van into gear, 'all right, we go.'

It was fortunate they had no mechanical breakdowns or worsening weather conditions on the way to the village, but the going was certainly treacherous and although they drove at a maximum speed of about fifteen kilometres per hour, they aquaplaned across many a snow-soaked roadway. They were lucky not to have drifted totally off the side of the road on more than a couple of occasions.

A little over an hour of this hair-raising experience, the two men entered the village, with more than some small cheer erupting from each of their lips. 'Thank you for coming with me,' said the old man as he dropped Rob off in the centre of the village.

'You're welcome,' replied Rob jumping from the van out onto the road. 'I'm just glad nothing went wrong.'

'Yes, me too,' said the old man with a toothless smile. 'Goodbye.' Rob closed the van door and headed for the general store, where he knew there was a telephone. There, the proprietor, a Chinese man by the name of Lee, greeted him and gladly accepted his credit card as payment for a long-distance call.

Rob took out Clare's number and hoped she wasn't asleep and if she was, well, that was just tough luck, because he figured that saving her life, might be worth the forfeiture of her slumber. He connected with the operator, dialled Clare's office first in Melbourne, and was surprised when she picked up the phone in the first three rings. 'Hello, Clare Carbone, here.'

'Hi, Clare, it's Rob Swift. I'm calling from Tibet.'

'Oh, my God,' Clare replied with unrestrained surprise. 'Rob, how are you?'

'I'm sorry Clare, but there isn't time for pleasantries. There's a bomb in the police station and you have to get everybody out. I saw it in a vision. You need to make sure you block off the streets a hundred metres either side of the police station. There's going to be power poles coming down and electrocuting people. Hurry, Clare.'

'Do you know where it is, Rob?'

'No, just evacuate the place and hurry!'

'Okay, thanks, Rob,' said Clare as she hung up the phone. 'Tony,' she screamed at the top of her voice, 'there's a bomb in the building. I want you to sound the alarm. We need to get everybody out, right now.'

Tony hit the evacuation button on the nearby wall and the whole police station seemed to light up as sirens blared and lights flashed as a hundred well-trained police exited the building on Clare's instructions. She used her mobile outside the building to contact both the commissioner of police, who in turn contacted the head of traffic branch to seal off the area, to prevent injuries if the bomb went off.

'So, this is all on the say-so of your psychic, Mr. Swift, is it, Sergeant Carbone?'

'Yes, sir,' replied Clare, 'but I believe him. He wouldn't have called from Tibet if he didn't believe what he saw to be true. I trust him.'

'I know you do,' replied the commissioner's gruff voice over the phone, 'and he has done us some favours in the past. Well, it's all on you, if it turns out to be untrue. Are you prepared for that, Clare?'

'Yes, sir, I am, but like I say, I trust him. We need the bomb squad down here to check this place out and either give us the all clear to go back to work, or deal with whatever's been planted.'

'I'll make sure they're on their way,' said the commissioner. 'Keep me posted.'

'Yes, sir,' replied Clare. She ended the call and waited outside the evacuation zones, which had now been taped off with crime scene tape that stretched across entirely across St. Kilda Road's three lanes of traffic. She rang Tony on his mobile phone and found him in the nearby crowd.

'So what do we do now?' he asked.

'We wait for the bomb squad to come and do their thing. If they don't find anything, I'll personally be on the next plane to Tibet, where I'll find Rob Swift, and slowly strangle the life out of him.'

'Sounds like a fair deal,' said Tony with a laugh.

From behind them, came a loud rumbling and the St. Kilda Road Police complex exploded upwards and outwards into the street. Even from the distance at which they stood, it was plain to see that the building had crumbled inwards and that ravaging fires inside were now burning off whatever property or furnishings were contained within the interior. Rob had also been right about the power poles coming down in the middle of the street and had anyone been in contact with those deadly electrical snakes, they'd surely have lost their lives.

'Jesus, it was lucky he called,' said Tony. 'There would've been a couple of hundred coppers in that building when that thing went off.'

'Yeah, not to mention, the passersby, too,' said Clare. 'It would've been a disaster.'

Clare's mobile phone rang in her pocket. She fished it out and put it to her ear. 'Hello, Clare Carbone, here.'

'Hello, Clare, it's Commissioner Davidson here. I need you and Green in my office within a half hour, is that understood?

'Yes, sir,' replied Clare. 'May I ask you what it's in relation to?'

'There's been a list of demands delivered to me, and the perpetrator has taken responsibility for his actions. He calls himself Fire of the Sun and says that Melbourne will look like the fire of the sun, if we don't acquiesce to his demands, thoroughly and quickly. We'll talk more when you get to my office.'

CHAPTER TWO

Rob boarded the little plane and sat in the back passenger seat, beside a young American man, who reminded him of his colleague, Matt Dearborn, who'd been murdered in the Esplanade hotel, with his movie-star looks, blonde hair and muscular physique.

'Hi, I'm Danny,' said the American holding out his hand.

'Yeah, I'm Rob, glad to meet you.'

'You're Australian, aren't you?'

'Yeah, that's right. So, where in the states are you from?'

'I, my good friend, hail from the honourable state of Texas.'

'So, what does a Texan do in Tibet?'

'I'm a doctor,' replied Danny, 'at least I will be, once I've done this rotation and get the credits for my medical degree.'

'So, you'll be like an M.D?'

'Yeah, that's right,' drawled the Texan.

'Have you got any plans to specialise?'

'I haven't made up my mind yet,' replied Danny. 'I've only just managed to get through my degree. I wouldn't mind working for a few years, for some international organisation, like the World Health Organisation. I kind of liked it here. The people are beautiful, in their own special way.'

'That seems very noble, very worthwhile,' said Rob with a smile. 'I'm sure you'll learn a lot and be a help to a great many people.'

'What about you, Rob, why are you in Tibet?' Danny asked as he tried to take his mind off the plane, as it bounced along the rough runway and burst upwards into the air, causing audible sighs of relief from the passengers and pilot.

'I studied for a while at a monastery,' replied Rob. 'It was a good place to take some time out.'

'I see,' said the American, 'so you're going back to the good old land of Oz?'

'Yeah, I'm heading to Melbourne. My plane takes off from the main airport in Delhi at six in the morning. I'll have to find some flea-bitten hotel to hold up in for the night. Then it's a straight shot to Oz, with a one night stopover in Singapore.'

'I'm in the same boat,' said Danny with a laugh. 'My plane doesn't leave there until eight, so I'm going to have to find a place to sleep, too. Could we look together? I noticed more than a few people seem to have a severe dislike of Americans. It might be better to have you do the asking, without the bias that goes with my accent.'

'Sure,' said Rob. 'I'll help you to get a room. In fact, if the two of us chip in, we might be able to afford a suite in one of the more expensive establishments.'

'Sounds like a plan to me, brother,' said Danny with a smile.

The plane drifted on through the sky, thrown about by ever-present turbulence, resulting from thermal winds that came off the mountains, which caused it to plummet a thousand feet or more in a few seconds and felt like it could crash at any moment. After many hours of this fly-by-the-seat-of-your-pants type experience, the Cessna came to a wobbly landing at the Indian airport of Delhi.

'Wow, that was really something,' said Danny as the two of them disembarked from the plane and looked around.

'You know, I haven't been near a city in over a year,' said Rob. 'The monastery's pretty isolated.'

'Me either,' said Danny with a laugh, 'I've been spending my time in the villages and when I wasn't doing that, I was trekking to other obscure places to provide medical aid. I wouldn't mind a drink, to tell you the truth.'

'Sounds good to me,' agreed Rob.

The two of them grabbed their gear, threw it onto their backs, walked away from the airport, and jumped into a taxi, which turned out to be an old Beetle, almost on its last legs. The driver was a nice old fellow, who helped them with their luggage and took them to a bar.

'What's the best hotel in town?' Rob asked as he paid the driver, adding a significant tip as he removed his and Danny's backpacks from the trunk of the car.

The driver continued to follow them inside. 'Probably, you want the Peregrine hotel, sir. My cousin runs it. If you want me to make a booking for you, I can.'

'What sort of rooms do they have there? Danny asked. 'Can we get like a suite with a few rooms and a good television? I haven't watched TV for an eternity. Oh, and we need something in the bar as well.'

'I think I can arrange that, sir,' said the old fellow who brought out a pen and wrote both their names on a scrap piece of paper. 'You'll find it if you turn left as you come out of the bar and walk for about five minutes along the main road. It is easy to see, a big, white place. The name is out front.'

'What are the chances of taking our stuff there with you?' Rob asked. 'There's another tip in it for you.'

'Yes, not a problem,' replied the driver, 'that is, if you don't mind putting them back in the trunk. My cousin and his staff can get them to your rooms from out of the car. I am a bit of an advanced age for that sort of exertion.'

'Okay, what can I get you two fellas?' asked a grey haired from behind the bar.

'I'll have a scotch, with ice,' replied Danny.

'I'll just have a beer,' said Rob, 'anything Australian will do, if you have it.'

'No problemo,' said the middle-aged, Australian man who served them.

'We'll be back in a minute,' said Rob, 'we've just got to go and put our backpacks back into the taxi.'

'No worries,' laughed the bartender, 'it'll probably take me that long to get them ready.'

When the two of them arrived back, Rob's beer and Danny's scotch were waiting on the bar. They sat down and Danny pulled out a fifty-dollar American note and handed it over to the bartender. 'It's my treat,' said the young American, 'and well-deserved thank you, Rob, for helping me to get a room with the minimum of fuss.'

'If you insist,' laughed Rob. 'It was nothing, really. I'll only accept if you let me buy you breakfast in the morning.'

'Then it's a done deal,' said Danny with an almost boyish chuckle, 'now drink up, my fine Aussie friend.'

The two men spent the evening consuming about half a dozen drinks each, and talking to the bartender, who was a native of Perth and had purchased the bar with his wife, an Indian national.

They felt somewhat inebriated as they exited the bar, walked out into the street and made their way to the Peregrine hotel. It was just getting dark, and the street seemed to have transformed into a market in the time they'd been inside. Vendors sold every conceivable type of goods from stalls located along the street fronts and food was available in abundance. There was a festive feel about it, as music played from speakers placed in the corner of a crossroads, and bright lights lit up the street as each stall tried to outdo each other, trying to attract the most customers. The streets were quite crowded and many passing people smiled at the two men, as they made their way through the throng, and headed toward the hotel.

At last, they arrived at the Peregrine, which was just as the taxi driver had described it. What he hadn't done was to explain the sheer beauty and majesty of the place, which had more than a passing resemblance to Tara, from *Gone with the Wind*.

'Wow, check this place out,' said Danny with a wide, slightly drunken smile. 'Are you sure we can afford it?'

'Yeah, come on, let's go,' replied Rob leading the way.

They walked into the plush foyer and headed straight for the main desk. There, they spoke to man called Tee, who explained he was the cousin of the taxi driver and told them their rooms were ready, and all they had to do was to show identification and their credit cards. Rob and Danny produced their passports, their credit cards, signed the guest register, and were promptly escorted to their three-bedroom suite on the second floor of the building by a man in a polished red and blue uniform. Rob decided to take the stairs when the elevator became slow. 'It's only one flight up, how far could it be?'

'Not that far, I guess,' replied Danny, 'I'm game.'

'Which way is it to the stairs?' Rob asked the little man in the uniform.

'That way,' replied the porter, 'but it is highly irregular for a guest to take the stairs.'

Rob laughed. 'Then I guess that means we're not regular guests. Coming, Danny?'

The two of the found the stairway and began the ascent. About halfway up, Rob stopped the young American and asked him to look down. The plush foyer was aglow in a soft, gentle yellow light and was captivating by any standard. 'If you took the lift, you'd never get to see that.'

'Yeah, I guess you're right,' said Danny wistfully.

The little porter followed them up the stairs with a smile on his face and led them to their rooms, which he unlocked and gave over possession of the keys to Rob, who tipped him with an Australian twenty-dollar note. 'Thank you, sir, very generous,' he said as he backed away from them and then turned back into the hall.

The suite itself, like the rest of the hotel, boasted plush and comfortable furnishings, like the two queen-sized beds contained in each of the bedrooms. They each had their own separate mini-bar and television.

'Quite a setup,' said Rob as he selected a bedroom, stowed his stuff and came out holding three small bottles of scotch and three cans of beer. 'I'll tell you what, how about I swap the scotch here, for the beers in your fridge? I hate to mix drinks.'

'You got a deal,' replied Danny with a laugh, 'just give me a minute and I'll bring them out.'

Rob walked out and inspected the sunken lounge room, with its enormous black leather lounge, and the big screen TV embedded into the wall above him. 'Yeah, not bad,' he nodded with approval as he wandered into the kitchen, which was spotless and clean to the point of sterility. He looked in a cupboard above his head and found some large glasses, took two down and placed them on the bench in front of him. He also found some ice in the freezer, which he was sure Danny would be glad of anyway.

A short while later, the young American emerged from his bedroom, carrying the alcohol. He'd changed his clothes and now only wore only a t-shirt, a pair of tracksuit pants and some woollen slippers, obviously acclimatising quickly to the warmth of the room. 'It feels good to get free of all that heavy shit you gotta wear out there. I feel like I've lost five or ten pounds by just taking it off.'

'I'm not going to stay up late,' said Rob putting the beer into the fridge, grabbing the tray of ice from the freezer, and placing it down on the bench for Danny to see. 'I've got to get to the airport early in the morning. Therefore, I might just have one or two beers in front of the big TV and then head off to bed. 'Could you do me a favour, if you would, Danny?'

'Sure,' replied the American, 'just ask.'

'Don't turn your telly up loud during the night. After sleeping for a year in that monastery, I need quiet to get to some shuteye.'

'No worries, Rob, I'll be as quiet as a church mouse.'

The two men sat in the living room of the suite and put on the television. The bombing of the police headquarters in Melbourne was big news. One of the reporters at the scene, a nondescript man dressed in a dark suit, said it was a miracle no one had been hurt or killed. 'No group or individual has yet taken responsibility for the carnage,' he added speaking into the camera, 'so the authorities are unaware as to whether the bomb had a terrorist angle to it, or whether it was planted by some disturbed, disgruntled person in the community. There's no way to know that yet.'

'Man, that's a trip,' said Danny, 'I hope they catch the bastard.'

'Yeah, they will,' replied Rob.

'How do you know?'

'Because I'm going to help them get him.'

'Are you a cop or something?'

'No,' laughed Rob as he finished off the last of his beer and stood with some tired effort. 'Well, they've actually offered me some employment, but I'm not officially a cop, per se. Anyway, it was nice to meet you, Danny, and I hope your trip goes well.'

'Thank you,' said the younger American man extending his hand, which Rob took. 'It was cool to meet you, too, Rob, and I hope you have a good trip back to Oz.'

The two of them separated as Rob took off to his bedroom, leaving Danny to catch up on the news in the living room. He entered his bedroom and lay on the bed for a moment, thinking, and then picked up the phone receiver from the cradle, on the bedside table. He entered his details with the operator and became connected to Clare Carbone's mobile phone in Australia.

'Hello, Clare Carbone here.'

'Hi, Clare, it's Rob. Sorry we couldn't talk much the other day when I phoned you. Other things took priority, at the time.

Clare laughed aloud. 'Thank God you did call. You saved many lives, you know. So, have you seen something else?'

'No,' replied Rob, 'I just wanted you to know I'm coming back to Australia. I'd like to help you with your little problem. Can you get the paperwork together, to get me assigned as the "admin" person assigned to the case, before I get there? It might make things a little easier.'

Will do,' replied Clare, 'I've just come from a meeting with the commissioner. I don't really want to say anymore on the phone, but I'm glad you're joining us. When do you get here?'

'The day after tomorrow, your time, at about nine in the morning, I think.'

'Okay, I'll organise to meet you at the airport, if I can. Welcome aboard.'

'Okay, see you then,' said Rob, putting down the phone. He managed to set his alarm for seven, and then completely crashed onto the bed and for once, he didn't dream, but slumbered like a baby, until the terrible realisation of the next day came thundering down upon him, crashing through his brain like a bulldozer in a landfill.

'Oh my God,' he wheezed as he reached out and turned off the alarm. He managed to get himself out of bed and went to the bathroom, where he splashed water over his face to wake up. He looked at his reflection in the mirror, letting the cool droplets fall from his chin to his chest and was not at all pleased with what he saw. 'God, you look like a fuckin' train wreck. Coffee, Jesus, I need coffee.'

He went to the kitchen, turned on the light and found an ample supply of milk, contained in small sachets, in the fridge, along with the other condiments needed to provide a morning beverage. He checked the electric jug for water, washed it out, then filled it and snapped on the button as he replaced it in its stand. He sat for a while at the kitchen table and just rubbed his eyes as he got his thoughts together. 'Panadol,' he mumbled as he retreated into his bedroom and retrieved a packet of the painkillers, which he placed on the long, white table and went to prepare his coffee. 'Yep,' he said to himself; 'not more than twenty-fours out of that monastery and you're already having a coffee and Panadol breakfast.'

He took his coffee with two sugars and gulped down three Panadol with the first mouthful and then finished it off, with a somewhat dreary, tired look on his face, as he came to terms with both what he had to do, and the after effects of the six beers he'd had last night. When his coffee was a memory, he headed for the shower and freshened himself up, with a long soaking, and an invigorating drying off, as he made his way to his bedroom and dressed in a fresh set of clothes from his backpack. He looked at the clock, saw that it was almost five-fifteen, and knew that he didn't have a whole lot of time to get to the airport.

From his bedroom, he called the reception desk and arranged for a taxi to take him to the terminal in half an hour. He finished dressing, in his jeans, with his sneakers and woollen socks. 'Tell the driver that I'll give him a good tip,' he added as he hung up the phone.

Rob took a notepad and pen from the writing desk in the corner of the room. He opened the pad and left a two-word note, which simply said 'breakfast and Panadol'. He tore out the page, leaving it with a fifty-dollar note and two of the headache pills on the coffee table in the living room, for Danny to find when he woke.

'Okay, I'm outta here,' said Rob as he picked up his backpack and headed for the foyer. He closed the door behind him, making sure it didn't bang on the way out and then made his way down the staircase and into the main foyer of the building. 'Hello,' he said to the woman behind the main the desk, 'I'm just checking out. My name's Rob Swift. I just wanted to pay for a phone call to Australia I made last night.'

'Very well, Mister Swift, I can arrange that,' she said with a bright smile.

He handed over his credit card and then after signing some paperwork, his checkout was completed.

'Thank you for staying with us, Mister Swift,' she said with such a genuine note of sincerity Rob thought she might even have meant it.

'The pleasure was mine,' said Rob flashing a shy, hungover smile. 'I ordered a taxi to be here. You by chance, haven't seen it?'

'If you go to the main entrance, I think you'll find the car you are waiting for,' she replied. 'The taxi drivers here can be very patient for a good-paying Australian fare. He'll turn up as you leave the front doors and will already be parked a short way up the road, even as we speak, keeping an eye out for you.'

Rob laughed and then took a second look at this beautiful woman, with the tied back hair, gorgeous dark eyes and the dry sense of humour. 'Thank you... Elizabeth,' he said reading the name from her uniform badge.

'You're welcome, Mister Swift,' replied the girl who smiled again and returned to her duties behind the desk.

Rob walked out to the front of the Peregrine and lit up a smoke, like some pseudo-protection from the chill of the early-morning air. He dragged on his cigarette for a couple of minutes, until a car horn blared and a small Mitsubishi van showed up in front of him. The driver opened the back door and Rob threw in his backpack and jumped in, glad the temperature inside the taxi was warm, and although it might have been a little ripe on the nose, it was still better than freezing his arse off out in the darkness. The driver was an older man with a balding head and a Fu Manchu moustache, who spoke little on the way to the airport. Rob was grateful for this small mercy, because the last thing he really felt like doing was engaging in witty repartee with another member of the human race. He asked the fellow in the front to call him when he got to the airport, arranged himself on the seat and promptly went back to sleep.

'Hey, Aussie-man, taxi here, at the airport, just how you want,' said the driver to wake Rob in the back seat.

'Oh, great,' replied Rob sitting up and stretching his arms. He looked outside the van and was glad to see the airport, except for maybe forty or fifty people, was almost deserted. There were plenty of places to sit, no long queues and if he found a corner and made himself comfortable, he might gain an extra half hour's sleep, before it was time to board.

He checked in his ticket and backpack, and then found a seat in the lounge. He sat for a moment, but was unable to doze as he had planned. He spied a newsagent not too far away and decided to go and look at what type of reading material was available. If he was lucky, he might strike upon a half-decent novel to wile away the hours before he got to Melbourne. He stood and headed across the tiled floor and went inside the mini bookstore, where much to his delight, he found a wide array of literature from which to choose. There were classics contained on the shelves such as Charles Dickens and Oscar Wilde, but also more contemporary novelists like Dean Koontz and

Stephen King. He opted for a smaller novella, *The Picture of Dorian Gray* by Oscar Wilde. He already knew the story and had a long time ago read the tale, but even today, the story still filled him with fascination, having left an indelible mark upon him during his teenage years. He remembered the hours he'd spent pondering the story as a young man, wondering about the duality of human beings, to be simultaneously both courageous and cowardly. It reminded him that the only thing he knew about people, was he knew little about people. He decided in the end, he was just better off keeping to himself, which was something being at the monastery had taught him well, with its huge walls and quiet halls of contemplation.

Shortly after he'd paid for the book, a loudspeaker sounded overhead, which informed him his plane would soon be departing and he needed to join the queue to hand over both his ticket and boarding pass. Rob went back to the lounge and took a place in the forming queue. It looked as though the plane was going to be loaded to capacity. There was huge line and many of the passengers in the lounge didn't even bother standing up, instead opting to wait for the line to recede. It seemed to Rob that the whole crowd had somehow managed to crawl out of the woodwork. He knew that they weren't there when he went to buy the book.

He got talking to an older Australian couple from Sydney, who told him that many of the people here now had asked specifically asked their drivers to bring them here at the last possible moment, given that Indian Airlines are at the best of times, unreliable. 'They're always running late, or getting grounded, or something,' said the old woman, 'but we like them,' she added, 'because they're cheap.'

'That they are,' agreed her husband. 'Hi,' I'm Don and this is Dawn Osborne,' said the older fellow extending his hand to Rob who took it and shook.

'I'm glad to meet you both,' he replied as they made their way onto the plane. 'I'm Rob... Rob Swift.'

'You're getting off in Sydney, too?' Dawn asked.

'No, I'm heading for Melbourne. I might even get off at Sydney, look around and take the sleeper train down, I'm not quite sure yet.'

'Yeah, I've done that,' said Don with a smile, 'for my business, a couple of times. It really is a very pleasant experience. If you get a sleeper cabin, you get breakfast provided, brought right to your door, and you can have a shower before you get off, to help freshen you up.'

'I think you've sold me,' laughed Rob as he handed over his ticket to the admin person at the boarding gate, who smiled and waved him on. Rob marched through the appointed gate, and found his way outside. A female airport staff member directed him over toward a Boeing 747, in front of which, a set of portable stairs were in the process of connecting to the door of the plane. He waited in line with the other passengers and then followed them blindly, when another female staff member announced it was now safe to cross to the plane begin boarding.

Rob held his place in line and then made his way through the queue and up onto the actual aircraft, where he gained a window seat on the left hand side of the plane. He noticed the temperature on board was quite comfortable, so he fished out the copy of *Dorian Gray* from his coat and then placed his gloves into the pocket of the parka. The parka itself he took off and stowed in the overhead storage compartment above his seat. He casually checked as he sat back down, that his wallet and passport were still in the back pocket of his jeans and breathed a silent sigh of relief when he discovered they were.

A red light flashed on above the cabin crew area, which proclaimed that all passengers must now be in their allocated seats, with their belts fastened. The captain said a few words over the PA, informing them the flight would be proceeding from Delhi to Singapore, where there would be a twenty-four hour stopover, before the plane headed to Sydney in the morning and then to Melbourne after that. 'We will be flying at an average altitude of thirty-six thousand feet. I've checked the radar and there are no major disruptions to weather patterns in the area, so we should arrive in Singapore at about eight in the morning. I hope that you all enjoy your flight. If you have any questions, please speak to our delightful cabin crew.'

Before the plane began to taxi down a main runway, the cabin crew performed the usual lectures about aeroplane safety and the correct procedures to undertake in the unlikely event of a crash, complete with whistles, inflatable lifejackets, and much pointing to the nearest available exits. They then seated themselves in the galley as they began to move. Rob looked out of the window and watched as the plane surged down the runway and took off into the sky, gunning its powerful jet engines as it climbed higher, as though it were escaping, leaving the city of Delhi behind like a spurned lover. Rob was pleased to find he didn't have to share the two seats with anyone else and thought he might even get some sleep on the way to Singapore.

The plane climbed for about ten minutes, and then levelled off. A red overhead sign lit up, informing the passengers they could move about the cabin. One of the flight attendants announced that trolleys would be soon be coming down the aisles, with food and drinks and should any of the passengers wished to purchase any of the goods, could they please have their money ready. She added they had both Australian and Indian currency and would happily provide change. Rob took ten dollars from his wallet, placed it in the top pocket of his t-shirt and began to read *The Picture of Dorian Gray*, while he waited for the cart to show up. It was an interesting book, beset with old language, almost forgotten by today's young people. He thought it a shame young people don't read as much these days. He could hardly blame them though. Everywhere they went, there were hugely expensive promotions, advertising this movie, and recommending that game. It must be a confusing world for a young person, with so much technology and information available at the flick of a switch, he thought as he put the book down and concentrated on the cart of goods in front of him.

'Hello, sir,' said a pretty, young Indian woman. 'Is there anything you'd like from our selection?'

'Yeah, I'll have a couple of cans of soda and that ham and tomato roll, if I could.'

'That'll be nine dollars, sir,' said the flight attendant handing over the roll and cans of cola.

'Thanks,' said Rob as he paid for the food. 'Keep the change.'

'Thank you,' said the flight attendant with a smile, as she moved onto the next row of seats in front of her.

Rob cracked a can and opened the plastic package, which stored the roll. He happily ate and then read for a couple of hours before finally stretching his arms and yawning. One of the flight staff offered him a pillow and blanket, which he gladly accepted and he went off to sleep, stretched across both seats.

CHAPTER THREE

Clare sat and listened. Just the timbre of the voice was chilling. Some sort of modification system altered the sound, so it'd be unrecognisable. Instead, the voice had a kind of quality to it that seemed almost robot-like, which made it even more menacing, due of its lack of emotion. It was as though the person behind it had no mercy, no semblance of compassion and that not giving into the demands could result in the deaths of many people, when the owner of that voice decided to unleash his fury on an unsuspecting world.

'Clare, what do you think?'

'I don't know, really, commissioner,' replied the sergeant, 'I guess I'm still trying to get my head around it all. This guy, says that he, The Fire of the Sun, is going to systemically destroy Melbourne if we don't give in to his demands and that the bombs are already in place, all around the city and suburbs.'

'That's correct,' said the commissioner. 'I received another email this morning. A statement that there are thirty bombs planted all around Melbourne. He's hinted that one of the explosive devices might be of nuclear origin. We have no reason to doubt him or the lengths he's willing to go to, to achieve his objectives. The police station was an example. He was willing to kill two hundred people without warning. He would have succeeded, too, if not for that Rob Swift of yours. '

'Jesus,' sighed Clare, feeling the blood drain from her face as the commissioner uttered the word nuclear. 'I assume, sir, you've already been in contact with the ASIO?

'Yes, both ASIO and the Australian Federal Police have been informed. They tell me that they'll have a team of Feds down here from Canberra by the morning.'

'Then there's not much to do until then,' said Clare. 'Is there a time limit, as far as the demands go?'

'Yeah, they've said the first bomb will go off in forty-eight hours. After that, they'll detonate one every forty-eight hours, until all demands are met, or the city's been destroyed.'

'Jesus, he's not mucking around, is he?'

'We don't think so,' said the commissioner. He stood and walked around his desk when he saw the door open and his personal assistant bring in a tray of coffee and tea. 'Would you, Clare, or any of you other gentlemen, care for a cup?'

Several of the high-ranking officers and department heads in the room took up the offer and made themselves a beverage while the commissioner continued to speak.

'I've decided we're going to have to form some sort of taskforce to deal with the crisis. I want all the cases currently under investigation by every member of the major crime squad dropped immediately and priority given to the bomber. That's not a request, by the way,' smiled the commissioner, 'I can assure you it's an order.'

'Yes, sir,' replied the group of suits in unison.

'That should provide you with a further six detectives and seven, when Ray Owen gets back from his holiday. He's already called me and told me he's on his way.'

'That's a good start,' said Clare.

'Yes,' agreed the commissioner. 'We'll pull detectives from both the armed robbery and the homicide squad as well. I personally want to make sure this bastard doesn't get away.'

'All right,' said Clare, 'let's go back over his demands. There might be something in them, which gives us a clue as to his identity.'

'He wants fifty million dollars, in fifty and twenty dollar notes,' replied Tony, 'nothing more and nothing less.'

'What about the Fire of the Sun? Clare asked. 'Where could that have come from? It could be something to do with some political movement. Tony, would you look up the Fire of the Sun on our database and cross-reference it with the feds?'

Tony retreated to another computer across the room. He called up the search engine and entered the Fire of the Sun into the blank space provided. 'There's over a hundred-thousand sites,' he called out to Clare. 'It'll take a while to find what we're looking for, if it's even there.'

'Then you'd better get started,' said the commissioner, which meant that the meeting had officially ended. 'I'll get more detectives to you, as soon as they become available, Clare.'

'Thank you, commissioner,' said Clare as she rose and shook the hand of the most senior policeman in the state of Victoria, 'I know you will.'

Tony and Clare left the commissioner's office and headed down the hallway to the elevators. 'So, where are our offices going to be, now that we've been blown out of St. Kilda Road?'

'You're not a big one for paying attention some of the time, are you Tony?'

'Not when I've got you there to listen for me,' laughed the detective. 'My eyes glaze over in the presence of big-knobs. I'm just a simple copper.'

'Well, we, meaning, you me, and the taskforce will be located here, in the commissioner's building. We don't want to advertise too widely either, not with a bomber on the loose.'

'Yeah, fair enough,' conceded Tony. 'Jesus, if this guy has his way, he might destroy half the city. He might do it anyway, even if he gets the money.'

'I just hope the commissioner isn't considering calling his bluff and waiting to see if the first bomb does go off.'

'Yeah, now that's a thought,' said Tony as the elevator reached the ground floor of the Whitlam building on Elizabeth Street. The door opened and nobody got in, so it closed again and made its way down to the basement car park.

'So, what do you want to do?' Tony asked as they approached the dark blue Ford.

'Not much we can do, without Rob Swift here. I wish he'd hurry up. If he can do for this guy, what he did with Clarence Grafton, we might be able to find him before he does too much damage.'

'How far away is he?'

'I'm not sure, but I think he might be flying Tibet, to India, to Singapore and then back here, so I don't think we should expect him for at least another twenty-four hours. Until then, we're on our own.'

'Will you be meeting him at the airport, Clare?'

'Yeah, I was hoping to. You sound like you want to come and meet him when he arrives.'

'I wouldn't mind,' replied Tony shyly. 'I liked Rob a lot. He seemed like a good sort of guy, for the short time I knew him. He did change my mind about the power of psychics to help us with our work.'

'Okay, I'll let you know when he calls and the two of us can go get him together.'

'Not a problem, boss, you can call me anytime.'

Clare drove to Tony's house, due to his own private car was now locked in the underground St. Kilda Road complex, where it would remain for the time being, until the place had undergone a complete examination for evidence.

'I hope your car's not too damaged when you get it back,' said Clare as she dropped him off at his front door in West Brunswick.

'Do you want to come in, Clare?' Tony asked as he opened the door. 'Jenny's at home tonight and I'm sure she'd love to see you. I think she actually finds you more interesting than me.'

Clare laughed. It felt good to laugh. 'I remember the last time I said yes to a similar invitation from you and Jenny, Tony, after we'd sorted out the mess left by that Grafton bastard. I've never felt so sick and hungover in all my born days and I never want to go through that again.'

'I bet you do, if we catch this prick,' said Tony with a laugh as he got out into the street and slammed the door behind him.

'If we catch this arsehole, then all bets are off,' Clare retorted, as she put the stick into gear and headed for home. Clare decided to put her work car in the underground car park, rather than out in the street, when she got home. The whole situation with the Fire of the Sun – or FOTS as some of the taskforce team were already calling the operation, freaked her out a bit. Right now, she didn't even know what sort of technology he had available to him. If he had the right sort of gadgetry, he might even be watching her now, or had already figured out the identities of the senior police in charge of the case. If he could do that, she wouldn't put it past him to plant a bomb under the car of a senior police officer, which would show they was serious and would strike a severe blow to the morale of the cops as a whole, not just the taskforce.

'Stop it,' she said to herself as she pulled the car in, 'you're getting ahead of yourself. You don't know if he's even capable of that.'

Clare turned off the engine and used the remote control from her keyring to close the garage door. She got out of the car and locked the door behind her with the remote, used the stairs to walk up to her apartment and then used two others keys, to open the steel safety door and unlock a deadbolt on the thick, wooden main door leading her into the apartment.

Once inside, she turned sharply to the left, flipped up a plastic covering, and entered a four-digit code into the alarm system. She let out a sigh of relief; glad she'd been able to get to the code in time, without it going off. It was a new thing in her life and she'd had a few of mishaps over the last couple of months, which had disturbed the neighbours, who were understanding and discreet enough not to make any comments to her about the incidents. She'd tried to apologise, but the elderly couple just waved her off with a smile, telling her she didn't have to apologise.

'It happens to everyone who puts in a new alarm system. We've seen a few owners come and go in their time.'

She made sure the deadlocks were fastened before she moved further into the flat. She turned on a light as she walked through the gleaming white kitchen, and then further into the living area, turning on lights as she passed. She thought about cooking something, but dismissed the idea, thinking she might as well just order in some Chinese food and look at the reports involving the case. She took out her mobile phone and looked in the contact list, where she saw the name of the Fountain Court Chinese Restaurant. She pressed the dial button and a female Asian voice answered the phone. 'Hello, this is Fountain Court, how may I help you?'

'Hello, is that Leah?' Clare asked with a smile.

'Yes, this Leah, who are you?'

'Hi, Leah, this is Clare Carbone. Would it be possible to get my usual order delivered?'

'Ah, yes, hello, Clare. I remember you, cop lady, huh?'

'Yeah, that's right. You still have my order written down?'

'Yes,' replied the Chinese woman with a giggle, 'we have your order pinned up on back wall, along with many others.'

'Leah, I don't want to sound paranoid, and I guess it's a cop thing, but could either you or your son, Jimmy, deliver the order? I just want to know it wasn't tampered with on the way.'

'Yeah, sure,' said Leah, 'I will bring it up myself to your house, in say, half an hour?'

'Yeah, that'd be great,' replied Clare. 'I wouldn't mind a shower before I ate. It's been one of *those* days, I'm afraid.'

'No worries, Miss Carbone, will be seeing you then.'

'Yeah, thanks,' said Clare and hung up the phone.

The shower was luxurious and Clare just stood there for a moment after she entered the water, her hands pressed up against the walls as she let the water invade every part of her body and soothe her troubled mind. She left her bedroom door open and listened to the television news, still focussed on the bombing at St. Kilda Road. There of course, had been an uproar made by the public, on sensationalist, current affairs programs, who interviewed the uninformed and said they were disgusted that such an act of terrorism could be committed on Australian soil.

'Just wait till you get the latest news,' she said to the television, 'about the FOTS and their demands. No doubt, then you'll all be blaming the police about not doing our jobs properly and you know what? You might actually be right. We somehow allowed a terrorist to go about his business, right under our noses.'

Just as she was putting on a pair of soft, light blue cotton pyjamas, there came a knock at the door, which she assumed would be her delivery from the Fountain Court.

'Come in, Leah,' said Clare with a smile, 'I've got the money for you right here, along with a tip, of course.'

'Thank you, Miss Carbone,' said Leah entering with two plastic bags. Clare took one of the bags from her, put it on the kitchen table and watched as the old woman followed suite. 'Here you are,' said the detective handing over a fifty-dollar note. 'Please, keep the change.'

'Thank you, Miss Carbone,' said Leah with a bright smile as she tucked the note into her top pocket. 'You're very generous.'

'You gotta be generous to get good service,' said Clare with a laugh.

'Yes, that's true,' agreed Leah. 'I must get back now, the restaurant is very busy.'

'Sure, I'll just walk you out.'

'Thank you, Miss.'

'You can just call me Clare, you know, Leah. You don't have to bother with the Miss. Clare's just fine.'

After the old woman left her apartment, Clare went and got some dishes from the cupboards and sorted out the Chinese food on the table. She brought her laptop out and booted it up while she shovelled all sorts of Chinese delights onto her plate.

There was something about the wording of the Fire of the Sun. She found it vaguely familiar on some level she couldn't identify, as if it was stuck down deep inside her memory, where she couldn't touch it, as though it was on the edge of her lips and then suddenly slipped off. She looked it up on the Internet and like Tony said, there were a hundred-thousand sites linked to that phrase and it'd take more time than they had to get through them all. She looked over the reports again. She noticed nothing new in terms of intelligence of which she was not already aware.

She sighed, folded her arms, lay back on her plush leather couch, and watched TV, in the back of her mind, hoping Rob Swift would arrive soon and have a chance of helping them out of this madness. With a full belly and her tired mind, Clare fell asleep on the sofa as the telly blurted out the words of David Letterman engaged in some mindless celebrity interview.

She slipped so casually into a dream that it almost went without notice and found herself on a huge slide, barrelling towards the bottom at a phenomenal speed, so fast that she found she was unable to scream, the desperate sound caught in her throat. Just as she hit the bottom of the slide, she woke and sat bolt upright on the sofa, soaked in perspiration and thankful the experience had been nothing but a figment of her imagination.

'Jesus,' she said as she went to the refrigerator to get a drink of water. She drank directly from a jug, not worrying about retrieving a glass and took the container into the living room, where she made a brief inspection of the files she'd scattered on the coffee table when she'd first entered the apartment. She picked up a DVD and looked at it for a while as she consumed more water from the jug and let out the satisfied sigh of a quenched thirst.

'Who are you?' Clare asked as she retrieved the DVD from the case and placed it into the player, which sat underneath her television. She grabbed the remote, turned on the TV, and sat on the sofa as she waited for the DVD to load. Soon after, a distorted image appeared on the set. It sat statue-still, without moving in the slightest, which was unnerving in itself, but the voice that accompanied the still image was even more unsettling. It was a deep voice, perhaps deeper than the natural voice of the speaker, due to the distortion, but the lack of emotion attached to it was truly creepy and made a shiver sneak down her spine. The speaker had made his demands, as if ordering a hot dog, or composing a grocery list, as if the possible deaths of thousands of people were of no concern to him at all. She wondered how someone could come to a point in his or her life, where causing the deaths of others meant nothing at all and was but the means to an end.

It was frustrating that the lab techs had no luck trying to decrypt the distortion and one of them had hazarded to guess, even if they had been successful, they would have seen nothing but a shop-store manikin, or some other type of dummy placed in front of the camera. The complete lack of movement suggested the speaker had in all likelihood, placed some sort of recorded message near or on the lap of the dummy and was probably standing completely out of view, operating the camera. They weren't taking any chances and even if the lab techs had been brilliant enough to remove the distortion, which they weren't, the taskforce would've seen nothing that would have led them to the perpetrator, anyway.

Clare replayed the DVD repeatedly, trying to discern something, anything from the background, but in the end, she just didn't have any sort of clue as to the speaker's whereabouts or identity. She sighed, relaxed back on the sofa, reached for the water and took a deep drink, then stood, and headed back to her bedroom, just as the day was beginning to break in the east. She saw a picture of Rob's face in her mind as she dozed off and wished for him to hurry up.

CHAPTER FOUR

Rob opened his eyes and realised straight away he'd been lying on his arm, which had gone to sleep and felt numb from his fingertips to his elbow. He adjusted himself and was surprised for a moment to find he was still on the plane, heading towards Singapore. He wiggled his fingers to get the blood flowing in his arm and asked a passing flight attendant how long it would be until they reached Singapore.

'We'll be landing in a little over two hours, sir. Can I get you anything?'

'Yeah, I wouldn't mind a glass of water, if you have one. I'm a bit parched after my sleep.'

'Of course, sir,' replied the flight attendant with a bright and cheery smile, 'I'll be right back.'

Rob looked out the window and saw nothing but darkness and the occasional fleeting cloud as it crossed over the wing of the plane. He looked around and accepted the drink from the flight attendant shortly afterwards. 'Thanks,' he said as he took a sip of the cool liquid.

'You're welcome, sir. Is there anything else I can get you?'

'No thanks, I should be okay.'

The flight attendant gave him another bright smile and disappeared into the darkness of the cabin. Rob finished his drink, placed the plastic container into the rubbish bag in front of him, and then looked around. The plane was quiet. The only thing that disturbed the darkness was the sporadic snoring that emanated from a passenger a few rows back. He slipped on a set of earphones from beside his seat and fell silently into sleep to the doleful sounds of a jazz quartet.

Rob awoke in complete darkness, punctuated by the only source of light, being the many stars, in the dark sky above him and while fascinating, they weren't luminescent enough for him to see his hand in front of his face. It was silent, unnaturally so, and it sent a chill up his spine. He decided to sit down, get his bearings and relax for a while. If something were supposed to happen in this dream, he'd let it come to him, rather than do the chasing. He felt soft grass beneath him, stretched out his body and lay on his back on the ground, breathing in the fresh-tasting air, glad to be out of the confines of the aeroplane. He looked up at the stars and marvelled at their distant beauty. He remembered as a kid, a teacher telling him the light from those stars he was now seeing would've emanated from those far off bodies, thousands of years ago and was now only just reaching the Earth. It was a humbling thought and made him feel insignificant and small in such a vast and complex universe. It was also something of a privilege to glimpse the light that had travelled such incomprehensible distances, through other alien galaxies, to reach its final destination in the retinas of his eyes. He wondered who else might be gazing up at those same stars right at that moment.

Rob's calming thoughts abruptly ceased, disturbed by a sudden rumbling in the distance, accompanied by the sound of distinctly Australian voices. As he looked on, he saw three army tanks, on which sat a group of soldiers, come crashing across the field in which he stood. A searchlight shone bright from the top of one of the vehicles and pointed out into the night, highlighting several structures, which stood about a half-mile away.

As the tanks came to rest about twenty feet away, a loud, commanding voice silenced all talk, and ordered the tanks to fire.

'Yes, sir,' replied an obviously subordinate voice in the darkness.

The armoured vehicles began a deafening and sustained barrage of fire upon the distant structures, which caused Rob to place his hands over his ears. In the distance, by the light of the exploding shells, Rob could see people running back and forth, trying to escape the savage, unexpected assault. He noticed with some distress that there were children silhouetted by the yellow of the flames of the now burning buildings, hugging tightly to the chests of their parents or hurriedly led away into the adjoining fields, out of the line of fire. He also noticed there was no resistance to the attack. Nobody fired back, or even yelled at the soldiers in defiance of their actions.

'Hold your fire,' said the commander, just as the sun moved over the horizon.

'Hold your fire,' repeated another unseen voice.

'Wait until the sun's up, and then send a squad of men to inspect the village. Make sure we've destroyed it and move the leftover people on, under threat of arrest, if you have to. I don't really want to take any prisoners, if we can help it. I don't want to go dragging a group of fuckin' ragheads through the desert. We have more important things to do.'

'Yes, sir, I understand.'

'Oh, and make sure the squad set explosive charges in any buildings left standing. That'll fix them from coming back to this god-awful place.'

'Consider it done, sir.'

As the sun emerged, Rob was able to get a better look at the soldiers who'd bombarded the village. There were the three tanks, a barrage of four-wheel drives, and a personnel carrier, which stood behind the armed vehicles. A sergeant jumped off one of the tanks and marched to the personnel carrier, from which a squad of heavily armed soldiers emerged. He ordered the soldiers to enter the village under the command of a corporal. He gave orders prior to their departure that no structure was to remain standing. 'The citizenry of the village are to be dispersed with a warning they're not to return to the area. 'Do you all understand?'

'Yes, sergeant,' came the chorused reply.

'If they offer you any resistance, they are to be treated as hostile. Is that clear?'

'Yes, sergeant,' repeated the squad.

'What about the dead, sergeant?'

'Let the dead lay where they are. The jackals can feed off them and the sun can bleach their bones white, for all I care. This'll be a lesson to the people of this land that they cannot fuck with the Australian army, without severe and unrelenting consequences. These fuckers killed some of your friends and colleagues, just a few days ago. They'll think twice before they try something like that again. Are we all clear about this?'

'Yes, sergeant, we're crystal clear,' replied the corporal.

'Good,' said the sergeant, 'now head out.'

The corporal ordered the squad of twelve soldiers split up into three groups of four and approach the village from different directions. Two of the groups would enter in four-wheel drives along the flanks of the village and the personnel carrier would enter via the main road.

'Maintain radio contact, at all times,' said the corporal as each of the designated groups moved towards their respective vehicles. 'If it looks as though there's anything in there that qualifies as intelligence, check it out before you grab it. I don't want to lose any more men this week because they were stupid enough to grab some wired up papers.'

The soldiers re-entered the personnel carrier and the hatch-door located at the rear, slammed shut with a loud metallic clang. The engine started with a low rumble that grew louder as the driver revved the engine. As it began to move off, Rob saw an opportunity and jumped onto the outside of the vehicle, holding on for dear life as the bulky carrier bumped and teetered over the rough terrain on its way to the village.

All three vehicles entered the village simultaneously as according to their plan. Many of the villagers stood dumbstruck as the soldiers stopped at each entrance to the village, as though they were a herd of deer caught in the headlights of a car. Many of them placed their hands in the air in surrender.

'All right,' ordered the corporal jumping out of a four-wheel drive, 'let's get this job over and done with. Group one. I want you to start moving these towelheads out of the village. Group two. I want you to search every house. You know what to do if you come across any hostiles and group three, you're with me. We'll follow the second group, one house behind, and start placing explosive charges in each of the houses once they've been cleared.'

Rob jumped off the top of the carrier and walked towards the centre of the village. He could feel the sun burning his back despite wearing a shirt. He passed the helpless villagers, herded like cattle out into the surrounding desert by four soldiers, who seemed to have little compassion for their captives. He wished he could do something for them, but knew these were circumstances already passed, on which he could have no bearing whatsoever.

One group of soldiers began searching the first of the houses. When one of them yelled clear, the second group moved inside and although he couldn't see them, he knew they were setting the explosive devices. It saddened him that his compatriots could undertake such wonton destruction of a place so obviously ancient. This process went on for several hours, until finally, all of the thirty odd dwellings were primed with explosive charges. The soldiers jumped back into their vehicles on the corporal's orders and headed back up the hill to their commanding officers, except for the four soldiers who'd been herding off the occupants. They waited up the road with the villagers, who stared back despondently at their homes, knowing their way of life would soon be no more.

'Watch this,' said one of the soldiers laughing. 'Should be quite a show.'

As Rob looked on, the major at the top of the hill gave a signal and there came an enormous noise from the first of the houses, which exploded into a pile of rubble and dust in a matter of moments, causing the guarding soldiers to roar with laughter. Then all of the houses began to explode one after and another and each time another dwelling disappeared, the soldiers burst into further fits of guffawing, while the people watched in both shock and horror.

Finally, when one of the village men could stand the insult no more, he attacked one of the young soldiers, punching him in the face and sending him to the ground, where he dropped his gun. For a moment, there was a distinct silence between explosions, as both the soldier and the villager eyed the gun. The soldier drew a pistol, just as the villager reached the rifle and shot the man, point-blank in the head. He stared with disbelief at the soldier for a moment and then dropped dead to the ground, a deep pool of blood gathering around the wound. A moment later, there came a cry of absolute anguish as a woman and a young boy ran to the man, picked his head up out of the dust, cradling him and crying and, although Rob had no way of understanding their language, he could see this was obviously the dead man's wife and son.

After a moment, the boy looked up at the soldier. 'You will all pay,' he said in perfect English and a disarming calmness. Rob believed what the boy said and knew that the whole mess in Melbourne was not primarily about the extortion of money, but rather about the revenge for a broken and bitter heart.

Rob woke as an announcement of the plane's imminent landing in Singapore blared over the loudspeaker and a flight attendant asked him to adjust his seat to the forward position.

CHAPTER FIVE

Clare walked into the office and was greeted by Ray Owen, much to her surprise, who called out to her from his office across the room. 'Hi,' she said as she approached, 'how was your holiday?'

'Good,' replied Ray with a sad smile. 'I came back as soon as I heard the news.'

As Clare ventured further inside, she noticed a man in dark suit seated on the chair opposite Ray's desk.

'Clare,' said Ray, standing, 'I'd like you to meet Commander, Peter Bell, from the Federal Police in Canberra. He'll be assisting us with the taskforce, along with a dozen other federal officers assigned to the case.'

Peter stood. 'It's good to meet you, Clare,' he said extending his hand. 'You've got quite the reputation for solving tough cases.'

'Thanks,' replied Clare taking his hand and shaking it. 'I do my best.'

'Your exemplary reputation quite precedes you,' said Peter with a smile. 'You should think about joining the feds someday. I'm sure we'd love to have you.'

Ray laughed aloud. 'Now, Peter, please don't go trying to poach my best officers, at least until we get this whole mess cleared up. Then, she can go and join the dark-side, or do whatever she likes.'

'Fair enough,' said Peter. 'Just to let you know, Clare, there'll be a meeting in half an hour in the conference room, so we can all get to know who's who, in the taskforce and bring everybody up to speed.'

'Okay,' said Carbone, 'I'll let Tony and everybody else know. I looked forward to working with you,' she added with a smile as she left Ray's office. She walked into the open planned area where the rest of the taskforce desks were located.

'Hey Clare,' called out Tony entering the office bringing coffee for the both of them in a cardboard tray he deposited on her desk. He was followed by numerous other police officers that appeared to have caught the same elevator. 'How's it all going?'

'Good,' replied Clare taking a sip and breathing a delighted sigh. 'The feds have arrived. Their boss is in with Ray.'

'I noticed all the new faces,' said Tony seating himself at his desk and taking a sip of his coffee.

'I wouldn't get too comfortable. There's going to be a briefing in about twenty minutes, in the conference room.'

Whilst they were sitting there, the place seemed to fill up with furniture removalists, bringing in new desks for the federal police officers and technicians, who were opening boxes filled with new computers and arranging connections to the Internet and the police Intranet.

'They're certainly not sparing any expense on this, are they?'

'No, they want to catch this arsehole, sooner rather than later. The commissioner has the press on his back and we need to get some results, bloody quick.'

'Speaking of results, have you heard about where Rob Swift is?'

'No,' replied Clare, 'but I assume he would've hit Singapore by now, which means he should get to Melbourne, by early tomorrow morning.'

'That's good, we sure could use his help,' said Tony. 'I'll let everybody know about the briefing.'

'Thanks, Tony, that'd be good.'

The twenty minutes between when Tony and Clare spoke and the beginning of the briefing quickly elapsed and soon after, all the taskforce officers gathered in the conference room, eyeing each other and wondering who was who. The briefing began with an address from the commissioner, who thanked the gathered crowd for attending, and told them they were the best and the brightest of the both the Victoria Police and the AFP. He added he had no doubt this group would detect and apprehend this terrorist, or group of terrorists, quickly and stressed that many lives depended on their actions.

'Okay, I won't waste any more of your time and leave you to it. Good luck ladies and gentlemen,' he finally finished.

Once the commissioner left the room, both Ray Owen and Peter Bell took the stage. Ray gave an update, as to the actual threat made, played the emailed message on a television screen and provided a rundown of the damage to the St. Kilda Road complex.

'I want to talk to you all about what each of actual your duties will be,' said Commander Bell, rising. 'The federal police officers assigned to this case are specialists in their respective fields. Four of the ten officers are experts at gathering intelligence from all manner of sources, including interrogation of foreign nationals, and the other five are expert surveillance officers, both physically on the ground and via satellite use, from their desks. We also have one officer, who'll work as a full-time liaison with ASIO.'

The commander took a deep breath, as if he was carefully considering his next words. 'I don't want to beat around the bush, that's not the sort of man I am and neither is Ray Owen, so I'm just going to speak plainly and make my message clear: this taskforce will not be burdened with any of that state versus federal rivalry shit. You're all here to compliment each other and to bring a positive outcome to this case. Anybody caught indulging in such misconduct will face severe penalties. Is that understood by one and all?'

'Yes, sir,' chorused the gathered officers from both organizations.

'Okay,' said Ray, taking centre stage again, 'there'll be two separate, but cooperating teams here. I'll be commanding the state police team and Peter Bell will head up our federal brother and sisters. The second in command of both teams will be Sergeant Clare Carbone, who you'll refer to in all matters should you find Ray or me absent.'

Whilst everyone was listening to Ray hand out various assignments, the door to the conference room opened and one of the administrative assistants assigned to the taskforce, quietly walked around the room asked Clare in a whisper if she could take a phone call.

'Can't you take a message?' Clare asked.

'I think you might want to take this call, Clare,' said the admin assistant who was unfazed by the all the eyes upon her, 'I think it might be important.'

'Excuse me,' said Clare, standing. 'I'll be back in a moment.'

When they got out of the room, the admin assistant told her that it was Rob Swift on the phone calling from Singapore.

'Thanks, Jenny,' said Clare to the younger woman. 'You're right, it is important.'

Clare rushed to her desk and pressed the flashing light to connect her. 'Hi, Rob, it's Clare here.'

'Hi, Clare,' said Rob's familiar voice. 'I think there's something you need to know. Australian soldiers in Afghanistan made the fellow you're looking for an orphan. I don't know his name, or when this happened, only that it did. I don't think the bombs he's planted are about getting money, it's about revenge on the people who killed his father.'

'So, it looks as though we were viewing this guy from the wrong angle, right from the start,' said Clare. 'Instead of the Fire of the Sun, we should have been thinking, fire of the SON. As far as the money goes, yeah, that makes sense. Anybody with half a brain knows that the government won't pay off terrorists. It would set too bad a precedent. The demand for money was probably just a way to throw us off his real motive. Thanks for that. I'll let the taskforce commanders know, as soon as I hang up. How are you doing?'

'I'm okay. I'm staying at Raffles in Singapore City, which is nice. I should reach Melbourne at about eight in the morning, your time.'

'Tony and I will come and meet you. Have you arranged for anywhere to stay yet?'

'No, I haven't. I guess I'll work that out when I get there. I'm sure my sister, Michelle would be okay about me staying at her place for a while. I haven't seen her or my nephew and niece in over a year.'

'No worries,' said Clare. 'If you get stuck, you can always stay with either Tony or me. My place would probably be better. Tony's got himself a new woman and you wouldn't want to be a third wheel in that equation.'

'No, I guess not,' said Rob with a laugh. 'Okay, I'll see you when I get there.'

'Okay,' replied Clare, 'stay safe.'

'Always,' said Rob as he hung up the phone.

Clare hung up and started back towards the conference room. She was halfway up the hallway, when the door opened and she found herself almost barrelled over by the onrush of police coming out of the briefing at a run.

'Get your coat and gun,' said Tony meeting her in the corridor, 'there's been another bomb.'

CHAPTER SIX

When Clare and Tony arrived at the Safehaven supermarket in Northcote, located in the northern suburbs of Melbourne, neither of them were the least bit prepared for a scene of utter devastation and carnage.

'Oh… my… God,' said Clare as she got out of the car and absently closed the door, unable to take her eyes from what she was seeing.

There were at least fifty dead, some of them retrieved from inside the burning building, laid out on the ground and covered with white sheets provided by the too few paramedics who ran frantically around the scene trying to assist those who'd been in the car park, and within close enough proximity of the explosion to suffer extensive burns.

The constant screaming in the background, which emanated from the burns victims and distressed relatives, who'd arrived at the supermarket, after hearing of the explosion on the news, made Clare think of what it must be like to be in hell, with all the eternally suffering, tortured souls.

'Come on,' said Tony pulling her back to reality. 'We need to see what we can do to help.'

The two of them rushed over to one of the parked ambulances and introduced themselves to an older female paramedic, who seemed as if she'd taken charge of the situation. 'What can we do?' Clare asked her.

'Glad to have your help,' said the paramedic. 'We can sure use it. We need to get a team together to go inside and check for anybody else who might be alive. We've found a few, so far, who were lucky enough to be shopping in the aisles farthest away from the blast, but they're not the majority. The trouble is, once we have them out, we need to apply first aid, and get them to the nearest emergency room. So going back in becomes a problem. We're filling the ambulances to the brim, but there just aren't enough of us.'

'Okay,' said Clare. 'Are there are any breathing apparatus we can use?'

'Sure,' said the paramedic jumping up and going into the back of the vehicle, where she retrieved two tanks of air, connected to facemasks and harnesses. 'Sorry, I should have introduced myself. I'm Jane Deen.'

'I'm Clare Carbone, and this is Tony Green,' said the detective as she fitted on the harness and placed the mask on top of her head, ready for use. 'You right to go, Tony?'

'Yeah, no worries.'

'Here, take these, too,' she added as she passed the pair a couple of two-way radios, 'and keep in touch.'

'Okay,' said Clare, 'we will.' She looked around and noticed that none of the other police from the taskforce had yet arrived. 'Ray Owen and Peter Bell are our bosses, and they'll get here, soon,' she said to Jane. 'Could you make them aware of what we're up to?'

'Not a problem,' replied the paramedic. 'Good luck.'

'Thanks,' said Tony as the two of them took off and rushed towards the still burning building. Once close to the blown-out front doors of the supermarket, they flipped down the breathing masks, turned on the switches that would allow for an influx of air, and checked their radios to make sure they could communicate.

'Okay,' said Clare, 'stay close, there's liable to be a lot of smoke in there. It'd probably be better if we kept down low, that's where the bodies will be anyway.'

Tony chuckled slightly. 'Clare, we did the same fire training course, remember?'

Clare looked at him and smiled. 'Come on, let's go,' she said, leading the way.

The first thing the two of them noticed were that the electric lights had gone out and the place was dark and shrouded in smoke. They were able to get a clear look around most of the store, due to the large hole in the ceiling near the cash registers at the back, which was sucking out smoke like an improvised chimney and because both the front and rear doors had been blown off their hinges and out into the street.

'I didn't think to bring a flashlight,' said Clare feeling a little irritated with herself.

'Hang on,' said Tony, 'I'll go and look on the shelves and see if I can't find some torches and batteries to go with them.'

'All right,' said Clare. 'I'll start on this side of the store and work my way towards the back. I'll meet you back there, near the storeroom. Don't be long.'

'I won't,' said Tony crouching and moving, 'I think I might just know where they keep them.'

Clare moved to her left and over to the far side of the store. The first thing she saw at the beginning of the first aisle was a bloody, amputated leg, just lying on the floor, and its owner nowhere in sight. There were other body parts, too, some of which were distinguishable, like hands and feet, even a decapitated head, with the hair all singed off, and other less identifiable remains, which resembled large chunks of barbecued meat and made her want to vomit into her mask. She resisted the urge to purge, by swallowing hard, and started to make her way down the aisle, when she thought she heard a noise, like a child's whimper. She stopped moving for a moment and listened, trying to locate the origin of the sound. After a moment, she called out. 'Hello, can anybody hear me? I'm a police officer, here to help.'

'Over here,' called out a weak and exhausted voice, 'I'm here... I'm alive.'

Clare looked through the darkness and smoke ahead of her, but couldn't see the man. 'Keep calling,' she yelled back. 'My name's Clare... just keep saying my name.'

'Clare,' said the man, 'Clare.'

The detective moved ahead into dimmer light, checking at her feet and on the floor in front of her, hearing the volume of the voice increase with every few steps she took. 'Keep saying my name,' she urged him, 'I'll find you soon.'

'Clare,' said the voice, 'I'm over here, Clare.'

She looked down and thought she must almost be on top of him, but still she couldn't see anything other than a pair of legs sticking out of a storage cupboard under one of the aisles and then as she looked closer, she saw one of the legs move and knew that it was the owner of the summoning voice. 'It's okay,' she said in her most reassuring tone, 'we're going to get you out.'

'My legs are pretty bad, aren't they? I felt them burn when I dived in here. I just couldn't fit my whole body in. It's a bit small. Now I can't feel much of them at all.'

Clare couldn't see his face, because it was stuck inside the cupboard and she was glad, for he would've seen her reaction to the condition of his legs. He'd been wearing a pair of polyester track pants, which had melted onto his body. She had difficulty trying to ascertain where his skin began and the pants ended and, for the second time in less than ten minutes, she wanted to be sick. 'Tony,' she called out, 'get over here, we got a live one.'

'Okay,' replied Tony coming up from the back of the store, his path illuminated by the light of a torch.

'Okay, Mister, what's your name?' Clare asked.

'My name's Craig... Craig Boyce.'

'All right, Craig, the first thing have to do, is get you out of the cupboard. Can you help us with that?'

'Sure,' replied Craig. 'My hands and arms are good. I should be able to push myself backwards, with a little help from you and the other guy you just called out for.'

'Yeah, that's Tony, he's a colleague of mine.'

'Hey,' said Tony in greeting, looking to see what was going on and quickly assessing the situation.

'We need to help Craig get out of the cupboard,' said Clare. 'His arms are strong enough, but he's got no feeling in his legs.'

'All right, hang on a second, there might be something here to give us a hand,' said Tony, as he stood and shone his torch, inspecting the goods in the aisle. He reached out and grabbed two beach towels. 'If we put one of these towels under his stomach, see in that space, between the edge of the cupboard and the floor, we can both lift him as he pushes out. Then we can roll him onto the other towel and drag him along the floor and out to the front.'

'You're pretty smart, for a young fella,' said Craig's muffled voice from inside the cupboard.

'I'm not just a pretty face,' retorted Tony as he rolled up one of the towels and gently passed it to Clare, through the gap between Craig's stomach and the floor. 'I got to tell you, Craig, it was pretty smart of you to think of getting in there when the bomb went off.'

'I'm a veteran,' replied Tony. 'Vietnam. I was in the infantry. It was just an automatic reaction, I guess, to a bomb or a mine going off.'

'Yeah, well, it probably saved your life,' said Clare.

'Okay, are we all ready?' Tony asked taking a firm grip on the end of the beach towel.

'Yep,' replied Clare feeling sweat beading off her forehead and down into her eyes.

'Yeah, me too,' said Craig.

'All right, on the count of three, you push Craig, and we'll lift you out.'

Tony counted and then the three of them together moved Craig out of the storage cupboard and onto the floor. Clare spread the other beach towel on the floor next to him and the two detectives rolled him over and onto the towel. 'Grab hold of each side,' she said, 'and don't let go, whatever you do.'

'Righto,' said the old man with a good-natured chuckle. 'I'll hang on like my life depended on it.'

Before they started to move him, Tony grabbed his radio, which he had hooked onto the belt of his pants. 'Jane, we've got a live one here,' he announced. 'We're bringing him out now. Can you have somebody waiting at the doors?'

'Okay,' replied Jane. 'It looks like your colleagues and the fire brigade have arrived, so you can expect some help inside soon.'

Tony didn't reply. He replaced his radio back onto his belt and grabbed the top of the towel. 'All right, let's get him out of here.'

The detectives pulled and slid the towel along the floor, carefully avoiding the numerous obstacles that stood in their path and were soon at the front door of the supermarket, where several paramedics greeted them and lifted the old man up onto a gurney and began applying first aid to his damaged legs.

'Thanks,' said Craig lifting his head from the gurney pillow, 'I won't forget this.'

'Don't mention it,' said Tony. 'It's all just part of the job.'

'What a load of crap,' said Craig with a laugh, 'I know how brave the two of you have been. Don't try bullshitting a bullshitter.'

Clare laughed beneath her mask and was just about to return into the store, to look for further victims, when a fire-brigade lieutenant stopped her. 'I appreciate your help, but you can leave it to us now.'

'You won't get any argument out of me,' said Clare.

'Me either,' agreed Tony. 'You can have it all to yourselves. By the way, there are no other victims alive in the first aisle, furthest to the left. Clare came down one way, I came down the other, and we covered the whole floor in that area. Craig was the only one.'

'Thanks,' said the lieutenant, 'that should save us some time. Now you two can go and take a break. You did well.'

Clare and Tony moved out to the front of the supermarket, into the car park, dodging the dozen firefighters who pushed passed them, eager and anxious to get inside and do their jobs.

'Hey, you two,' said Ray Owen approaching them with Peter Bell in tow. 'You got here quick.'

'That's the beauty of local knowledge,' said Clare, removing the mask from her face and harness from her back. 'Much quicker than a GPS'

The four of them looked on as the fire brigade sprayed water on the sections of burning roof. 'It's probably going to fuck up the crime scene,' said Peter, 'but there's not much we can do about it.'

'I'll bet he was counting on it,' said Clare. 'Oh yeah, there's something I need to tell you as well, it might help with our profile of this creep. Rob Swift let me know, when I was on the phone to him, just before we all took off, so I didn't have a chance to tell you.'

'What's that?' Ray asked.

Clare told them about the bomber being the fire of the SON, rather than the Fire of the Sun. 'So he's motivated by his emotion and his need for revenge on the troops that killed his father.'

'Or just Australians in general,' said Tony. 'It doesn't look like he makes any distinction.'

'No, it doesn't,' said Clare, 'and if he's got a nuclear weapon in this country, he's sure going to use it to cause maximum damage, no matter who he kills.'

'Jesus,' said Ray looking up at the burning supermarket, 'if this is just the beginning, I'm afraid to think what the end is gonna to look like.'

CHAPTER SEVEN

Rob looked around and found he was sitting in a grassy field that seemed to go on as far as his eyes could see. It was warm day, probably summer and a cool breeze wafted though his hair and over his skin. He looked up and saw the branches and dark leaves of a huge fig tree above him.

'I know this place,' he said thinking aloud. He looked down and saw a picnic basket sitting beside him on the grass. He opened the lid to see the delicious array of food packed inside and almost began salivating on the spot. He pulled out a bottle of wine, found a corkscrew hiding in a side compartment, and proceeded to remove the cork. Once opened, he took a swallow straight from the neck of the bottle and then searched the basket until he came up with a crystal glass, which he filled to the brim. He had just taken a mouthful of the wine when he heard a familiar voice call out to him.

'Hey, there, save a glass for me,' said Aroha walking up a nearby hill.

Shocked by the sight of her Rob spat the wine out and coughed, feeling as if he was choking for a moment. 'Aroha,' he said when he could finally get her name out.

'Hello, my love,' she said, sitting and kissing him. 'You taste nice,' she said, licking her lips as she pulled back from him. 'I do like that wine, I selected it especially to bring today.'

'Is this real, or just a dream?' Rob asked her.

'Does it really matter, Rob? The important thing is we're together. Don't you think so? Let's just enjoy the moment.'

'Of course,' said Rob, taking her face gently in his hands and kissing her with great passion. 'I'll take whatever I can get.'

Aroha laughed and Rob almost cried thinking about how much he missed the sound of her laughter, the almost musical expression of her joy as it filled the air around him.

He grabbed a glass from out of the basket, filled it with wine, and handed it to her. 'I think this occasion calls for a toast,' he said as he raised his glass.

'To us,' said Aroha, tapping their glasses.

'Yes, to us,' agreed Rob, who gulped down the wine and almost finished his glass in a single swallow.

'Hey, take it easy, tiger,' said Aroha, removing his glass and placing it on top of the basket with her own, 'we've still got a bit of time together.'

'I wish that everyday could be like this,' he said as he pulled her to him and held her close, wishing for the moment to go on forever.

Aroha leaned back into his chest, took his hands, kissed his fingertips, and slowly, sensually, taking each finger into her mouth individually, and running her tongue over them. 'I do so miss the taste of you, Rob,' she said as he wrapped his arms around her.

'Why did it have to end like that? Why did you have to die?'

'There are lots of answers to that question,' she replied, 'but probably not a whole lot that you'd understand with your present mind, in your limited plane of existence. Some perceptions require more than vision to confirm belief, some things require feelings that go deeper than you could ever imagine. I guess the easiest way to explain it, for now, would be to say that it was my time to go.'

'You make it sound as if it's better to be dead, than it is to be alive.'

Aroha laughed. 'All of us, Rob, have to cope with whatever reality is in front of us, we've no other choice. You simply have to play the cards dealt you.'

'Yeah, I guess so. I have a feeling you've come here to talk to me about something else, as well, something important.'

'Yes, I have,' she said, 'but that doesn't mean I can't enjoy the experience, too. We'll get to that soon, but right now, I really want to make love to you, right here, under this tree.'

'Who am I to say no to a request like that,' said Rob with a laugh as he pulled her close and kissed her on the mouth.

CHAPTER EIGHT

Mark Andersson covered his chin and cheeks with an adhesive, using a shaving brush and applied first, the dark moustache and then the beard, which he'd flecked grey with powder to give it a more authentic appearance. He waited until it dried, pulling it slightly to test its strength and was satisfied with his work. He then took the dark wig from the bed and pulled it down over his head until it fit comfortably. He looked into the mirror, made sure that it covered his blond hair and grinned, amazed he could look so completely different with minimum effort and a single visit to a theatre supply shop. He smiled at the recollection, of how he'd explained to the proprietor that he was an actor in an amateur stage production with a local theatre company, and would require appropriate props to fit the character he was portraying. 'I'm David, by the way,' Mark lied in his heavy Swedish accent as he extended his hand to the old man.

'Yeah, sure, I can help you,' replied the old fellow shaking his hand. 'I'm Doug and I've been acting in the theatre since I was a kid. That's why I bought this place, so I could supply artists with just the right stuff, selected by an experienced hand, not just some bum off the street. I know just what you need, so come right this way.'

He led Mark into the back of the shop and there, he showed him a variety of make-up, and useful props. He also showed him how to apply them, so he could completely change his appearance. When they'd finished and Mark had selected everything he needed, he thanked the old man for his trouble and killed him, by snapping his aged neck like a twig, robbing the cash register, and setting fire to the shop.

Mark dressed in an older man's wardrobe, consisting of a brown blazer, matching pants, a white shirt and dark tie, which he'd selected with care from the Salvation Army store down the street, a week before. He inspected himself in the full-length mirror on the door to his wardrobe. He looked middle-eastern, no doubt about it, which was just what he wanted anyone who saw him to think. It surprised him how much he actually looked like his dad and wondered if he had done so subconsciously, which made sense, for it was for him and his mother that he'd take revenge on the bastards that killed the two of them, and had changed his destiny, inexorably and forever. The time had come and his plan had already begun. Many were now dead and many more would soon follow. Before it was over, much of this city would burn with the fire of the son and he would laugh and find joy in their suffering, as did those Australian soldiers, who'd shot his father and driven his weeping, wailing mother to her grave when he'd been but a boy

Mark closed the wardrobe and made his way out of the room. He listened before opening the door, to make sure there was no one in the corridor and then stepped out. He looked up and down the hallway and then moved away from his room, trying to distance himself from it, so if seen, he'd seem like just another guest from a different room in this cheap dive of a hotel, where people came and went largely without others noticing, in their drunken or drugged-out states.

He passed several rooms on his way to the back staircase, heard a man beating his wife in one room, two junkies having an argument over stolen goods in another, and heard someone watching Miss Universe with the volume turned up too loud, probably to disguise the sounds of masturbation through the paper-thin walls. He liked the place, because it was colourful, cheap, and best of all, because you could just about hide an elephant in plain sight and no one would be any the wiser.

He reached the staircase and made his way down in the darkness, stepping over the broken stairs he'd seen when he came up. He approved of the fact that the hotel was so badly maintained that they didn't bother to change the globe that was supposed to illuminate the staircase, which probably left them wide open for litigation when someone finally fell down and broke their neck, but for his purposes, it worked well, hiding him like a shadow encased in darkness.

He stole though the car park at the back of the hotel and jumped into the white Toyota Camry, which he'd stolen a couple of days ago. He took the car because it was common, both in model and in colour, making it easier to blend into its surroundings and because the opportunity to steal it had unexpectedly landed right in his lap, when a drunken fool stumbled out of the pub and attempted to start the vehicle with the wrong key. Mark had offered to drive him home and now his un-breathing body lay comfortably in the trunk.

He set the GPS for the docklands and started the car using the owner's keys. He sat for a while, listening to the radio while the engine warmed up, then put the car into gear and drove out of the hotel, switching on the lights when he was about leave the car park. He wound down the window, letting the breeze wash over his face, looking at and contemplating the people in the other cars and those that travelled on foot as they crossed in front of him.

He contemplated the fact that most people are like sheep, stupid and predictable, which only made them so much easier to eradicate, knowing the majority of them would never really contribute anything worthwhile towards the society to which they belonged. Most of them were just a waste of space, taking up good air, munching on their fast food like pigs, gorging at their perennial troth, and fiddling with their unneeded electronic gadgets, before they died of coronary heart disease, while sitting at their desks in their overpaid, useless, pen-pushing jobs.

'Turn left in one hundred metres,' ordered the electronic female voice of the GPS.

Mark followed the direction and soon found himself on the outskirts of the docklands. He parked in the shadows at the end of the pier carpark, grabbed a set of binoculars from the glovebox, and a small backpack from the floor of the front passenger side. He jumped out of the car, locking it behind him. He looked up at the dark sky, filled with infinite stars and wondered at the greatness of the universe before lifting the binoculars to scan the far horizon of the ocean. There, in the distance, he saw the oil tanker, glowing like a Christmas tree out in the darkness and nodded with approval. It was going to be on time, and would dock in Melbourne as scheduled, in approximately an hour.

He decided he had some time to kill before the ship arrived, so went for a walk and found a small, out of the way café, not too far from the docks. He sat down, ordered a strong black coffee, and spent his time reading a daily newspaper. He first read about his latest exploit in the supermarket and the bravery shown by both members of the public, two major crime squad detectives, and the fire brigade who'd responded when the bomb had gone off, rescuing the few survivors of the blast, regardless of the risk to themselves, the building collapsing, or there being another device.

Mark looked at the picture of Clare Carbone and Tony Green taken by a newspaper photographer as they came out of the burning building, their faces full of anguish for the survivors and the dead, and anger for the perpetrator of such a ghastly deed. He recalled his initial anger, when he first realised that they'd found the bomb in the police station, prior to its detonation. It was supposed to kill many of the serving officers, demoralise them and make their investigation into his activities that much more difficult, but for reasons he couldn't explain, it hadn't worked out that way.

'Clare Carbone,' he said under his breath, 'and Tony Green, perhaps we'll meet sooner than you expect.'

He finished his coffee, paid his bill on the way out, and made his way back to the docklands, where he pulled out his binoculars. He watched and waited until the ship tied up and the crew headed down the gangplank to wait upon processing by customs officials before leaving the dockland area.

It seemed by their jovial language that the crew was ready and enthusiastic for rest and recreation of the carnal kind in the fleshpots of the city while they were in port, before they started again on the long journey back to the oil-producing nations to collect another load of petroleum.

He waited for another hour and when he was satisfied the ship was almost deserted, made his way to the pier. He crossed the gangplank, walked up onto the ship, found his way to the captain's stateroom on the second tier and knocked on the door.

'Come in,' said a man's voice on the other side.

Mark opened the door and saw three men sitting and eating breakfast. It was obvious as to the identity of the captain, who seemed to dominate the room with his presence. He was a large man, obese and bearded, who sat at the head of the table, while his two senior officers sat one each side of him.

'You've come for the delivery? You're Arkmed, I assume,' said the captain with a heavy Russian accent.

'Yes, that's right, I'm Arkmed. I believe you are holding something for me.'

'Please,' said the captain gesturing towards the food, 'come in and join us.'

'Thank you,' said Mark as he sat down and hung his backpack on the arm of the chair, 'I don't wish to take up much of your time.'

'No, that's all right,' said the captain turning to one of his subordinate officers. 'Please, go and get the silver case from my cabin and bring it back here.'

'Yes, captain,' said the officer who wiped his mouth, stood and exited the room.

Mark poured himself a glass of orange juice and sipped it to keep his hands busy and so disguise his nervous anticipation in light of the coming delivery.

'It seems you have friends in high places,' said the captain as he munched on a slice of buttered toast.

Nothing disgusted Mark more than people who spoke with their mouths full. It was the absolute epitome of bad manners in his view, and showed nothing but the utmost disrespect to the listener. He managed though, to hide his revulsion, sipped on his juice and looked at the captain. 'I also have friends in low places,' he replied.

The captain guffawed and almost choked on his toast. 'Apparently so,' he said when he managed to compose himself.

A short while later, the ship's officer returned to the stateroom carrying a silver suitcase, which he placed on the table in front of the captain.

'Now, could the two of you please leave Arkmed and myself alone? We have some private business to discuss.'

'Certainly, captain,' said the other officer pushing away from the table, rising and taking his coffee with him as he and his colleague made their exit.

When the two of them had left the room, the captain retrieved a key from around his neck and opened the lid of the case. 'Come here, my boy, and see the toy your friends have sent you.'

Mark took his backpack from the chair and moved over to where the case sat. He placed his backpack on the floor underneath the table and looked at the complicated machinery contained inside. 'It seems that the Japanese don't have a monopoly when it comes to creating big things in small packages.'

The captain laughed again. 'No, the KGB was pretty good at it, too, before the fall of communism. A once, proud, idealistic nation were we and now, everything is for sale, including miniature nuclear weapons. This thing might be small in size, but you can be sure it'll deliver quite a punch.'

'That's my hope,' said Mark. 'I'll need the codes to arm it and set the detonation time.'

'Of course you will, my boy,' said the captain closing the lid and handing over the key. He went then to the far side of the room and opened a cupboard in which there was a small wall safe. He pressed a six-digit code into the front and pulled it open. From it he took a small white envelope, which he gave to Mark. 'Here are the codes. I don't want to know whom you are working for, because it's none of my business. I was paid very well indeed for my courier services, but if you could tell me when you are planning to set it off, I will make sure my ship is underway at the time, and as far from the blast as possible.'

Mark looked at the captain and wondered for a brief second whether he would resemble a roasted pig if caught in a nuclear blast. 'I'm not certain, but I'd be out of here in the next two weeks, if I were you.'

'Very good, very good,' said the captain. 'I think our business is now concluded, yes?'

'Yes, I think so,' replied Mark extending his hand, while at the same time, gently pressing his foot down onto the backpack under the table, setting the timing sequence of the incendiary device contained inside. Mark took the case and then he and the captain walked out onto the deck.

'It is a nice night,' said the mariner looking up at the star-filled sky, 'and good to be in port, instead of out on the rough ocean. A man needs to be in a port now and again, it's good for the soul.'

'I'm sure it is,' said Mark bidding the Russian goodbye and moving off into the night. He returned to the Camry, placed the case on the floor in the back seat, and then started the engine, put the car into gear and drove off, as fast as he could manage without drawing attention. He was about a half a kilometre away when the bomb went off, but he still felt the ground shake through the body of the car and heard the blast, followed by a further succession of thunderous explosions, which he assumed was the petroleum igniting in the hold of the tanker. He looked into the rear-view mirror and saw the yellow of the flames in the background, lighting up the horizon like the beginning of a new day.

He drove to the other side of Melbourne, by which time it was midnight. He parked the car in a do-it-yourself car wash, in Reservoir, inserted some coins into the appropriate slots, put on a pair of leather gloves, and thoroughly cleaned the interior of the car, erasing any fingerprints or DNA he might have left in the vehicle.

When he was sure that nobody was watching, he opened the trunk, gave the owner's body a thorough squirting down with a high-pressure hose, and filled the trunk with water, making any forensic investigation of the murder difficult, if not impossible. They'd know that he had died from a broken neck, but it would be difficult to tell anything else.

When he was satisfied he had taken care of every conceivable thing that could connect him to the car, he drove to a nearby train station and left the vehicle in the car park. He grabbed the suitcase from the back and a shopping bag from the passenger seat, walked to the rear of a set of nearby shops and ducked into a laneway.

There, he removed his make-up and changed his clothes into others he'd brought in the shopping bag, placing the discarded clothes back into the shopping bag. He then inserted the blue contact lenses from his pocket to change the colour of his eyes. He looked at his face, using the mirror from a compact, assuring himself the adhesive was gone from his cheeks. He also inspected his hair and saw that there were several dark roots, which had started to show through. He'd soon need to take a trip to the hairdresser to maintain his Aryan looks.

Feeling good about everything, he walked further up the laneway, removed a set of keys from his pocket, and opened the door of a waiting Volvo. He placed the case and the shopping bag on the floor in the back and headed for home.

Mark laughed as he drove along, thinking about how normal everything would seem tomorrow, when he resumed his job as an attaché in the Swedish embassy. He would frown and show the same concern as his colleagues when informed of the terrible things that had occurred over the weekend, but on the inside, he'd be laughing at them all, knowing there was so much more to come.

CHAPTER NINE

'So, what was it you came here to tell me?' Rob asked, as he lay naked with Aroha, looking up at the sun bouncing off the leaves of the fig tree.

The beautiful, raven-haired woman turned around and raised herself up onto her elbows to face him. 'There's going to come a time, soon, when you'll be forced to make a decision about your future. It'll be the biggest decision you've ever made and the outcome could have catastrophic implications for others if you hesitate.'

'Can't you be a little bit more specific?'

'No, I'm afraid not,' said Aroha leaning forward and kissing him on the lips. 'I can't tell you what to do, and neither can anyone else. It's going to be totally up to you. I just wanted you to know it's coming and I love you. I also wanted you to know that those people who love you the most are near you, Rob and always will be, until you join us.'

'Is this your way of telling me, that I'm going to die soon, because that's the feeling I'm getting?'

Aroha smiled, her face enigmatic. 'I'm afraid I've told you everything I can. It's time for you to go back now, you have things to do.'

'I really wish I didn't have to go,' said Rob, 'and we could just stay right here, forever, and make love for the rest of eternity.'

'That's a beautiful thought,' said Aroha. 'Hold onto it,' she added and kissed him again.

Rob opened his eyes, taking his lips from Aroha's mouth and found himself sitting in his plane seat. For a moment, he thought he could still smell her on him, but her perfume quickly faded, leaving him feeling disappointed, but happy to have seen her, no matter in which realm of reality or plane of existence.

'Sir, please place your seat in the upright position,' said a young, female flight attendant who smiled at him. 'We'll be landing in Melbourne in just under ten minutes.'

Rob complied with the request. He smiled, wondering why they always asked passengers to place their seats in that particular position prior to landing on the tarmac. It didn't seem as if it'd make the slightest difference to the aircraft if everybody reclined their seats and came in to land while snoring their heads off, but then, he had to admit, he wasn't any kind of expert in the field of aerodynamics. He looked out the window as the plane came in to land. He saw the sun in the distance as it rose above the horizon, a bright, glowing orb that lit up the dew on the nearby grass, as though a carpet of sparkling diamonds surrounded the airport.

Once the plane came to a stop, he remained in his seat, letting the other passengers grab their belongings from the overhead compartments and queue in a long line, while they waited to disembark. When the majority of people had left the body of the aircraft, he jumped up and grabbed the small knapsack he had acquired in a Singapore market from the compartment above his head, and wandered down to the front of the plane.

'I hope you enjoyed your flight, sir,' said a flight attendant smiling mechanically. 'I hope you'll fly with us again.'

'Yes, I did, thanks,' replied Rob as he walked off the plane, up a small corridor and out into the main terminal building of Tullamarine airport. The airport was crowded, there seemed to be people everywhere he looked, shopping, eating, chatting, reading, and waiting for relatives to disembark, or planes to take off. It surprised him how much he'd grown to hate the sight, thought, and feel of crowds and that very moment, he would've given anything to be back in Tibet, enjoying the simple lifestyle and the hard training, often without saying a word throughout the whole day. The plane from Singapore hadn't been so bad, mainly because he and almost everybody else had slept for the majority of the journey.

'Hey, Rob,' called out a familiar voice.

Rob turned and saw Tony Green and Clare Carbone walking towards him. The moment he saw Clare's face, he knew that there'd been terrible things happening since he'd last spoken to her on the phone. He could clearly see the stress of coping etched into her countenance like small lines on a roadmap. She looked tired and overworked.

'Hi, guys,' said Rob with a smile.

'It's so good to see you,' said Tony hugging him like a long-lost brother.

Clare stood back a little and watched the interaction between the two men.

Rob glanced at her over Tony's shoulder and saw the glint of a tear in her dark eyes, and although she said little, he could feel her enormous relief brought on by both his presence and offer of assistance. 'Come on, we have to get my bag from the luggage carousel.'

The three of them walked through the airport and waited with the other passengers, until Rob picked up his backpack. Before they left the airport, Clare suggested they stop and grab a cappuccino each for the drive back to the office. 'Are you hungry, Rob?'

'No, I'm okay, I ate on the plane.'

Tony bought a ham and salad roll and Clare purchased a small salad in a plastic container, which she put in her handbag and handed out a coffee each before paying.

'I gather from your silence that things aren't good?' Rob asked the detectives as they reached the carpark.

'No, they're not,' replied Clare. 'I'll tell you more once we're safely in the car.'

Tony put the backpack in the trunk and insisted Rob take the front passengers seat so that he could eat as they drove. Clare put her coffee down in the centre console and started the car. She drove to the ticket booth at the far end of the carpark, showed her police identification, and the attendant waved them through. She then picked up her coffee again and began consuming it in small sips as she watched the road in front of her.

They'd only travelled about a hundred metres from the terminal, when Rob felt himself hit by a wave of nausea that almost made him vomit on the spot. 'Stop the car,' he demanded jamming his hand over his mouth, 'I need to be sick.'

Clare pulled the car over into the emergency lane on the down ramp, which headed towards the freeway and Rob jumped out of the back, fell to his knees, and began to vomit up the contents of his stomach.

'What's the matter?' Clare asked as she knelt down beside him, a consoling hand rubbing his back.

'I don't know,' replied Rob standing, 'but it's something bad,' he added as he began to walk off back towards the terminal. He then had a sudden jolting feeling as if a fist had punched him in the side of the face and he again fell to his knees. He looked up and saw the main airport terminal building explode, and proceed to collapse inwards, sending a giant cloud of dust and black smoke billowing high up into the air and gigantic yellow flames bursting through the glass windows and doors as they shattered, spraying glass all over the place.

'Oh, my God,' said Tony hardly able to believe what he'd just seen.

'Fuck,' said Clare in almost a whisper as she bent down to pick up Rob, without taking her eyes from the inferno in front of her. 'Tony, get on the phone and call the fire brigade and the ambulance. Here, Rob, let me help you up.'

'No,' said Rob pushing her away, 'just leave me here for a little while. I can hear the screaming echoes of hundreds of people, who've just crossed into the void.' When the sound of agony and outrage became too much to bear, he closed his eyes and blacked out.

CHAPTER TEN

Rob woke, sat up, rubbed his tired eyes, and found he was in some sort of office, lying on a comfortable leather couch. He could still hear the voices of the dead in the back of his mind, but they soon faded, travelling back into the void as he progressed further into consciousness. He sat up and saw that his shoes were no longer on his feet. He looked around and saw them beside the sofa on the carpeted floor. He leaned over, put them on, and walked over to look out of the huge window, which sat behind the enormous wooden desk that dominated the room. He saw he was high up in some sort of skyscraper in the middle of the city as he watched the people and cars, which moved along below him. They appeared like children's toys, miniature representations of their real-life counterparts.

Rob turned around when he heard the office door open. He gasped when he saw a little red-haired girl, who he estimated to be about four or five years old, standing there smiling, attired in a blood-soaked summer dress, with half her face blown off, so that her much of her skull was clearly visible. She walked over, took Rob by the hand without saying a word and led him out of the office, up a long corridor and into some sort of conference room, where there were another twenty or so people seated around a large, oval table. The little girl took him to the head of the table, and as Rob passed each of them, he saw that each individual had sustained horrific injuries, including severe burning and amputation of various limbs, which he assumed occurred because of the bomb blast at the airport. The little girl pulled a chair out from the table and pointed to it, instructing Rob to sit down, and then placed herself on a chair next to him, continuing to smile cheerfully, which sent a shiver up Rob's spine.

'I'm so sorry,' said Rob to the gathered group. 'I wish I could've known sooner what was going to happen. I would have tried to warn you.'

Everyone in the room turned to him at the same time, as if it was a choreographed movement and nodded their heads in acknowledgement of his words, as if they understood and felt his sorrow and then those that still possessed moveable limbs, lifted their index fingers to their mouths, as if telling him to be quiet.

A fellow, whose skull appeared so mangled, he would have been unrecognisable to even his loved ones, stood, lifted up an old film projector, and placed it on the table in front of a large whiteboard at the front of the room. He turned it on, and as it began to whir and flicker to life, he moved over to the far side of the room and turned off the lights, so that the place was plunged into darkness, except for the light from the projector.

Rob looked on as the film, also without sound, displayed the face of a young boy, which he instantly recognised as the child whose father the Australian soldiers had killed in the desert. His surroundings though, had now changed and it seemed as if he no longer lived in a desert habitat. He passed by green trees, lush lawns and European-style houses as he skipped down the street with a small group of friends, seemingly on his way either to or from school, judging by the uniform both he and the other children wore. He said goodbye to the other kids at the corner of his street and ran down the road, apparently eager to get home. As he jogged along, he pulled out a drawing from his schoolbag, which he gripped in his hand, letting it flap in the wind as he ran.

He reached small, tidy, red brick house in the middle of the street, opened the gate, and ran up to the front door, smiling from ear to ear in his child-like way. He opened the door and it appeared that he was calling for someone, which Rob guessed was probably his mother.

When she didn't respond to the sound of his voice, a concerned look seemed to pass over his features and he began searching the house in earnest. He first tried his mother's bedroom, but caught no sight of her there and then he tried the backyard, but found it empty. He returned inside and went from room to room, until he reached the bathroom and there he found her, inside the bath, her wrists cut, and the warm water in which she lay, coloured a deep red by her blood. The boy stood frozen for a few moments, as if he was taking a mental picture of the moment and at the same time, trying to process it into his infant mind. He then started to cry and tears fell from his eyes, which he rubbed away with his fists, but still they came, a continuing stream of sorrow and grief. He walked over to the bath, slid into the crimson water beside his mother, and held her in his arms, kissing her cheeks and talking to her, as if somehow his words and affectionate hugs could bring her back from the void where she had gone in order to escape the intense grief of losing her husband and the atrocities to which she'd been subjected.

At that moment, the soundtrack from the projector became audible and Rob heard the boy vow to kill all the Australian soldiers who'd murdered his father and had driven his mother to this. 'One day, when I'm big,' he said, 'they're all going to pay for this.'

Rob wondered about the sound of his accent, which didn't sound the least middle-eastern and more European, although he couldn't make out the exact country of origin, based on such a small sample of his speech. A moment later, the film in the projector ran out and flapped mechanically inside the reel. The man with the mangled skull, again turned on the lights, changed the film, and then sent the room back into darkness with a flick of the light switch.

When the next reel opened, it showed the same boy, but he was slightly older and seemed to be residing in some sort of institution, along with many other children of similar age. He was withdrawn and sullen and it appeared many of the other children chose him to be the butt of their jokes and ridicule, which only reinforced his anti-social attitude and behaviour. He also became violent when he'd had enough of the name-calling and having his bed pissed in by the other residents. It seemed that on several occasions, he'd beaten other boys senseless and had even assaulted a teacher, who he felt had treated him badly and whom he had built up an intense resentment for over many months.

'Jesus, this kid really copped it bad,' said Rob to himself. He continued to watch the screen and saw a couple arrive at the institution, agree to foster him, and to take him into their home. They seemed like a nice couple, but in appearance very different to the boy, in that they were both very blonde, with deep blue eyes. The child had dark hair, dark eyes, and an olive complexion. It would have been easy to tell he was not their own. Still, they showered him with affection, taught him right from wrong, and treated him as if he was their own biological son. They enrolled him in an expensive, private school, where began another saga of torture from the students who sensed his difference from the moment he walked in the front gate. This experience only served to increase his hatred of the Australian soldiers who he blamed for him being there in the first place.

Rob felt sorry for the kid and could see where his motivation for killing Australians had originated, but even so, those that died because of his actions, didn't in the least, deserve the fate that had befallen them. Rob knew the people in this room had come to show him the man's past as a way of stopping his actions in the present. This man's hatred, no doubt, consumed him every moment of the day, and there was no telling what he would do, or how far he would go to fulfil his lust for revenge. All Rob knew was that it was going to get a lot worse before it got any better, and he didn't need any sort of psychic insight to tell him that, he could feel it in his bones.

A short while later, the film flickered off and the lights returned to illuminate the room. The little girl with the blood-splattered dress, rose, took Rob by the hand, and led him out of the conference room, back to the office where she'd first found him. She smiled and waved once at him as she turned, left the office, and closed the door behind her. Rob felt tired and collapsed onto the comfortable cushions on the sofa and fell asleep.

He awoke later to the sound of voices, finding himself in the same office, but this time, populated by a group of people all engaged in an ardent, heated discussion. He sat up, saw his shoes were by the sofa on the floor, and put them on as he looked around to see Clare, Tony, and some other people with whom he was unfamiliar.

'Hello, Rob,' said Carbone. 'How are you feeling?'

'Yeah, all right, although I could use a drink, my mouth's dry.'

'Here,' said Tony pouring a glass of water from a jug on the desk and offering it to him.

'Thanks,' said Rob gulping down the cool liquid as though he'd been walking in the desert. 'How did I get here?'

'You don't remember?' Clare asked him. 'You collapsed for a while on the roadway and then got up and into the car. The airport was on fire, and another bomb went off, so it was too dangerous to go in. The bomb squad's checking it out for more explosives as we speak. We all came up here together and you just fell asleep on the sofa. I took your shoes off, I hope you don't mind.'

'No, not at all,' replied Rob. 'So, where exactly are we?'

'This is the commissioner's office,' replied Clare. 'He'll be here in a minute. I'd like you to meet the taskforce commanders. This is Ray Owen and this is Peter Bell.'

Rob stood and shook the hands of the two men. 'Good to meet you both, I've met you before Ray, haven't I?'

'Yes, that's right,' replied Ray, the last time you were in Melbourne. You did us a great service.'

'Oh, that's right,' said Rob as recognition set in, 'I remember now.'

'Anyway, it's good to have you back again, although we all wish the circumstances were better,' said Ray. 'Clare said that you have some information which might help us to catch this guy.'

Rob grimaced, thinking about his next words. It would be just too weird to tell them he'd just attended a daytime matinee with a bunch of dead people, where the main feature had been the bomber's early life. 'Yeah, I do,' he said. 'Just don't ask me where I got it, because you might not like, or even believe the answer.'

'Look,' said Ray, 'I personally don't care if you pulled it out of your arse, as long as it helps us to bag this terrorist. Last year, I saw some very weird shit go on, as far as you're concerned, but in the end, you helped us immeasurably. So, both I and everyone in this taskforce will take what you say as truth and anybody that doesn't feel that way is going to find themselves directing traffic in Bourke Street at peak hour.'

'Thanks for your confidence, Ray,' said Rob.

A moment later, all eyes looked towards the door, as the commissioner entered the room. 'Clare, Peter, Ray,' he said acknowledging the presence of the officers as he sat down at his desk, 'and this must be the famous Mr. Swift I've heard so much about.'

'Yes, that's right,' said Rob moving over to the desk in order to shake the commissioner's hand. 'Glad to meet you, sir.'

The commissioner laughed. 'You can call me Ron, or Mr. Rouse. After all, you're not officially employed by us, yet.'

'And after that, what do I call you?'

'Sir, in public,' replied the commissioner with a smile. 'Okay, let's get down to business. I need to give some sort of press conference in less than hour and right now, I just don't have a clue as to what I'm going to say and as you can imagine, that displeases both the minister and I, greatly.'

'I'm sorry, sir,' said Ray, 'but there isn't a lot to tell you. It seems this bomber, whoever he is, is exacting some sort of revenge for the death of both his parents. The title of Fire of the Sun was somewhat confused and it is in fact, The Fire of the Son, as in offspring. We don't think money is his primary motivation, and he just used that to throw us off the track. We also think he's trying to tie up all of our resources, making investigation difficult.'

'Yeah, well, he's doing a pretty good job of that, isn't he? Do we have any positive leads?'

'We may have one lead,' said Clare. 'We think our suspect blew up the petroleum freighter at the docklands. Our investigation revealed one of the ship's officers who had some small interaction with the suspect and the captain, managed to survive the blast. He's badly hurt and currently in intensive care at the Royal Melbourne. The doctors have him in a medically induced coma. If he comes to, we're hoping to get a description.'

'What makes you think it's the same man?'

'Two things, sir: the first is, obviously, a blast like that, in view of the other recent bombings, has to be more than a coincidence and second, the initial forensic investigations have revealed the same sort of explosives were used on each occasion.'

The commissioner smoothed back his silver mane of hair. 'Can we trace the explosives to any particular batch? We might be able to find out where it was sold and who bought it, or where it was stolen from.'

'We've got the labs working on it around the clock,' chimed in Peter. 'We should know something soon, hopefully.'

'Good,' said the commissioner, rising, 'keep me informed. I now have to attend a meeting with the minister and brief him before we face the T.V. cameras. Oh, and get this fellow here, signed up,' he added pointing at Rob. 'I want him on the job as soon as possible.'

'Yes, sir,' said Ray. 'It'll be done before the day's out.'

'Very good,' said the commissioner, heading for the door and what seemed like an army of personal assistants that waited outside the office for him. 'Carry on.'

Once the commissioner had exited the room, it seemed everybody let out a relieved sigh.

'So, where do we go from here?' Clare asked of no one in particular.

'I think we need to reorganise,' replied Ray. 'Pete and I spoke to the commissioner and he's agreed to ask for help from interstate, and to get more bodies and forensic teams down here, from both South Australia and Queensland. I think we're going to end up with too many crimes scenes for all of us to investigate efficiently.'

'I know this is far-fetched,' said Clare. 'Can I make a suggestion?'

'Sure,' replied Ray, 'nothing you say is going to hurt matters, that's for sure.'

'Well, I've been thinking about the ship and the bombing. It kind of doesn't make any real sense. The other bombs were set to cause maximum damage and casualties. Whilst the bomb at the docklands did cause significant damage to the docks, it didn't really result in much loss of life and that just seems out of character for this suspect. I think, and believe me, I hope I'm wrong that he may have been trying to hide something.'

'Like what?' Peter asked her, his face turned ashen, as if he knew the answer she was going to provide before she even said it.

'Like the delivery of a weapon,' replied Clare.

CHAPTER ELEVEN

Tony Green sat on the tram headed for Brunswick and sighed. To say today he'd had a bad day at the office may well have been the understatement of the century. He doubted that anybody else in the whole country had as bad a time at the office as he and his colleagues had experienced over the past few days. He looked at the papers held up by the other passengers, which screamed headlines at him as though the whole mess was somehow his fault. He felt guilty, too, just like everybody else in the taskforce. So far, the loss of life had been off the scale, unprecedented, and it was hard to know how to handle, or even process it. There were times when he just wanted to sit down and cry and other times, when he became so incredibly angry with the suspect, he could feel himself just itching to punch a hole in the nearest wall. So far, he'd managed to restrain the compulsion.

He jumped off the tram at Lygon Street and walked past the Greek social club, with its elderly male patrons sitting outside, drinking strong black coffee and watching the last rays of the sun disappear over the rooftops of the nearby houses. He said a quiet hello as he passed, and the old men nodded and smiled back at him. It was strange how life just went on, that ordinary things just kept happening, that people continued to drink coffee, to smile, to laugh, to go on shopping sprees with their credit cards, and to spank their children in supermarkets, when all around them, there were ticking bombs just waiting to explode and blow them into little pieces.

Tony grabbed his house keys from out of his pocket as he walked up the garden path of the little weatherboard house. He was a little pissed off that Jenny wasn't there. It wasn't her fault, though. She'd told him over breakfast this morning she had a late meeting and wouldn't be home until well after dark. He just wanted to feel the softness of her, to hear her voice tell him everything was going to work out and it would all be all right, that she had confidence in both him and Clare to solve the case, but she wasn't, so that was that.

He wandered around the place for a bit, walking from room to room, seeing but not looking, contrasting the quietness of the house to the noise of the thoughts constantly running through his head. He thought about taking a long, hot shower, but then decided he needed to do something to tire himself out physically, otherwise he knew he wouldn't sleep that night and he hated to bring work home, or even the memory of it, as it seemed like too much of an invasion of his Jenny's privacy.

He changed his clothes, removing his dark suit, which he placed on a hanger in the built-in wardrobe that sat adjacent to the foot of the bed, along with the light blue tie Jenny had given him as a birthday present and threw his shirt into the laundry hamper in the corner. He searched the wardrobe drawers until he found a pair of shorts, some white sports socks and an old t-shirt, and retrieved his sneakers from under the bed, all of which he put on. He grabbed his hiking backpack, went to the bathroom, and shoved in some shampoo, a face-washer, and some deodorant. He returned to the bedroom, where he found a pair of boxer shorts, another pair of socks, and an extra t-shirt, which he also placed into the bag. Before he left the house, he stopped by the kitchen and left Jenny a note, telling her he had gone for a run and a workout at the gym and that he'd be back by eight. As an afterthought, he added that he'd pick up some Chinese on the way home. He attached the note to the fridge, held in place by a magnet in the shape of Australia and headed up the hallway. He fiddled with his keys as he reached the door and opened it, letting in a cool breeze that made him shiver. He found the key he was looking for, turned and eased it into the lock on the security door, just as the dark figure appeared beside him and hit him hard in the back of the head, sending him sprawling down to the ground, groaning, shocked, and trying to come to grips with what had just happened.

He looked up at the man, silhouetted by a streetlight, so that his features remained dark and indistinguishable. He came towards Tony, with what looked like a baseball bat and hit him once again, before he had a chance to move, sending him into the blackness of unconsciousness.

CHAPTER TWELVE

Rob and Clare sat in the doctor's office and waited for her to finish her ward rounds, so they could speak to her about her patient.

'Do you think they'll let us get near him?' Rob asked.

'I honestly don't know,' replied Clare, 'I guess all we can do is ask and see what she says.'

'Hello there,' said a middle-aged blonde woman, entering the office wearing a white lab coat, which signified her position as a medico. 'I'm Doctor Helen Harris. I understand that you're both here to see Mister Petrovski.'

'Yes, I'm Clare Carbone and this is Rob Swift, we're both assigned to the bomber taskforce. We think the man you're holding may have some vital information.'

'Terrible business,' said the doctor, seating herself at her desk. 'I'm afraid Mr. Petrovski will be of little help to you. He's still under heavy sedation and is currently unable to speak. We placed him in a drug-induced coma, due to the extent of his injuries.'

'How bad is he?' Rob asked, looking through the large glass window into the unit, where he saw Petrovski, plugged into what seemed like a million wires, monitoring his heart rate and other vital bodily functions. The scene reminded him of the time in Alice Springs, when Aroha had found herself in almost the same situation and he had to admit, it felt more than a little eerie.

'He's got burns to seventy percent of his body. In all honesty, we don't expect him to last more than the night, maybe a couple of days.'

'I know this is asking a lot,' said Clare, 'but could we have some time with him alone, with the curtain drawn?'

'Whatever for? You can't get any information out of him,' replied the doctor.

Clare looked at the doctor for a long moment, trying to choose the right words, but in the end, she reasoned that no matter how she said what she was about to say, it was going to come out sounding crazy. 'Rob, here, has a psychic ability that has been of great help to the police before in situations similar to this. We think he might be able to extract the information without having to speak to Mr. Petrovski, or even wake him up.'

The doctor became quiet for a moment, placing her fingertips on her chin, as though engaged in pensive thought. 'I don't suppose it can do any harm,' she conceded. 'Would you mind if I stood in, both to witness this process, and to provide care for the patient?'

'I can't see any harm in that,' replied Clare. 'What about you, Rob?'

'It's okay with me. All that I ask is that you don't touch me when I go under, it just tends to complicate things.'

'Certainly,' said the doctor. 'Could you two go and get a drink at the canteen and we'll meet back here in a few minutes? I'll arrange for all the visitors to leave. It's almost time for visiting hours to finish, anyway. I'll just tell them we're doing some kind of special procedure, which requires quiet and concentration. I'm sure they'll all understand. I know it's a lie, but it sounds more plausible than the truth.'

'Sure,' replied Clare. 'Come on, Rob, I could do with a coffee, anyway.'

The two of them headed out of the ICU and took an elevator downstairs to the ground floor. There, they found the hospital canteen and each retrieved a cappuccino from out of an automated machine. They sat down on one of the wooden tables dotted throughout the place and drank their coffees in silence, glad for the temporary reprieve from the constant cluster of noise that seemed to surround them over the past few days.

Once Clare had finished the cappuccino, draining it to the last drop, she broke the comfortable silence between them. 'I guess we'd better get back.'

'I guess so,' replied Rob, taking both his and Clare's cup, standing, and depositing them into a nearby bin. 'All right, I'm ready, if you are.'

'Before we go up there, Rob, I just wanted to tell you how much I, and all of us, really appreciate what you're doing.'

Rob smiled. 'Don't mention it,' he replied with a shy smile.'

The pair made their way back to the ICU, where Doctor Harris met them at the office and informed them everything was ready. 'Please put these on,' she said, handing out gowns and rubber gloves.

'I'll need to be able to touch Petrovski's skin for it to be able to work,' said Rob.

'That's okay,' said the doctor. 'You'll need to thoroughly wash and disinfect the hand that'll be out of the glove to prevent possible infection.'

Once they were appropriately dressed, and Rob had scrubbed his hand almost red-raw, the doctor led them into the unit and to Leonard Petrovski's bedside.

Rob looked at the man below him and for a brief moment and had a flashback to when Aroha lay in the ICU in Alice Springs. He also remembered her last moments of life and the sword sticking out of her chest. He tried to put it out of his mind and concentrate on the job at hand, although he found those visions to be somewhat disconcerting.

'You'll need to touch him, here,' said Helen pulling the curtains around the bed and pointing to his foot. 'It's one of the few places that he wasn't burnt, because he was wearing shoes and woollen socks.'

'No worries,' replied Rob taking a deep breath. 'All right, here goes,' he said as he placed his fingers on Leonard's right foot. Rob remembered some of the lessons he'd learnt at the monastery. One of which, was to centre his being and to slow his breathing, which helped him to concentrate. His teachers had taught him to see himself at the top of the world, looking down at all creation and to see the psychic patterns of everyone all at once, like seven billion unique fingerprints and then, to colour red the pattern of the person he wanted to look at. He'd done it under guidance, without having to touch anyone physically, since his psychic skills had advanced, thanks to his stay at the monastery, but without Mr. Betung here, it did make the process easier and more concrete for him, having the man's physical being underneath the tips of his fingers. He knew that he was a long way from mastering everything that his teachers had shown him. One of the things that did stick in his mind, though, was that there was no better way to master a skill than to actually use it in real-life circumstances and that his skills would improve with practice, each use of them helping him to become more adaptable.

Rob looked down from what felt like a high mountaintop and saw below him a long red trail, stretching out like an immense ribbon, flapping wildly in the wind, which he knew he had to follow. He'd practiced and succeeded at what he was about to do, more than a hundred times, but it still made him nervous. He heard the laughing voice of Mr. Betung in his head, encouraging him, assuring him that everything would be all right.

'Go, Rob, jump,' he said, 'follow your heart and you will prevail. Trust me, but most of all, trust all you are and all you can be.'

Rob took a few steps backwards and then ran and took a running jump off the cliff. He felt himself falling for a moment and then composed his thoughts and stopped still in mid-air, floating, feeling as light as a feather.

'I'll never get used to that,' he said as he directed his thoughts towards the blazing trail below him. He began to fly, picking up speed, watching mountain ranges and streams slip by in a blur. He passed over townships, pastures and meadows, over oceans and seas, moving with the speed of a jetfighter, until he finally recognised the city of Melbourne and the docklands below. There, he saw the trail lead onto the tanker, which had exploded a day ago, but here, in this reality, it was still intact, full of petroleum and seaworthy, as opposed to the condition he'd seen it in on the television news. It'd resembled a relic from some fierce war battle, completely burnt out and half-sunk to the bottom of the seabed.

Rob willed himself to land on the nearby pier and followed the red trail up the ship's gangway and onto the tanker itself. The ship was deserted and he remembered from the news story that the majority of the crew had escaped the inferno, having been on land, enjoying shore leave when the tanker had gone up. He followed the psychic trail, which led him further inside the ship and stopped at the captain's stateroom. He heard voices from behind the walls and then continued moving, passing through the steel of the barrier in front of him as though it didn't exist. Inside the room, he saw four men. One was obviously the captain of the ship and the two other younger men seemed to be his ship's officers, but the fourth man seated at the table, looked decidedly out of place. He had a long, dark beard and hair, and eyes that seemed to dart all around the place, taking in everything around him. He shifted uncomfortably in his chair as the captain spoke to him, his Russian accent distorted by his mouth full of toast. He heard the captain address him several times by the name

Arkmed. Rob took a closer look at the man and committed his likeness to memory, so that when he returned to the physical world he'd be able to compile a description for Clare and her colleagues. The closer he inspected him, the more he couldn't help but feel as if there was something false about him, as if his eyes didn't match the rest of him and were somehow younger, or more vibrant than the image he was attempting to convey.

The captain ordered one of the officers to leave the room, retrieve a silver case from his cabin and to bring it back to the stateroom, while he and the mysterious stranger continued with their breakfast. Rob stood in the background, anxiously waiting, somehow knowing in his gut that what the missing officer had gone to retrieve wasn't going to be good, and it had the potential to frighten the life out of him. The officer returned a few minutes later, carrying the briefcase, which the placed on the table in front of the captain, who then requested the younger men leave the two of them alone to conduct their business. The two younger officers left the stateroom, with quizzical looks upon their faces, both seemingly disappointed they hadn't been able to share in the captain's secret, nor see just exactly what was in the case, even though they were his most and senior crewmembers.

Rob remained in the room and witnessed the exchange between the captain and the bearded man. The seaman took a key from around his neck and opened up the case to reveal a machine of some description, which contained a red digital readout and several bright coloured switches. Rob noticed, too, there was a universal insignia for radiation plastered on the inside lid and he knew then, without any doubt, that a nuclear bomb had been brought into Australia. It made him feel sick with anxiety at just the thought of the scale of destruction this killer was intending to inflict on so many innocent people.

'You fucking piece of shit,' Rob shouted at the man and, although he knew his voice wouldn't reach their ears, or gain any acknowledgement whatsoever from the pair, it made him feel better for having expressed his anger.

When he managed to settle down, he listened to what they said to each other and this only confirmed what he already knew. It was a nuclear bomb. The captain left the table, walked over to the other side of the room, and opened a hidden safe, from which he removed an envelope, telling the mysterious man that inside were the codes required to arm and detonate the device. The captain asked when the other man was going to detonate the bomb, as he wanted to be out at sea and far away from the blast area.

'I'm not certain, but I'd be out of here in the next two weeks if I were you,' came the reply. Rob wished he could've been more specific, but at least he now had some sort of timeframe to deliver.

Once they'd finished their business, the captain walked the other man out onto the deck and looked up at the stars. 'It's a nice night,' he said looking up at the sky, 'and good to be in port, instead of out on the rough ocean. A man needs to be in a port now and again, it's good for the soul.'

'I'm sure it is,' agreed Arkmed, who went off into the night.

Rob attempted to follow him, but found himself restricted by the psychic trail he had chosen to follow. 'Damn,' he said. A moment later, there came a terrible rumbling, like approaching thunder as the ship exploded and the petroleum ignited below the decks, sending out flames a hundred feet into the air. He looked on as the captain and the two ship's officers became engulfed in flames. Of them, Leonard was the only one to make it over the side of the tanker and jump down into the water.

Rob opened his eyes and found himself back in the hospital, standing at the base of Leonard's bed, his fingers still lightly placed on the foot of the injured sailor.

'We need to talk,' he said to Clare. 'This is not good.'

'Is that all there is? You were only in your trance state for about two minutes,' observed the doctor.

Rob smiled at the medico. 'Time is relative,' he replied. 'Come on, Clare, we need to get back to the taskforce and talk to Ray about this.'

As they drove back to the office, Rob explained to the detective all he'd seen in his vision.

'Jesus,' said Clare. 'I think we're going to have to evacuate the city. At least, though, we still have some time to try and find this bastard before he sets that fucking thing off. You said about two weeks, right?'

'Yeah, that's what I heard, but you never know, this arsehole could be pretty unpredictable.'

'I think that both the commissioner and the minister for emergency services are just planning on saying something to the public about people remaining in their homes and not visiting any public places, at least for the time being. We can't really sit on this for too much longer. I guess when the time comes, they'll have to issue an evacuation order for the whole city, which is going to be a fucking logistical nightmare.'

Suddenly, Rob screamed and doubled over in his seat.

'What's the matter, Rob? What's going on?'

'It's Tony,' Rob wheezed, 'he's been taken by the bomber.'

'Christ, how do you know?'

'He just called out to me. He's being tortured and he needs our help.'

R.B. Clague • 100

Clare pulled the car up on the side of the road with a screech of brakes, causing several drivers behind her to swerve and swear at her as they passed.

'Can you tell where he is?'

'I honestly don't know,' replied Rob sitting back up, the pain now gone from him. 'Maybe if we go to his house, I can touch something that belongs to him. It might help, but I can't be sure.'

'All right,' said Clare, grabbing her mobile phone and dialling Ray Owen's number. 'We need a team to go straight to Tony Green's house. We think he's been taken by the FOTS bomber.'

'Shit,' said Ray. 'All right, I'm on it. Do you now how long ago?'

'No,' replied Clare. 'Rob just had a vision. He said Tony's being tortured by the prick. We're on our way there, now,' said Clare, banging the phone shut and leaning over to the passenger side, where she flipped open the glovebox, pulled out the flashing blue light, which she jammed into the cigarette lighter, and placed on the roof of the car over her head. 'Hang on,' she said to Rob as she switched on the siren and pressed the accelerator hard, sending the car rocketing out into the roadway, causing several cars to almost collide as they stopped suddenly to let her pass.

'Tony lives in East Brunswick, doesn't he? How long will it take to get there?'

'Normally, about ten minutes,' replied Clare as she ran a red light in the middle of Lygon Street, ignoring the multitude of blasting horns and screams of motorists who initially failed to see the police lights and hear the siren, 'but I reckon we can get there in two.'

As they went speeding down the street, Rob did his best to look out for obstacles that might impede their progress and to warn Clare in advance. In any other circumstance, he might have called Clare reckless and irresponsible and that dodging cars in this manner was paramount to committing vehicular suicide, but that seemed to matter little right now. Their friend was hurt and in danger and all other considerations seemed to pale in comparison.

Clare swore as they hit a traffic jam at the corner of Lygon and Rathdowne Streets, brought about by a reversing semi-trailer who'd hit another truck and had left his vehicle in the centre of the road, as he exchanged angry words with the other driver on the sidewalk. The detective honked her horn several times and when the driver failed to respond, she jumped out of the car, grabbed her gun, and put it to his head.

'If you don't move that truck out of my fucking way in the next ten seconds, you're going to be dead in eleven. You got that?'

'Yeah, yeah,' conceded the burly, overweight, middle-aged driver putting his hands in the air, 'whatever you want, lady, you're the boss.'

'Glad you could see it my way,' said Clare, who tucked her gun back inside her jacket, turned, and ran back to the car.

'You really are one tough bitch, Clare,' said Rob as she hopped back into her seat.

'When I have to be,' replied the detective who honked the car horn to hurry up the truck driver.

The driver pulled his rig over up onto the sidewalk and waved a hand for Clare to pass. She'd already put the car into gear and revved the engine, sending white smoke from off the tyres into the air as she took off. She stopped briefly at the next intersection, making sure it was safe, before slamming her foot down on the accelerator and squealing the tyres on the bitumen as she headed again for Tony's place.

They arrived in Tony's street a couple of minutes later and jumped out of the car, leaving the doors open and sprinted to Tony's front door, which they both noticed was ajar. Clare drew her gun and hit the light switch, illuminating the porch and the hallway in front of them, which led to the main body of the house.

'Stay behind me, we need to check out the house, before we do anything.'

'Look,' said Rob pointing the floor, 'that's blood there, isn't it?'

Clare led the way into the house, her firearm raised in front of her, checking out each individual room as she went. When finally she was satisfied there was no one inside, she returned to the kitchen, where she noticed the note left by Tony on the fridge.

'It looks like he was heading to the gym when he was taken. Judging by the blood on the floorboards, I'd say our FOTS guy ambushed him as he opened the door, probably whacked him over the head.'

Outside the house, the sounds of wailing police sirens increased, coming closer with every passing moment. A few seconds later, both Clare and Rob saw the flashing red and blue lights that bounced off the walls all the way up to the kitchen.

'Clare, Rob,' said Ray Owen, running up the hallway, a look of deep concern and stress spread across his features. 'No sign of Tony?'

'No, he's gone,' replied Clare, 'but we're going to try like hell to find him. Rob thinks if he can touch something belonging to Tony, he might get a handle on where he is.'

'Well, let's not stand around talking about it,' said Ray impatiently. 'Rob, do your thing.'

'I've got an idea,' said Rob, leaving the kitchen and walking back out to the front door. He bent down, stuck his index finger in the blood patch on the floor, and smeared it between his finger and his thumb.

'I get it,' said Clare as she and Ray joined him. 'The blood is part of Tony, so it's just like touching him.'

'That's the plan,' said Rob sitting on the hallway floor, closing his eyes and letting his mind take him to wherever it would. He could feel himself start to drift away, but a moment later, the sound of a woman screaming at the top of her lungs broke his concentration and brought him back to the house.

Clare grabbed the dark-haired woman and held her in a hug as she came running into the hallway.

'Where's Tony? What's happened here?'

'Come with me, Jenny,' said Clare leading her towards the kitchen, 'and I'll explain everything. Rob, get on with it, I'll take care of this.'

Rob sat there for a moment longer, feeling for the woman, unable to rouse his focus straight away. Nothing he'd seen so far had been as personal as this. He knew that, as soon as his mind drifted to wherever it had to go, he was going to see Tony, either in the midst of being tortured, if not dead, and he wasn't sure if he could handle it.

'I know this is hard,' said Ray leaning down and placing a hand on Rob's shoulder, 'but you're the only chance we've got to get Tony back alive.'

'Okay,' said Rob taking a deep breath and dipping his finger into the pool of blood on the floor. He again smeared the blood between his finger and his thumb and brought it up to his nose, hoping this would provide an extra boost to his senses and get him to where he wanted to go in quick time.

He closed his eyes and found himself in a dark room, the only light provided by a dim globe suspended from the roof, under which was Tony tied to a chair, wearing only a pair of boxer shorts. Rob tried, immediately, to find the exit so he could work out exactly where he was and inform the police, but for some reason, he was unable to move out of the room. He tried several times to pass through the walls, but to no avail. They were as concrete to him as if he was there in person. He figured Tony may have been unconscious all the way here and had woken up in the chair, so his psychic trail was blank in between his place and this room.

'Shit,' Rob hissed in frustration. He looked back over to where Tony sat and saw a dark figure emerge from out of the shadows. He watched as the figure placed another chair beside the detective and unfolded a small table, on which placed a large, bowie knife and several lighters.

'What the fuck are you gonna do?' Tony asked the man, his voice trembling with fear. 'Look, you don't have to do this. It's only going to be worse for you when they catch you, you know.'

'Mr. Green, please be quiet,' replied an electronic voice which came from the mouth of the figure, 'we'll get to our business, soon enough.'

Rob walked over to where Tony sat. He saw that the figure had on a long black cape and hood, which covered the colour of his hair and that on his face he wore a Darth Vader mask that must have contained some sort of electronic device, which altered the sound of his voice, making him sound like the character from Star Wars. The man in the cape picked up a knife, which glinted silver under the globe and showed it to Tony.

'Let me show you how sharp this is,' he said cutting a single line across Tony's chest and drawing blood, which began to leak down his front and onto his stomach. 'I can fix that,' he added picking up a lighter and heating the blade, until it turned black. He then ran the hot blade over the cut, cauterized the wound, and stopped the bleeding, causing Tony to scream out with pain.

'Now, I'm going to ask you some questions and I need to have some honest answers. Do you think you can do that for me, Detective Green?'

'Sure, fire away, you fucker,' replied Tony between gritted teeth.

'How did you find out about the bomb in the police station?'

Tony was silent for a moment considering his answer. 'A couple of rookies stumbled across it by accident.'

'Now, now, Detective Green, lying will not help you,' said the man in the mask as he heated up the blade of the knife again and placed it flat on Tony's breastbone. He dragged it for about six inches, causing the skin to burn and blister and for smoke to emanate from Tony's chest, the smell of which almost made Rob sick.

'Now, I'll ask you again, Detective Green. I know no one stumbled across the bomb, because I hid it too well for that to happen. 'So, tell me, how did the information come to you of its existence?'

'Go screw yourself, you sick fuck, I'm not telling you fuck all.'

'Oh, but Detective Green, you'll tell me everything and in short time, too, for I have been trained to torture by the very best in the business,' he said as he put down one lighter and picked up another. 'You can scream and shout all you want, but nobody can hear you. I have nothing personal against you, Detective Green, but I can't say I don't gain a certain amount of enjoyment and pleasure from your pain. You'll tell me what I want to know, and yet, you may even live.'

Tony managed to laugh through his tears and his agony. 'Piss off. Do you honestly think I'm some sort of dickhead? You're going to kill me, whether I tell you what you want to know, or not.'

'If I was going to kill you, why would I wear a mask? I could just as easily show you who I am. If I injure you, however, and get the information I require, it will be a severe blow to the morale of the police, knowing I could take and toy with one of their own as I see fit.'

'When Clare Carbone gets a hold of you, arsehole, she's going to blow a hole in you the size of a fuckin' fist. You just wait, you piece of shit!'

'Ah, the esteemed Ms. Carbone, we've yet to meet, but no doubt, she'll be sitting in that same chair, not so long after you've vacated it.'

'If you can get to her now, you must be good. Because by now, she and the top knobs in the force will be aware of what's going on and they'll be right on guard against you, so good luck with that.'

'Anyway, that's enough chatter,' said the man in the mask as he put the lighter down and then placed the heated blade on Tony's genitals, causing him to scream out in agony and collapse into unconsciousness, his mind unable to grapple with the pain or the realisation of what'd just occurred.

Rob came to, sitting again in the hallway of Tony's house and swore at not being able to discern the location of where the detective was being held, or even by whom. He could do nothing but weep tears of frustration, sadness, and horror.

'Can you go back?' Clare asked him.

'Yeah, but I don't know if it'll do much good. I can't see where he is and all I'm doing is witnessing his torture, which may have already occurred. I don't care how tough Tony is; he's going to tell this prick everything he wants to know in the end. No one could stand that type of torture for long.'

'So, then,' said Clare, 'we can assume he's going to know about you.'

'Yeah, I guess that's a pretty fair assumption,' replied Rob. 'Oh, one thing I did gather, Clare, is that he's coming after you, too, but once he knows about me, I guess I'm going to be his main target.'

'Yeah, that's right,' said Clare. 'You're the only one who has the potential to fuck up his plans and he won't stand for that. It might, though, give us an opportunity to use you as bait to catch this arsewipe when he makes his move. What do you think?'

'It's sure worth a shot. Nothing else has worked so far, so I guess we gotta get radical.'

R.B. Clague • 108

CHAPTER THIRTEEN

Rob, Clare, and the rest of the taskforce sat in front of the television as the commissioner and the minister for police and emergency services faced the cameras for the umpteenth time that week.

'Ladies and gentlemen,' said a ministerial spokeswoman, 'Minister Harding will first make a statement and will then answer a few questions, thank you.'

The minister stood behind the microphone. From what Clare could see, he appeared to have aged ten years over the past few days and looked just about the way she felt, with his drawn, stressed face and grey hair that seemed to have turned almost white since this bomber had first made his presence known.

'Ladies and gentlemen of the press and my fellow Victorians, I come before you today with a grave undertaking. Our beloved city of Melbourne has come under siege by a person or persons who identify themselves as The Fire of the Sun. The commissioner of police has received a communication from this person, or group, claiming there are thirty bombs similar to the bomb that destroyed the St. Kilda Road Police complex, the tanker at the Melbourne Docklands, and the supermarket in Northcote, planted in various locations all around the city. We are urging all citizens to remain their homes and not to visit any public facilities unless it is vital, at least for the time being. We would ask that anyone who decides to evacuate the city, please do so in an orderly fashion.'

'Like that's going to happen,' said Ray. 'The highways are going to be more clogged than a constipated arsehole.'

'I'd have thought that you and Peter Bell would've been at the press conference, to lend support,' said Clare.

'Given what's happened to Tony, the commissioner thought it best to limit our personal exposure to the press.'

'A joint taskforce,' continued the minister, 'consisting of approximately thirty state and federal police officers, was several days ago established to deal with this matter and we believe it's only a matter of time before this terrorist or terrorists are apprehended and face the full weight of the law. We would also ask that members of the public keep an eye open for anything suspicious that may lead police to potential suspects and to inform the FOTS Taskforce on the 1800 number which will appear now on your screen. I will now hand you over to Commissioner Ron Rouse, after which we'll answer a few of the questions from the journalists present. Thank you for your patience.'

Ron Rouse took centre stage as the minister backed away from the microphone. He, too, looked like a man under immense pressure, and had large, dark circles under his eyes as though he hadn't slept in a week.

'Jesus, I wouldn't want to be his personal assistant right now,' commented Ray. 'He's a moody, bad-tempered bastard when everything's going well. I can't imagine what a pain the arse he'd be at the moment.'

The police commissioner reiterated the initial message given by the minister, urging people not to go to work, or to use any public facilities for the time being. 'So far, we've only been able to identify one man. We believe that this man goes by the name of Arkmed, although it might well be an alias. We have made an identikit drawing of the suspect, which will now appear on your screen. Should you see this man or know him, please contact the FOTS Taskforce immediately. Thank you. Now we'll take a few questions from the press gallery.'

Rob looked at the drawing of the suspect when it appeared on the screen. With its dark eyes, dark hair, and grey-flecked beard. The same feeling of falseness crept over him, as though this was some sort of disguise, perhaps meant to fool the public if anyone actually survived the tanker blast. 'I don't think he looks like that anymore,' he said.

'Probably not,' agreed Ray. 'I mean, take a look at the drawing, it's almost stereotypical. We're going to get a thousand phone calls in the next few hours, reporting every Muslim, Orthodox Jew, Seikh, and old man with a beard in the city of Melbourne. You got to hand it to this guy, he's bloody brilliant at covering his tracks and clouding the waters.'

'Yeah, he's so brilliant, it makes you think he might have had training in that area,' said Clare to no one in particular.

'What do you mean?' Ray asked.

'I think guy has, at some point, had some involvement with some sort of terrorist organisation. Maybe he's on his own, you know, gone rogue, or he could be working for someone. Although, no terrorist organisation is going to accept responsibility for detonating a nuclear bomb, killing innocent citizens, it's not very good publicity for whatever cause they believe in.'

'That could be,' interjected Peter. 'I've got agents looking into anyone who might be involved in terrorist activities. They've been bringing people in and questioning them around the clock, but so far, with no luck. If anyone knows about this shithead, they're either too scared to say anything, or simply just don't know. He's a fucking ghost with a bomb and that's just about my worst nightmare.'

'Yeah, mine, too,' said Ray, who stood and turned off the television. 'Clare, I want you to take Rob and have him issued with a firearm. Then take him to the range and teach him how to shoot it without shooting himself. Rob, please don't give me any argument about you not wanting a gun, it just won't fly. Now listen to me very carefully, the both of you, I don't you to be out of sight of each of each other for a minute. If one of you goes to the toilet, the other is to wait outside. With what we know about this lunatic from Rob's last vision, he's going to come looking for one or both of you and I want you to be prepared. That's an order, do you understand?'

'Sure, boss,' replied Clare.

'Got it,' said Rob.'

'I'll also be issuing you both with locater devices that can be hidden in your clothes and assigning a detail to protect you both, and if FOTS makes a move to snatch either of you, we'll be there. I don't want either of you to go home and I'll arrange for a hotel where you can stay. I'll have someone go to your house and pick up anything you need, Clare. Just make a list and leave it with me. Rob, your stuff is still in Clare's car. Is there anything else you need?'

'I'm pretty right. I will need to get some essentials, like shaving stuff, razors, foam, and some soap, but I'm okay for now with what I've got.'

'Clare, after you've taken him to the range, take him, and buy him a suit and tie. You can charge it to the department and get him a haircut while you're there,' said Ray handing her a departmental credit card. 'If he's going to be a copper, then he at least, needs to look like one. I don't want to bring the force into disrepute, by having the papers say that we have a fucking hippy in our employ. Rob, you just look too distinguishable from the other coppers and that could single you out to FOTS. Let's not make his job any easier, if we can avoid it. When you've done all that, I want you both to go over the individual crime scenes and see if you can't come up anything new. Rob, we're working on trying to locate fragments of the actual bombs. If we can do that, do you think you could use your gift to try and see something that could help us?'

'I'll give it a try, Ray. I'll certainly do my best.'

'Good,' said Ray. 'Okay, the two of you can get going. Oh, and just one more thing, Clare, you are to call me every hour on the hour on my mobile phone, until the protection team show up. I'll assume if your call is fifteen minutes late, you're in trouble.'

'Okay,' said Clare. 'So, where do we go to get fitted for the locaters?'

'I've called tech services. They're now in the Royal Air force building in St. Kilda Road. That's where you'll be picking up Rob's firearm as well. You'll also be using the Air Force firing range, to practice with the firearm. Got any further questions?'

'Do you know which hotel we'll be staying at?' Rob asked.

'Not yet,' answered Ray with a smile, 'but I'll try to make it a good one, because of the inconvenience.'

'Do we get a minibar?' joked Clare. 'I could sure use a drink.'

'You two need to be one your toes, so, no, no minibar, I'm afraid.'

'All right,' said Clare, standing, 'we're outta here.'

'Don't forget,' said Ray, 'call me every hour, and that's an order.'

'We won't,' said Clare heading out the door.

'I'll remind her,' said Rob with a smile as he followed the detective.

The two of them took the elevator down to the basement of the building, riding in silence, their thoughts occupied by what Tony must be enduring at that very moment. They'd both tried to put on a brave face, but knew the longer it took for him to be found, or turn up somewhere, the more likely the chances of his never making it back to them.

'Damn,' said Clare, kicking the elevator wall in frustration as tears began to well in her eyes, 'I just wish there was something we could do. I've never felt so fuckin' useless in my whole life. I love that man as if he was my younger brother and I know he's out there somewhere, hurt and in pain and there's not a thing I can do to stop it.'

'I know,' said Rob. 'I wish I could be more help. I have this so-called gift, but I might as well be walking around blind.'

Clare fell into Rob's arms and began to sob into his chest and it surprised him, because she was always so together, so collected and calm. Still, it was good to see she had a human side, a part of her that still recognised the pain of others, despite all the terrible things she must have seen throughout her career.

Rob realised as soon as it happened, that it must have been that moment of vulnerability, the complete surprise of seeing her emotions come to the fore that stripped him of his own control and sent him reeling back into Clare's past. He found himself standing before a huge lake, the water glistening as sunshine fell from a perfect blue sky. He looked over from where he stood and saw an old man and a young girl sitting on a pontoon looking out onto the water, their fishing lines dangling into the deep below them. They seemed happy in each other's company, as if they were good friends.

Rob walked up the pontoon and knew from first sight he was looking at Clare, but that she couldn't have been more than thirteen or fourteen years old. She had the same dark hair and penetrating brown eyes and yet, they were softer, more innocent, not yet hardened by the career that she'd one day choose. She spoke almost reverently to the old man and Rob wondered who he was in relation to her. He seemed too old to be her father and after listening to their conversation for a little while, he heard her call him Nono, which he knew is the Italian word for grandfather.

'There's something that I need to tell you, Clare,' said the old man.

'I thought so,' she replied as she adjusted her line.

'How did you know?'

'It seemed kind of strange you would invite me just fishing without the rest of the family. I thought you might want to say something.'

'You're a smart kid, you know that?'

'I get it from you,' said Clare with a smile.

'Can you guess what is?'

'I've thought about it all week,' said Clare, 'ever since you phoned the house and Mum told me you wanted me to come with you. I don't know exactly, but I don't think it's good. Mum and Dad have been kind of strange for the past couple of weeks and I heard Mum crying in her room one night.'

The old man smiled. 'Yes, your mother can be a bit emotional at times. She lost her mother not long ago and I guess the news that I'm dying, too, has struck her hard.'

Clare turned and looked at the old man. A single tear ran down her cheek and she held him close, sobbing into his chest in the same way she had with Rob in the elevator. 'I thought that was what it might be,' she said between her tears. 'I guess I just didn't want to hear it said it out loud.'

'I know,' said the old fellow, with great gentleness. 'I could hardly believe it myself, although it didn't come as a complete surprise. I've been feeling a bit tired lately, as if I've run a long race and it's time to rest. When your grandmother passed away, I felt as if something broke inside me and I think somewhere deep inside, I knew I'd soon be joining her.'

'Nono, do you think that you will go to be with Nona? Do you think that there's a heaven?'

'It's funny you should ask that,' said the old man, running his hand along Clare's dark hair, which shone under the rays of the sun, 'because I've been giving it a lot of thought, lately. I've attended church my whole life, mostly at your Nona's urging. I've prayed to God and I've accepted communion, but truth is, my darling, I don't know what's out there, with any certainty. I feel, though, in my bones, that if there is any justice in the universe, then your grandmother and I will one day be reunited and then she can nag at me for the rest of eternity.'

Clare laughed and Rob couldn't help but to chuckle, too. He must have been some old man with a sense of humour like that.

'Don't worry, though, Clare, I'm going to be around for a while yet, so we'll still be able to spend time together.'

'So what's the matter with you, Grandpa?'

'I've had leukaemia for about five years now. It's not a fast acting disease, but it's got to the point where the doctors don't think they can do much more for me. I was in, what they call a remission phase for a while, but it started up again and they can't seem to slow it down this time.'

'So, how long have you got, did the doctors say?'

'They give me anywhere from six months to a year, which is a lifetime, if you think about it. I mean, you can do and say a lot in six months, and even more in a year. I guess it's better than getting hit by a bus and not being able to say everything you want to the people you love.'

'Yeah, I guess it is,' said Clare hugging him tight.

'When I'm gone, Clare, I want you to know, that if it's possible, I'll be looking out for you from wherever I am. I know you'll become a fine, outstanding woman and do great things in the world and I'd really like to see that. My only disappointment is that I won't be there to congratulate my favourite granddaughter in person.'

'You know I'll never, ever forget you, don't you, Nono? If I ever do get to do great things in the world, I'll always think of you.'

'Anyway, that's enough morbid stuff, for the time being. So, tell me Clare, have you given any thought to what you want to do with your future?'

'Not a lot,' answered Clare, looking out onto the water. 'I mean, it seems so far away. I've thought about becoming a cop, the same as you were in Italy, when you helped put away all those mafia criminals. I thought that was pretty cool.'

'Joining the police is a fine calling, Clare. I always felt proud to protect and serve the people of my state and it's not bad money the further you advance, either. Not that money was my main consideration, but it certainly helped your Nona and me to have a comfortable life back in the old country, and for us to move to Australia when I retired, so we could be closer to your family.'

'I remember when you and Nona first came to Australia,' said Clare with a laugh, 'and you picked me up and hugged me at the airport. I didn't know you and you seemed like you were seven-feet tall then, but I remember I felt safe and warm in your arms and in Nona's, too.'

The old man laughed. 'You still remember that?'

'Like it was yesterday,' replied Clare.

'That's nice,' said the old fellow smiling warmly, 'because a cop needs a good memory.'

Rob looked around when he heard a woman, who looked remarkably like the adult Clare step out onto the porch of a nearby house and yell out to the pair. 'Gino, Clare, come inside and have some lunch.'

Clare and the old man wound up their fishing lines, packed up their tackle and headed towards the house. Rob watched as the old man put his arm around her shoulders as they walked. He didn't feel right about going up to the house, as if it'd be some sort of invasion of their privacy and he already felt like something of a voyeur, having seen the interaction between the two of them.

'She's grown up to be a good woman, hasn't she?'

Rob turned around and saw Gino standing there, a wide smile spread across his face.

'Yes, she has. She's one of the most dedicated, sensitive, and intelligent people I know,' replied Rob.

'I like to think that she got her smarts from me,' laughed the old man, 'but it's more likely they came from her grandmother.

'Oh, I don't know,' said Rob. 'It seems like you were pretty smart yourself, in your day.'

Gino laughed. 'I like to think I was a good leader, but the truth is, I had many smart people looking out for me when I was a cop. The best rule you can follow as a detective is to surround yourself with smart people. Clare knows that, and that's why she relies on you so much.'

'I don't think of myself as being particularly smart,' said Rob. 'She could probably do a lot better.'

'You may not be a trained police officer, but you're talented, Rob, that's for sure, in ways most people can't even comprehend. I just wanted to take the opportunity to tell you that I'm glad you and Clare are working together and you've become friends, because by the time this is all over, it'll be your friendship that makes the difference between life and death.'

'You're talking about the choice that Aroha said I'd have to make?'

'I am,' replied Gino. 'There'll come a time when you're faced with the choice of risking everything, to maybe survive, or taking the alternative route and saving the lives of people that you have come to love and moving onto a higher plane. It won't be easy, but I'm sure when the time arrives, you'll know what to do. Just follow your heart, Rob, it'll lead you along the right path.'

'It's not an easy thing, knowing I'm probably going to die,' said Rob as he picked up a smooth stone from the bank and skimmed it across the water. He watched as it planed the surface five or six times and then plopped into the drink.

'No, it's never easy to know you're going to die,' agreed Gino, 'but in some ways, it's harder for those left behind. It's something you can come to terms with, and help others to as well, if you say what you need to, to the people you love before the time arrives. I was lucky, I had more than a year, but you might not have so long. Make sure you do it, Rob, or it might be something you regret for a very, very long time.'

'I will,' said Rob already contemplating what he'd like say to his sister, her husband, his niece, and his nephew.

'Good,' said Gino, 'it would be best. I must leave now, and you need to return to the world. Would you do me a favour when you get back?'

'Sure, just name it.'

'Would you tell Clare you saw me and that I'm well and very proud of her and have been keeping an eye on her progress, like I said I would? I think it'd mean a lot to her.'

'Yeah, okay,' said Rob, 'I might leave out the bit about me dying, though. I think she has enough on her plate right now, without that.'

'A good decision,' said Gino extending his hand. 'I'll be seeing you, Rob, take care.'

'Yeah, you too,' replied Rob as he grabbed the other man's hand in a firm grip and then found himself back inside the elevator, Clare's head resting upon his shoulder.

'I'm sorry,' said the detective moving back and taking a handkerchief from the pocket of her jacket, 'I don't usually let things get to me.'

'That's okay, Clare, you don't have to explain, I understand.'

'Thanks,' said Clare dabbing her eyes and fixing her smudged makeup using a small compact she took from her bag, 'and not a word to anyone, all right?'

'Cross my heart and hope to die,' said Rob with a sad smile. 'You're secret's safe with me.'

The two of them stepped out of the elevator in the basement of the building and headed towards the dark blue Commodore parked a couple of lines back. Clare grabbed her keys from her jacket pocket and opened the car from about thirty feet away. Just as they reached the vehicle, another car pulled up at the rear of Clare's, which contained two men, both of which looked not the least bit like police. The driver had a long, dark beard and wore overalls, as though employed in some sort of trade. The second man, sitting in the passenger seat, had dark skin and dreadlocks down to his shoulders. He also wore a denim jacket, which had a large marijuana leaf fixed over one of the breast pockets.

Clare moved her hand inside her jacket, and grabbed the handle of the Glock.

The driver wound down the window as they pulled up to Clare. 'Sergeant Carbone, g'day, I'm Russell Downy,' said the bearded fellow extending his hand out the window, 'and this Le Mar Johnston, we're part of the surveillance team that's going to be looking out for you.'

Both Clare and Rob breathed visible sighs of relief. 'Jesus, I'm glad you identified yourselves,' said Clare as she took his hand. 'To tell you the truth, I was just about ready to shoot the both of you. So, where did they pull the two of you from?'

'We're narcotics unit, undercover,' replied Russell. 'There are six of us, in all, who've been assigned to look after both you and Mister Swift. You'll meet the whole team once you get down to technical. The rest of the guys are waiting down there.'

'I don't know about Rob, but you can cut out the Sergeant Carbone thing and just call me Clare, unless we're with the brass, all right?'

'Mister Swift was my father,' said Rob with a laugh, 'I'll be happy with just plain old Rob.'

'Yeah, no worries,' said Russell with a smile. 'Here, take this,' he added handing over a small two-way radio. 'Keep this with you at all times, Clare. It'll just help us to keep an eye on you and make sure you have it turned on. Not much good having a radio if we can't talk to you.'

'Yeah, not a problem,' replied Clare who inspected the device and turned a switch to the on position at the top. She pressed the signal send button on the side, spoke into the face of the radio, and heard her voice echo from the pocket of Le Mar's jacket.

'Good,' said Russell. 'It looks like we're clear to go. We'll give it another test when we're on the road, just to be sure, but technical say it's good for up to about three or four kilometres.'

'So, you'll follow us down to technical?' Clare asked as she started to move towards her own car.

'That's the way surveillance generally works,' replied Russell with a laugh. 'We follow you, not the other way around.'

'Ah, a smartarse,' retorted Clare as she opened her car door. 'I can see I'm going to like you and your team already.'

Clare and Rob waited for the automatic door to open in the basement and then drove out into the city. The first thing they noticed was that there was an inordinate amount of traffic for that time of the day and, as Rob looked at the faces of the people in the passing cars, he would see that many people were frightened and heading for home, wanting to be away from anywhere a bomb might go off.

'I guess a lot of people must have just chucked it in and took off from work.'

'Yeah, it looks that way,' said Clare, also noticing the frightened looks on people's faces. 'That means the traffic out of the city is going to be clogged up for a while, but once everybody gets out, things should ease up a bit.'

Rob jumped when the radio went off inside Clare's pocket and Le Mar asked in his Jamaican accent if they were receiving their signal.

'Could you get that, Rob?' Clare asked tossing him the radio.

'Yep, no worries,' said Rob into the radio. 'You're coming in loud and clear.'

'Good,' said Le Mar. 'It doesn't look like we're going to be at technical anytime soon. We're about six cars behind, but we have a good visual on you. So, take it easy and just enjoy the relaxation while you have the chance. We'll check in every half hour or so.'

'No worries,' said Rob.

Clare switched on the stereo and auto-tuned it to Triple J. 'I remember this from when I was kid,' she said with a laugh as an old Skyhooks song radiated from the dash, all electric guitars, bass, and the distinctive voice of Shirley Strachan as he belted out lyrics about living in the 70s.

'Yeah, me too,' said Rob smiling. 'Speaking about being a kid, you look a lot like your mother, don't you, Clare?'

'Yeah, well, I did, before she died, but how do you know that? You've never seen a photo of her. I'm not really one for bringing that sort of sentimental crap into the office.'

'I know,' replied Rob, 'because I saw your mother call you and your grandfather in for dinner on the day he told you he was dying. You were fishing off a pontoon, in a lake near his house.'

'When did you see that?'

'In the elevator, on the way downstairs, when you touched me, I couldn't help it. I just suddenly found myself back there.'

'Well, just to clarify things for you, that wasn't our actual house, it was our holiday place, in Kinglake. I grew up in Doncaster, but we used to go up there on holidays and on weekends, sometimes. My dad and Gino went halves in it. God, I haven't been back there for years.'

'There's something else, too,' said Rob.

'Oh, what's that?'

'I spoke to Gino. He wanted me to tell you he's well and very proud of you and that he has been watching you ever since he left this plane of existence.'

Clare felt the tears beginning to well in her eyes as she thought about the old man, with his thick silver mane of hair that glistened in the sunlight of the lake and his kind, compassionate eyes that always understood her heart, even when no one else could. She reached down, pulled her kerchief from her pocket, and dabbed at her eyes.

'That's the second time today that I've cried, and in the last hour,' she laughed. 'I'm turning into a big girl.'

CHAPTER FOURTEEN

The snow-capped mountains loomed large in the distance, foreboding, as if they were omnipotent gods, ready to take on all challengers that dared to transgress their borders. The men sat in front of their fires and devoured their meagre rations without speaking. The sun scorched down upon them. The leader of their party told them to enjoy it while they could, for soon, they would be heading to the mountains to undertake intense guerrilla training.

Mark knew just what meant, and that it wouldn't be pleasant, having been through the routine on several occasions over the past three years and although he knew the hell he had to look forward to, it would still be hard, especially for the new recruits. It was necessary, though, for not only did it toughen them up physically, it also served to increase their hatred of the enemy, to blacken their hearts to mercy and to blame the infidels who lived in comparable comfort and luxury for their hardship and pain.

Mark stood, threw his paper plate into the flames, and walked out into the desert, found himself a spot where he could be alone and lit up a cigarette. He loved the desert, the feeling of complete isolation you could find if you just stepped fifty feet away from the rest of your party. When those welcome, but seldom-realised breaks from killing, patrolling, or training had arrived, he'd found time to meditate in the great nothingness of broken stones and sand. In the immense deafening silence that surrounded him, he'd sometimes felt as if he was about to be bestowed with some great insight, or revelation, but the feeling just as quickly slipped away, like a vague memory, leaving him feeling unsated and in pain. In those times, his need for vengeance, to see others suffer as he had, seemed more intense, more palpable, in the absence of anything else and he would seethe with rage for days after.

'Arkmed,' called a voice from the camp, 'come on, we're going.'

Mark stubbed his cigarette out in the dirt and placed the butt into his jacket pocket, leaving no tangible trace of his presence. He looked once more at the mountains in the distance and then turned and walked back to join the other men.

He returned to the campsite, jumped into the front passenger seat of one of the old U.S. army jeeps the group had commandeered during one of their many raids on the infidels and sat back, letting the driver take him further into the desert towards the far off snow peaks. It took them almost four hours of driving, stopping only once to stretch their legs and to refuel the vehicles with gas that sat in the back of the jeeps, to reach the base of the mountains. Once there, the group emptied the supplies from out of the vehicles and hid the jeeps in a secluded cave, placed brush, camouflage canvas, and dirt over the entrance to hide them from prying eyes, or enemy patrols that might stumble upon them, although the chances of that were relatively slim. The enemy were many hated things to him and this group of freedom fighters, but one thing they weren't was stupid. They didn't venture this far into the mountains. There were too many places where they could be ambushed and either captured and interrogated for information, or just killed outright and not even the foolhardy American, English, or Australian soldiers would try that, at least not for the time being.

Mark knew that one day they would come in force and then they'd be forced to move on to someplace else. Staying alive was imperative for him and his group. They had many missions in far off places to complete before they finally made their way to heaven, or the great void, or whatever else waited out there for them, once their time on this planet ended. Until then, though, Mark and his band of brothers would cause as much disruption and death as they were able to manage, until those bastard infidels left this land of his ancestors, or indeed, they were all dead.

Each of the men grabbed a heavy pack, lifted it onto their shoulders, and made sure that their automatic weapons were locked and loaded, ready for use, before heading off in single file on a trail that led upwards into the mountains.

After about an hour of constant marching, the group took a rest on a rocky ridge and looked down from where they'd come. Their breath came in tired gasps and no one spoke as they laid their heavy burdens down onto the ground and collapsed into the dirt, glad for even the slightest reprieve from the relentless uphill march.

It took but a few minutes for the sweat on the inside of his jacket to turn freezing cold once he'd rested, now that they'd reached the snowline. He lit up a cigarette and drew in the smoke, glad for the reprieve, but also wanting to get moving soon, so he could warm up again. He let the smoke drift away from him and listened to the silence that surrounded him. He liked silence, but at the same time, he hated it, for sometimes in those quiet moments, he could hear his own voice screaming inside his head. If he concentrated, he could block the sound out, but always it was there; the need for revenge, which he knew would always enslave him until the day he took his last breath. He would always find another enemy onto which he would vent his anger and he wondered sometimes, if the infidel, whom he worked hard to destroy were, in fact, the other enemy, second only to his own self-hatred and loathing.

'Come, we must be going,' said the group commander. 'It is not too far now and you can all rest there for the night, before your training begins in the morning.'

The group stood and again shouldered the heavy packs, without a word of complaint. That was one thing Mark noticed the most in terms of the differences between these men and the men who fought for Europe, and the West. Their motivations were completely different. Those men in the West, in places like Australia, America, and Britain, would've complained about having to get up and climb up a mountain in the freezing cold and almost impenetrable darkness, but these men thought what they were doing was a sacred duty, a part of a greater holy war that Allah had directed them to undertake.

Mark didn't believe in Allah, or in fact, any god at all. His time at university had turned him into a confirmed atheist and existentialist, although he went through the motions and prayed with the other men, five times per day, bowing and scraping on his prayer mat, professing a love of the almighty Allah and adhering to the strict behavioural norms of the Muslim religion, but only because it served his purpose. These extremists had what he wanted and needed; connections, and international networks that had both the motivation and access to the type of weapons he wished to employ for the purposes of his vengeance and they also provided him with the training he required to use them to maximum effect.

In a lot of ways, he thought both sides were as bad as each other, killing indiscriminately and for no good reasons when it really came down to it, but it'd been those Australian soldiers who'd chosen his side for him, on that fateful day in the desert and in that bathroom in Sweden. Every hardship he endured on this journey only stiffened his resolve to hurt them even more and hurt them he would, in ways they could never imagine. When the time was right, he would systematically destroy as many people in that country as was humanly possible.

Finally, after what seemed like an eternity of drudgery and exhaustion, they found the entrance to the basecamp, located inside one of many caves that bore deep into the mountainside. The commander of the group waited until the twelve of them had entered the cave, instructed them to proceed in single file and then came in at the rear, and produced a flashlight to help them guide their way. He gave the torch to another member of the group and grabbed a straw broom hidden inside the dark recesses of shadow and swept away their footprints as he trailed behind, so that following them to their destination would be impossible.

'Here,' he said, handing off the broom to another of the troupe, 'make sure you get all the footprints. Your life may one day depend on it.'

Mark had been inside this cave about a dozen times in the last three of years, but even so, he couldn't have found his way to the camp, if his life depended on it. It was a very tightly guarded secret, so that only a dozen men knew their way, and there were a number of alternative routes in and out, which made it even more confusing. He'd been told, that should any of the fighters be captured by the enemy, even with torture, they would be unable to give up either the location of the cave, which was always approached in darkness, or the location of the camp inside, due to the confusing twists and turns that one had to take to get there. It was rumoured those men, who did possess the knowledge, made a vow to commit suicide if faced with capture, rather than disclose the location of the base. Allah would supposedly forgive their suicides, if their deaths resulted in the greater good.

The group's leader kept the beam of the flashlight focused on the floor of the cave so, for those who didn't know their way, would see no landmarks to give away their position. The group travelled through the darkness in silence, nary a word uttered between them, except for when the leader ordered them to change direction and proceed down a different tunnel. The only other sound was the constant sound of the sweeping broom behind them. They moved along in this manner for about a half hour and then without warning, they walked into a huge cavernous area, which Mark estimated to be about half the size of a stadium. There, they saw about a dozen fires, which men sat around, talking in whispers and sleeping on cushions and improvised bedrolls.

Their initial appearance caused some suspicion and several automatic weapons were raised and pointed in their direction, until someone recognised the group's leader and to his surprise, Mark himself, who'd always tried to keep under the radar and remain as inconspicuous as possible.

'Welcome,' said an older bearded man who jumped up from one of the fires, strode over to the group, and hugged the commander. 'Allah be praised you made it here, safe and well.'

'Yes, praise Allah,' agreed the commander returning the hug. 'My men are hungry and tired. Would you see to it that they are fed and accommodated?

'Of course,' said the older man smiling and turning to the group. 'Please follow me.'

'Just leave your packs over there,' said the commander pointing to a spot in the sand. 'I'll have someone sort them out in good time.'

The men complied with the order and dropped their packs with many sighs of relief. They then proceeded to follow the old man, stretching and rotating their shoulders as they moved along.

'The prophet wishes to see you, as soon as you've eaten and washed.'

'Very well,' replied the commander, dropping his own pack on top of the rest. 'You may tell him I'll be there shortly.'

Mark, of course, was well aware of just who they were talking about. The man, simply known as the Prophet, was the leader of the whole movement, a man who'd planned and carried out many successful attacks on foreign soils and had sent many a martyr to their deaths with bombs strapped to their bellies. He was a man that all the western governments wanted to get their hands on; in fact, he was *the* man, who would be the poster boy for the war on terror if they ever caught him. There was a twenty-five million dollar reward on his head for anyone who could provide information that led to his capture. Yet, despite this, he had so far, managed to elude the long arm and complex nature of such governments for almost two decades, and from what Mark could tell, would probably continue to do the same for many years to come.

The old man, whose man was Yousef, led the group to the far end of the cave, where an improvised kitchen stood and informed the men they could help themselves to what food was available. He also informed them where they could secure extra bedrolls and recommended that they get to sleep early, as training was due to start at first light. Many of the exhausted men needed little encouragement to eat just enough to stave off hunger and collapse in front of the fires, almost asleep before their heads touched their pillows.

Mark woke early the following morning, placed a couple of pieces of wood from a nearby pile onto the fire in front of him, and warmed his body by the flame as he smoked a cigarette. The only other people awake at that time, were the three men stationed to keep watch at the entrance. They smiled and waved at him as he stood and made his way to the kitchen, where he prepared a pot of strong, Turkish coffee and ate some bread, which he chewed listlessly as his mind began to awaken. He looked around and saw that there were about one hundred men of differing nationalities who slept around the fires. Of course, he couldn't well who was who at a mere glance, but on his previous visits, he'd come to know a few of the other fighters and was somewhat surprised by their diversity. Some of them had never set foot in Afghanistan before. They were the descendants of parents who'd long ago fled the country, when the Russians had unsuccessfully tried to occupy the land, before the current force that now occupied the country. There were others, who'd betrayed their own countries for ideological reasons, because they didn't believe in what their compatriots were doing. However, the majority of those that fought for the liberty of this country were people like him, who'd been harmed and damaged by the occupying forces, so determined to break the people and turn the place into another United States of America, or a little Australia.

What those forces hadn't bargained on, was the ferocity of the Afghans to resist those armies and to become organised under the banner of the Prophet and that, thought Mark, was the fundamental difference between the occupying forces sent here and those people who claimed this as a homeland far back into antiquity. They arrived here, based on orders from the generals and politicians, who sent them, and they received a salary, but the people who fought for the land, did so out of passion and a wish to sustain their culture, as it has been for thousands of years. The other thing the western forces hadn't foreseen was the ability of those freedom fighters to move the war back to the countries that sent it here in the first place. To take it back to Mr. and Mrs. Citizen, who sat back in their comfortable armchairs, in their middle class neighbourhoods and saw the conflict from a distance, as if they were watching a movie produced out of some Hollywood studio. When he got his chance, the people of Australia would see the conflict close up, as they'd never seen it before.

Before long, other men began to emerge from out of their bedrolls and make their way to the kitchen, ready to fill up their stomachs before the day's training began. After all the men had eaten, the entire collective pulled out their prayer mats and offered up ritualised praises to Allah, as the sun rose, while they faced Mecca and another of the group sang out passages from the Koran.

When their supplications ended, three commanders divided them up and took command of a group each. The first of the groups moved into an adjoining cave, where they would practice hand-to-hand combat, the second were led outside to a firing range to master both their accuracy with pistols and their sniper techniques, and the third, of which Mark was a part, were led outside for what Yousef called endurance training.

Mark's group walked again in darkness, blindly following the group leader, but this time through another series of connecting tunnels and out into the light of day. The commander ordered each member of the group to remove all of their clothing except for their pants and to place them in a pile at the mouth of the cave. The men stood in a single line, shivering in the intense cold of the mountains and the snow that already ached their exposed feet.

Mark remembered the first time he'd undertaken such training, and at the time, he thought he'd die, but he hadn't and it only served to make him stronger and more intent on his revenge. The majority of the men thought they were actually there for endurance training. Mark knew, though, it really was just a technique for creating extremism and hate for the enemy. Once this day was over, some of the men would be dead, for if they couldn't stand the rigours of such brainwashing they were no good to the collective. Those who failed were subtly taken to some isolated place, allowed final prayers to Allah and then had a bullet lodged in their skulls, their families informed anonymously later that they'd died martyrs for the cause. Those who passed this test would be so proud of themselves and their achievement they'd feel invincible, and deeply, almost spiritually, bonded to the collective. This invincibility and bonding, tethered to their hatred of the enemy were the perfect ingredients to create an extremist, or a terrorist, as the west liked to call them.

'Arkmed,' called out Yousef, 'you were selected to take this training again for two reasons. The first is that you have already passed it before and the second will be to explain to this group how to complete it. Please come out here and tell them what they'll experience and how to get through it.'

Mark broke away from the line, and walked out to stand beside Yousef and faced the line of shivering men. 'There is a tree, approximately three miles from here, along that path,' he said pointing to a rough track that led further into the mountains, 'each of you are required to touch the tree and to make it back here within the hour. The path is rough, strewn with sharp, hidden stones, potholes, and snow, and getting to the tree will require much courage and personal endurance. The way to make it through is to take the pain and direct it towards your enemy. Every time you cut your feet, you must curse them and tell yourself that you'll seek revenge for the pain and hardship you're enduring. This will help stiffen your resolve to make it back. You may help others along the way, but if in doing so, you arrive back outside the allotted time, your time within this collective will be at an end, and so will your life. There is a man stationed at the tree, who will mark your hand with a felt pen to show that you made it to the tree. Good luck, brothers and pray that Allah smiles upon your journey and your courage.'

'Thank you, Arkmed,' said Yousef, looking at his watch. 'Now, go,' he called out to the group and pointed to the pathway.

Mark was the first to take to the path. He immediately felt the rocks begin to cut into his feet and swore under his breath, taking his own advice and directing the pain towards the Australian soldiers who'd killed his father. He didn't look down at the damage, for he knew the sight of his own blood would only slow his progress. Nor did he listen to the protests of the others that followed him, or stop to assist any of the men who slipped over in the ice that covered much of the trail. They were on their own, just as he was.

Mark slipped into a kind of trance as he ran, ignoring the outside world and concentrating on his breathing, letting the air enter through his nose and exit from his mouth and moving his legs to the rhythm of his breath. He ran, knowing his life depended on him finishing this course, for he didn't intend to become one of the men taken to an isolated place, killed for their unworthiness, and buried in some unmarked, anonymous grave.

He came the bank of a fast flowing, icy stream and before he had time to even think about it, he was inside the torrent, half wading, half swimming across to the far side, feeling his body go numb beneath him, but pushing on regardless of the lack of feeling. He reached the bank and pulled himself out of the water using a large exposed root from a nearby tree, collapsed on the ground for a moment, until the surrounding cold started to make its presence known and then got up and proceed on, cutting his feet even more, which had become soft due to the immersion. He turned around as he ran and saw the terrified faces of the men who followed him, waved once for them to come on, and then took off up the trail, disappearing around a bend. He heard the numerous splashes of the group behind him as they entered the stream and swore at their enemies as they attempted to cope with the bitter cold.

The next obstacle between him and the tree was a large snowdrift that extended for about a mile upwards. Mark looked at it and then jumped in, extending his stride so that his feet touched minimally upon the ground. As the snow touched his wet shorts, he felt them become crisp, the water freezing inside the cotton material. Nevertheless, he kept moving, feeling the sweat upon his body turn to ice as soon as it emerged through the pores of his skin. He reached the top of the hill and saw the tree below him, about a half-mile away. He started down the hill, feeling his breath coming in deep, sour-tasting gasps and then fell into the snow, slipping on a covered rock and falling, sliding, and crawling, made his way to the halfway point. There, he stopped for a few moments, took a drink of water from a canteen offered to him by the soldier stationed there and stood, held out his hand and received the mark, before he started to make his way back the way he'd come.

He climbed to the top of the hill again and saw the majority of the men who followed him making their way through the snow, using his footsteps to help them move along at a swifter pace. They cursed at their enemies, uttering profanities, and calling America, Britain, and Australia a bunch of imperialist dogs, while swearing by their god to kill every soldier who'd entered their country, as well as their families, and friends, too.

Yes, thought Mark, the hatred the Prophet wanted drilled into these men, was by increment ingraining itself into them with every passing second and every difficult obstacle put in front of them. By the time they reached the end and arrived back at the cave, they'd associate their pain with their hatred of the enemy in a way that'd be impossible to distinguish.

Mark smiled at them as he came down the hill, and many of them patted him on the back as he passed, telling him he was a true patriot, praising his skill and endurance. He mumbled some half-hearted words of encouragement in reply and kept going, ignoring the stones that bit at his feet like wild dogs, just wanting this episode to be over with, so he could enjoy his lunch in some warm clothes beside a comforting fire.

By the time he reached the stream, he could feel his physical strength dwindling, badly depleted by the constant exertion and was glad that this was the last major obstacle he'd face on his way back. He knew, though, there were some men in the group who'd drown in the stream, unable to conjure up the strength to get across to the other side, taken downstream by the raging torrent and fished out later, their bodies hidden from the enemy in some dark, damp hole. For a moment, felt bad for them and their families, but if they were not up to it, it was their own bad luck for lacking the determination and zeal it required to become a part of this collective. This was a test and the consequences of failing were to pay the ultimate price. Each of them realised before they signed up, they may be required to go to their deaths for the sake of the cause and each of the men accepted that condition with the understanding that a reward awaited them in heaven for their martyrdom, if they gave their lives.

Mark jumped into the stream and gasped at the freezing temperature of the water. He took several deep breaths and made his way to the centre, where he stood for a moment, looking for the best place to cross the rest of the way. He misjudged his footfall and stepped into a deep hole, finding himself suddenly submerged and carried a short way downstream by the current. He didn't fight the water, there was no point in doing that, he knew he'd only exhaust himself further, but waited until his feet found a shallow point on the bed of the stream and then steadied himself and made for the bank again. This time, he judged the depth of the water correctly and made it to the far side, pulling himself up onto dry land by using the native grasses that grew beside the stream. He lay on his stomach for a moment, shivering, his breath coming in shallow spasms, and feeling an overwhelming desire to go to sleep, but knew he dare not. He had no doubt he was suffering the effects of hypothermia, and was aware that if he fell asleep now, he'd never wake and would die right there on the bank of the stream, drifting off into some delicious fantasy of warmth and comfort. He had too much to do and couldn't afford to die quite yet.

Mark opened his eyes and forced himself to his feet. He had to concentrate to put one foot in front of the other, but with focussed determination, he managed to do so, and soon, he was moving along at a jog, stumbling on the stones like a drunken man and now, even he cursed aloud at his enemy, swearing deliriously to take revenge for all he'd been through. He ran with his head down, too exhausted to lift it and trying to avoid the stones on the trail, with little success, hardly able to control the movements of his own body, and only looked up when he heard Yousef's welcoming voice ahead of him. He stumbled to the mouth of the cave and collapsed into the older man's arms. Yousef gently lowered him to the ground, gave orders that he was to be dressed and immediately returned to the base camp, so he could undertake a medical examination, and fed hot soup to stave off the cold inside him.

'You have done well, Arkmed. I had no doubt you'd be the first back here. Go now, rest, and recover, you've earned it.'

Mark opened his eyes and looked around. It took him a moment to realise he was no longer in Afghanistan. He threw his feet over the side of the cot and ran his hand through his hair, yawning as he came to terms with his wakefulness. He reached down to the floor, grabbed a cigarette from out of a packet, and lit it up, drawing the smoke deep into his lungs as he pondered what he'd do next. The information he had taken from the detective had proved invaluable. The police had a genuine psychic, who could see his movements if he came into contact with any object he'd touched, or any person with whom he made contact, with the mere touch of his hand and even more fascinating, this Rob Swift, could sometimes see the future. He wondered how he could use that information to his advantage, in a way to cause more confusion and devastation. No doubt, it would come to him, but for now, he had another duty to perform. He stood, grabbed the

Darth Vader mask from off the end of the bed, and placed it over his face. He adjusted the straps, turned on the voice modulation control, and tested it to make sure it was operating. When he was satisfied, he put his sneakers on his feet and exited the room, making his way into an adjoining room, where detective Tony Green lay slumped over, unconscious in his chair.

Mark, without speaking, approached the detective and removed the bowie knife from his jacket pocket. He then used his lighter and heated the end of the blade, which had turned black from previous use, until it began to smoke and began to work on Tony's chest, ignoring the agonised screams of the police officer who suddenly woke with the pain, carving a message he wished both the police, and specifically, Rob Swift to see.

CHAPTER FIFTEEN

Rob raised the muzzle of the Glock and aimed at the paper target located twenty metres from where he stood.

'Remember,' said Clare beside him, 'just squeeze the trigger gently, and try not to jerk, otherwise you'll miss for sure.'

Rob did as he was told, but at the last moment, closed his eyes and missed the target altogether, which caused Clare to laugh.

'Jesus,' said the detective, 'if you're ever going to hit anyone, they'd better be standing about a foot from where you are.'

'I'm sorry, Clare, but guns are just not my thing.'

'Apparently not,' agreed the detective, 'but we can get in some more practice later, after we've met the whole protection team. They should all be up there by now. Come on, let's go,' she added as she took Rob's gun, turned on the safety and placed it into his shoulder holster inside his jacket. 'Just make sure you keep that thing with you. You never know, you might by accident, manage to hit the right target. Stranger things have happened.'

The two of them removed their Kevlar vests, placed them on a bench behind the firing range, and headed for the elevator. They rode up the two floors in silence, listening to some bland country and western muzak. When the door opened, they moved down a long corridor and into a conference room, where sat three men and a trio of women.

'Hi, Clare, Rob,' said Russell rising to his feet. 'I'd like you two to meet the team who'll be looking out for you. I'll introduce you by each of the teams selected to work together, although, the truth is, we'll probably mix and match as we go. We've decided each team will consist of both a male and female officers, which looks less conspicuous in any situation and is a tried and true method we've used in the drug squad since God was a boy.'

'Sure,' said Clare, 'sounds quite reasonable.'

'Okay,' said Russell, moving through the room. 'You already know Le Mar, here. His partner will be June Haleo, that's the woman sitting next to him, with the jean jacket and long, dark hair. Next, we have Annie Chow, who'll be working with me. The bloke with the beard here is Marcus Longhorn… we give him shit about his name all the time. Last, but not least, is Josie Weiss,' said the cop, touching the shoulder of a gorgeous blonde woman who'd have looked perfectly at home on the cover of a men's magazine, 'the woman with supermodel looks, guaranteed to turn the head of any man who isn't gay, and has the brain to match.'

'Glad to meet you all,' said Clare.

'Yeah, me too,' added Rob. 'It's good to know we have such experienced people looking out for us.'

'Yeah, well, I can tell you not all of us are particularly pleased to be taken off other cases, to play babysitter to you two,' said Russell, 'but we do understand the gravity of the situation and that one of our own has been taken by this prick. We won't let that happen to you, or to Rob. What we do need, though, is your cooperation, or the whole exercise is pointless. We need to know where you're going and when you're going, so we can keep track of you. Speaking of which, has there been any sign of Tony?'

'No,' replied Clare, her tone despondent. 'Nor has there been any sort of ransom demand as yet, but I'm not giving up hope on him.'

An audible sigh escaped from the officers as the words fell from Clare's lips and the group was reminded that Tony Green, a brother officer, was in the hands of some maniac. There was a silent acknowledgement it could've happened to any of them, given the dangerous nature of the occupation they undertook and the ruthless people they dealt with on a daily basis.

A door opened behind Clare and a young man in a lab coat, glasses, carrying a large cardboard box stepped inside. 'Hi,' he said with a shy smile, 'I hope I'm not interrupting anything. I'm Larry Batts, chief scientist from technical. I've come up set you up with the tracking devices and explain to you how they work.'

'We've used tracking equipment before,' said Annie, rolling her eyes. 'You can just leave the stuff on the table and tell us where the base station is.'

Larry laughed good-naturedly. 'You might have used tracking stuff before, but not this gear. It's the newest stuff from Japan, just arrived. Very simple to use, it'll only take a few minutes and there's no base station.'

'Okay,' said Russell, 'not a problem. Just set your box down here,' he added pointing at the conference table.

'Thanks,' said Larry laying the box down and pulling out the equipment, which was still wrapped in plastic bags. 'Now, as I understand it, there'll be three teams of two.'

'Yeah, that's right,' replied Russell, picking up one of the smaller plastic bags and raising an eyebrow as he gave the equipment inside an inspection. 'So, what's so good about this stuff?'

'You'll see,' replied Larry, chuckling with nervous enthusiasm. 'If you could all get into your teams, just stand beside your partners around the table.'

When the six detectives had gathered in their pairs, Larry handed out three flatscreen iPads. He then gave each of them a printed number on a piece of paper and informed them that this would enable them to login to the screen.

'I'd advise you to memorise it and to get rid of the paper as soon as possible. I keep an inventory of all login numbers in my office, so don't worry if you forget it. You can just call me, confirm your identification with a few personal details from the COPS database, give me your police ID number, and I'll give it to you. Okay, so turn on the unit, wait a moment for it to boot up and then enter the login number.' Larry then went back to the box and retrieved three smaller plastic bags, which he placed on the table. He removed them from their packaging, inserted some batteries in each of them, and informed the group that these were the tracker devices, which the handheld devices would find, within a radius of up to twenty kilometres. He switched them on and watched as the faces of the detectives lit up with amazement.

'This is like a portable GPS, in real time,' said Annie, 'it actually gives the address of this place, street name and all and shows just where each of them are. That's the three little red dots, yeah?'

'That's right,' replied Larry, attaching a small transmitter underneath the collars of both Rob's and Clare's jacket and asking them to move around the room. When Clare stood at the opposite side of the room, he asked the detectives to press a button marked 'separate' on the devices and the screen divided into three and showed each tracker device in a separate screen. 'That's there to use in case Rob and Clare get separated. If you look at the data output screen, it also details just how far they are from each other and in which direction. The third tracker is to be placed inside the car, somewhere inconspicuous, just in case.'

'That's fucking amazing,' said Annie. 'We couldn't lose this pair now, if we tried, and sorry, too, about my earlier crack.'

'That's okay,' replied Larry, 'you couldn't have known. If you have any problems, please don't hesitate to contact me,' he added, handing out his personal card. 'I'll be stationed in this building, downstairs, until they sort out the mess with St. Kilda Road.'

'Thanks,' said Annie with a smile. 'I might call you, sooner than you think.'

Larry blushed, his face turning a deep shade of red, as he handed out leather pouches for each of the tracking devices, packed the empty box with the leftover material, and then fumbled his way out of the room, looking back once at Annie who laughed at his awkwardness.

'He is kinda cute,' said Josie smiling, 'in a nerdy, scientist, kinda way.'

'Hands off, Wonder Woman,' retorted Annie laughing, 'I saw him first.'

The door opened again and Ray Owen entered. His face looked drawn, thought Clare, no doubt the stress of the situation was getting to him. 'Hi,' he said, 'I've just come down to grab your house keys, Clare, and to let you know you and Rob have a suite reserved at the Hilton Hotel, which you can pay for with the credit card I gave you. Rob, a salesperson will arrive at the suite in the morning, to outfit you with some more conventional clothes. We don't want you two going out in public right now. I've also come to give this team a full briefing about what's going on. The commissioner wants the pair of you to concentrate on finding the device. You'll have back up, of course, some of the feds and some of the Victorian coppers. It's the top priority right now and both the commissioner, Pete Bell and I, think you two have a better chance of doing it than anyone else.'

'The device,' said Russell, raising a concerned eyebrow. 'I don't know if I like the sound of that.'

'Yeah, neither do I,' added Marcus, 'sounds ominous.'

'Well, you're going to hate it even more once I tell you all about it,' replied Ray, as he removed a DVD from his briefcase, inserted it into the player at the front of the room and turned on the television set. Russell stood and hit the lights, plunging the room into momentary darkness, until the screen illuminated in front of them. The police officers sat in silence, watching the recording made by the Fire of the Son and several of them swore under their breath, when they fully comprehended the type of damage and devastation that FOTS was about to inflict on the people of Melbourne.

'Holy shit,' said Russell as he turned on the lights and sat down back into his chair. 'Has the existence of the nuclear device actually been verified?'

'Yes,' said Ray, casting a surreptitious glance at Rob. 'We have it on good Intel it was brought in by sea and the ship which ferried it, was the tanker destroyed at the docklands two days ago.'

'Christ in a bucket,' June exclaimed as she stood up. 'I need to get my family out of the city. My kids are only nine and six.'

There was a general clamour as panic set in amongst the police, who feared for the safety of their friends and family.

'All right,' said Ray, 'please calm down. You can all call your families if you want, but the existence of the device is to remain a secret, at least for now. Tell them you're unsure about the placements of the conventional weapons, if you want and get them out of the city, but nothing about the nuke. Many people are already evacuating the city, so it won't seem out of the norm. We believe he's going to set if off in about twelve days and we hope to God we find him before then, but if it gets back to him that we've confirmed its existence, and we know what we're looking for, he might detonate it sooner and we can't take that chance.'

'All right,' said Russell, 'look, I know this is disturbing, to say the least, but we need to stay focussed. There's a possibility that FOTS is going to make a grab for either Rob or Clare. I daresay Rob will be his preferred target.'

'Why's that?' Annie asked. 'In fact, why is Rob involved with this case at all? From what I can gather, he's not a trained officer, either.'

'Rob has certain talents and intel gathering devices that have helped the police in the past,' replied Ray. 'All you have to know is the commissioner has complete faith in him.'

'You know what I think,' said Josie rising from her chair. 'I think that's a load of crap. If I'm going to put my life on the line, then I want to know all the facts, not just the ones you decide to dole out to me at your convenience.'

'Yeah, I agree,' added Annie.

'Me too,' said June. 'At the end of the day, we're the ones who're sticking our necks out, so we want to know why. I don't think that's one bit unreasonable.'

'Looks like you're outvoted, boss,' said Le Mar with a laugh.

'Outvoted and outgunned,' added Marcus. 'We want to do a good job, but we can't if we don't have all the tools. Any good cop knows that the most useful tool to have is information and correct and current information, at that.'

Ray stood silent for a moment and cast a glance at Clare. 'All right, I'll tell you, but nothing said here is to leave this room, is that understood?'

There were murmurs of agreement from all the gathered cops, who sat waiting in anticipation of what info Ray was going to impart to them.

'Do you want to tell them, Clare? It might sound better coming from you, since you were so close to what happened the last time.'

The surveillance team sat in silence, casting glances at Rob as Clare went through the Clarence Grafton case, relating what had happened and how Rob had formed a psychic link with the killer, from the moment he had touched one of his victims in the morgue. She further explained how Rob had assisted them to both catch Grafton and find the kidnapped Aboriginal artist, Willow, in the process. When Clare was finished, the team of officers just sat there, stunned, hardly able to believe what they'd just heard.

'It's all true,' said Ray. 'We need to look out for Rob. He may be our best chance to get this shithead, either as bait, or through his visions. He's already been an invaluable help to us. We can't afford to lose him.'

'That's right,' added Clare. 'Rob is a protection priority. If it comes down to saving him or me, I need to know you'll save him. He's much more important, and that's an order. Saving Rob could help to avoid our city becoming a nuclear wasteland and potentially save millions of lives. Do you all understand?'

'Yeah, we do,' said Russell with a nod. Now you've given us all the facts, I'm sure everyone here will do their best, isn't that right?'

'You can count on us,' said Marcus, 'and I think I speak for the whole group.'

'I find the whole psychic thing pretty amazing,' said Annie, 'and I don't mean to pry or sound like I don't believe you, Rob, but is there any chance of you giving us a demonstration on how that works, some time?'

Rob pondered the question for a moment. 'I can't really control what I see,' he replied. 'Sometimes, the visions aren't pretty and I don't know if you'd want to know what the future holds for you, if that's where I went.'

'Yeah, I guess so,' conceded Annie.

'Besides that,' chimed in Ray, 'Rob's not some sort of circus sideshow act. I don't want his talents to be used up on people's curiosity, when there are more important things at stake here.'

'Fair enough,' said Russell, casting Annie a disapproving look. 'All right, I want to organise some logistics. Rob and Clare will be heading back to their suite, shortly. I want Marcus and Josie to head over there and check out the rooms before they get there. You two will be crashing in the suite, keeping an eye on things from the inside. Le Mar and June, I want you to find a spot halfway to the hotel and stop there. Annie and I will follow Clare's car and we'll do a switch, when we reach you. After that, I want the hotel entrances to be covered both front and rear. Keep in radio contact, every hour on the hour. Anybody have questions?'

'Nope,' said Marcus answering for the entire group, 'I think it's all pretty clear.'

'Very well,' said Russell with the air of a commander, 'carry on, then.'

'Looks like we've got a bit of time to kill, Rob,' said Clare. 'Fancy a bit more time on the firing range?'

'Yeah, why not?' replied Rob. 'It can't hurt.'

Just as Clare and Rob were about to leave the room, Ray's phone rang and he waved a finger at the two of them, asking them to remain where they were for the time being. He gave several replies to the person on the other end of the line, thanked them, and then closed the phone, ending the conversation.

'It looks as though the ship's officer from the tanker has died,' said Ray, 'resulting from complications of his burns, so we won't be getting any further info from him. We've also had some luck in finding some of the bomb fragments in the supermarket, which we'll be sending over to the hotel. They should get there, shortly after you arrive. See what you can do with them, will you?'

'I'll do my best,' replied Rob. 'I can't make any promises, though, you know that.'

CHAPTER SIXTEEN

It was a great honour to meet with the Prophet. Few people had actually seen him up close, or could even provide a description and those that could, kept their mouths closed, under threat of death for such betrayal. Mark supposed that keeping his identity a secret had a twofold purpose: the first being to build up a kind of god-like, iconic mystique, and the second, so that he could escape and hide amongst everyday people if the enemy got too close for comfort.

When informed that the Prophet had requested specifically to see him, Mark immediately thought it could only be for a couple of reasons. He had either somehow discovered Mark was not as spiritually loyal to the cause as he led people to believe, or that the Prophet had some special task or mission he wished to assign him. Either way, he knew that his summons before the leader would mark a significant moment in his life. He could only hope it was the latter. The invitation had arrived discreetly, whispered into his ear by a man he'd never seen before around the camp, although obviously known by several of the more senior members who nodded in his direction when he arrived. Mark assumed he was an aide to the Prophet.

'You will come with me, now,' he said in Arabic as though the invitation was not a matter of choice. 'Bring with you, your prayer mat.'

Mark complied with the request and was led further into the labyrinth of surrounding caves and blindfolded with a medical bandage. He could see a vague light as he walked along, which he guessed was the illumination from a flashlight, but even so, he wouldn't have been able to find the hiding place of the Prophet, even if the man had removed the blindfold from his eyes at any time during the journey. They moved through the caves for what Mark estimated to be a good half hour, without speaking, the silence as oppressive as a great weight, as if the roof would suddenly fall, or the walls cave in around him upon utterance of a word. They stopped several times and Mark was provided with water from a canteen and informed it wouldn't take them long to arrive at their destination.

'You enter the domain of the Prophet,' said a voice from out of the darkness in front of the pair. 'Speak, and be recognised.'

'It is I, Ali,' answered the man who led Mark by the arm. He recited a passage from the Koran, which Mark assumed amounted to a kind of password and then the two of them gained admittance to this inner sanctum of the Prophet.

Mark could see the bright yellow flames of a fire through the blindfold and remained standing for a minute by himself, while Ali walked off to attend to some other business.

'Don't remove the blindfold until you're instructed to do so,' were his parting words.

'Okay,' replied Mark, 'I won't.'

A short while later, Mark felt the warmth of another person's breath on the back of his neck. It surprised him that anyone could approach with such stealth and get so close to him without detection.

'Are you loyal to the cause of freedom?'

'Yes,' replied Mark without hesitation, 'I am loyal.'

'Good,' replied the voice in almost a whisper. 'Are you loyal to me also?'

Mark immediately realised that the man standing behind him was none other than the Prophet himself. He fell to his knees in feigned supplication. 'Yes, great Prophet, you are the messenger of God, sent to free this land from the infidel. I would give my life for you.'

'That is as it should be,' replied the voice. 'Now, take the bindings from your eyes.'

Mark removed his blindfold and was surprised just how normal the Prophet looked. He was of average height and weight, with a long dark beard that reached almost down to his waist. He was dressed in white, free flowing Arabic garments. His smile was warm and welcoming, but his eyes were intense and intelligent and felt as if they bored into Mark's soul, seeing the things he'd tried so hard to hide from everyone.

'Arkmed, it is good of you to come. I would like to talk to you after we've said our evening prayers and have feasted in your honour.'

'It is I who am honoured,' said Mark, 'to meet with you.'

'I can tell you are a good man,' said the Prophet. 'Come, place your prayer mat next to mine and we will pray to God, together.'

There were five men gathered in the cave and by candlelight and with the aid of a recording of sacred passages of the Koran, the men prayed, bowing to the creator of heaven and earth, remembering those martyrs who'd gone before them and seeking assistance to maintain their courage and bring others into their fold. When they had finished their prayers, they washed themselves and readied to eat. The Prophet clapped his hands and a feast of delicate, spicy meats, specially prepared in the halal method, were brought before them, along with a selection of fruits and vegetables, which made Mark's mouth water at the sight.

'Please, eat, help yourself,' offered the Prophet smiling. 'It has been a while since you've enjoyed such food as this?'

'It feels like a lifetime,' replied Mark filling his plate. 'The food in the camp is adequate, but not like this.'

The Prophet laughed aloud. 'No, the food there is not like this. If it were, it would make the men soft and in fact, the food we usually eat is not this extravagant. The feast is in your honour, Arkmed.'

'You feast in my honour?' Mark asked, washing his food down with fresh orange juice. 'What have I done to deserve such a privilege?'

'It's not for what you have done, Arkmed, but for what you will do. This is a martyr's feast. It will be the last you'll have with us, before you go off to fulfil the will of God. You are to become an instrument of terrible destruction, against the infidels, in their own land. You will take our struggle to them and neither they, nor we, will ever forget your name. You'll become a hero for the people of our cause.'

Mark was dumbfounded. 'You're sending me to Australia, aren't you?'

'Yes, Arkmed, I am. I know what the Australians did to your father, your mother and, in turn, to you. Your hatred of those people shall motivate you in a way nothing else could, but you must be patient and bide your time. The plan I have in mind, will take some years to implement, but when all the pieces are in place, it will be perfect and the harm you will cause the enemy will be unprecedented. They will think hell has come to their shores and its name shall be Arkmed, sent by the Prophet.'

Mark smiled, hardly able to contain his glee. He felt almost drunk with happiness, giddy at the realization of what would one day occur and he would be at the centre of that destruction. It had worked out just as he had planned and now it was only a matter of time, and time was one thing he had in ample supply.

Mark had accepted the forged passport offered to him by the Prophet, which said that he had spent the last three years moving through Europe, but made no mention of Afghanistan, or any other middle-eastern country. The passport had been stamped with the Dutch insignia on many occasions, so it appeared, he was just another

Swedish hippy, smoking dope and getting laid in Amsterdam, for a year after leaving University, leaving there when his visa ran out, and returning for more of the same within a short timeframe.

'Is there a real Mark Andersson?'

'Oh, yes,' replied the Prophet with a knowing smile, 'or at least there was. I'm afraid he was, unfortunately, lost at sea a few months ago. He obtained a master's degree in political science from the University of California, Berkley, and a bachelor in the same discipline from Stockholm University, prior to going to the U.S. His parents, like yours, are dead, both killed in a car accident when he was a child. He was chosen for a few reasons, namely for his lack of parentage and associated relatives and because of his eligibility to obtain employment within the Swedish Diplomatic Service. His name was also an added bonus. We know that your anglophile name is Mark, too. When his identity was brought to me, you were the first person I thought of.'

'You knew of me before this, Prophet?'

'Yes, Arkmed, I've been keeping a personal eye on you since you arrived back in Afghanistan. I hatched this plan many years ago, but needed just the right individual to pull it off and I believe you are just the man. All your years in Sweden will come in very handy. You're familiar with the language and its customs. You'll need to change your appearance somewhat, but that shouldn't be too much of a problem. When you return to Sweden, you will return as Mark Andersson. I have friends in the Swedish Diplomatic Service, who will make your entry into that Service, perhaps a lot smoother and quicker than usual. You'll have to go wherever they send you for the first two or three years, while you complete your training, but after that, you'll be free to request a transfer to wherever you deem fit. Australia, for instance.'

'What happens if I come across somebody who knows the original Mark Andersson?'

'Andersson is the second most common name in Sweden, after Karlson. It was another reason this identity met our selection criteria. If you encounter someone who knows Mark Andersson, you can simply say you have the same name, but are not the same person and if that person gets a little too inquisitive, well, you can always dispose of him or her. You've had enough training in the art of killing, so it shouldn't be a problem, if you don't let it escalate.'

Mark smiled. 'It won't be a problem, at all.'

'Once you're out of Sweden, the chances of meeting someone who knew the original Mark Andersson will be less than negligible,' said the Prophet, 'and your deniability to being that person will also increase. Don't worry too much, Arkmed, or should I say, Mark, I'll have people looking out for you. You won't see them, but they will be there, in places you might not even expect. From time to time, someone will contact you and reassure you everything is proceeding according to plan. All plans, unfortunately, contain some element of risk, but trust God, that the risk will be minimal and the outcome will be the one we desire. We will prevail, for we fight on the side of the righteous.'

Mark opened his eyes and looked at the suburban Kew house in front of him. For a man who had reached a colonel's status in the Australian army, it wasn't that impressive. It was a simple, modest, red double-bricked residence, with three bedrooms and a study out back, certainly a lot more functional than decorative. There were two moderately priced cars in the garage and a neatly trimmed rose garden and manicured lawn out front, which he could spend time on, now he'd retired. After a lifetime of killing innocent people, raping women and stealing from the poor, Mark thought the man would've had significantly more to show for his efforts. He thought it somewhat ironic that a man, who'd possessed so much power throughout his career, would end up reduced to such bland mediocrity in his latter years. It almost seemed like a shame to kill him, as if letting him live his pathetic life would be the greater punishment for his reprehensible deeds, but death was long overdue for the colonel and tonight, he would stare it directly in the face. He lifted the binoculars from the seat next to him, pointing them at the front room of the residence while he drank the last drops of his coffee, which had long gone cold. He looked at his watch, saw that it was almost ten-thirty, and knew that the man and his wife would soon go to bed.

For three months he'd stalked this man, watched his every move, followed him to the supermarket, to the barber's, to his children's houses, to his friend's, and in that process, he'd managed to locate a lot of the regiment to which he had once belonged, but he hadn't yet seen the other three men he sought. When he did, though, each of them would fall, until finally, he'd be the only individual who'd carry the terrible memory of their deeds to his own grave, but they would pay before that, by God, they would pay.

Mark checked he had everything he needed in the little backpack beside him. When he was satisfied, he exited the car, closed the door behind him, slipped the backpack onto one shoulder, and headed for the house. He was glad that he could now go to work on his bastard, and wished he could've some time ago, but the need to gather information was more pressing. He wanted to kill the whole pack of dogs, not just the leader, and now he knew how to locate them, there was no reason to hold back. Tonight was a night of quiet celebration and he imagined the flowing blood of the colonel as the champagne he'd use to toast his victory.

Having witnessed the couple's nightly ritual for months, he knew exactly where to go. He moved to the back of the house, opened the backdoor, and slipped into the kitchen. He waited for a few moments, just to make sure they remained seated in the living room, watching the last few minutes of a chat show and then stole up the hallway and into the master bedroom. As usual, the bed was made up to a military standard, all hard and crisp corners, and the couple's pyjamas and robes lay out neatly on the end, left there by the wife for easy access, once they'd completed their ablutions in the bathroom.

He heard the television switch off in the living room and the old man yawn, telling his wife he was ready for bed. She agreed and together, the two of them made their way to the bathroom, turning off lights and locking doors as they went. Mark slipped behind the bedroom door and into a space between the wardrobe, the rear wall, and the doorframe, his presence covered by two large wet-weather jackets that hung on hooks on the back of the door. He waited until the sound of water and an electric toothbrush buzzed down the hallway and then reached into his backpack, pulled out the nine-millimetre Beretta, attached the silencer to the end of the barrel, pulled the black balaclava down over his face, and waited.

A few minutes later, the elderly couple entered the bedroom and began undressing, placing their clothes on chairs on opposite sides of the bed. They talked about the garden, what the weather would be like the following day and for a moment, Mark wondered if they would have spoken of such mundane, banal subjects if they had known what was going to happen next. Mark moved with practiced ease from behind the door. He clubbed the man on the back of the head with the butt of the gun, sending him facedown to the floor and into unconsciousness. The old woman looked around and opened her mouth wide to scream. Before she could utter a sound, Mark put a bullet through her forehead, creating a neat little hole that dripped one single droplet of blood, while some of her brains and skull matter exploded out the back of her head and landed on the wall behind her as she went sprawling backwards onto the bed. The room was silent. Mark hit the old man with the gun again just to be sure he wouldn't wake while his back was turned. He went back to the inner side of the door, retrieved his backpack and took from it a roll of thick gaffer tape, tore a length off, and placed it over the old man's mouth to prevent him from screaming, should he revive unexpectedly. He put the tape and the gun back into the backpack, which he threw over his shoulder, grabbed the old man and dragged him from the bedroom, stopping to turn off the light and plunging the room into darkness.

Mark moved the old man into the study at the rear of the house. He dropped his body into the heavy leather recliner that sat at his expensive oak desk and taped his hands to the side of the chair, his feet, and legs to the bottom. He then ran the tape around his torso several times, taking it around the back of the chair and making it utterly impossible for him to move.

When he was completely satisfied the colonel had no way to escape, he wandered down to the kitchen and opened the refrigerator door, looking inside for something to cool his thirst after such intensive labour and saw a bottle of orange juice and checked out the used-by date, which was still intact. He placed the juice on the bench and opened the freezer, from which he took an ice-tray filled with frozen cubes, which he also placed on the bench, while he grabbed a large glass from an overhead cupboard. He half-filled the glass with ice and then poured in some juice. He lifted up the bottom of the balaclava and sipped from the glass and sighed, pleased with the taste of the juice and with his progress so far.

He stood in the kitchen for a while, enveloped by the darkness, amused by the feeling of being almost invisible, as one with the darkness as anyone could be. He opened the door of the refrigerator, leaving it slightly ajar, using the light while he searched the cupboards for a jug, into which he placed the remainder of the juice in the bottle and the ice from the tray, closed the fridge door, returned to the study, and left the jug on a bookshelf away from the sleeping colonel. He walked back to the kitchen and washed out the glass from which he'd been drinking, removing any trace of DNA evidence and then cracked the glass with the butt of a knife he kept in a scabbard on his waist. He placed the broken glass into the kitchen bin, making it look like an ordinary domestic accident, which could've happened at any time before his entrance into the house.

Mark moved back into the study and grabbed the jug, emptying the contents over the old man's head, waking him abruptly from his enforced slumber. He mumbled something intelligible under the tape and then began to struggle when he realised he'd been bound into the chair.

'Okay,' said Mark removing the Beretta from his backpack and placing it against the old man's head, 'I'm going to remove the tape from your mouth. If you try to call out, you'll be dead before the first word gets out. Do you understand? Just nod if you do.'

The old man nodded his withered, bald, head, signifying his agreement to comply with the conditions. Mark grabbed an end of the tape and yanked it hard from the old man's mouth, causing him to grimace with pain.

'Where's my wife? What have you done with her?'

'She's dead,' replied Mark. 'It's probably better she is, otherwise she'd have seen what a piece of shit you are, Colonel Daniel Murphy. You don't mind if I call you Danny, do you?'

'You killed her, you cold-blooded son of a bitch. She never even said a bad word to anybody in her whole life, and you killed her?'

'Yes, I killed her, Danny,' replied Mark, 'that's just the way the cookie crumbles. You would call it ... what's the term? That's right, collateral damage.'

'Who in the fuck are you?' Colonel Murphy demanded to know, struggling futilely with the bonds that kept him restrained in the chair. 'Why don't you show your face, instead of hiding it like a fuckin' coward?'

'I'm sorry, but no,' said Mark from underneath the balaclava. 'I need to avoid being seen by a certain psychic. You wouldn't recognise me, anyway. It's been a long time since we met and I was only thirteen years old. You stood on your tank, like some supreme being, watching as your cronies destroyed the village of my family and then, killed my father.'

'You're Afghani?'

'Yes, that's right, but I've taken the identity of another. Do you not notice my accent, too? It's Swedish, that's where my mother and I escaped to as refugees, when we left Afghanistan, after you and your men shot my father and gang-raped my mother. Don't you remember that? I really thought you would. I stood by, helpless and watched you and those animals treat her like dirt. When you were finished, you left us both in the desert to die and we very nearly did, too, but for the kindness of some freedom fighters that took us in and led us to safety. I made a promise to myself and to my parents, that one day, when I was old enough, I'd return to Afghanistan and fight with those men and then I'd come for you and those jackals that killed my father with a gun and my mother, slowly and by degrees. I did that, too. I killed more Australian soldiers than other fighter in the desert. I lived to kill your countrymen, but most of all, I've lived to kill you.'

'I do remember and I'm sorry,' said the colonel bowing his head in shame, 'but you have to know the context in which it happened. We had a dozen of our men killed in an ambush only a few days before. Most of them had wives and children, too. We were angry and wanted to get back at those attackers in any way we could. It was war. I felt terrible afterwards, but by then, it was too late, we couldn't have found you again if we wanted to and we couldn't take the chance you would report us to the military police. Our lives, our careers, would've been over.'

'War? That wasn't war,' said Mark, seething with anger. 'War is a thing of honour, where brave men kill each other and accept their fate. What you did was a crime and both you and your people are going to pay for it.'

'I accept my fate,' said the colonel. 'I accept I should be executed for what I've done, but there's no need to hurt anyone else.'

'I'm afraid it's a little too late for such noble, altruistic gestures,' said Mark with a laugh. 'Your people are already dying and a lot more will by the time I'm finished.'

'You're the bomber, aren't you? You're the one who's been setting off the explosives all around the city.'

'Yes, that's right,' replied Mark, 'and there are a lot more to come. By the time I have completed my mission, you country will be left in tatters, just as mine has been.'

'Is this all because of me, and my men?' asked the colonel, bowing his head as tears rushed from his eyes. 'I turned you into the person you are. What have I done?'

Mark smiled, a cold, callous grin that spread across his face. 'Yes, Colonel, in a way, you did create me. You gave me the motivation to learn what I had to, to come and find you and the Prophet gave me the opportunity and the means. In repayment for his services, I'm going to devalue your dollar, demolish half the city and last, but not least, for my finale, I'm going to set off a nuclear device in Melbourne and turn it into a desert.'

'You don't have to do this,' pleaded the colonel. 'You can have me and I'll tell you how to find all the men that hurt your mother. I even remember the name of the man who shot your father, even though it was an accident. He killed himself not long afterwards, said he couldn't cope with you and your mother crying over the body.'

'I already have you, colonel,' said Mark with a soft laugh, 'and yes, I will take the addresses of the other three men who also raped my mother. As far as my father goes, I know it was an accident, those things happen in war. Perhaps, if you'd let it go at that, I may have forgotten about my revenge and just lived out my life, happy just to be with my mother in Sweden, but you didn't and now there will be consequences.'

'I'm ashamed of who I am and what I've done,' said the colonel, 'and I do deserve to die. Can you make it quick?'

'I'm sorry,' replied Mark, 'but I've waited a long time to meet you and I just wouldn't be satisfied if I let you slip out of my hands too quickly.'

'Have it your own way,' said Murphy, 'but that just makes you as bad as me in the end, doesn't it? Maybe even worse, because you plan to kill so many more innocent people than I ever did.'

'Before we get to that, though, there's something I need for you to do,' said Mark, reaching into his backpack and pulling out a large, folded vanilla envelope. He reached inside, grabbed a single piece of white A4 paper, and placed it on the desk in front of the colonel. 'It's a written confession, detailing the rape of my mother. I want for you to sign it before you die.'

'That might prove a little difficult in my present position.'

'Just a small problem,' said Mark with a laugh as he pushed the chair further into the desk and retrieved his knife from his side. 'Which hand do you write with?'

'My right hand.'

'Very well, I'm going to release your arm, so you can sign the confession. If you make a wrong move, I will slit your throat and watch you bleed to death in front of me.'

'Yeah, I understand,' said the colonel. 'I'll sign the fuckin' thing, even if it's only to ease my own conscience.'

Mark sliced through the tape and grabbed a pen from out of one of the desk drawers, which he placed in the colonel's hand. 'Now sign at the bottom,' he said.

Murphy sighed and placed his moniker at the bottom of the page. 'It actually feels like a weight off my shoulders. I'm glad it's the last thing I'll ever do. I just wish I could've said goodbye to my wife.'

'Don't worry, colonel, you'll be seeing her again, very soon,' said Mark as he retaped the arm of the old soldier back to the chair. 'Now, I assume you have the names and addresses of the other men who also raped my mother, somewhere here, too.'

'Yeah, there's an address book I keep beside my bed. You'll find them in there.'

'What are the names of the men?'

'Captain Michael Marshall, Sergeant Chris Knight, and Corporal August Richers,' replied the old man. 'You'd better watch out when you go to get Richers, I've heard he's a mean drunk nowadays, with a penchant for handguns.'

'Thanks for the advice,' said Mark as he taped up the mouth of the colonel, 'I'll try to remember that.'

When the colonel was again secure in the chair, Mark told him that it was now time for him to die and that it was going to hurt, which caused the eyes of the old man to widen with fright. 'You see, for revenge to be perfect, the punishment has to fit the crime exactly, anything less is just not justice.'

Mark pulled down the pyjama pants and boxer shorts worn by the old man and exposed his genitals. He then used the knife, cut off both his scrotum and penis, and held them up for the colonel to see. As the old man looked on, bleeding profusely, Mark placed the genitalia on the desk and separated the penis from the testicles, then ripped off the tape and shoved the penis into the old man's mouth, stopping the screaming as he gagged and resealed his mouth with the tape.

'There, don't you think that the punishment fits the crime?'

Mark stood back, away from blood pooling on the carpet beneath the colonel's feet. He watched the old soldier die in a matter of minutes, whimpering like the pathetic animal that he was, and felt satisfied with what he'd accomplished.

When the last glimmer of life left the old man's eyes, he went back to the kitchen, selected a sharp, heavy, carving knife from a drawer, and returned to the study. He moved to the side of the body, as he avoided leaving footprints in the rapidly expanding crimson pool, leaned over, and grabbed the confession from the desk. He pierced the paper at the top, so that it hung to the hilt of the knife and drove the blade into the back of the colonel's neck. It would be the first thing whoever discovered the body would see as they entered the study, by which time, he would've found and disposed of the other three and would be ready for his great finale.

Mark left the house, after locking all the doors and closing any curtains left open. He knew from watching them, it would be a while before anybody missed the old couple and that was just the way he wanted things.

He went to his car, opened the trunk, and checked that Tony Green was still alive. A steady pulse still beat in his wrist. He didn't want the detective to die. It just wouldn't serve his purposes. He was a terrorist and fear was what he most desired. He wanted to put the fear of God into the police and for them to know that he knew all about them, but most of all, he wanted Rob Swift to fear him, and for that fear to interfere with his psychic abilities and slow him down. He knew this Swift was his greatest threat and the police would be keeping him under constant guard. It was the inevitable consequence of taking this detective and, though he would have no opportunity to eliminate him physically, he might be able to wage a disabling psychological war against him. Even without possessing psychic abilities of his own, he knew they would soon meet and only one of them would emerge from the encounter. He didn't care if he died, he just needed to accomplish what he set out to do, before he let that happen.

Mark closed the trunk, jumped into the car, and removed the balaclava. He wiped the sweat from his face with it and threw it to the floor of the passenger side, and started the engine. He looked at his watch and saw it was almost nine-thirty. He was amazed that he'd spent almost two hours in the house, and smiled at the thought of time flying while he was having fun. Nine-thirty was good, it wasn't late enough for the police to notice his car and pull him up for a random breath test, or licence check. There were still plenty of people about to cover his presence, even though a lot of the population had decided to desert Melbourne in the wake of the bombings. Still, such an inconvenience would place him in a certain time and place, which was something he wished to avoid. The less that anyone knew of his comings and goings, the better.

He drove the car through Kew and down to the Yarra River in Fairfield. He steered the vehicle off the road and down under the bridge, which separated the two suburbs, where he knew many old drunks would congregate to sleep later in the night. He parked the car in the shadows, lifted Tony out of the boot, and placed him at the base of a large gum tree that looked out over the river. He threw his wallet about ten metres from where he sat, knowing it would be found later, when police searched the area. He checked his pulse and then moved off into the surrounding darkness, sure the blood on the front of the detective's t-shirt would alert even the drunkest of fools into calling an ambulance.

He returned to the car, stripped off his overalls, placed them into the trunk along with his balaclava and his backpack, and headed back towards the city and his apartment. Tonight, he had a date with a beautiful German woman who had been of great help to him since arriving in this country. They would share a late meal and a drink, at her apartment, where they would screw until they were both utterly exhausted and then he would murder her, taking away any connection to her that he might have. Before he did that, though, he would need to change his appearance, back to Arkmed; the man she'd so foolishly fallen in love with.

CHAPTER SEVENTEEN

Both Clare and Josie grabbed their guns and aimed them at the door as soon as the knock sounded. A moment later, Josie's mobile phone rang and Russell, stationed in the basement with the hotel security, gave the all clear, having seen Ray Owen approach the room through the closed-circuit television units located on each floor.

'It's okay,' said Josie holstering her weapon, 'it's only Ray.'

Clare opened the door and only holstered her Glock once Ray was safely inside the room and the door both closed and latched behind him.

'I've brought over some of the bomb fragments for Rob to have a look at,' said Ray as he placed a small cardboard box on the coffee table in the centre of the living area. He opened the lid and from the inside, retrieved three plastic bags, which were marked as evidence. 'Each of these bags has been taken from the three different crime scenes. Forensics seems to think they're the same sort of device, possibly manufactured by the same person, probably at the same time, but other than that, they can't tell us much else. We have ASIO and both the FBI and the CIA in the U.S. going through their databases, trying to determine if the bombs have any signature qualities left by the maker, but we've not heard anything from them, yet. I was hoping, Rob, you might be able to come up with something more concrete in the meantime. All this fuckin' waiting around for the next thing to happen is driving me up the bloody wall.'

Rob sat down on the lounge adjacent to the coffee table. 'Okay,' he said picking up and opening the first bag, 'let's see what happens.' He took hold of what looked some burnt electrical wires, which he rubbed between his forefinger and his thumb. He closed his eyes and sat back on the couch as the familiar feeling of building electricity began to escalate within him. When he opened his eyes, he found himself standing in a dark deserted room, lit by a single lamp that looked down onto a workbench, cluttered on one side with all sorts of unrecognisable equipment and tools. He moved over to the workbench and, although, he had no training in engineering, or anything that even resembled it, he certainly recognised the packets of clearly labelled C4 explosives laid out in neat little rows on the opposite side of the bench. There were ten of them in all and it appeared the bombs were not yet fully assembled.

A moment later, a door opened and a light sliced through the darkness, temporarily blinding him from seeing the two people who entered the room in all but silhouette from the doorway. Once the door closed, he could see it was man and a woman, who both walked over to the workbench and took up stools next to each other. The man carried a large, brown, leather suitcase, which he lifted carefully up onto the bench and zipped opened the top.

'There are my babies,' he said in an almost reverential whisper.

'Hang on,' said the woman, in what Rob thought was a German accent, as she slid off her stool and turned on a radio, which played classical music, hidden in shadow from an overhead shelf, 'I need music to work by.'

'Of course you do, Petra, my dear,' replied the man who kissed her on the lips as she returned to her place on the stool.

'Now, don't distract me, Arkmed,' she said, pushing him away in jest, 'unless you want to end up a pancake, to be scraped off the ceiling.'

Rob looked into the suitcase and saw there were ten devices, each neatly placed side by side and packed with old rags to prevent damage. He watched as Petra removed one device at a time, and attached to each a packet of C4 and then set it aside to move onto the next. 'So, you are going to say there are thirty devices, when there are only really ten of them?' Petra asked him.

'That's right,' replied Arkmed, taking the last of the devices from her, setting it down carefully on the bench, and then placing the case on the floor. 'Ten bombs are bad enough to know about, but having the police and the general population think there are thirty, or forty, placed all around the city, will create much more fear and panic and that's precisely what we want. I also have another surprise, a much bigger surprise for them, once the bombs we create here, have detonated.'

'Oh, really, what's that?'

'It's probably better if you don't know everything, Petra, but trust me when I say, even an experienced bomb maker like you will be surprised.'

'Of course I trust you, Arkmed,' said Petra leaning over and kissing him on the mouth. 'Once this is all over, I want to marry you and spend the rest of our lives fighting for the freedom of the oppressed peoples of Afghanistan.'

Rob looked at the woman in the lamplight so he could provide the police with a description of her once he re-entered the world. She was tall, he imagined she was almost six feet and she had dark, wavy hair and emerald green eyes that seemed to glitter under the lamplight. He also saw that she had a beauty spot to the right of her nose and a small scar on the left-hand side of her forehead. He noticed, too, as he walked around her, trying to discern any further distinguishing features that she had a small tattoo of a dragon on the base of her back, which stuck out of her jeans as she leaned over the bench to work.

'Now for the tricky bit,' she said as she grabbed a box from the other side of the bench and removed several small items, which she placed onto the bench.

'Those are the detonators?' Arkmed asked looking closer at the little metal cylinders in front of him.

'Yes, that's just what they are,' replied Petra. 'Tonight, we'll be arming two different types of devices. The first nine will be connected to a timing device and the last one will be a device that can be set off using a remote control.'

'You are a destructive genius,' said Arkmed, kissing her lightly on the cheek. 'The movement is fortunate to have you within its ranks.'

'I was fortunate to be selected,' replied Petra, 'both by the movement and by you.'

Arkmed kissed her again. 'Come, time is wasting and we need to be getting on with the mission. You have a long drive ahead of you over the next week.'

'Yes, you're right, of course,' agreed Petra as she began the delicate and dangerous work of fitting the timers and detonators to the devices. Once that was done, she connected a radio receiver to one of them and produced a television remote control unit. 'I gutted the inside of this and have replaced the inside with alternative electrical circuitry, so that it will seem less conspicuous. All you will need to do to set off the explosives is to push the play button. It would be better if you didn't insert the batteries into the remote until you're ready to go. If it is knocked by accident and the play button pushed, it might not produce the outcome you want and if you're near it when that happens…'

'I see,' said Arkmed. 'I will make sure that doesn't happen.'

'Yes, you'd better not,' said Petra with a laugh. 'If you blow yourself up, I'll kill you.'

Once the work was completed, the two of them loaded the suitcase again with seven of the ten devices. They carried it carefully outside between them, covered by the night and placed it into the trunk of a small Daihatsu hatchback and Arkmed closed the trunk with a soft thump. Rob looked at the numberplate, which was LAG 201. He committed the number to memory, so he could give it to Ray once he returned to the hotel. He also noticed they'd just walked out of a small garage, hidden in a back of an alleyway, behind a line of suburban residences, probably hired by the pair for storage from the householder. It was a fair bet whoever owned the house, more than likely had no idea about the covert construction of explosive devices at the bottom of their back garden. Alternatively, the place may have belonged to one of them. He didn't think they'd be stupid enough to construct the devices so close to home, just in case something went wrong, but then, Arkmed seemed to have a lot of confidence in Petra's skills and perhaps, she was confident enough to think she wouldn't let an explosion shed any light on what she was doing. He'd have to wait and find out where they went back to, after storing the bombs in the trunk.

'Shall we go and have a bite?' Petra asked. 'All that work has given me an appetite, I think we should go and eat.'

'Sounds like an excellent idea,' said Arkmed placing his arm around her waist. 'I'm going to need all my strength to make love to you all night, before you go off in the morning.'

The two of them walked off arm in arm down the street. Rob attempted to follow them, but could get no further than the trunk of the car, stopped by what felt like some sort of invisible wall.

'Shit,' he said in frustration, realising the link was only to the bomb fragments, but not to Petra herself. He looked around, trying to make out where he was, but the surrounding darkness stopped him from reading the nearby street sign. He squinted and thought it said Lee Street, but wasn't one hundred percent sure.

'Rob,' said a familiar voice, 'you need to wake up.'

Rob opened his eyes to find he was again sitting on the sofa in the suite of the Hilton hotel. Clare sat next to him, touching him lightly on the arm, tears streaming down her cheeks. He looked at her and immediately knew something major had occurred in his absence. 'What is it? What's going on?'

'They've found Tony,' replied Ray in almost a whisper. 'I just got the phone call from the hospital.'

'He's alive,' added Clare, 'but he's not in good shape from what the doctors say.'

'At least he's alive,' said Rob putting his arm around Clare, who sobbed with relief into his chest.

'Come on,' said Ray, we need to go and see him. Getting there isn't going to be a problem. It's getting away from the hospital that might prove a bit tricky.'

'Why's that?' Rob asked.

'Because, if I was FOTS,' answered Ray, 'I'd have followed the ambulance to the hospital and would be watching the place, knowing both you and Clare would go there to see Tony. It may be the only reason he was allowed to live.'

A moment later, Ray's phone rang. He grabbed it from out of his shirt pocket and flipped it open. It was obvious he was speaking to Russell. A minute later, he closed the phone and a huge smile spread across his face.

'We'll take the cars to the hospital and Russell has just told me he's arranged for the air ambulance chopper to transport us from the roof of the hospital, back to the helipad on the roof of this hotel. Let's see if the bastard's expecting that. Russell's on his way up as we speak.'

'That's a great idea,' said Josie. 'That's why he gets paid the big bucks,' she added with a laugh.

'So, Rob, did you see anything useful that might help us?'

Rob smiled as he stood. 'As a matter of fact, I did. FOTS has an accomplice and her name is Petra. Sorry, but I didn't get a surname. She's in love with FOTS, or Arkmed, as he calls himself. She was the one who made the bombs, and there are only ten of them, not thirty, like we originally thought. He only said that to create more fear. He had seven of them and she had three. The two of them spoke about her taking some sort of trip for a week or so, in her car. I gathered she might be going somewhere interstate to plant the devices, although I don't know exactly where.'

'Did you get a good look at her?'

'Yeah, I did. I can give you an accurate description of her right up to the dragon tattooed on the base of her back and, I got the numberplate from the car.'

'Good work,' said Ray. 'I'll get that to Peter Bell. He might have some info on her, if she's come across the Federal or ASIO radars before now. He can pass it on to the FBI and CIA and see if they have anything on her. ASIO can contact the German Intelligence services. She might have a profile in that country, too. In the meantime, I'll arrange for a police sketch artist to be here, when we get back. If you could work with the artist, we might have a second face to present to the public, which brings us that much closer to getting to the nuke and the other bombs, too. At least we're making some progress in the case.'

'Not a problem,' said Rob. 'I'm glad I could help.'

Ray opened his phone again and walked off into Clare's bedroom to get some privacy and let Peter Bell know what was going on.

A minute later, Josie's phone rang, letting her know Russell was traversing the corridor and would be knocking on the door in a moment. 'All right,' said Josie, 'we'll try not to shoot you.'

Even though the two detectives knew who it was on the other side of the door, they out of reflex grabbed their guns, but held them by their sides until they were sure it was Russell who knocked.

'Not a bad place to crash,' he said as he looked around the well-appointed suite. 'Got anything to chew on? I feel like I haven't eaten for a week.'

'Yeah, there's some leftover ham and bread from last night in the fridge,' replied Rob. 'Help yourself.'

'No caviar and champagne?' he joked as he made his way to the kitchen.

'I'm afraid not,' retorted Clare. 'Best we could come up with are ham sandwiches and Coke. You can blame Ray for that.'

Russell grabbed the meat platter from the fridge and placed it on the kitchen bench. He placed several pieces of ham between two slices of bread and began to outline the plan and their approach to the Queen Victoria Hospital between mouthfuls of food.

'I've already spoken to the other teams. Annie and I will go ahead of the rest of you. She'll drop me off out the front. I've arranged with the hospital administrator to deck me out as a janitor. I'll keep an eye on the front foyer. Annie will go undercover as a doctor and stay on the ground floor, keeping an eye on the rear of the place. The rest of you will travel in convoy. Marcus will go with Josie, driving out front. You'll have Clare in the back seat. June and LeMar will drive behind you, with Rob in the rear of your car. It's important we keep in constant radio contact throughout the journey. Once we get close to the hospital, the two of you will get down on the back seats, so you won't be immediately visible. We'll drive to the front foyer of the hospital. My feeling is that he'll expect us to go to the rear, so we'll do just the opposite. We'll get as close to the entrance as we can with the cars and let the two of you out, to make a dash to the foyer, using the cars as cover. I'll be keeping an eye out while you make your way inside and make sure the foyer's empty of people who might get in the way. We don't need any more innocent victims associated with this case. The real danger point will be heading in. If he's placed somewhere with a rifle and a telescopic sight, well... I guess I don't have to explain. We have Kevlar vests in the trunks of the cars and we all keep an extra one, just in case. I want everyone to wear one. They won't stop a headshot, but if we exit the cars quickly enough and get inside, hopefully, he won't have the chance to get a good shot off. It's almost one, now,' said the detective looking at his watch. 'You'll head off at two, after the lunchtime rush is over. That'll decrease your chances of separation in traffic while you're driving. Annie and I will head off in a few minutes. Is that all right with everyone? I think I've covered every possible contingency.'

Ray re-entered the living room just as Russell finished speaking. 'I heard what you said. I've spoken to Peter, and he's going to place a team of fed snipers on the surrounding buildings. If that fucker tries to take a shot at you two, he'll give his location away. They'll fire to wound, but not to kill him. We still need to find the location of the nuke. As much as I hate to say it, we need the prick alive.'

'Even better,' said Russell, cracking a can of Coke from the fridge. 'We can use all the cover we can get.'

'Sure sounds like a plan to me,' said Josie as she snatched the can from Russell and took a large gulp.

CHAPTER EIGHTEEN

'Okay, Clare,' said Marcus, 'we're about two blocks from the hospital. Time to get down and out of sight.'

'Yeah, no worries,' replied the detective, popping her seatbelt and lowering herself down onto the seat. 'I hate that this arsewipe has reduced me to this.'

'Don't we all?' agreed Josie, 'I mean, look at the city. You'd think it was a public holiday. The place is fuckin' deserted.'

'I guess you can't blame the people who've left,' said Marcus as he pulled up at a set of lights. 'I'd get out, too, if I could. I'm just glad my wife and kids could. They've gone to my sister's in Whittlesea until this is all over. I felt like a bit of a prick lying to her and not telling her about the nuke. I've never lied to Kelly before, but I guess the main point is, they're in the country and away from all this shit.'

'Yeah, that's right,' said Josie. 'I asked my parents to go and they steadfastly refused. You know my parents are American; my dad's from Texas and he's real old school patriotic. You know, that "I refuse intimidation by terrorists" idealism, shit. If he had his way, there'd be a lynching once they caught FOTS.'

Marcus laughed behind his beard. 'I guess he wouldn't be the only person looking up at that piece of shit dangling from a rope, with a smile on his face. To tell you the truth, I think they should bring back capital punishment for scumbags like FOTS.'

'Yeah, me too,' said Clare. 'I guess the best we can hope for, though, is we catch him alive, that he gets life in prison and is gang-raped every day of his life. As much as I hate crims, the jail population doesn't look too kindly on pricks who kill innocent women and children. I hope we do take him alive. I only wish I could put a bullet in his balls before they take him away.'

'You're such a lady, Clare,' said Josie with a laugh, 'a woman after my own heart.'

'All right,' Marcus informed Clare, 'we're coming up on the hospital entrance. Open your door and get ready to go.'

'Okay,' said Clare, slipping her hand into her jacket and removing her Glock from its holster. She grabbed the door handle, pulled it, and pushed, opening the door slightly as the Commodore pulled up to the main entrance of the hospital. At the same time, Josie informed the rest of the team they'd arrived. Le Mar responded to her call and told her that they were about a half minute behind with Rob.

Clare opened the door and slid out headfirst onto the ground, keeping herself below the line of the windows as she moved. She closed the door behind her, scoped out the entrance, and estimated there was about thirty feet of open ground between the car and the sliding glass doors that led inside to the main foyer. She looked over and saw Russell glance at her, armed with mop and bucket and disguised as a janitor, cleaning the sterile white floor tiles of the outer foyer, appearing oblivious to what as going on around him, although Clare knew better. He was a man who'd spent so much time undercover that he could divide his attention without anybody noticing his focus. When she looked closer, she could see the radio wire that led from his overall pocket and into his ear and the slight bulge under his jacket, where he kept his firearm.

A moment later, the second car pulled up and Rob slipped out, ducking as he used the car to cover his presence. He looked at Clare and she indicated to him with hand signals that they would dash inside on the count of the three.

She held up one finger and Rob breathed deep, trying to stem the nervous energy building inside him.

Clare gripped her gun and hit the slide, sending a bullet into the firing chamber and then held up a second finger. She saw that Russell was making his way out of the foyer, having grabbed a broom and was pretending to sweep the bricks in the driveway. When Clare held up her third finger, the two of them sprinted to the entrance, and made it inside without incident. They headed straight for one of the elevators, followed by Russell, who'd stopped it on the ground floor, using a key he'd procured from the head of the janitorial department. Russell turned the key to the express mode, so it'd go straight to their destination without stopping, and pressed the fourth floor button, which would take them to the High Dependency Unit where Tony was located. Once the elevator started moving, he grabbed his radio, informed the team they'd made it to the lifts, and asked each of them to go to their assigned stations and look out for anyone or anything unusual and to keep in radio contact every twenty minutes.

'That seemed just a little too easy,' said Clare, who replaced her gun back into her shoulder holster, but left it unclipped.

'I know,' said Russell, 'I was just thinking that, myself.'

The three of them looked up and watched the yellow lights and the highlighted numbers as each consecutive floor passed. A bell sounded as they reached the fourth floor, and they were relieved to see Annie's smiling face as the elevator door opened.

'Hi,' she said, 'glad you could make it.'

'Annie, you stay out here and look out for anyone that comes up the elevator or the stairwell,' said Russell. 'I'll keep an eye on the intersecting corridor around the back of the unit and both the service lift and the fire escape staircase as well. The other guys have the place covered from the outside and the snipers will remain where they are and keep an eye on things until you guys leave.'

'I don't think the prime minister himself gets this much protection,' said Clare.

'Probably not,' said Annie, 'but then, Rob's more important than the prime minister right now and I'm sure the PM would most likely agree.'

'You want to know something funny? Russell asked them. 'The prime minister knows exactly what's going on and those were, or so I'm told, more or less, his exact words.'

'Hello there,' said one of the nurses pushing through the translucent doors that led inside the unit, her features covered in a surgical cap and mask. 'I'm Janice Brown, Nurse Unit Manager for High Dependency. I take it you're the police officers who've come to see Detective Green.'

'That's right.' I'm Clare Carbone and this is Rob Swift. We both work with Tony. How is he?'

'Did you say that your name's Swift?' Janice asked, ignoring Clare's question.

'Yeah, that's right. Rob Swift.'

'You'd better both get dressed and come inside straight away. There's something you ought to see.'

Janice asked them both to turn off their mobile phones, explaining they interfered with the equipment and provided the pair with full-length gowns, surgical gloves, masks, caps and white rubber boots, telling them the get-up was important to prevent infection to the patients inside the unit.

'Sorry about the inconvenience, but Tony is very susceptible right now, in his condition.'

'How is he?' Clare asked again, not liking the sound of things already.

'He's in critical condition,' replied Janice. 'We've put him into a drug-induced coma for the time being, to help with his healing and to prevent shock. I need you both prepared for what you're going to see. He's been through a lot and he's lucky to be alive. The next twenty-four hours are going to be important. I can tell you one thing, though. He's a fighter, that's for sure.'

Rob looked at Clare's eyes over the top of her mask and the fear and trepidation he saw there mirrored his own. He took hold of her hand and turned to face the nurse. 'Okay, we're ready,' he said, 'take us in.'

'This way,' Janice directed them, pushing the door with her back to maintain the sterility of her hands. She held the door open with her body and waved the two of them inside.

Rob and Clare entered the unit and the stark contrast to the fluorescent illumination outside was immediately apparent. It was darker and without sunlight, bathed in a kind of manufactured dusk, which emanated from soft lights placed over the patients' beds. The only bright points were the downward pointing desk lamps that sat on opposite sides of the nurses' station, so they could verify drug labels, fill up syringes accurately, and complete administrative work. The place was silent, except for the sounds of the complex monitoring machines that beeped and buzzed at regular intervals at the bedsides and the whispered voices of the nurses and medicos, who conferred between themselves and spoke to the bedridden patients about the strength of their pain, or other medical matters.

Rob's mind flashed back to the Alice Springs Hospital and the first time he'd gone to see Aroha. He looked over to the side of the unit and for a moment, saw her sleeping there, her arms filled with tubes and a ventilator assisting her to breathe like some mechanical automaton. He knew it was a memory, but at that moment, it seemed so real, so incredibly vivid, he felt as if he'd been transported back there, caught unaware by one of his visions.

'Are you okay?' Clare asked him.

'Yeah, I'm fine,' replied Rob, shaking his head to rid himself of the memory. 'I think I've just spent too much time visiting places like this over the past couple of years.'

'This way,' said Janice, leading them past the nurses' station to a smaller room on the far side of the unit. 'He's in there,' she informed them, pointing at a large, glass window that looked into the room, but for the time being was temporarily blocked off by a drawn curtain. 'Wait here for a little while, we're in the process of changing some of his dressings, and you two will only get in the way. I'll come and get you in a couple of minutes.'

'Sure,' said Clare, almost glad for the temporary reprieve from entering the room, 'take your time.'

While they were waiting, they heard a soft bell sound and one of the nurses left the station and moved out through the entrance. She returned a few moments later with an envelope. 'This is for you, Detective Carbone,' said the nurse handing over the envelope. 'It was delivered to reception this morning. Sorry about the delay, but nobody knew of you at the time, and then your colleague asked that the main foyer be vacated for a while. I guess it got put in a tray and left for a time.'

'That's okay,' said the detective, eyeing the package with suspicion. She walked over to the nurses' station and asked if they had a penlight she could borrow for a few minutes. She held the envelope up by the edges and used the light to look through the paper to make sure there were no mechanical devices or white powder inside. She looked at the front of the envelope and saw her name, Clare Carbone printed in blue pen. She noticed there was no reference to her as a police officer, which probably added to the confusion of finding her. She knew it was from FOTS before she even opened it. It couldn't have been from anyone else. No one knew she'd be here this morning. She didn't even know herself. Ray didn't get the call until after midday, informing him of Tony's admission to the emergency room. The hospital staff didn't know who he was, at first, his identity was only discovered when uniformed police made a search of the area and turned up his Police ID in the grass, metres away from the place where some drunk had discovered him in the morning, on his way to the local soup kitchen for breakfast and called an ambulance.

'I'll be back in a minute,' she said to Rob as she headed out of the unit. Clare grabbed a spare pair of surgical gloves and a mask from a cupboard as she passed through the reception area. She headed around to the back of the unit, where she found Russell waiting in the corridor keeping an eye on the service elevator and the stairwell. He could tell there was something wrong as soon as he saw the look on Clare's face.

'What's up?'

'I think I've got a letter from FOTS,' she replied holding out the envelope.

'You haven't opened it, have you?'

'No, I wouldn't put anything past that bastard, as far as sneaky goes. Can you give Larry Batts at technical a call and see if we can't get it to the lab? I think it needs thorough examination before we open it. It could be soaked in some biological agent or explosive. As I say, I wouldn't put anything past him. Here, take these gloves, mask, and gown. Put them on before you handle it and warn Larry, too. It might be overdoing it, but I suggest we take as many precautions as possible until it gets the all clear. Make sure you use your phone first, before you touch it, we don't want any kind of cross-contamination.'

'Yeah, fair enough,' said Russell as he began to gear up, dialling his phone as he dressed. 'Hello, Larry,' he said. 'We need for you to get down to the Queen Victoria Hospital, as soon as possible. It looks like we got a letter from FOTS.'

'Jesus,' said Larry, 'whatever you do, don't open, or knock it against anything. Does it seem as if it contains any sort of mechanical device?'

'No, Clare had a look inside, using a penlight and it doesn't seem to have anything like that in it.'

'Okay, that's a relief,' said Larry with a sigh, 'but we need to consider that it may be impregnated with some sort of solution or biological agent, too. Can you get Clare to go back to the unit and get a bag for the disposal of contaminated biological products? They should have them there. They're big yellow, sealable bags with ties at the top and then get her to ask for some sort of sealable container, too, to place it in. I'll be there as soon as possible. Also, make sure she throws her gloves into it. Was it handled by anyone else?'

Russell removed the phone from his cheek and hit a button to place it on speakerphone. 'Did anybody else handle it?' Larry repeated.

'Yeah, the nurse who gave it to me,' replied Clare, 'although I saw her take her gloves off afterwards and throw them in the yellow bin. It was also probably handled by the staff at main reception. They wouldn't have had gloves on, either.

'Okay, you need to go and get the bag from the bin and tie it up. Then you need to get to the person at reception as quickly as possible and isolate them. Take down gloves, masks, and gowns and if there's more than one staff member in reception. Gown them all up and isolate the lot of them. I'll call the hospital administrator while I'm driving and have them get a room quarantined. Hurry, Clare, before it gets out of hand.'

'All right, Larry,' said Clare, 'I'll see you when you get here and hurry.'

'On my way,' said Larry and then the phone went dead.

Clare and Russell rushed back to the reception area of the HDU. Russell grabbed a pile of surgical gear and told Clare he'd head straight down to the reception area.

'What's wrong? Annie asked as came around the corner.

'No time to explain,' said Clare as she grabbed a biohazard bag from the cupboard, placed the envelope inside, peeled off her gloves, placed them into the bag as well, and sealed it at the top. 'Go with Russell, he'll tell you on the way down to the foyer,' she said as she snapped on a second pair of gloves, grabbed another biohazard bag, and rushed back into the unit.

'What about guarding the two of them?'

'Don't worry about them right now. They'll be safe inside the unit. We have a larger, more immediate problem to deal with. 'Here,' he said throwing a surgical outfit at her, 'put these on and that's an order, Annie.'

'Fuck, if you're giving orders, Russell,' said Annie as she gowned up, 'it must be really serious.'

'Come on,' he said, 'we need to get down to reception.'

The two police officers bypassed the elevators and took the staircase at a run. They practically hurled themselves down the flights, almost jumping from one landing to the next, hardly touching the actual stairs themselves, while Russell breathlessly explained the situation to his colleague. As the detectives burst through the ground floor doors, they grabbed their police identification and held them in the air.

'We are the Police,' Russell yelled at the top of his voice. 'This is an emergency situation. We need to evacuate this area, right now.'

'You stay right where you are,' said Annie to the three reception staff. 'Don't move or attempt to go anywhere.'

There was something of a momentary panic, as both visitors to the hospital and staff started running in all directions, leaving the foyer deserted in less than a minute.

'Annie, go close and lock all doors to this area,' ordered Russell, as he threw the gowns and other apparel at the reception staff and told them in no uncertain terms to put them on. He then went and pressed the buttons on each of the elevators, bringing them down to the ground floor and ushering those people who were already in them, outside as quickly and quietly as possible. He then locked each elevator in turn with his key, preventing them from moving, and told Annie to keep an eye on the stairwell.

A moment later, there was a loud crackling sound, as the hospital public address system sounded and the hospital administer, ordered that all staff and visitors were to remain where they were for the time being and further informed that the main reception area was at this time, out of bounds. He went on to say, an all-clear announcement would sound, when it was safe to re-enter the foyer and reception area.

'Okay, that covers everybody inside the building,' said Russell. 'Now for the outside,' he added as he grabbed his radio from his pocket and contacted each of the external surveillance teams and gave them orders to prevent anyone from entering the building. 'We'll have uniforms down here, soon,' he said, 'but for the moment, it's up to you guys.'

'Okay,' said Le Mar, 'we'll move the car to the front and put the flashing light onto the roof, but it's probably going to blow our cover.'

'Screw your cover,' said Russell with a laugh, 'you can always get a haircut, Le Mar.'

'No worries, boss,' responded Josie, 'Marcus and I got the rear covered.'

'Okay, people, good work,' said Russell. 'Larry Batts is on his way and so are the Hazchem unit. Make sure to let him through when he arrives.'

'I guess you did call him sooner than he thought, Annie,' said Josie over the radio.

'Very funny, Wonder Woman,' replied Annie with a chuckle, 'very funny indeed.'

CHAPTER NINETEEN

Clare walked into the high dependency unit, asked to see Janice Brown straight away, and explained it was an emergency. One of the other nurses went to Tony's room and relieved her, where she was busy assisting in changing the many dressings the detective required over his wounds.

'What's up?' Rob asked. 'I just heard the announcement over the speaker.'

'It's not good,' replied the detective in a whisper. 'The letter that arrived for me was probably from FOTS. We're not taking any chances that it might contain either explosive, or some sort of chemical or even a biological weapon.'

'Do you want me to come with you?'

'No, you stay here. You've still got your Glock holstered, haven't you?'

'Yeah,' replied Rob, 'not that I'd do much good with it, anyway.'

'I'll be back in a little while. Go in and see Tony.'

'You wanted to see me?' Janice asked approaching the nurses' station.

'Yes,' replied Clare who went on to explain the situation to the nurse manager. 'We need to empty that bin,' said the detective, 'and place everything in it in a biohazard bag.'

'All right,' said Janice, grabbing the bag from the bin, sealing and placing it inside another biohazard bag. 'Is there anything else that I can do for you?'

'Yes, could you get hospital security up here, just to keep an eye on things?' said the detective. 'The lifts are out by now, if I know Russell. We just need to have the staircases covered, just in case.'

'Not a problem,' said Janice picking up the phone. 'Rob, you can go in and see Tony now. It looks like they've finished his dressings,' she added pointing to the curtain that was now open in the room.

'Yeah, go on,' said Clare. 'I'll come up and join you soon. I just need to deliver these bags to Larry in the foyer and make sure everything's all right.'

'Okay,' said Rob, 'I'll talk to you later.'

'Yeah, okay,' said Clare, taking the yellow biohazard bag and moving out of the unit.

Rob turned and headed to Tony's room, followed by Janice. He gasped when he saw the many bandages Tony had placed all over his body. His face, too, was almost completely covered, except for his eyes, nose, and mouth, right down to his feet and a steel frame placed over the centre of the bed, to prevent the sheets from touching his skin, Rob thought to stop infection and to prevent cotton from the sheets entangling in his wounds.

'I wish I could shoot,' said Rob to himself, 'I'd sure as hell put a bullet into the fucker, if I ever got the chance.'

'Are you okay?' Janice asked him.

'Yeah,' replied Rob. 'What was it you wanted Clare and I to see, Janice?'

The nurse drew the curtains across the window again and told Rob that what he was going to see might shock him, so he should prepare himself. She then went to Tony, removed the sheet from the frame, and drew it back to the bottom of the bed. Rob felt tears of anger and sadness begin to well in his eyes as he looked at the body of this man, who he'd come to know as a friend. Carved deep into his chest in capital letters was one word – SWIFT. The letters of his name were large, angry, blistered, and filled with blood. Rob knew from his vision of Tony's torture, the name was cut into Tony's chest and then a knife heated and traced over the wounds, both to stop the bleeding and to prolong the agony that this poor man must have had to endure.

'Oh... my... God,' Rob said, almost collapsing onto a chair against the wall before he fainted. He looked again, compelled to, hardly able to believe the evidence of his own eyes and felt the contents of his stomach begin to rise. He made for the door and Janice directed him to the staff toilet behind the nurses' station. He rushed inside to one of the cubicles, lifted the lid on the bowl, pulled down his mask and vomited several times, resting his head on the cool floor between episodes, until the image surfaced again in his mind and he was forced back.

A few minutes later, Rob heard the bathroom door open and footsteps approach. He looked up and saw Janice's gentle eyes behind her mask. 'Take this,' she said, offering him a towel to wipe his mouth and helping him to sit up. 'You're not the only one to do this,' she consoled him with a gentle hug, 'a couple of my younger nurses had the same reaction and they didn't even know the man, much less have their name carved into his chest. I don't blame you and neither does any of the nursing staff here. We know you want to catch this bastard and we all support you, wholeheartedly.'

'Thanks,' said Rob wiping his mouth and breathing deeply, trying to put the image of his friend out of his mind, 'that means a lot.'

'You can stay in here for as long as you need to,' said Janice. 'When you're ready, come out and I'll make you a nice cup of tea in the break room. Tea's a good thing for settling the stomach and you can trust me, I know, I've had to settle a few stomachs in my time.'

'Thanks,' replied Rob, 'that'd be really good.'

'You don't have to go back in and visit your friend, but if you want to, you can, we've covered him over again.'

'I'd like to just sit with him for a while, once I'm feeling a bit better.'

'Okay,' said Janice rising to her feet. 'You'll need to change your gown and gloves. It happens that vomit and leaning over the toilet bowl are not exactly conducive to a good, sterile environment.'

'No, I guess they're not,' said Rob with half a laugh. 'Thanks again.'

'Stop thanking me,' said Janice as she headed to the door, 'it's what any decent human being would do. I'll have one of the other nurses bring you in a change of gear in a few minutes.'

Rob stood and went to the sink, where he washed out his mouth and splashed water over his face, repeating the action several times until he at last felt better. He looked into the mirror opposite and noticed he suddenly looked older, as if the shock of seeing Tony in such a deplorable state had somehow changed him physically, along with the strain and pressure of trying to catch FOTS over recent days. His hair seemed just a little greyer on the sides of his face and his skin seemed stretched and slightly more wrinkled than when he'd looked in the mirror this morning. There were dark circles under his eyes, too, but he remembered them already being there, caused by the lack of sleep he'd endured ever since he'd arrived back in Australia.

'Here you go, Detective Swift,' said one of the nursing staff as she entered the bathroom and placed a change of surgical gear on the bench next to where he stood.

Rob was about to tell her that he wasn't a detective, but couldn't be bothered with the hassle. 'Thanks,' he said.

'You're welcome,' replied the nurse who exited the room just as quickly as she'd entered.

Rob kicked off the rubber boots and changed his surgical gear, leaving the soiled garments inside a hamper next to the door, along with others that appeared to need laundering. He washed his hands thoroughly and put on the gown, boots, and mask and then grabbed a set of surgical gloves from a box on the bench, which he put on and used his body to push open the door, and walked back out into the unit.

'Glad you could make it,' said Janice, noticing his entrance. 'The coffee room's over there,' she added, pointing to a door just up from the nurses' station. 'Take your time, Rob, there's no hurry.'

'Is Clare back yet?'

'No, I'm sure she's not far away, though. They've just given the all clear over the loudspeaker while you were indisposed. I expect she'll be back presently.'

'That's good,' said Rob, heading towards the tearoom, 'about the all clear. I guess that means they've got everything under control.'

'Yeah, it looks that way,' said Janice from underneath her mask, 'and a good thing, too. My nurses are due to finish their shifts soon and the afternoon shift is about to start. Let me tell you, there's nothing pricklier than a tired nurse who wants to go home. Make a terrorist seem like a boy scout.'

'I'm sure they would,' agreed Rob. 'By the way, Janice, thanks for the laugh, I needed it.'

'That's why they pay me the big bucks,' retorted Janice, winking over the top of her mask.

Rob pushed the door inwards and was immediately struck by the brightness of the room, lit up by fluorescent lights, so that every corner was visible, which was such a contrast to the unit outside. It took him a moment to adjust his eyes, blinking a few times to cope with the sudden and dramatic change. The first thing he noticed was a sign on the wall in front, telling him to remove his gloves upon entering and to discard them in the biohazard bin beneath the sign.

Once he'd oriented himself, he complied with the direction and then headed for the cupboards, where he found a huge mug and the ingredients to make a brew. He concocted himself a strong coffee with two sugars, because he felt like a bit of extra energy. It was something he'd always done for as long as he could remember when he wanted to be good to himself.

Rob sat down at the table located in the middle of the room and looked up at the opposite wall, plastered almost to the roof with cards from previous patients and relatives from those that'd made it to recovery and others who'd been less fortunate and had lost their battle to live. He noticed that even the cards from the relatives of those people who'd died, had something good to say about the treatment their loved ones had received whilst in the unit, under the excellent care of the doctors and the nursing staff.

'Well, it looks like Tony's in the right place, at least,' he said to himself.

He finished his coffee, washed out the cup, and placed it back where he found it in the cupboard. He used some disinfectant placed near the sink to cleanse his hands and then grabbed another set of gloves and pulled those on. He took a deep breath to steady himself and headed back out to see his friend. He moved quietly back through the unit and Janice asked him if he was okay to go back in by himself.

'He's covered up,' she said, 'and I've got some other stuff I need to take care of.'

'Yeah, I should be okay,' replied Rob, 'at least I know what to expect now.'

'All right,' said Janice, 'I'll send Detective Carbone in as soon as she gets back.'

Rob entered Tony's room without making a sound, almost reverently, not wanting to disturb him in any way. He stood looking at him for a time, watching his chest move up and down, and the fluids dripping into his veins via the lines that hung above his bed. He thought again of Aroha and for the briefest instant, he saw her, lying on the bed in Alice Springs, her life sustained by what looked like a million machines.

Rob returned from the memory and moved the chair at the foot of the bed closer to his friend. He wanted to say something to him, anything that might ease his pain, in some small way, but couldn't find any words adequate to the task. Instead, he placed his gloved hand on his arm and squeezed it, hoping the physical touch would say more than his words ever could. Rob in that sudden instant found himself on a station, standing amongst other commuters who were waiting for the train to arrive. He wondered, at first, how he'd arrived there, but knew it had something to do with touching Tony's arm. It didn't usually happen like this, not while he was wearing gloves and separated from the physical being, but he figured the intense feelings he'd undergone when he'd seen his friend's condition and the affection he held for him, must have had something to do with it. Perhaps the power of the vision was, in some way, exponentially increased by his recent experience. He couldn't think of any other explanation, and somewhere deep inside him, knew he was right. He looked around at the other people who stood on the platform and recognised Jenny, Tony's partner, who he'd first seen on the day of his disappearance, glancing through a magazine while she waited. As he cast his eyes further afield, he saw Clare, Ray Owen, and some of the other police he'd come to know over recent times. All of them waited patiently, without speaking, occasionally glancing down the line to see if a train was approaching, and then returning to their reading, or just staring straight ahead.

Rob walked through the crowd of passengers. He occasionally bumped into someone as he moved along and received a smile from that person, but not a word exchanged. He purposely bumped Clare's shoulder and she turned to look at him, smiled and moved aside to let him through, but showed no sign of recognition. He tried the same thing with Ray and elicited the same response.

'This is weird,' he said.

'Not as weird as you might think,' said a familiar voice from behind him. 'It's all relative, really.'

Rob turned and saw Tammy Parks standing in front of him. She was at least thirty years younger than when he last saw her and in the prime of her life. Her hair was dark now and without a fleck of grey, her muscles seemed toned and her eyes were bright, as though a spark flamed beneath them. 'Death becomes you,' he said with a laugh.

'Yes, it does,' agreed Tammy throwing her arms around Rob's neck and squeezing him. 'It's so good to see you again.'

'You too,' said Rob returning the hug. 'I can't believe how good you look.'

Tammy laughed. 'Yes, I was a bit of a dish when I was young. My husband still tells me that now. He's not too bad himself, these days, either. A spirit is always young, ageless, despite the ravages of the physical body, prior to its departure.'

'So, where are we?' Rob asked.

Tammy smiled knowingly. 'This is Tony's life, in the present,' she replied. 'The trains heading down the track represent his past and the trains moving up the track represent his future.'

'So, that's why there are people here I recognise?'

'That's right, Rob.'

The two of them watched as a train pulled into the station. Rob saw that there were already many people aboard, each carriage filled with passengers. 'Who are the people already on the train?'

'They're people who've come from Tony's future life, but are becoming a part of his past, people he met briefly once or twice, or associations that have faded away.'

The two of them watched as the waiting passengers boarded the train and sat down, or remained standing, clutching the passenger rails that ran the length of the carriage, some of them continuing to read their magazines or newspapers, while others simply gazed out of the windows. A minute later, a loud whistle sounded at the other end of the station and the train moved off. Rob looked again around the platform and saw there were now about a dozen people standing and waiting. Clare was still there, as was Ray, Jenny, and so were some of the nurses and doctors from the high dependency unit, who still wore their gowns and surgical masks.

'So, I gather these are the people who'll have an immediate impact on Tony's present life.'

'That's right,' said Tammy. 'It seems you're catching on. You always were a quick learner, Rob. Our train will be along in a few minutes. In the meantime, would you like to go and have a cup of tea?'

Rob laughed. 'You always were a bit of a tea freak, weren't you?'

Tammy laughed, too. 'If there were no tea in the afterlife, I would have insisted on reincarnation.'

'Can you do that, insist on reincarnation?'

'All things are possible, Rob, in a universe with no boundaries,' she replied. 'Come on, let's go get a cup each of nice, hot tea and perhaps a treat, too.'

Tammy led Rob to the far end of the station, and into a little café located in the main building. She asked him to get them a table, somewhere, preferably in the sun and went off to order their refreshments.

Rob sat down at a little wooden table and looked out of the window beside him at the train tracks, and the few suburban houses that lay beyond the boundaries of the station, partially hidden by a line of gum trees and native bushes. The sun felt nice on his face. He craned his neck and stretched, letting the tension slip out of him, as though the warming rays provided him with a kind of ethereal massage that helped to relieve his stress and apprehension.

'There you are,' said Tammy, arriving at the table with a large plastic tray, on which were placed two cups of tea and a couple of blueberry muffins. 'I love muffins with tea,' she said as she placed the tray onto the table, removed the cups, the muffins, and some packets of sugar, and then placed the tray on the next table opposite them.

Rob grabbed his tea, tore open a satchel and stirred in a single sugar, while Tammy did the same. 'So, I gather if we're catching a train to Tony's future, that he's going to live.'

'My, my, you could be Sherlock Holmes with such brilliant deductions,' said Tammy, taking a sip of her tea and smiling broadly.

'I'm right, though, aren't I?'

'Yes, you're right, Rob, now drink up, we only have a few minutes. You're not allowed to eat or drink on the train, it's against the rules.'

'Whose rules are they?'

'The rules of the universe,' replied Tammy as she opened her muffin and split it, leaving half on the plastic packet, and placing some into her mouth, which she chewed and swallowed before continuing to speak. 'Sometimes, for no apparent reason, they mirror the rules of the physical world. Don't ask me why, I haven't quite figured that out, yet, but give me time.'

'I'm sure you will,' said Rob who took a large bite of his muffin and washed it down with a swallow of his tea. 'It always amazes how on this plane of existence, I can do something, like eat a muffin and it tastes the same as in the physical world. I mean, it even feels the same.'

Tammy smiled at him. 'Existence is existence. Didn't the sorcerer once tell you the mind is a desert and you can put what you want into it?'

'Yeah, I remember that. It kind of amazed me at the time.'

'Well, think of the afterlife as a larger extension of that concept. Except you can do things on a larger, even grander scale.'

'I guess there are certain things that make being dead quite appealing,' said Rob, picking up his cup and finishing the last of his tea in a swallow. 'There's also Aroha to look forward to, as well. I guess I don't have to tell you how much that means to me.'

'No, you don't,' said Tammy finishing her tea and the last bite of her muffin. 'Come on,' she urged him, 'we need to get going, the train's coming.'

Rob stood and helped to place their scraps back onto the tray, which Tammy retrieved from the other table. She stood, took the tray back to the counter, and thanked the young woman who had served her. Then she and Rob moved out onto the platform, just as the train was pulling in. They stood there for a moment, waiting, and then boarded the carriage nearest to where they stood. Tammy took a seat near a window and gazed out at the world beyond as they pulled out of the station and began to pick up speed. Rob remained on his feet facing her, also looking out at the passing scenery and the parade of people and different houses, feeling almost hypnotised by the rhythmic sound of the steel wheels as they moved along the tracks.

A few minutes passed and then the train slowed and pulled into another station. 'Come on,' said Tammy, heading for the door, 'this is your vision. We wouldn't have stopped here unless there was something you were supposed to see.'

Rob jumped off the train and followed Tammy through the main body of the station and out through a turnstile. Instead of arriving in a street outside the station, the two of them found themselves standing in the living room of Tony's house. Rob looked closer at his friend and saw that he had two long, think scars that ran down each side of his face, from below his eyes and down to his chin.

'Here, baby,' said Jenny, carrying a toasted sandwich on a plate, which she handed to Tony who sat in front of the television. She sat down beside him, placed her hand on his leg, and stroked it slowly. 'Are you okay?'

'Yeah, I'm all right,' he replied taking an absent bite of the sandwich. 'It just feels weird to be back here, after being in the hospital for so long, and look at me, I look like some kind of freak. I don't know how I'm ever going to go outside ever again, much less work.'

'Tony,' said Jenny reassuringly, 'you don't look like a freak at all. The doctor said the scars on your face will heal, so you'll hardly notice them and there's no need for you to go back to work until that happens. Don't worry, my love, you've just come home today, it's going to take a while to adjust. Clare said she'd come and see you tomorrow, once you've settled in. Tony, the people who love you will always be there. I just thank God you're alive and I didn't lose you. It would've been too much for me to bear. In the meantime, we can cover the scars with makeup if we have to go anywhere. Did you forget that I'm an expert with makeup? I'll make you look like a supermodel.'

Tony began to laugh and Jenny joined him. They hugged, kissed, and cried together and Rob felt uneasy about being in the room during such a private moment.

'Can we get out of here? I feel like a voyeur, seeing something I wasn't supposed to.'

'Of course,' replied Tammy. 'Follow me, Mister Swift, your carriage awaits you.'

Rob and Tammy headed for the front door of the house. 'Just keep going,' said Tammy, 'we can walk right through it.'

The two of them passed through the door like ghosts and were soon found standing once more at the station. They passed again through the turnstile and found the train waiting for them at the platform. They boarded the same carriage, and the doors closed behind them as the train moved off.

'So, what's next?' Rob asked taking a seat.

'You'll have to wait and see,' replied Tammy taking a piece of candy from her bag, which she unwrapped and put in her mouth. 'You want a piece?'

'No, thanks,' replied Rob. 'So, every station is some sort of episode from Tony's future?'

'I don't talk while I chew things,' said Tammy covering her mouth with her hand, 'it's very bad manners.'

A few minutes later, the train stopped again and the two of them disembarked onto another platform. Rob led the way this time through the turnstile and out into a charming old country church, where he saw Tony and Jenny in the midst of saying their marriage vows, overseen by a grey haired old pastor as many well-wishers looked on.

'It's lovely, isn't it?' Tammy asked as she took a seat in the last pew.

'Yeah,' agreed Rob sitting next to her, 'I'm glad he's so happy. I guess I'm a bit jealous, too.'

'I can't blame you, Rob, I probably would be, too, if I was in your position.'

Rob looked at the gathered crowd and saw Clare holding hands with a man a few rows from the front of the church. 'So, she finally found someone. I'll bet he's a cop, too.'

'Of course,' said Tammy with a laugh. 'She married him about six months before this took place. Go and look at him, I think you'll be surprised at who it is.'

Rob walked up the aisle to the front of the church and peered down the pew to where Clare stood with her husband. It took him a moment to realise it was Russell, although now he was without the beard, the long hair, and the overalls. They both looked happy to be there and happy to be with each other. He was glad she'd found someone to love. Her life had seemed somewhat empty in all the time he'd known her. She was a great detective, and he had the utmost respect for her, but her life seemed consumed by her occupation. At least now, she had someone who both loved her and understood her passion for her work.

'I now pronounce you husband and wife,' said the minister. 'You may kiss the bride.'

Tony leaned over and kissed Jenny with scaring passion on the mouth and the whole congregation erupted in applause and cheering, although the happy couple seemed oblivious to the noise around them. Rob smiled, walked back down the aisle and found Tammy.

'Okay, let's go,' he said.

'Hang on a minute,' said Tammy. 'Do you know why you've been brought here? Is there anything you see, or don't see, that grabs your attention?'

Rob looked around the church, at all the gathered people and at the bride and groom. It suddenly struck him that he wasn't there, and he knew if he'd been alive, he'd never have missed such an occasion.

'It's me,' he said looking at Tammy. 'I'm already dead when this happens, aren't I?'

'Yes, you are,' replied Tammy. 'I think you were brought here for two reasons. The universe took you to Tony's house to see he'd recovered enough to leave the hospital, so that you can go on doing what you're doing and catching that man who's wrought so much damage and misery to others. You were brought here to see something you would otherwise have missed out on and to know the people who you've held dear, are going to be all right, if you make the right decision when the time arrives.'

'Why can't you just tell me who this FOTS guy is and save us a whole lot of trouble?'

Tammy stood and placed a reassuring hand on Rob's shoulder. 'Even in a universe where there appear to be no limits, there are rules of conduct. You need to learn certain lessons before you depart the physical realm, as have all those before you. You'd be incomplete if you didn't. The lessons you will learn just prior to your death are the most important ones. I'm afraid there's just no getting around it, my friend.'

'Is there a hell?' Rob asked. 'Is there some place where all the evil people go, after they die?'

'No, there isn't a hell,' Tammy replied. 'Those people who don't learn the lessons of their physical existence, just don't make the transition to the afterlife. They're so consumed with themselves that their spirits spontaneously combust as they die and they're simply no more. They become a part of the great void that surrounds us. Sometimes, they're sent back, given a second chance, but the opportunity is rare and far between.'

'So, reincarnation is real?'

'All things are possible,' said Tammy, 'sometimes, and with the right conditions.'

'Can we get out of here?' Rob asked. 'I want to get back to the hospital. Clare might be back now and there are things we have to do.'

'Of course,' said Tammy with a smile, 'follow me.'

They left the church by the front entrance and found themselves again on the railway platform. This time however, the train wasn't sitting at the station. 'Fancy a cigarette, while we wait?' Tammy asked, pulling some Marlboros from her bag.

'Yeah, thanks,' said Rob as he pulled one from the packet. Tammy handed him a lighter and the pair of them stood without speaking, watching the blue plumes of smoke drift away, sailing through the air until they disappeared altogether, carried by a soft, gentle breeze that brushed past them.

Rob put his cigarette out in a nearby ashtray, just as the train came up the tracks and stopped at the station, this time heading in the opposite direction. He jumped on board followed by Tammy and took a seat. 'So, all this, the thing with Aroha and Clare's grandfather, it's all about preparing me for leaving?'

'Yeah, I guess it is,' replied Tammy. 'I don't make the plays. It's the universe that arranges everything. I'm glad to have seen you, Rob, but I didn't ask to be here. I was just as surprised as you were to find myself on the platform at the station.'

'So, you're saying that there's a higher power, at work here? Is it God?'

'I don't know, Rob. I can't say that since I've been dead I've met God, or even heard any mention of a supreme being as such. My feeling is that it's just another plane of existence, but I don't know for sure. The search for knowledge doesn't stop once you've left your mortal coil. It's an eternal quest. I learn new things almost every day.'

'I guess it's good to keep your mind occupied,' said Rob, standing as the train pulled up. 'You don't want to spend an eternity bored out of your brain.'

Tammy laughed, stood, and hugged Rob. 'It's anything but boring, my dear friend.'

'Goodbye, Tammy,' said Rob, releasing her and heading towards the door, 'I guess I'll see you soon. I don't suppose you can tell me how it's going to happen, can you?'

'No, I'm afraid not,' replied Tammy as she walked him to the door. 'That's something you have to find out for yourself.'

'I didn't think so,' said Rob with a sad smile, 'but I had to ask, anyway.'

'I know,' said Tammy. 'Goodbye, Rob,' she added as the doors closed and the train began to depart the station.

Rob stood for a moment on the platform and watched the train as it moved off down the tracks and then disappeared around a bend. He turned, walked to the rear of the station and through the turnstile, and found himself again sitting beside Tony in his hospital room.

'Hi, Rob,' said Clare who stood at the foot of the bed, her eyes red, as if she'd been crying, 'I didn't want to disturb you, I could see you were… busy.'

Rob looked up at the detective and smiled under his mask. 'He's going to be all right,' he told her, 'I've seen it with my own eyes.'

Clare sighed. 'I was hoping you'd say that. Janice showed me some photos of what FOTS did to him and told me how you reacted. I can't say that I blame you. Are you okay?'

'Yeah, I'm all right now,' replied Rob letting go of Tony's arm and standing. 'I'm glad I came. I'll tell you about what I saw on the way back to the hotel.'

'Okay,' said Clare who moved closer to the bed and placed her hand on Tony's unmoving arm. 'I promise you, Tony, I'm going to catch this bastard if it's the last thing I ever do.'

'Take it from me,' said Rob with a gentle laugh, 'you'll do plenty more, after you've done that.'

'What do you mean by that?' Clare asked as she followed him out of the unit.

CHAPTER TWENTY

Mark knocked twice in quick succession on the front door of the apartment. Putting his ear to the frame, he listened for the signs of movement emanating from the inside and noticed the vague sound of a toilet flush and a door close on the opposite side of the flat. A few seconds later, he heard approaching footsteps and a fastening chain slide and clink, before the door opened and a pair of green eyes peered out into the hallway and looked at him. He smiled and held up the bunch of red roses he'd purchased from a florist on his way there.

'Hello, Arkmed,' said Petra, opening the door wider to allow him admission. 'Are those flowers for me?'

'Of course, my love,' he said handing them over and kissing her cheek. 'Flowers for a flower.'

'Thank you, you've never done that before,' said Petra, smelling the aroma from the petals. 'I'll just grab a vase from the kitchen to put them in.'

Mark scanned the lavish apartment; her good taste a product of her wealthy parents, who still resided in Berlin and against whom she had constantly rebelled since her days in university. He looked for anything, no matter how obscure that might link them together. He saw an old, woollen jumper he'd lent her one cold night, and an aeroplane ticket she had paid for, when they'd gone for a vacation on the Gold Coast, but that was all he could detect, for the time being. He would make a more thorough inspection later, after she was dead. Killing her wasn't something he was particularly looking forward to, but it was a necessity of his mission and just something that simply had to happen. Eventually, the authorities would understand her part in the conspiracy and under interrogation she'd have divulge all she knew.

Petra placed the flowers on a cabinet to the side of the living room, where they could gather from sunshine from a nearby window. She returned to the kitchen and brought out a bottle of wine and two glasses, which she placed on the coffee table in front of her large, leather sofa.

'I know that you don't ordinarily drink, but I think this is a special occasion. Our mission is now complete and come midday tomorrow, this country will receive a destabilising blow like never before.'

Mark took the glass she offered and smelled the vintage wine before taking a sip and gave her a look of approval. 'Yes, on this occasion, I think it will be all right. Besides,' he added with a smile, 'I know you'll never tell anybody.'

'Of course I wouldn't,' Petra assured him with a kiss. 'You know you can trust me to take any secret you share with me to the grave.'

'Of course I do,' said Mark kissing her again, 'of course.'

Petra made him a delicious, traditional Afghan meal consisting of lamb, specially prepared by an Islamic butcher, rice, Nan-bread, vegetables, and an orange for dessert, which they consumed while sitting on the floor. The two of them ate with their fingers, using their right hands, in the traditional manner, which Petra still considered something of a novelty, having grown up using both knife and fork, although for Mark, it was a way of life and his pretence being the use of cutlery to fool those around him. They laughed and watched television as they devoured their food, finding the constant news bulletins about the bomber, who'd so far evaded capture, to be highly amusing.

'We'll be gone from this country before they have a clue as to who we were,' laughed Petra, 'and we'll be heroes when we get to Afghanistan. The Prophet will commend us in front of all our comrades-in-arms.'

'Yes, we will be heroes,' said Mark leaning over and kissing her, tasting the citrus from the orange still on her lips.

'I can't wait to be your wife,' said Petra, standing and extending her hand. He took her fingers in his own and she led him into the bedroom, where they undressed each other and made love until the daylight arrived through the bedroom curtains to greet them and then Petra fell asleep, exhausted and blissfully unaware of her impending fate.

Mark looked at her serene sleeping features and the exquisite shape of her breasts as her chest rose and fell in the dim light of the room. She was beautiful, both physically and spiritually and if the mission didn't take precedence, he may well have taken her for his wife and fled back to his homeland, although he was unsure as to how she'd cope in such a harsh environment. However, her knowledge of his activities and the fact that several European states wanted her for acts of terrorism and murder made her nothing less than an unacceptable liability to him in this country. Her profile was too high and eventually, her guard would slip, she'd be recognised, and arrested. She was good at what she did; building explosive devices, seducing men and avoiding capture for almost a decade, but the fact she'd given her heart to him made her vulnerable and if he left her and she gave it to someone else, the whole cause could be put at risk. She was too gentle for capture and he knew she'd never survive prison, or intense interrogation. She didn't have the training to deal with such situations, and it was just not in her nature. Petra, he thought, was a middle-class terrorist and really had no idea of how things worked in the world. Protected by her middle-class, idealistic associates, in their middle-class houses, secretly accepting money from her parents, she had no concept of actual hardship, or what living the ideal, really meant. She thought she was fighting for freedom, but was really just a recalcitrant child, poking her tongue out at her parents and schoolteachers.

He leaned over, kissed her on the cheek, and watched her stir briefly, elicit a tired smile, mumble something incoherent, and then fall back into peaceful slumber. He wanted to remember that picture of her, sleeping peacefully, without a care in the world. He wasn't normally a man prone to sentimental feelings, he couldn't afford to be, but close emotional encounters were so rare in his world he felt almost sad as he placed his hands around her neck and began to squeeze.

It took Petra a moment to wake and another moment to realise what was happening. She struggled, kicking her legs, flailing her arms, and attempting to scream as her face turned bright red and then purple, all the time looking deeply into his eyes, as if searching his face for a reason as to why he was killing her, when she'd only ever shown him love and loyalty.

'I'm sorry,' he whispered to her as she lost consciousness. He picked up her limp body in his arms, held her close for a moment, and then in one swift movement, snapped her neck and killed her. He laid her body down back onto her pillow and sat there for a while before moving, breathing deeply, letting the adrenalin in his body settle so he could think, in order to make his next move.

When he thought he'd gained his composure, he stood up naked from the bed and headed for the bathroom. He looked at the clock on the living room wall as he grabbed his backpack and saw that it was just after six in the morning. He went into the bathroom, looked at his reflection in the mirror above the sink, and then peeled off the beard that bordered his chin and placed it into his backpack. He used Petra's moisturiser to remove the adhesive that stuck to his chin, rubbing it deeply into his pores until his skin was bare and naked. He shaved, using one of Petra's razors, which he obtained from the cabinet from under the sink and then smiled at himself. He was just about to hop into the shower when he remembered the wig sitting on the top of his head. He removed it carefully, placed it into the backpack, and fluffed out his dyed-blonde hair he'd flattened to his scalp with hair oil. He wished he could've stayed in the shower for an hour, just sitting there and thinking, but all his time in the desert had conditioned him into taking quick washes and he rarely had a shower that lasted for more than a couple of minutes. He thought about one of his old commanders, who had stressed the importance of water for drinking and not as a convenience for washing.

'We smell like men. It is the way of the desert. This precious liquid is to keep you alive, not for washing in. It is the infidel who uses it daily to remove their stench of sin, not us, the fighters for freedom.'

Mark dried himself and strolled naked back to the bedroom. He threw a sheet over Petra's face to cover her statue-like stare and dressed in the outfit he'd worn the previous night. Once he was fully clothed, he returned to the bathroom, picked up his backpack, and carefully emptied it out onto the bathroom bench, taking out one article at a time. He removed one of the explosive devices that Petra had constructed first, took it into to the living room, and set it down with care on the coffee table and looked towards the bedroom where Petra lay lifeless and smiled. 'It's ironic that you'll be cremated by the bomb you, yourself created. If there's a heaven, or a hell, I'm sure you're really laughing about that now.'

Mark returned to the bathroom, flattened his hair with gel, and then refitted the wig to his head. He looked into the mirror to make sure it sat evenly and that his hair didn't show from underneath and then reached into the backpack and extracted a tube of adhesive. He squeezed a small amount of the clear adhesive onto his index finger, and smoothed it evenly under his nose. He reached back into the backpack again and removed a small plastic bag and took from it a thick, dark handlebar moustache, which he placed under his nose and moved about before the adhesive set, so that it sat naturally and then waited for a moment for it stick in place. He searched the cabinet, found some eyebrow pencil, and darkened his brows so they matched both his hair and moustache. He stood back and looked at himself in the mirror, but wasn't quite satisfied. He thought for a moment and then grabbed Petra's toothbrush from a holder above the sink and looked again through the contents of the cabinet until he found some baby powder. He sprinkled some over the brush and then held it under the tap so that a few drops of water mixed with the powder and rubbed it gently into the toothbrush with his finger, turning it into a smooth paste. He used this to streak both the moustache and the sides of his wig, giving him the appearance of a much older man.

When Mark was happy with his look, he packed up his gear into his backpack, returned to the living room, and set the timer on the bomb for fifteen minutes and placed it beside Petra on the bed. He grabbed the jumper he'd loaned her from the living room, the ticket stubs, and pulled on a baseball cap of hers, emblazoned with the New York Yankees insignia, from a hatstand beside the door, put on a pair of dark sunglasses and headed out into the hallway, pulling the door behind him so it locked.

He thought about taking the elevator to the ground, but dismissed the idea; it was only two floors down and waiting for it would be nothing but a waste of time. He wanted to get as far away from here in the fourteen minutes he had left, without seeming to rush and bring himself to anybody's attention. He walked to the end of the landing, pushed the door to the stairwell, and descended into Kensington Street outside the row of expensive townhouses that lined Benny Street. He liked Kensington. It was inner city enough for a diversity of strange and weird people to live there without anyone raising an eyebrow. He walked a block to Macaulay Road and caught a tram headed for the business district. He was entering North Melbourne, when the bomb went off. He was far enough away not to be connected to the huge black plume of smoke that rose up into the air, but close enough to see the results of his handiwork in the distance.

Mark jumped off the tram in the city. It was strange to see just how deserted it was now. The usual crowds of people who crammed the sidewalk on their way to work just didn't exist anymore. People were just too scared of being one of his next victims and he had to say, it pleased him no end. That is true terrorism: creating the fear inside of people that they might be killed or injured in the next act of organised violence.

He jumped on a bus, paid for his ticket, and sat at the back, watching the faces of people as they passed by his window and was glad that he hadn't become a sheep, blindly following the human flock of pointless activity into a life that meant nothing and a death that meant even less. He got off the bus in Exhibition Street and walked into the park located across from his apartment. He found the public toilets he knew would be locked at this hour of the morning and picked the padlock. He locked the door behind him and removed his makeup and wig, using the moisturiser he'd procured from Petra's apartment. He put in his blue contact lenses, fluffed up his hair, put everything in his shopping bag and then left the toilets. He walked over to his apartment block, took the elevator to the third floor, and let himself inside.

He undressed in the living room while watching the television and saw the news report of the bombing in Kensington. The female reporter said the police had cordoned off a block of flats and both the arson and forensic units were investigating. She also said that, although nothing concrete had surfaced, there were some unfounded rumours it was the work of the same bomber who'd been terrorising the city for the past week.

Mark switched off the television and had another quick shower to wash the gel from his hair. He dried and dressed in his sparsely furnished bedroom and selected a white cotton shirt, an expensive, black Armani suit, and a red Pierre Cardin tie from his walk-in wardrobe to wear to work. Once attired, he went to the living room, grabbed his backpack, returned to the bedroom, and emptied the contents into the bottom drawer of his wardrobe. He then went to the unit beside his bed and removed the remote control device, which he placed into the backpack, along with two batteries, which he put into a separate pocket.

Just before he departed the unit, he gave himself a once over in the full-length mirror attached to the door of his wardrobe. He smiled at himself, the innocent looking Swedish attaché, who got on well with everybody, was compliant to the ambassador's every whim and who'd never hurt a fly. He nodded his approval, turned, and left the apartment. He took the elevator to the basement, where he found his work Volvo sitting in its usual place, started the engine and pointed the car in the direction of the embassy. Today was going to be a good day, he thought to himself as he patted the backpack beside him on the passenger seat.

CHAPTER TWENTY-ONE

'Jesus,' said Peter Bell as he stepped into the study and got his first look at the lifeless body of the former Colonel Danny Murphy, 'it sure looks like someone had an axe to grind.'

'You can say that again,' agreed Ray Owen, handing him a pair of gloves and bringing Peter's attention to the confession embedded into the back of Danny's throat.

Peter spent a minute reading the contents and frowned. 'So, this guy's saying that the good colonel here and some of his men raped his mother in Afghanistan.'

'Can you find out who he was stationed with in Afghanistan?' Ray asked. 'I assume you'll have access to Department of Defence records, being the feds and all. We need to get hold of whoever else raped that woman before FOTS does. If we get to them before him, we might get a confession out of them, so we can prosecute, and with a bit of luck, we might even be able put a name to the victim. That might bring us closer to catching FOTS himself.'

'Yeah, it shouldn't be a problem,' replied Peter. 'So, we're assuming that it's FOTS, aren't we?'

'As soon as I read about the mother, I assumed that it was the Fire of the Son. It has to be the son of the same woman; too much of a coincidence not to be. He's seeking revenge on both the soldiers that raped her and on the country of their origin. It's too bad he didn't give her name, but then, he's not that stupid, either.'

'Can't say I blame him, in a way, for this,' said Peter. 'If somebody did that to my mother, I'd probably be more than a little pissed off myself.'

'Yeah, me too,' said Ray, stepping out of the way as the crime scene investigators made their way into the room.

The two men proceeded down the hallway of the house and into the master bedroom, where the wife lay on the bed. 'It looks like she was killed quick, with a single shot to the head. The husband was the primary target. He got all the attention.'

'None of the neighbours heard anything?' Peter asked.

'No, we've got uniform doing a canvas of the nearby houses, but there are no reports of any disturbances last night. Most of the people in the street are elderly, and would've been in bed early. By the look of it,' added Ray, taking a further look at the wife's head wound, 'he used a small calibre handgun, probably equipped with a silencer.'

'Yeah, real professional hit,' agreed Peter, crouching down beside the bed to take a closer look at both the entry and exit points in the head of the dead woman. He also examined the splatter on the wall behind and agreed that the killer had mostly likely used a small calibre handgun.

'We need to get those records and start processing them for names as soon as possible,' said Ray, 'before more bodies start turning up.'

'I have a nasty feeling, in the pit of my stomach,' said Peter, 'they're already waiting for us. This arsehole is just too smart to leave anything to chance, if you ask me. He's not going to risk us setting a trap for him, when he goes for the others. Who found the illustrious colonel, by the way?'

'It was quite by accident,' replied Ray. 'The colonel made a complaint about his reception to the pay T.V. company that supplies his cable. One of the technicians knocked on the door and when the old man didn't answer, he got up on the roof to take a look at the aerial and saw the body through a skylight.'

'So, it could be that FOTS wasn't expecting the body to be found for several days,' said Peter, thinking aloud. 'I think we can safely assume this chap would've done his homework, stalking the old man and his wife, knowing just who he visited and who visited the two of them, and when. If I were in his place, I would've killed him at a time when the next visitor to the house would be furthest away. That way, I'd have time to do the others, before they found this old bastard.'

'That might give us a bit of time,' said Ray. 'In the meantime, I'm heading into the lab. Larry Batts has asked me to come in. There's been an interesting development with the envelope from the hospital. You can ride along with me, if you like. Leave your car with one of your men and pick it up later, when I head back to the office.'

'Sure,' replied Peter, 'that'll give me some time to make a couple of phone calls and see if we can't get those records delivered to the office before we get back. I know it's asking a lot of him, but could we get Rob Swift to do his thing on the colonel? He might be able to come up with some useful info on the rape victim.'

'I'll ask him,' replied Ray. 'Clare just phoned me before. They're both back at the Hilton, the chopper dropped them off not long ago. She told me, too, Rob had a bit of a hard time at the hospital. Apparently, FOTS carved his surname into Tony Green's chest. Clare saw some photos and said it was bloody horrific and it understandably, shook Rob up a bit. All I can do is ask him and see what he says. He's with a sketch artist I sent over there, as we speak, trying to put together a likeness of the Petra woman who helped FOTS make the bombs.'

'That's good,' said Peter as they exited the room. 'As soon as they've completed the Identikit, get it faxed to the taskforce office. I'll have one of my men, circulate it, and send it to ASIO, Interpol, the FBI, and the CIA. If that bitch has come to anybody's attention, anywhere in the fucking world, she'll be on record.'

'Good call,' said Ray as the two of them reached the front door of the house, walked out onto the pathway, and tore off their gloves. Peter lit up a cigarette and offered one to Ray who declined. 'I could sure use a beer, though.'

'Sorry,' said Peter, patting his pockets with a smile, 'fresh out of beers. Give me a minute,' he added, 'I'll just hand over my car keys to one of my men, and be right back.'

'Sure,' said Ray as he made his way to the dark blue Commodore parked at the curb. He opened the driver's side door, jumped in, leaned over and popped open the glovebox, from which he retrieved a packet of spearmint chewing gum. He removed a stick, fiddled with the wrapper for a moment and then popped it into his mouth. It felt good to rid himself of the taste of death that every cop incurred at the scene of a murder, when the escaping gases from the deceased, mixed with the same air that those closest to the bodies were bound to breathe. He wished he'd brought some Vaporub, but gum would do for now, until later when he could wet his whistle with a stiff whiskey, followed by a nice beer chaser.

'Okay,' said Peter, stubbing his cigarette in the gutter and entering the car from the passenger side, 'I'm right to go.'

Ray started the car and put the gear lever into drive. 'I just want to stop and take a look where Tony was found before we head into the city. I hope you don't mind.'

'No, that's fine,' said Peter, doing up his seatbelt as they moved off. 'You never know what a fresh pair of eyes can come up with.'

'My thinking, exactly,' said Ray as they joined the flow of traffic that moved into Kew Junction. The car moved slowly, caught in congested traffic caused by a tram up ahead of them, as it stopped and started every few hundred metres, letting people on and off as they headed home from work in the heat of the summer sun.

Peter took the opportunity to call Rick Wells, an old friend and connection he had at the Department of Defence, and gave a brief explanation that his inquiry related to the murder of the colonel and potentially other members of his old command, by someone with a grudge against the military. He put the phone onto loudspeaker and introduced Ray, knowing he might also provide some valuable input into the conservation.

'I can't give you any specific details about the case, of course, but if you could get the names, file and addresses of those soldiers who served under Colonel Murphy to me as soon as possible, that'd be great.'

'Hang on a second, and I'll see what comes up on the database. I trust you'll be sending me the appropriate paperwork and that it's already in the mail,' said Rick with a chuckle.

'Of course it is,' said Peter, 'don't I always?'

'Yeah, better later than never,' said Rick with a good-natured sigh. 'Okay, he wasn't a colonel when he served in Afghanistan, he was a major, and commanded an armoured field division of commandos. He received orders to return to Australia after facing disciplinary action. He, apparently, led some troops into an ambush and a number of them lost their lives. He wasn't supposed to be out there in the first place, from what I can see. It looks like they sent him home and promoted him into a desk job. There's also a psychological report here that says he had some power issues,' added Rick. 'From what I can gather, he thought he was a modern-day MacArthur.'

'I suppose he knew what was going to happen to him, once his troops were killed,' said Ray, 'and he would've been pretty bloody angry, maybe wanting to take it out on someone.'

'Yeah, I got to agree with you there,' said Peter. 'Maybe we can narrow things down a bit, too. I wouldn't think the rape of a woman and the threat of exposure would be something the major would want everyone under his command to bear witness to. I think it would only have been the senior officers, which would have been privy to and participated in the event. Rick, can you get the names of the seniors under Murphy's command for me?'

'Yeah, shouldn't be a problem,' answered Rick. 'I'll send the files to you by courier. They should arrive in a couple of hours.'

'Thanks, Rick,' said Peter. 'I owe you one for this.'

Rick laughed on the other end of the line, 'And you bet I'm going to collect.'

'Yeah, thanks, Rick,' added Ray as Peter pressed the cancel button on the phone, ending the call.

'Okay,' said Peter as they pulled up at the bridge. 'It looks like we might be moving a little closer to finding this arsehole.'

'None too soon,' said Ray, opening the car door. 'We're running out of time.'

The two officers jumped out of the car and headed towards the tree where Tony had lain until discovered. They ducked under the crime scene tape that surrounded the area and heard a voice call them. The two of them turned and saw a uniformed officer stationed there to guard the scene overnight.

'Can I help you?'

Ray and Peter produced their identifications and handed them to the young cop, who briefly scrutinised them before handing back the wallets. 'There's not much to see here,' he told them. 'Forensics has been all over the place. They've made some plaster casts of some shoe prints and some tyre tracks, which they think came from the car, which held Detective Green before the prick dumped him here, but other than that, there's not much to go on. They're going to take another look first thing in the morning, so me and my partner got the short-straw and ended up here for the night.'

'So, where is your partner?' Ray asked.

'She's gone to get us something to eat and a coffee,' replied the cop.

'Look, I'm not going to say anything, but take it as a lesson learned,' said Ray gently. 'This arsehole is completely unpredictable and he, apparently, gets off on killing cops. Being here without backup is an unnecessary risk. Make sure it doesn't happen again. If one of you needs to go and get something, get some relief down here and you can tell your sergeant, Senior Sergeant Ray Owen from the Major Crime Squad said that's the way it is, like it or not. There's been enough tragedy associated with this case so far and we don't want any more, is that understood?'

'Yes, sir,' replied the young cop nervously. 'I'm sorry sir. I guess we just didn't think.'

Ray smiled. 'We'll stay here until your partner gets back. What's your name, kid?'

'Mike... Mike Collingburn, sir.'

'Well, Mike, like I say, think of this as a lesson. How long you been in the force?'

'Just under a year, sir.'

'That's not long,' said Ray, 'just make sure you don't do anything like this again and you'll stay alive long enough to make it a career.'

'Mike,' said Peter, 'could you show us where the forensics team took the plaster casts from?'

'Sure,' said the young cop, leading them to a slightly muddy trail located about ten metres from the tree. 'I was talking to one of the scientists, who said the car was parked here, that's where they found the deepest, clearest imprint from the tyres.'

Ray looked at the position of the trail, as opposed to the location of the tree for a moment. 'He was strong,' said Ray rhetorically, 'otherwise he would've pulled right up to the tree. Why didn't he?'

'He didn't want to be seen,' replied Peter. 'He left the car in shadow.'

'Who would see him?'

'Maybe some of the hobos who crash under the bridge,' replied Mike. 'They're down here every night. It was one of them who found the detective.'

'Have they all been spoken to?' Peter asked.

'I guess it's a bit hard to keep track of them,' said Mike. 'They just come and go as they please and most of them don't want anything to do with the cops, I bet.'

'Yeah, you can bet there are probably a few outstanding warrants amongst them. I think we need to talk to them, though.'

'Good luck with that,' said Mike with a chuckle.

'We just need to provide the right sort of incentive,' said Ray, pulling his wallet from his back pocket and taking out twenty-dollars, which he handed to the young cop. 'Mike, I want you to go to the local bottle shop and pick me up a flagon of cheap moselle, as soon as your partner gets back.'

'Yes, sir,' replied Mike as a smile spread across his face. 'I guess they didn't think of that, either.'

'Live, and learn,' said Ray with a laugh, 'live, and learn.'

Just as the words left Ray's mouth, the headlights of a police car lit the underside of the bridge and came to stop beside Mike. A young woman in uniform stepped out and handed Mike a brown paper bag. 'Here's your falafel,' she said looking towards Peter and Ray. 'So, are they friends of yours?'

Mike smiled. 'That's Peter Bell from the feds and that's Ray Owen from major crime. They've come down to check out the crime scene. Gentlemen, this is Constable Julie Jordan, my partner.'

'Nice to meet you, Julie,' said Ray. 'Sorry to send you off before you've eaten, but we have a job for the two of you.'

'We're supposed to stay here and guard the scene,' said Julie.

'Never mind that,' said Mike ushering his partner back towards the car, 'I'll explain on the way. They can look after the place while we're gone.'

'Yeah, okay,' said Julie a bewildered look on her face as she back into the passenger seat.

'Oh, before you go,' said Ray approaching the car on the driver's side. 'Have you got a flashlight in there? It's starting to get a bit dark. I've got one in my car, but I'd like for Peter to have one as well.'

'Sure,' said Mike, reaching down beside his seat. He pulled out a large, stainless steel torch, which he handed out through the window. 'See you soon.'

'Thanks,' said Ray taking the flashlight, 'see you soon.'

The detectives watched as the car moved away, pulling out onto the main roadway, and disappeared from sight. 'All right,' said Ray, 'let's go and get that flashlight while we're waiting.'

The two of them stood by the car awaiting the return of their uniformed colleagues, when Peter saw something in the distance. He brought Ray's attention to a light, flickering about a hundred yards from where they stood.

'I think it's a fire.'

'Yeah, me too,' said Ray, 'a campfire, on the other side of the river.'

'You want to go check it out?'

'Yeah, come on, let's go.'

Both men trod carefully through the uncut grass, waving their flashlights in front, watching out for any obstacle that might hinder their progress or cause possible injury. They walked up a slight hill and crossed the waterway via an improvised bridge made of a dozen old fallen logs stretched out over a narrow bend in the river. As they walked across, they could hear the sound of running water about ten feet beneath them.

'Be careful,' Ray advised with a laugh, 'I don't think that workers comp covers something like this.'

Peter laughed, too. 'You mean you don't get compensation for injuring yourself in a reckless endeavour? I am surprised.'

The two of them made it across the stream without incident and onto a small, dirt track that led away from the water. They walked about another fifty yards, came out into a small clearing and saw the fire burning ahead of them. As they drew closer they saw a dozen or so men crouched around the fire; some sleeping, some sharing a bottle of red wine they passed between them.

'It's the coppers,' said a slurred voice from out of the darkness.

'Yeah, but they're not uniform, so they're not here to move us on,' said another man who gulped from the bottle and then looked up at the detectives. 'So, what the fuck you want? We're a quiet lot here, it's the young bucks down under the bridge that makes all the noise, with their fucking drugs, not us.'

'We're not here to move you on,' Ray assured them. 'We were wondering if any of you might be able to give us a hand with something.'

'So, what's in it for us? I never heard of a copper helping us out, but they come here sometimes, expecting us to do the right thing by them.'

'I've got a full flagon of moselle on its way here, if you can give me some info,' replied Ray.

'What sort of info you want? We got all sorts of info for sale here,' said the old man, 'and a full flagon sounds just about the right price, too.'

'A car pulled up near the bridge, last night,' said Peter. 'We're hoping one or more of you might have got a look at it, maybe tell us what sort of car it was, or even the colour, although it was probably too dark to see.'

At the mention of a full flagon of moselle, a number of the men who, at first glance appeared to be sleeping, sat up and looked over the fire at the two detectives. They seemed to be mostly older men with tough-edged faces and red eyes, typical of people who'd lived hard lives ruled by the bottle. The unmistakable smell of stale alcohol permeated the air as they breathed in the direction of the police officers.

'I might know what you're talking about,' said a man who sat at the periphery of the group, his face was half-hidden by deep shadows. 'I was here last night and I saw something you might be interested in knowing.'

'Oh, what's that?' Ray asked.

'I'll tell you, but I don't want my name mentioned. I got some outstanding troubles and I don't want any contact with your sort.'

'Fair enough,' said Peter. 'We just want to know what you saw, that's all.'

'I saw a car pull up near the bridge just after dark, last night.'

'Do you know what sort of car it was?' Ray asked him.

'I got a fair idea,' replied the drunk, 'but I'm not saying, 'til I see the flagon, safe and well in my hands.'

'Okay,' said Ray, 'if you come with us, back to the bridge, I'll hand it over without any fuss whatsoever.'

The informer looked at the two of them with what they thought was disdain. 'I'll come with you, but if it's a trap of some sort, I'll clam up and I won't say a fuckin' word.'

'Yeah, fair enough,' said Ray. 'I give you my word it's not a trap. We just want the information. It could save a lot of people's lives.'

The man stood on trembling legs and for a moment the two officers thought he might topple over. He managed to steady himself and after a moment, he joined the detectives on the other side of the fire. 'I'm Bradley,' he said extending a hand to Ray, who shook it, despite some trepidation of catching something contagious and made a mental note to wash thoroughly later.

'I'm Ray and this is Peter, glad to meet you.'

'So, Bradley,' asked Peter, 'nobody spoke to you today?'

'Like I said before,' replied Bradley, 'I don't want contact with you lot, if I can avoid it, so I didn't hang around. I don't stay here during the day, anyway, too much of a hassle, what with rangers patrolling the place and cops constantly trying to move you on, 'cause you disturb the nice people having picnics in the park. I usually take off at first light and head to the local soup kitchen for breakfast. You have to eat a good breakfast every day when you're on the grog. It's the malnutrition that gets to you in the end and not drinking enough water, too, that'll kill you.'

'You seem to know how to look after yourself,' said Peter as the three of them traversed the track back to the river.

Bradley laughed aloud. 'No, I'm fucked and heading for an early grave no matter what I do. AIDS will do that to you. Some fucker raped me in the police watchhouse one night when I was pissed out of my brain. I hardly remember a thing about it, so I've decided to stay drunk until the end comes. There's worse ways to go.'

'I'm sorry,' said Ray. 'Can't you get some treatment? I've heard they can prolong the lives of people for a long time now, with the right combination of drugs.'

'Nah, not interested,' replied Bradley dismissing the notion. 'I hate hospitals worse than I hate fucking AIDS, can't stand the stinking smell of disinfectant, makes me want to throw up, every time.'

As the three of them crossed to the other side of the river, they saw the lights of the police divisional van as it pulled up. 'Don't worry,' said Ray, 'I promise you it's not a trap.'

The trio walked over and stood in the lights of the van. It was there that the symptoms of Bradley's disease became evident. His face was dotted in small black sores that Ray guessed were cancers associated with AIDS, and although he tried to hide his shock, the look on his face must have given him away.

'You can see them, can you?' Bradley asked. 'They're all over me. I'm pretty much fucked.'

'If I gave you the number of a doctor, would you go and see him?'

'I occasionally go to the free clinic, that St. Vincent De Paul runs, when I'm sober enough. I got it covered, but thanks.'

Mike and Julie approached the front of the car and Bradley saw the flagon carried by the young, male cop. 'Is that for me?'

'Yeah,' replied Ray, 'here,' he said taking the flagon and placing in it Bradley's hands. 'Now, what can you tell us about the car?'

Bradley ripped off the tab from the flagon, held it up above his mouth, and took a long swallow and smiled with approval. 'I used to be a mechanic a long time ago, in another life, and I'm pretty sure it was a Volvo, I could tell by the shape of the lights. I worked on a few of them, when I could work.'

'Did you see the colour?' Peter asked.

'I can't be sure,' said Bradley taking another swallow of the wine, 'but I think it was either a light blue or a greenish colour. It's hard to tell from that distance, especially when you've had a skinful of port, but I thought I got a glimpse of the colour as it came off the road. I was just heading across the river when it pulled up and I stopped to make sure it wasn't the cops come to move us off. That's pretty much everything I can tell you.'

'That's okay,' said Ray, 'thanks a lot. You've been a big help, really.'

'No worries,' said Bradley holding up the flagon to look at the box. 'Can I go now?'

'Yeah,' replied Ray, 'you can go. Have a good night.'

'I sure will, now,' said Bradley as he strolled back off into the darkness, heading back towards the camp, carrying the flagon of moselle.

'Well, that was good luck and really good police work, Ray,' said Peter. 'We know now, that FOTS was driving a Volvo and we have a possible colour, which narrows it down even further. That's a starting point, at least. If he stole it, we might even be able to get a fix on where he is, if it's a later model with a tracking device. If it was his car, well, that's even better.'

'Yeah, it gives us something to go on. Come on, Peter, we need to get going and see what Larry has to show us.'

The detectives thanked the uniformed officers for their assistance, 'Remember,' said Ray as they hopped back into the car, 'never leave your partner alone.'

CHAPTER TWENTY-TWO

'No,' said Rob, looking at the laptop screen, 'her face was thinner, more tanned, and her nose was longer, too.'

'All right,' said Ashley Green, a police-sketch artist, who sat next to Rob on the plush sofa of their hotel suite, opening a different window on the computer, which displayed a variety of nose types and shapes. 'See if you can pick her nose from out of these.'

Clare laughed in the background at the unintended pun. 'You two want to take a break? I've just boiled the jug for coffee.'

'Sounds like a good idea to me,' said Rob rising and heading towards the kitchen.

'Yep, you twisted my arm, too,' said Ashley with a laugh as she placed the laptop on the coffee table in front of her. 'Don't worry, Rob,' she said as she joined the two of them and Russell in the kitchen, 'we'll get it.'

'I can still see her in my mind, as clear as day,' said Rob, feeling a little frustrated by the painstaking process.

'It seems you do have something of an incredible mind,' said Ashley, 'if all the things I've heard about you are true.'

'Just what are they?' Clare asked the artist.

'Well, I've been listening to the talk here throughout the day and heard that Rob can see the future and the past just by touching someone. Is it true? I promise not to say anything to anyone.'

Rob looked at Ashley, at her pretty face, her dark hair, her light green eyes, and for some reason he was unable to explain, he knew that he could trust her not to say anything. 'Yes,' he said in almost a whisper, 'it's true, I do have a gift.'

'It's important you don't disclose this to anyone,' said Russell as he poured out the coffees, 'we don't want it getting into the media. It'll turn the investigation into a circus.'

'Sure,' said Ashley, 'I understand.'

'Would you like a demonstration?' Rob asked her. 'I don't fancy looking into your future much, because I hate the burden of having to either tell you what I saw, or keeping it to myself, if that's more appropriate, but I could look into your past, just to show you how the gift works.'

'You don't always tell people about their futures?'

'No, not always,' replied Rob. 'Sometimes, it's better to keep quiet.'

'I guess I can understand that,' said Ashley. 'Okay, if you want to look at my past, then be my guest.'

Rob took hold of Ashley's hand. He felt the familiar build up of electricity and then found himself in an unfamiliar setting. He looked around and saw that he was in a green field, which by the look of it, had been recently ploughed. He saw a house in the distance, a pretty country cottage and began to walk towards it. The place had a nice feel about it and appeared old, with its dark slate tiles that covered the roof, whitewashed walls and old Tudor-style windows. Either it was a residence handed down through the passing generations, or was a very well done replica. As he drew closer, he decided that it was the former.

About thirty feet from the door, he heard a loud yelling coming from inside the place, which had the definite timbre of a man's voice. There was also the sound of anguished crying which accompanied the rage. Rob drew closer to the house and peeked through one of the front windows, where he saw a heavyset man, his face flushed red with anger, banging on what appeared to be a bedroom door.

'Come out, you fucking bitch, you're going to learn your lesson this time!'

'I'm sorry, Richard,' wailed a woman's voice from the opposite side of the door. 'I didn't mean to make you angry.'

Rob sneaked around to the side of the house, looked through the bedroom window, and saw that the woman was Ashley, but estimated she was about twenty years older than she was when he'd last seen her. As he looked at her, he could see her face was a mass of old scars from the many beatings she'd taken at the hands of this man.

'Open up this fucking door, or I'm going to break it down!'

'Richard, please,' pleaded Ashley, 'just go away. If you hit me again, you're going go to jail and then we'll lose the farm.'

'I don't give a shit about jail, or the farm,' said the man on the other side of the door. 'Open up, now!'

'Please, Richard, don't do this,' wailed Ashley.

Rob watched as the door burst open, fragments of wood flying across the room as Richard burst in and grabbed Ashley by the throat. He forced her down onto the bed, overpowering her with his bulk and began smashing her in the face, more times than Rob could count, turning it into a bloody pulp. When he'd exhausted himself, he fell down beside her on the bed, breathing heavily and said her name. When she didn't respond, he took a closer look and saw she was dead. He held her lifeless hand and then hugged her and began to howl with regret, asking himself why he hadn't listened to her and screaming his life was over.

Rob followed him from the outside of the house, as he left the bedroom and walked into the living room and grabbed a shotgun from behind one of the fireside chairs. He put his hand into his jacket and produced a couple of shells, which he placed into the gun. He lay down onto the sofa and placed the barrel of the gun into his mouth. Rob looked away as the gun went off and walked away from the house. He didn't look back and just kept walking across the field, imagining in his mind what the scene behind him looked like without actually having seen it. 'Jesus,' he repeated to himself as he trudged along, trying to cope with the shock of the two deaths he'd just witnessed, 'Jesus... Jesus... Jesus.'

As he walked along, he heard a familiar sound in the distance, which began to increase in volume, until it seemed to fill the air around him. He soon realised it was the sound of a mobile phone and if he was right, it was Clare's, calling him back to the physical world. He stopped walking, closed his eyes and willed himself back to the hotel.

When he again opened his eyes, he saw Clare pick up her phone. She unlocked it, had a brief conversation with the person at the other end, and ended the call. 'It looks like we won't be requiring your services to find Petra, Ashley. She's turned up at the city morgue... in pieces.'

'What happened?' Rob asked shocked at the news.

'There was a bomb this morning, in Kensington. They found her body at the scene, severely dismembered and burnt to a crisp. Because it was a bomb, the technician at the morgue sent the prints from the one hand they found, to the feds. They just got the results back and it seems as if it's our Petra. She's a wanted terrorist, convicted to life imprisonment in her absence in Germany, for acts of terrorism and murder. She was to stand trial, but escaped during the pre-trial period.'

'We could still use Ashley,' suggested Russell, 'if this Petra is burnt beyond recognition. We might be able to locate her associates if the identikit gets circulated to the public.'

'That's true,' agreed Clare. 'Right now, though, I want to take Rob to the morgue and see if we can't get some info from the body itself. Are you up for that, Rob?'

'I guess so.'

'So, what did you see when you took my hand?' Ashley asked.

Rob took a moment to look at Ashley, to take in just how beautiful she was and how she'd end up, if she hooked up with this Richard character. 'Will you make me a promise?'

'If I can,' replied Ashley searching his eyes for some clue as to what he was going to say.

'If you ever meet a man named Richard, just run the other way and don't even stop to look back. Can you do that for me? Trust me, you won't regret it.'

'You saw my future, didn't you?'

'Yes, I did. I didn't have a choice,' replied Rob, 'and it wasn't pretty.'

'Can you tell me about it?'

'No,' said Rob, 'I can't. I don't have time right now and it's not very nice to think about. Just make me that promise, will you?'

'All right,' replied Ashley, 'if I ever meet a man named Richard, I'll run, and not look back, I promise.'

'Okay,' said Rob with a smile, 'you'll be all right, if you do that.'

'Do you have a card?' Clare asked the artist, 'I'll give you a call when we get back if we need you.'

'Sure do,' said Ashley retrieving a card from her bag on the sofa, which she handed to the detective. 'Thanks, Rob,' she said as she headed for the door.

'You're welcome. Just remember that name, Richard, it's important.'

'Are you joking?' Ashley retorted with a nervous laugh. 'It's now etched into my brain. I'm not likely ever to forget it.'

'Okay,' said Russell after Ashley's departure, 'I'll go on ahead with Josie. June and Le Mar can take you, Rob, Marcus, and Annie can take Clare. We'll mix it up a bit and have Clare leave from the front of the hotel and Rob leave from the rear. Are you two okay with that?'

'Sounds good to me,' said Clare, finishing the last of her coffee.

'Me too,' said Rob.

'Good,' said Russell pulling his phone out of the front of his overalls and heading out onto the balcony so he could talk. 'I'll let the others know.'

'So, what did you see, as far as Ashley's future?' Clare asked when the two of them were alone.

Rob sat back down on the sofa and sighed. 'I saw her in about twenty years, get beaten to death by Richard, the man supposed to love her, and then kill himself.'

'Fuck me,' said Clare, 'no wonder you wanted her to run when she came across that Richard guy.'

'Yeah, it's not easy to tell someone. It gives me chills up my spine just thinking about it.'

'Yeah, same with me, and I wasn't even there,' said Clare, sitting down beside him, 'but you told her enough to save her life and that's a good thing.'

'Yeah, that's right,' agreed Rob. 'It always freaks me out when I hear about stuff like that,' he added, gulping down the last of his coffee. 'I just don't get it. How could a man who loves a woman, do something like that to her? It just doesn't make any sense at all.'

'You know,' said Clare, 'I've been a police officer for nigh on fifteen years now. It was the first job I got when I left school and the only one I ever wanted. I used to try and figure out why people do stuff like that and yeah, I've hear all the forensic psychologists explanations, which are great in hindsight, but at the time and in the direct aftermath of a terrible crime, all you can do is whatever you can. At least you can prevent something terrible from happening. Me, it's always been my job to come in and clean up other people's messes. If we catch this FOTS guy and stop him using the nuke, then I'll feel as if I've done something at least partially proactive for once, instead of reactive.'

'Have you ever been in love, Clare?'

'That's a funny question,' replied Clare seeming almost taken aback. 'Why do you ask?'

Rob thought back to the vision of her and Russell in the church holding hands and it gave him a warm feeling inside, taking his mind from the murder-suicide he'd seen in his vision. 'No reason, I was just curious. I guess in a job like this, it must be hard to meet anyone and I guess you must get kind of hard, from the things you see.'

Clare sat back on the sofa and sighed. 'The last time I was in a relationship was over ten years ago. There was a fella, Macca, who I met through friends. He was an architect. It just didn't work out for various reasons, but mostly because of me, my mindset being on my career at the time and all the different shifts that I had to do when I was in uniform. It was an amicable split and I still see him now and again. He's married now, with three lovely kids.'

'Were you in love?'

'I don't think so,' replied Clare. 'I mean it didn't gut me when it finished, or anything. I was just too busy getting on with things that I hardly even noticed. You were in love with Aroha, yeah?'

'Yeah, I was,' said Rob with a deep sigh. 'I can't imagine myself being with anyone else. She was one of a kind, that woman.'

'It must be really something to find the person you want to spend the rest of your life with. I'm thirty-five and I think I'll just end up on my own. I might make commissioner, but I'll be single all the way.'

'Well, you never know,' said Rob, rising as Russell re-entered the living room, 'these things have a way of working themselves out.'

'Do you know something I don't, Rob?'

Rob laughed. 'Being a psychic is just one of those things, where you get to see stuff you just don't expect to.'

'Well, at least you're not telling me to run for my life away from someone.'

'No,' said Rob as a smile crossed his face, 'I think you'll be fine.'

Russell came back into the apartment and closed his phone as he walked towards them. 'I'm going to get going with Josie. You two should be okay to get to the cars from here. They'll be waiting for you by the time you've ridden the lifts down to the ground floor. FOTS can't know you're here, so we don't need to guard you all the way down. Besides, the both of you are carrying pistols, right?'

Clare touched the bump under her jacket. 'It's like my American Express card.'

'Yeah, I got one, too,' added Rob, 'but it's pretty much an ornament. I'm more likely to shoot myself than anyone else.'

'Well, that may be,' said Russell, 'but you might fluke it and just shoot the right person.'

'Funny,' said Rob with a smile, 'that's just what Clare said to me, too.'

'Great minds think alike,' said Russell with a wink as he headed for the door. 'I'll see you both soon, at the morgue.'

'Righto,' said Clare. 'We'll give you and Josie a couple of minutes to head off and then we'll follow.'

'Good plan,' agreed Russell, 'see you soon.'

Clare closed the door behind the detective and turned to face Rob. 'I like Russell,' she said, 'he's a good guy who knows what he's talking about.'

'Yeah, he does,' said Rob smiling, thinking back to the vision at the church. 'I'm sure he likes you, too.'

'There's a really mischievous look in your eye, Mister Swift. You want to tell me what that's about?'

Rob chuckled. 'I don't want to spoil the surprise, so no, I don't.'

Clare shrugged and walked back into the living area of the suite. She sat down on the sofa, removed her Glock from the shoulder holster inside her jacket, and checked it was loaded and that she had an extra magazine of ammunition in her pocket. Once she replaced the gun back into its holster, she indicated that the two of them should make tracks for the elevator.

'Have you checked your gun?'

Rob opened the flap of his jacket, and showed the Glock to Clare. 'Yep, it's there, all right.'

'You'd never make a cop, you know,' said Clare with a smirk.

Rob lifted his finger to his mouth. 'Shoosh... don't tell anyone, but I know it, too.'

The two of them exited the hotel suite and headed for the lift without speaking and even though Clare knew that FOTS couldn't possibly know their location, she was still suspicious of every person they passed in the hallway and was ready to produce her gun at the slightest provocation. She was glad when the lift doors opened and they entered, feeling safer on their own, with the steel walls surrounding her and her charge.

As soon as the doors opened on the ground floor, the two of them split up. Clare headed for the main entrance and Rob went through the kitchen, walking amongst the busy chefs and kitchen hands to the rear door of the hotel. Once outside, he saw both June and Le Mar sitting in a blue Commodore awaiting his arrival. As soon as they saw him, they pulled up to the entrance and Rob jumped into the backseat and lay down, under the line of both vision and possible gunfire. It was a pain, but he knew it was for his own safety. As soon as Rob was in the car, June picked up a portable radio and informed Russell they had the package and were on their way. Marcus also confirmed Clare's pickup at the front of the hotel.

'All right,' said Le Mar in his cheerful Jamaican accent, 'off we go.'

The three of them drove through the city listening to Bob Marley playing on a CD, and Le Mar bopping away as he steered the car. The only interruption to the music was the static of the radio as Russell periodically checked in to make sure everything was okay.

It took them about fifteen minutes to reach the outside of the mortuary. Rob looked up and recognised the grey concrete building from his last visit, when he'd helped to identify Clarence Grafton by touching one of his dead victims. He only hoped this experience wouldn't lead to similar circumstances. He had no desire to make another psychic connection to another murdering nutcase.

The cars pulled around to the rear entrance of the building and Rob saw that Clare had already arrived. June and Le Mar dropped him off at the entrance and went to park the car.

Once inside, Russell stationed Annie, Marcus, Le Mar, and June at both the front and rear entrances of the building, respectively while Rob, Clare, Russell, and Josie accompanied Emmarentia Guilfoyle, the head pathologist to the mortuary proper. At the entrance, Clare asked Rob if he wanted Russell and Josie to wait outside, just in case it disturbed his concentration.

'No, it's all right if they come in,' he replied. 'The more the merrier.'

'Okay, follow me,' said Emmarentia as she pulled open a large steel door that led into the refrigerated interior of the mortuary, where the bodies lay in drawers, waiting to undergo examination, or to be shipped out to funeral homes for burial or cremation. 'I'm afraid she doesn't look too good,' said the pathologist, 'the blast made quite a mess of her.'

Clare reached into her jacket pocket and pulled out a jar of Vaporub, dipped in her finger and smeared some under her nose and then handed the jar around to the rest of the group. 'I'm betting she probably doesn't smell too good, either.'

'Good thinking,' said Russell as he repeated her actions and passed the jar on.

'I don't even think about the smell anymore,' said Emmarentia. 'I guess you just get used to it after a while.'

'I wouldn't have your job for quids, Emmarentia,' said Josie as she rubbed the lotion under her nose.

'Horses for courses, I guess,' said Emmarentia, 'and by the way, you can all call me Emma. This way,' she added directing them to drawer at the far end of the room.

The pathologist grabbed the drawer and warned the gathered police that if they were squeamish they might want to wait at the other end of the room. When no one answered, she pulled out the drawer to reveal the burnt and twisted corpse of Petra, wrapped in a large plastic bag, which Emma explained was due to the fragile state of the corpse.

'We think she was very close to the blast site and she was dead before the bomb went off.'

'How can you tell?' Josie asked.

'There was no burning on the inside of the lungs,' replied Emma. 'If the blast had caused her death, there would be signs of blistering, from where she inhaled the blast flames and in the absence of such signs, we are able to form the opinion that the blast occurred post-mortem.'

'Were there any personal affects that we might look at while Rob does his thing?' Russell asked the pathologist.

'There were a few things found in the apartment,' replied Emma. 'The thing you'll find most interesting is her driver's licence. It's in a false name, but I'm certain it's her in the picture. Here,' she said, handing Russell the keys to her office, 'her belongings are in an evidence bag on top of my desk, if you want to take a look. There's a box of surgical gloves on top of my filing cabinet.'

'That'll save us having to use a sketch artist to get a likeness of her,' said Clare. 'There's probably a really good photo of her from where she was arrested in Germany. We'll have to ask Ray to get a hold of that.'

'Okay, Rob,' said Russell, 'you do your thing here. I'll leave both Josie and Clare with you, and go and have a look at her stuff. There might be something that can help us. I personally doubt it, except for the licence, but you never know. I'll give Ray a call, too, and see if he can't arrange to get the German photo as well. How long does this generally take to do?'

'Not long,' replied Rob. 'Give me about ten minutes. That should do it.'

'Okay, I'll see you lot in a little while,' said Russell as he headed for the office.

'I get the feeling that Russell didn't want to be here for this,' whispered Clare in Josie's ear as Russell left the room.

'Yeah, he told me all this psychic shit freaks him out a bit,' replied Josie with a nervous laugh. 'To tell you the truth, I don't feel all that comfortable with it, either.'

Emma unzipped the bag, withdrew one of the blackened, charred hands, and placed it beside the body on the steel gurney. 'Whenever you're ready.'

Rob stepped forward, closed his eyes so he didn't have to see himself touching the burned skin. He took a deep breath and then grabbed the tips of the fingers in his hand. He felt the familiar build up of electricity as it ran rampant around the periphery of his body. He then felt his body, or his spirit, or whatever part of him it was that had the capacity for traversing the past, and future, travel to somewhere completely different.

He opened his eyes and saw he was standing at a gateway, which opened onto a long, curving driveway, and led to an enormous mansion. He wondered if this was where Petra had grown up. If it was, she'd obviously hailed from money, a great deal of money by the look of it.

Rob strolled down the roadway, past an army of beautiful, tall oaks, which stood like soldiers at attention on each side of the drive. He felt a cool breeze blow through his hair as he walked along and heard the whisper of the stirring leaves, as if they were talking to him in some complex, undecipherable language.

At the end of the driveway, he saw a late model Mercedes-Benz and a BMW parked in front of the house, contrasted by the brilliant white of the Roman columns that heralded the entrance to the residence and captured the oversized oaken door like a picture frame. The place would not have looked out of place at the head of an American cotton plantation in the mid 18th century overlooking the work of slave labourers. He noticed as he passed by, that the cars were the same colour of navy blue, and wondered if it was a mere coincidence. He somehow didn't think so.

As he came nearer to the residence, he thought he heard the sounds of voices somewhere, swallowed up by the cavernous house. He couldn't make out whether they were male, female, or child, but was determined to find out.

He stepped up onto the massive front veranda and passed through the wood of the door in his usual ghostly manner. The inside of the mansion was even more elaborate. Everywhere he looked, he saw original works by famous artists that hung from the walls and furniture, which could've come from some of the English and French kings of times past, and although he was no antique expert, even he could tell no expense had been spared in the outfitting and furnishing of this palatial residence.

Ahead of him, he heard voices and walked towards the noise. He found three people sitting around a large, antique table in a dining room. Two adults sat at each end of the table and a young girl child sat in the centre. They talked and joked as they consumed their food, served to them by servants who hovered around the table and acquiesced to their every whim.

Rob could tell the girl was Petra, the same woman he'd seen in his previous vision, although here, she was perhaps eight or nine years old. It was interesting to see the essence of her still remained, even though her features had changed with maturity. She laughed at the antics of the older man, who made funny faces at her and told her she was beautiful. Even though they spoke a foreign language, which Rob guessed was German he was able to understand their every word and remembered the same thing had occurred with the sorcerer, when he'd entered a dream and had spoken to the Aboriginal man.

Her father, a stern looking man with grey hair, beard, and cold blue eyes had a soft smile. Rob had the feeling that away from his family he wasn't the sort of man a person would toy with. He was, judging just by the house in which they lived and the cars that they drove, very successful in business and one didn't become this successful without being ruthless.

The woman who sat at the opposite end of the table looked to be of Spanish, Italian, or of Greek origin, with beautiful olive skin and dark brown eyes, and hair as dark as a raven's wing. When she smiled, she lit up the room and Rob could understand why a creature of such exquisite beauty could besot this wealthy, successful man. Even though she tried to be stern towards both her husband and her daughter, urging them to maintain a sense of decorum around the servants, she couldn't help but to smile and laugh at their comedic antics.

When dinner finished, Petra's mother ordered her to her room to complete her homework and then the three of them would take an evening walk through the garden. The child complained, but when her father informed her that if she didn't go, he wouldn't take her and would walk alone with her mother, she promptly stopped her whining.

'The quicker you do it, the sooner we can go.'

'Yes, Father,' said the child who dutifully trod off toward her room accompanied by an older woman, which Rob assumed to be some sort of nanny or governess.

After the child left the room, the atmosphere seemed to become decidedly tense, as if there was some sort of unresolved issue between the couple, of which they didn't speak, but hung in the air like a thick fog between them.

'I'm going to my study to have a cigar,' said the old man, rising from the chair. 'I'll meet you and Petra in the garden in half an hour.'

'Yes, enjoy your cigar, Berndt,' said the woman, emphasising the word cigar with a very sarcastic, bitter tone.

'Thank you, Carmelita, I will,' said Berndt as he strode from the room.

Rob followed the old man through the house as he made his way to his study. He took a set of keys from the pocket of his suit as he walked long and jangled them at his side while he hummed a tune. Berndt's study was located at the other end of the house and, to Rob's astonishment it took almost five minutes to traverse the entire residence. He couldn't even imagine what it must be like to be so wealthy. It was so far removed from his personal frame of reference it was like an alien reality.

He descended a set of stairs that led to a lower floor, walked down a sizeable hallway and unlocked the door to his study, which Rob thought was as about the same size as the last apartment he'd had rented in Alice Springs.

Berndt opened a bottle of cognac, lit up a huge Havana cigar, and sat down on an antique leather sofa that faced the biggest flat screen TV Rob had ever seen. He turned on the television and pulled a mobile phone from out of his pocket. He looked contact list and then dialled a number, while he sat back on the sofa and puffed on the cigar, letting the smoke drift up and over his head.

Rob only heard one side of the conversation, but it appeared that the old man had a mistress and had plans on meeting her later on in the night, after his daughter had gone to bed. Rob then understood the tension that existed between Berndt and his wife.

Berndt finished both the phone call and the cigar. He gulped down the remainder of the drink and left the study, locking the door behind him. Rob followed him back upstairs and watched as the little family strolled out in their expansive garden and went for their evening walk.

As they rounded a bend, the vision shifted and Rob still found himself in the same house, but there was something distinctly different about the atmosphere of the place and Rob felt a nervous tension building up in his gut. He watched as Petra, about thirteen years old, got out of a chauffer-driven limousine at the front of the house, and went running inside, calling out for her mother. As she ran up the stairs, she started talking about the day she'd had at school and an upcoming field trip her class would be taking to the zoo.

Rob followed her as she went barrelling into her mother's bedroom and heard a deafening scream just before he entered the room behind her. 'No,' Petra yelled as she fell to her knees. 'No. No. No!'

Rob looked up and saw that Carmelita had hung herself from the top of the four-poster bed in the centre of the room. A few seconds later, several of the house servants, including Petra's nanny and a man who appeared to be some sort of butler or valet, rushed into the room and attempted to revive her, but their efforts were in vain and they lay the poor woman on the floor, her lifeless body as still as a marble statue.

Rob walked over to the bed and saw were some papers scattered over the covers. He took a closer look and saw they were documents signifying an intention on part of her husband to divorce her. He understood why she'd done this, but thought Carmelita had been selfish in her irrationality and should've thought of her daughter before taking her own life. No doubt, this would have far-reaching consequences on the child's life. Rob wondered if that was why both she and FOTS had linked up, for his mother, too, had taken her own life.

The vision shifted again and Rob found himself standing amongst a large crowd of young people at a Rolling Stones concert. He saw Petra again; she was about twenty years old and very beautiful, having inherited many of her mother's exquisite physical traits. She swayed to the music coming from the band and looked up into the flashing lights with a kind of bewildered fascination.

'She's either drunk or out of it, on something,' thought Rob as he moved through the crowd towards her. He wondered why this occasion was significant.

As he watched, he saw a young man emerge from out of the crowd and hand her a drink. Rob moved closer to take a better look at him. It took him a moment to realise that the man he was looking at was Arkmed. He was younger than when he appeared in Rob's previous visions, but Rob would've bet money that it was the same man. He didn't have the beard, was clean-shaven, and he looked at Petra as though he was in love, or at least in lust with her, and who could've blamed him? She was, after all, exceedingly attractive and the type of woman a man would be proud to have on his arm on any occasion.

Rob waited around until the concert was over, and followed the two of them back to his car, which was an old blue Volvo. He jumped inside when Petra opened the door, sneaking in before her and sat on the back seat listening to them talk. They didn't say a whole lot that caught his interest. They spoke mostly about the Rolling Stones, and about how much they liked the band and particular songs they sang. Petra said she thought Mick Jagger was getting sexier as he got older.

Rob looked out the window and tried to figure out exactly where they were. It was a big town, and the signage on the passing cafes and streets were all written in a foreign language he had no hope of deciphering. He decided to wait and see what turned up.

They stopped at a café and grabbed some coffee and something to eat. While they were waiting for service, Rob spotted some American tourists chatting and discussing a map they held between them. When he looked closer, he saw that the map detailed Sweden. There were about a half dozen of what looked like students in the group, who were energetically discussing their next move. Some of them wanted to leave Sweden and go to Amsterdam so they could smoke some dope at the cafes, while others wanted to see more of the country before heading off.

'So, I'm in Sweden. That must've been the country where I saw him in my last vision. So, Arkmed, how did you get all the way from Afghanistan to here?'

Without warning, the vision shifted again. This time, he saw Petra with an older business-suited man, having sex on his desk. He looked at the two of them, feeling like some sort of voyeur and wondered what the vision was trying to show him. It made him nauseous having to wade through crap like this in order to get to the heart of the situation. He didn't like porno films, and having to see people having sex in real circumstances was something he found less than charming.

The old man was gasping, slobbered over Petra's naked back as he penetrated her and although Petra made the same noises of ecstasy, Rob could see that there was something more in her eyes than lust and she was just going through the motions, but not really enjoying the experience. He had the feeling this was the means to an end for her and the sexual satisfaction was something she was providing in order to get something back. This man was going to pay dearly for his moment of pleasure, Rob was sure of that.

The old man climaxed, fell to his knees on the floor, and came to rest with his back against the desk, sweat dripping from his forehead. Petra at the same time, called out as though she'd just experienced the greatest orgasm of her life, although Rob knew this was just acting on her part and then she slid down beside the old man and began kissing him on the lips, stroking his ego and thanking him for the pleasure he'd given her. Rob had to laugh aloud when she told him that he had an enormous member and was the best lover she'd ever had.

'Jesus, lady,' said Rob with a chuckle, 'you could win an Oscar with a performance like that.'

'Would you mind going to get me a drink of water?' Petra asked her companion, 'I do feel rather parched.'

'Of course,' replied the older man standing and pulling up his pants, 'there should be something cold in the break room.'

'Thank you,' said Petra as she rose, put back on her panties and picked up her skirt from off the floor.

The old man kissed her once and then left the room, closing his office door behind him. When she was sure she was alone, she went to her handbag and retrieved an explosive device. She set a digital timer with a date and time, but Rob wasn't quick enough to see just when the explosive would go off. She then placed it in the bottom cupboard of his desk and covered it with various personal items and papers. She closed the cupboard with a satisfied smile, walked around to the other side of the desk, and stood waiting for him, leaning back on the desk in a very alluring position.

Soon after, the businessman re-entered the office, carrying a bottle of water, which he handed to the beautiful German woman. 'Would you take me home, now?' Petra asked as she toyed with the open bottleneck, placing it between her lips in a most suggestive manner. 'I have to say, I'm really tired after that and I'm going to sleep like a log.'

'Of course,' said the older man looking at his watch. 'My wife is going to be expecting me soon, as well. Can I see you tomorrow night?'

'I'm sorry,' said Petra sweetly, 'but you caught me on the last leg of my trip. I'm heading back to Berlin early in the morning. Perhaps next time I'm in the country. I know your name now, Derek, and where you work, so it shouldn't be too hard to catch up again.'

'When will that be?' Derek asked her, kissing her and tasting the coolness of the water on her pouting lips.

'A few months, perhaps,' answered Petra. 'It depends on the company and what they want to do. If sales begin to slump again, they'll send me back. I can be a very persuasive motivator.'

'Christ almighty,' said the older man with a laugh, 'I bet you could sell ice to the Inuit.'

'How nice of you to say so, Derek,' she said, kissing him on the cheek. 'I think we should be going. I need to get some sleep. I have an early flight in the morning.'

The vision repeated itself soon after with another man. Except this time, the two of them engaged in sex on the floor of some sort of vast complex, a dim light shining from an upstairs office, where Rob assumed the two of them came from. This man wasn't as old as the other two, and decidedly better looking with dark hair and a well toned, muscular build. Petra actually seemed to be enjoying the experience more than she had in her previous exploits with the other executive. The two of them climaxed at the same time and from what Rob had previously seen, he thought she might have actually orgasmed. The two of them lay on the floor, completely naked and out of breath.

'So, you're not married, Richard...or should I say, Dick?' Petra asked with a laugh.

'Nope, divorced and single,' replied the executive. 'Would you like to come back to my place and see?'

'I would love to... for a little while,' said Petra, 'but I have to get up early in the morning and catch a plane back to Berlin. A car is coming to pick me up, so I'll need to get back to my hotel at some point.'

'So, did I fulfil your fantasy?' he asked her as he rolled over and took her in his arms.

'Of course,' Petra with a throaty laugh, 'I always wanted to be ravaged on the floor of the stock exchange at midnight by a handsome man.'

'Not only that, you got ravaged at the biggest of them all, the Sydney Stock Exchange.'

'Shit,' said Rob, realising her plan. 'She's trying to destabilise the dollar, blowing up the major stock exchanges. No wonder she had sex with them in their offices.'

'Would you mind getting me a drink of cold water? I don't think I can move.'

'Of course,' answered the businessman, standing naked and strolling off to fulfil her request.

Rob watched as Petra went through her familiar routine and retrieved the explosives from her bag. This time he watched closely, saw the date and time on the digital readout, just before she hid the device under the bottom of a bank of computers and scarpered back to her previous position on the floor.

'Fuck,' he swore aloud, 'that's today, that's now. I have to get back.' He closed his eyes, concentrated, and found himself back in the mortuary, returning with such speed it made his head spin. 'What time is it?' Rob asked of no one in particular.

'It's ten past two in the afternoon,' replied Clare. 'What's the matter? What's happened?'

'Fuck,' said Rob, 'it's too late.'

At that moment, Clare's phone rang and Russell came bursting back into the morgue. 'There've been two explosions, at the Sydney and Melbourne stock exchanges. Over a thousand people lost their lives in the blasts.'

'Petra planted the bombs,' said Rob, 'but he was behind it.'

'Why?' Clare asked in shock, hardly able to process this terrible information. 'Why would someone do something like that?'

'To cause maximum damage and to destabilise the Australian dollar, is my guess,' said Russell. 'If the stock exchanges and its brokers are killed, trading will stop and that will have a negative affect on the value of the dollar and the economy. This guy is sick, but he's a genius, in his own way.'

Clare answered her phone and heard a familiar voice on the other end. 'Have you heard?' Ray asked her.

'Yeah,' replied Clare, 'and I feel sick about it.'

'There's even worse to come,' said Ray. 'Can you get to the lab at technical, as soon as you can? Larry has something you have to see to believe.'

CHAPTER TWENTY-THREE

Mark sat in the meeting, feigning interest in what was going on. He looked at the other embassy staff and couldn't help but to feel disgusted. He felt especially abhorred when he watched the ambassador, with his neatly cut grey hair, his expensive silk suit, and his permanently aloof disposition. He was part of the old guard, thought Mark; a world that'd once been, brought up on ideals that no longer existed; a world of chivalry and fair play, where the good are always victorious, and the bad sent permanently into exile. Such was the fate of the ambassador. He'd once been an active minister of the Swedish government, in charge of foreign affairs, but an indiscretion with one of his ministerial aides had eventually turned into a major media affair. The scandal became so large that photographers and television news crews besieged his house and the party in its political wisdom decided it'd be best to demote him and send him to Australia until the scandal died down or his retirement arrived. It seemed most likely the latter of the two would be the case.

He accepted his fate with good grace, but on the inside, Mark could tell he died a little with each passing day. It would've been better just to shoot him and put him out of his misery. Mark considered the option and thought he just might do the ambassador the courtesy of a bullet to the cranium, before he was done. His affair with the aide would seem like very small potatoes once the public found out he was the Fire of the Son. The ambassador would have to take responsibility for hiring him and his continued employ and would, no doubt, be required to fall onto his political sword, sending him further down the pecking order, so he'd be fortunate to be placed in charge of a public tollgate at the end of his career.

To take his mind from the droning words of one of the other attachés, he let his mind drift away, out of the building and imagined himself flying over the city, watching the insignificant humans below who scurried around like ants in the summer. He flew out of the city and out into the countryside. He looked down as he passed over the many trees and the lush green fields, which catered for herds of differing stock and a multitude of planted crops, almost ready for harvest, baking under the warmth of the summer sun.

In the distance, upon a large green hill, he saw a wooden cabin nestled amongst gum trees and vegetation, the grass around it neatly mowed and beside it, a little vegetable garden that ran parallel to one side of the residence, catching the morning and afternoon rays of the sun. Mark found himself outside the cabin. He stepped forward, opened the door, and smiled at what he saw happening on the inside. Captain Michael Marshall strapped naked, facedown, gagged and tied to a double bed on one side of the cabin. His face was bloody, having sustained several severe beatings throughout the night and his back was covered in blisters, which looked very painful. He looked further into the shadows of the cabin and saw himself, dressed in black jeans and a white shirt, his face completely exposed, splotches of dried blood covering his torso. He hadn't worried about wearing a mask on this occasion. He would utterly destroy the bodies and make it seem as if it had been an accident, caused by the use of petrol and gas in too close a proximity to flame, by a man who publically drank too much and had become careless. It would be weeks before anyone discovered the truth and by then, Rob Swift's psychic talents would provide no assistance in the matter.

The former captain grunted under his gag, his eyes wide with fear, not knowing what was to come next. Mark walked towards himself and then became a part of the memory, rather than simply watching it from a distance. He walked over to the captain and removed his gag. He offered him a drink of water, but he refused, perhaps thinking anything he ingested might contain poison or some other substance.

'Well now,' said Mark with a smile, 'I guess we should have a little talk, shouldn't we? I suppose you want to know why I dropped in for a visit.'

'Who are you?' Michael asked almost timidly as if he didn't want to really know the answer, or perhaps he already did.

'No, I don't suppose you'd remember me. It was a long time ago and you're more likely to remember my mother, the woman you and the three others raped on the sand in the Afghani desert. Do you remember her?'

'Yeah, I do,' replied Michael realising the identity of the man who sat on the edge of the bed. 'You're the son. I knew we should've shot you both while we had the chance, but the major said to let the desert take care of it. He said you'd die out there of thirst before the end of the day. I guess he was wrong, huh?'

'Oh, yes,' answered Mark, taking a knife from a scabbard strapped to his belt. 'The colonel was wrong. Did you know he was promoted to colonel when he got back from Afghanistan?'

'Yeah, I heard that,' said Michael. 'How is the old bastard, anyway?'

'Oh, he's dead,' replied Mark nonchalantly, 'and not a very honourable death, I'm afraid. It seems he got his testicles and his penis stuck in his throat.'

'Yeah, well, he always was a bit of a dickhead,' said Michael with a bitter laugh. 'I suppose you're going to do the same thing to me.'

'Oh, no,' said Mark heating the end of the knife with a lighter flame. 'I pride myself on my sense of originality and taste. I have something completely different planned for you and the other two.'

'Okay,' said Michael, 'you might as well get on with it. I got nothing to live for, anyway, these days. Fucking Afghanistan, I wish I'd never heard of the place.'

'I suppose we all make good and bad decisions,' said Mark as he lifted the gag back over the former captain's mouth. 'It's just that some decisions have a tendency to come back and haunt us,' he added as he drew the heated blade over the skin on Michael's back, causing him to utter a muffled scream under the gag and blackout with pain.

Mark stood and walked outside. He opened the trunk of his car and stood back as the smell of faeces and urine permeated the air. He reached inside, grabbed the old woman by the back of her clothes, and threw her to the ground, sobbing pathetically beneath the gag tied about her mouth. He closed the trunk and made a mental note to clean it when he got the chance.

'There, there,' he said as he stroked the old woman's hair, soothing her as he clutched her by the collar of her nightgown and drew her up to her feet, 'I thought you'd be pleased to pay a visit to your son's house. I bet it's been a long time since you've seen each other.'

The old woman looked at the cabin in the fading light of the day as though she'd never seen the place before.

'Michael's never invited you here?' Mark asked her as he pushed and pulled her to the front door.

The old woman shook her head to answer his question and sobbed as she moved along.

'You're as pathetic as your son,' said Mark as he opened the door, cut the ropes holding her hands behind her back, and pushed her to the ground, causing her to cry out as she collapsed onto the floor. Mark turned on a lamp in the living room area of the cabin, bathing the place in yellow light. He looked up when he heard a whimper from

Michael on the bed, as he recognised his mother the moment the brightness lit up her features. Mark took his knife from the scabbard, kneeled down, and placed the tip of the blade under the old woman's chin. 'You stay here,' he ordered her. 'If you try and run away, I'll catch you, cut off your tits and make your son eat them while you watch. Do you understand?'

The old woman nodded, indicating her intention to comply and stayed where she was, visibly shaking with fear and trepidation, caught like a rabbit caught in headlights.

Mark went to the other side of the room and removed Michael's gag. 'It looks like we have a guest,' said he said with a cold laugh, 'I might as well get this party started.'

'Leave her alone,' said Michael struggling with the ropes that bound him to the bed, 'she didn't do anything to you.'

'Oh, but she did,' said Mark as he began to cut away the old woman's clothing. 'She gave birth to you, and you raped my mother. Somewhere in her DNA, or perhaps, even the way she brought you up, she gave to you the characteristics that enabled you to do something like that.'

'Look, I'm sorry about your mother, but it was war.'

'Yes, the colonel used the same excuse, but I'm afraid it just doesn't wash. What you did was not an act of war, it was a criminal endeavour, and I've always been a great believer in that old adage, an eye for an eye.'

'Please, just let her go. You can do whatever you want to me, but she's innocent.'

Mark laughed as the last of the nightgown slid from the woman's body. He threw it into a corner of the cabin, removed her gag, and pushed her down to the floor. 'Nobody's innocent, Michael. Human beings as a rule are a sinful species. Now, watch me commit the sin of vengeance.'

Mark pulled the old woman across the room and behind a freestanding filing cabinet. He made her lay so that her legs stuck out, but no other part of her body was visible. He then took off his clothes and lay down on top of the old woman. He didn't have either the heart or the desire to rape her. Instead, out of Michael's sight, he repeatedly pinched her throat in rhythm with his moving body, causing her to cry out in pain, giving Michael the impression he was raping her, which he knew would be just as psychologically damaging. He looked up to watch Michael's face and saw it contained a mixture of anger, disgust, and sadness. He struggled against the ropes that held him to no avail and in the end, he turned his face away and tried to stop the noise by pressing his ear into the mattress. Every so often, when the old hag seemed as if she would black out with pain and shock, he raised his hand and slapped her hard across the face, just to add a little spice to the experience. She would cry out in response to his violence. Michael would turn around to see what he'd done, and then Mark would smile and slap her again, just for his captive's benefit.

When he'd finished with her, he punched her hard on the chin, sending her into unconsciousness and dressed himself. He lit up one of Michael's cigarettes and made himself a coffee in the kitchenette. 'I do love a cigarette after sex,' he said as he pulled down Michael's gag and then sat down and drank his beverage on the kitchen table.

'Go fuck yourself,' Michael spat at him from the across the room. 'You're a fucking animal!'

'No, dear boy,' said Mark dropping the cigarette butt into the remnants of the coffee and listening to it sizzle out, 'animals don't commit such acts against each other. Cruelty is purely the province of human beings. Animals kill for need and survival, but we kill animals for pleasure and for sport and each other, for many reasons other than to survive and I have to admit, we do it well. The human being is, in the end, the most advanced killing machine ever to walk the face of this planet.'

Michael looked at him with almost total disbelief. 'You're really enjoying this, aren't you? Untie me and then we can go outside and the two of us can go for it. I promise you, I'll be a challenge. I'll show you just what a killing machine really is.'

Mark laughed. 'While that's a very tempting offer, Michael, it does have its drawbacks. I have a job and I do need to look very conservative and can't afford to appear as if I've been fighting. The second, is fighting you would be unfair. You'd be fighting in anger and rage, and bound to make mistakes. I'm afraid you'd be far too easy to kill and besides, I have other, more colourful plans for you. This is a three-act play and now, I must finish the first act before we get to the second and then, eventually, arrive at the finale.'

'What's the finale?'

'I shouldn't worry about that too much if I were you,' said Mark rising. 'You won't be around to see it.'

'I suppose you're going after August, too, are you?'

'Oh, yes,' replied Mark as headed for the door. 'Mister Richers, the colonel told me he might provide more of challenge than the two of you. It should be interesting.'

'Yeah, he's no pussy,' said Michael bitterly. 'I hope he rips your fucking guts out.'

'Oh, he'll get his chance,' said Mark with a laugh, 'but I don't think he'll actually live up to his reputation. None of you army types do, you're all just a bunch of grunts, with brains the size of peas.'

Mark walked out the door and went to his car. He opened the boot, removed a pump action shotgun from its cover, and returned to the cabin. Once inside, he loaded the gun with four cartridges and cocked it, making it ready to fire. He aimed the gun at the old woman on the floor and fired, creating a huge hole in the side of her face with the first shot and then removing her head altogether with a second.

'There,' he said looking at Michael, 'that's the end of the first act and now for the second.'

'I hope you burn in hell for what you've done,' Michael screamed as Mark came towards him and cocked the gun again. 'Go on, get it over with!'

'Now, now,' said Mark with a laugh, 'don't be so eager, because believe me, you're not going to like it.'

'Do your fucking worst,' said Michael as tears rolled down his cheeks, 'I don't give a flying fuck!'

Mark moved closer to the bed and inserted the end of the barrel into Michael's mouth. He pushed it hard into him, forcing the barrel into his throat, making Michael squeal with agony. He then withdrew it and forced it in again, laughing at the other man's pain.

'Fuck you,' mumbled Michael as he gagged on the barrel.

Mark pulled the trigger of the shotgun and Michael's throat and left shoulder exploded, sending flesh and blood onto the bed head and killing him. He aimed higher and fired again, causing Michael's brain and top of his head to fly off his body and smash against the end of the bed. Mark wiped off the gun with a tea towel from the sink and replaced it back into its cover. He then replaced it back into the trunk of his car and removed a small bag, which contained a change of clothes and a canister of petrol.

He returned to the inside of the cabin and took a shower, washing off the blood and gore, which had collected on him while he worked. He used one of Michael's towels to dry and when dressed, went back to the main area of the cabin and inspected what he'd done. He felt pleased with himself. It was a good day's work.

'Now, for the finale,' he said as he went to the stove and turned on all of the gas jets connected to the bottle outside. He closed all of the windows and then poured petrol over the bodies, and all around the cabin making sure the place would erupt into an inferno once he lit it up.

Mark trailed the petrol to the front door, grabbed his bag, and placed it into the car along with the shotgun. He then trailed the petrol away from the cabin right up to the trunk of his car, where he replaced the canister and his other belongings. He decided to wait until the cabin was full of gas, lit up a cigarette, and listened to music on some local country music station for while. When he was satisfied there'd be enough fuel inside to destroy the place without leaving a shred of evidence, he started the engine of the car and let it sit idling while he lit up a tissue and dropped it onto the trail of petrol.

He smiled as he jumped into the car, put it into gear, and drove off. He watched in the rear-view mirror as the place exploded in flames, feeling the shock from the blast from the inside of the car. 'That, Michael, was your finale.'

Mark found himself again sitting back in the meeting and hearing the ambassador suggest that it was ten minutes to two and they should all take a short break and convene back here just after two. 'I'm expecting a call,' he said to his staff, 'and I should have some good news when I get back.'

Mark smiled at the other staff as he rose, indicating he felt it had been a good meeting, although in reality, he'd hardly been there at all. He let the women in the room exit before him, holding open the door in a courteous manner and then headed for his own office down the hall. Once inside, he sat down behind his desk, looked out at the day, and then at his watch, trying to calm his breathing as he contemplated his next move. At one minute to two, he reached inside his desk drawer and pulled out the television remote control, and a packet of AA batteries. He rose, moved out from behind the desk, and entered his private washroom to the side of his office. He closed and locked the door and sat down on the closed bowl as he pulled the back off the remote and inserted the batteries and then pulled out an aerial from the top of the box. He looked again at his watch and saw that he had less than a minute to go. He stood up and onto the bowl of the toilet and pointed the tip of the aerial out of the angled windows at the top of the room.

He looked again at his watch and exactly as the hand moved onto the twelve, he pressed the play button and listened for the sound of an explosion. He heard the enormous boom in the distance, smiled, and got down off the toilet, removed the batteries from the remote, and flushed the toilet, just in case anyone had walked into his office in his absence. He put the box and the batteries into his pocket and returned to his office, and replaced the remote back into the drawer from where he'd retrieved it.

He left the office and went to the break room, where he knew there was a television set. He made a cup of coffee and sat with the secretaries, who were all curious about the sound of the explosion.

'Turn on the television,' said the ambassador's secretary, 'there might be some news. We've still got some time, the ambassador's still on the phone in his office.'

One of the other women switched on the set and started going through the channels. She stopped when she saw the serious face of one of Melbourne's best-known newsreaders and put the remote on the table in the centre of the room. The newsreader went on to report of a deadly explosion that occurred at the Melbourne Stock Exchange just a few minutes prior. She said that there'd been major damage to the building and the numbers of dead were in the hundreds, although the exact tally was unknown.

As she was reporting, another person slipped onto the screen and placed a piece of paper on her desk. The newsreader stopped for a moment, her eyes filling with tears, as though she could hardly believe what she was seeing on the page. She then gained control of herself, looked into the camera, and said that there'd also been another explosion, which had occurred simultaneously in, Sydney Stock Exchange.

'It is a sad day for Australia, when such acts of terrorism occur in this country. Please stay tuned and we'll bring you more news as it comes to hand.'

'Oh, my God,' said the ambassador's secretary, placing a hand over her mouth and heading for the door. 'I must go and tell the ambassador, at once.'

The three remaining women were still, unspeaking, their eyes glued to the television screen ahead of them. Mark wanted to laugh aloud, to tell them they were fools for feeling sorry for the pathetic dead, but instead, managed to restrain his vengeful joy and he, too, headed out the door and back to his office.

He switched on the radio he kept on a shelf above him, sat back in the chair behind his desk, and lit up a cigarette. He knew he wasn't supposed to smoke inside, but his lack of adherence to such mundane rules were the least of anyone's concerns at a time like this, when the whole country was in trauma over such a ghastly event.

He'd just finished his cigarette when the door opened and the ambassador came in and sat down, his brow sweating and a concerned and stressful look on his face.

'This is terrible,' he said.

'Yes,' agreed Mark lighting another cigarette and offering the old man one from his packet. 'Who'd have thought something like this could happen in Australia, of all places?'

'Not I,' replied the ambassador, taking the cigarette and a light from Mark, who pushed his ashtray between him and the old man, 'Not in a million years. We must, of course, offer our sympathies and condolences to the Australian government and people. If you could set up a phone call with the prime minister, Mark, I'd appreciate it very much.'

'Certainly, ambassador,' replied Mark, realising the irony in the situation. He almost smiled at the absurdity of it, but jammed his cigarette between his lips and sucked in the smoke before he gave himself away, 'I'll get to work on it, straight away.'

'I imagine there will be some sort of memorial service conducted in the near future. Please see to it we're included in such an event. I imagine ambassadors and their staff from all the embassies in Australia will want to attend and participate.'

'Certainly, sir, I will keep you abreast of any arrangements and let you know about speaking to the PM.'

'Thank you, Mark,' replied the ambassador, butting out his cigarette and rising. 'I don't know what I'd do without you. Oh, yes, the Swedish prime minister will be calling me within the hour. Could you please make sure I'm not disturbed during the call? I'll tell my secretary and if you could inform the rest of the staff.'

'Yes, sir,' said Mark, also rising and walking the ambassador out of his office. 'You can count on me, sir.'

Mark retreated back into his office as the ambassador departed. He sat down at his desk and laughed to himself. Without even planning it, he'd arranged a way to set off the nuclear device in a place that would cause the most damage to the country - at the memorial service. No doubt, the prime minister and most of the senior cabinet members would attend and it would be the perfect opportunity to kill all of them and completely demoralise the whole country. On the coattails of the ambassador, he'd waltz right in, an honoured guest of the proceedings. He wouldn't even have to bring the device into the church. If he could place it in the trunk of a car parked nearby, he could vaporise everything for a square mile, slipping discreetly away before the thing went off.

'Perfect,' he whispered as he picked up the phone and asked to be connected to the prime minister's office. 'Absolutely perfect.'

CHAPTER TWENTY-FOUR

'Okay,' said Larry Batts, removing a cooler from the lab refrigerator, 'wait here for a bit. I'll be back in a couple of minutes.'

'So, we think he was driving a Volvo,' said Ray, 'when he dumped Tony under the bridge.'

'That's interesting,' said Rob, 'aren't Volvos Swedish cars?'

'Yeah,' replied Peter, 'I think it's their most famous export.'

'In the vision I had of Petra's past, I saw her in Sweden with Arkmed. I saw him grow up, in an earlier vision, in some European country, but couldn't make out which country it was. It could well have been Sweden.'

'So, you think FOTS somehow made his way from Sweden to Australia?' Peter asked, as he grabbed for his phone.

'I'm not a hundred percent sure, but I think so,' said Rob. 'You can never tell with this psychic stuff. It's not an exact science.'

'All right,' said Peter, 'I'll have my officers contact the Swedish embassy and immigration and see if we can't get a list of all the Swedish people in the state, both tourists and citizens. Ray, could you phone the Road Traffic Authority and see if we can narrow down people of Swedish origin who own Volvos in Victoria? We'll need to cross-reference the lists and see how many possible suspects there are. There's bound to be a significant list, but if the info we have is correct, then he's bound to be on it, somewhere. Damn, we're starting to get somewhere, at last. At least it'll give the rest of the taskforce something to go on.'

'No worries,' said Ray, pulling out his phone, 'I'm on it.'

A moment later, Larry appeared again. 'All right,' he said, directing everyone's attention to a monitor that sat on a bench. 'I want to show you all what would've happened if Clare had opened the envelope at the hospital. If you look at the monitor, you'll see that the part of the letter contained inside the envelope has been torn off and is sitting in the middle of the floor of this concrete bunker.'

'Okay,' said Annie, 'enough with the build up. Get on with it.'

'Sure,' said Larry as he took a remote control in his hands and raised the temperature in the bunker. All of a sudden, the paper seemed to light up and then exploded with a deafening noise.'

'What the fuck was that?' Clare demanded to know, shocked by what would've happened had she been just a bit careless.

'The paper was soaked in some kind of explosive compound,' replied Larry. 'Had you touched it with your fingers, it would have raised the temperature enough for it have detonated and, in all likelihood, killed you and anybody who was standing near you at the time. This explosion occurred using only about one eighth of the page. The whole page would've been far more devastating.'

'Christ, I've never heard of anything like it before,' said Ray. 'Where did it come from?'

'So, this guy could potentially paint any surface with this stuff?' Peter asked the scientist.

Larry took a pair of reading glasses from the top pocket of his lab coat, put them on, and turned to his computer. 'From what I've been able to gather, I think it initially came from the Israeli Intelligence Service, Mossad, but the formula was either stolen or traded off by somebody on the inside while it was still in the development stage. The Israelis abandoned it as a bad idea, due to it being largely unstable and hard to transport. In answer to your question, Peter, yes, it is potentially possible to coat any surface with the compound. All it would take to set off the explosive is for the air temperature to rise, or for someone to touch that surface, even for only a few seconds and you've seen the results... not pretty.'

'So, why didn't it explode back in the hospital?' Clare asked.

'I think it was for a couple of reasons,' replied Larry. 'The first was your handling of the envelope, Clare. You only handled it by either the edges or the corners, so that your fingers didn't raise the temperature on the outside of the envelope. My guess is that this and the fact that hospital has constant air-conditioning, probably contributed to the lack of detonation. The fact that you were also wearing surgical gloves might also have had something to do with it, but I don't really know for sure, it's all just a hypothesis and not one I'm keen to test. I do know, though, that you're one lucky copper.'

'So, how did you know about it?' Annie asked, obviously impressed by the scientist's skills. 'I mean you couldn't tell just by looking at it, could you?'

Larry laughed. 'No, I'm a nerd and besides, this guy, whoever he is, seems to specialise in explosives. There was no reason to believe he'd changed his modus operandi. My only other concern was it might contain some sort of biological agent, but it's been checked out and given the all-clear.'

'That's good, at least,' said Ray.

'So, where do we go from here?' Russell asked.

'Okay,' said Ray, 'let's just add up everything we know so far. We think this lunatic is Swedish and he drives a Volvo. Australian soldiers raped his mother in Afghanistan. He's killed Danny Murphy, the previous commander, for his part in the rape and for sure, he's going to go after the other soldiers who helped him. I think we need to concentrate on finding them first. We might be able to trap him if we can locate them first, watch them. Peter thinks it's most likely the senior members of the platoon did the deed.'

'I have some files on their way to my office,' said Peter, 'from Defence. It should give us some clues about where to find them. If they're no longer at their listed addresses, we turn to their next of kin. That info will be contained in the files. I think we need to split up into two teams, divide up the names and start tracking them down, before FOTS gets to them, if he hasn't already.'

'Sounds like a plan,' said Clare. 'What about me and Rob?'

'I'll head one of the teams,' replied Ray, 'and you can come with me. Peter can head up the other and he can take Rob.'

'Okay, Ray and I are going to head back to the taskforce office,' said Peter. 'The files should've arrived by now. We need to brief the commissioner about what we have so far. He'll be anxious to know and I need to call my boss in Canberra and let him know, too. While Ray and I are doing that, I'll hand the file over to Clare to peruse. She can start dividing the names and handing out the assignments. When Ray and I are done with the briefing, we'll join you.'

'In the meantime,' said Ray, 'we'll have the rest of the taskforce, who aren't at the stock exchange crime scene, start cross-referencing the Volvo list with Swedish citizens in the state and start making physical enquiries.'

'It's going to take at least twenty minutes for us to get back to the office,' said Peter. 'I think you should use that time to go and get something to eat. I have a feeling it's going to be a long night and none of us are going to get much sleep over the next couple of days.'

'One more thing,' said Ray. 'I want everyone well-armed and to wear their Kevlar vests if entering a residence and I especially don't want Rob to enter a residence without someone checking it out first. This prick could be sitting somewhere, waiting for us to show up and I don't want anybody hurt. If there's the slightest indication any of the addresses are setup with traps, I want the bomb squad called in before you enter. Don't touch any doorknobs or knockers. This arsehole might well have coated them in the compound. I want everyone to be on his or her guard at all times. The slightest lapse in judgement could mean you die, or a colleague does. Is that clear?'

'Yes, boss,' chorused the detectives.

'Rob,' said Peter, 'you've been a great help to us, so far. I was a bit sceptical when I first heard about you, but you've turned me into a believer. I hope you'll continue to keep up the excellent work. It's an honour to have you on our team.'

'Thanks,' replied Rob with a shy smile. 'I'll try.'

'That's all we can ask,' said Ray slapping Rob on the shoulder.

'All right, you lot,' said Peter as he and Ray headed for the door, 'go get something to eat, then get back here and gear up. Make sure your firearms are loaded and checked and you have spare ammunition. Clare will call you and give you the addresses.'

'Okay,' said Russell turning to the rest of the team, 'you heard the man, fall out, and meet back here in half an hour.'

'I know where there's a good Chinese place, not far from here,' said Annie.

'Well, lead on,' said Russell with a smile. 'I like Chinese food.'

'Oh, a man after my own heart,' said Annie leading the way. 'We can walk there, too, it's not far.'

'I know it's a bit paranoid,' said Russell, 'but I'd prefer if we took Rob in one of the cars. 'I'd never be able to forgive myself if anything happened to him and the commissioner would tear us all a new one. Just give me directions and we'll meet you there.'

'Okay,' said Annie, 'if you go down to the end of the street and turn left, you'll see the Emperor's Palace just down the street, you can't miss it.'

'Okay,' said Russell heading for the door with Rob in tow, 'see you guys in a bit.'

'What about you, Larry?' Annie asked the scientist with a smile, 'You want to come and get some food too?'

'Yeah, sounds like a good idea,' replied Larry his face a blush with shyness, 'I've just got to lock up in here, and then I can go.'

'That's okay,' said Annie, 'I'll wait with you.' She turned to the rest of the officers and told them to go on ahead and the two of them would catch up in a couple of minutes.

Josie laughed as she made for the door. 'You know, Annie, you should give up the Victorian police, go to Canada, and join the Mountie's.'

Annie laughed, too. 'Very funny, superwoman, now get your arse out of here.'

Larry ran around locking up the lab, setting the alarm, and grabbing his coat, while Annie waited. When he was finished, they headed for the door. 'I know I'm a bit of a nerd,' he said, 'but what did Josie mean, when she said you should join the Mountie's?'

Annie laughed and took his arm as they walked out into the street. 'The Mounties always get their man,' she replied with a laugh.'

TWENTY-FIVE

The ambassador leaned back in his chair. 'Of course we'll cooperate,' he told the two law enforcement officers who sat on the opposite side of his desk. 'I'm just shocked to find out that a Swedish citizen could be this terrorist, Fire of the Son.'

'Yeah, I can imagine,' said Leigh Best, one of the leading federal investigators. 'Nevertheless, we still need to get the list of Swedish citizens who are currently in this country, both as citizens and as tourists. So we can start dismissing suspects.'

'Of course,' said the ambassador, reaching for his phone and dialling an internal extension, 'I'll put my best man on it, straight away. The ambassador waited for a moment and then heard a voice on the end of the speakerphone. 'Mark, could you come straight to my office?'

'Certainly,' replied Mark and hung up the phone.

'Mark Andersson is one of the best attachés associated with the embassy,' said the ambassador. He'll get you what you need.'

'Thank you, ambassador,' said Eddie Bakas from the state police, 'we appreciate your cooperation.'

'It's the least we can do,' replied the ambassador. 'I hope you catch this man. I'll inform my government of what you've told me and we'll see what the police in my country can do to help your investigation.'

A moment later, the door to the ambassador's office opened and Mark Andersson made his way inside. As soon as he saw the two men seated at the desk, he knew who they were by the slight bulges in the jackets and their haircuts, although he outwardly portrayed no signs of his recognition.

'Ambassador, you called me?'

'Yes,' replied the ambassador, rising. 'Mark Andersson, this is Mr. Best from the Australian Federal Police and Mr. Bakas from the Victoria Police, they're involved in a joint taskforce trying to track down the terrorist known as the Fire of the Son.'

'Good to meet you,' said Mark, shaking each of the men's hands in turn. 'How can I be of assistance?'

'We need to get a list of all the Swedish citizens and former citizens residing in Victoria and those that are here on temporary work or holiday visas,' said Leigh. 'The ambassador tells us you're the best man for the job.'

'That could take some time,' said Mark taking a seat at the side of the ambassador's desk, 'there are a lot of Swedish citizens in Australia at any one time. I'll need to contact immigration in Sweden and see if I can get a list. How far back are you looking at?'

'As far back as you can, I guess. We appreciate the enormity of what we're asking you,' said Eddie, 'but it could save a lot of lives.'

'I will, of course, authorise any overtime you need to take to get this done,' said the ambassador.

'Thank you, sir,' said Mark. 'If I go to work on it straight away, I could get it done I think by ten or eleven tonight. If you could possibly come back then, I'll try to have it for you. I'll be here on my own, so ring me on my extension,' he said pulling out one of his cards and handing it to the federal officer.

'Not a problem,' said Leigh. 'We'll see you then.'

'Very well,' said Mark with a smile, 'I look forward to it.'

Once the detectives had left the room, Mark pulled out a folder from under his arm and handed it to the ambassador. 'The Australian prime minister will call you in the morning at nine and the memorial service for all those killed at the stock exchanges will take place in two days at

St. Pauls Cathedral, here in Melbourne. There will be a simultaneous service conducted in Sydney. There will be limited space, but there are reserved seats for both you and your wife and for two of your senior attachés. As I understand it, the premier of Victoria has flown to Canberra and will conducting a joint press conference, later on this afternoon. The prime minister will be attending the Melbourne service. One of his aides told me that the PM has no intention of letting the Fire of the Son intimidate him into not attending and he wants to show solidarity with the people of Melbourne, after what they've been through.'

'That's good work,' said the ambassador, taking the folder to inspect the contents. 'You, of course, will be attending the memorial service with me?'

'Of course,' replied Mark. 'I just need to get these detectives out of my road, first.'

The ambassador smiled. Please, carry on. I know you'll do your usual thorough job. If we can help to apprehend the Fire of the Son, it might well be a feather in our cap, and it certainly won't hurt your career, my boy.'

Mark left the ambassador's office and walked down the hall to his own. He sat down and pulled out a bottle of whiskey and a shot glass from the bottom of his desk. He filled the shot glass and downed it one go and then poured himself another, which he sipped as he gazed out of the window down at the traffic below.

He wondered how the police had found out the Fire of the Son was a Swedish citizen, when he thought he'd covered all his bases. It had to be Rob Swift and his absurd psychic ability that'd provided the vital clue. He speculated about what else they might know and arrived soon at the obvious conclusion: he had to rid himself of the Mark Andersson identity and become someone completely different. The more he thought about it, the more the thought of becoming Leigh Best appealed to him.

He could have provided the information that the two law enforcement officers requested within a couple of hours. However, getting the two of them to return later on in the night, when he'd be at the embassy alone, had been an inspired improvisation. This would provide him the opportunity to kill Mr. Best and his partner and take their identities, so that he could get close to the prime minister and members of his cabinet, to set off the nuclear device with the minimum of fuss. Before he got to that, though, there were three other things to take care of, and two of them were August Richers, and serving Sergeant Chris Knight.

CHAPTER TWENTY-SIX

Clare sat looking at the files in front of her and, for a change, was glad to be doing some sort of administrative work as opposed to sitting in the next office with Ray and Peter, who'd had to bear the brunt of the commissioner's anger and frustration. He bellowed at the top of his voice that he wanted this Fire of the Son fucker caught, yesterday. 'People are deserting Melbourne in fucking droves. The place is turning into a bloody ghost town.'

Both Ray and Peter tried to placate him by filling him in on their progress, but the commissioner was not to be placated and continued to yell at the top of his voice until he stopped to consume a large glass of whiskey. He thoughtfully offered one to both men and then went on venting until he finally managed to calm himself down.

After that, there was a teleconference with the federal commissioner of police from Canberra, who manifested an equally livid mood. He told the trio he'd been on the phone to both the premier of Victoria and the prime minister only minutes ago and both men were equally displeased with the progress of the case and wanted results, immediately.

'Are you aware that this man has singlehandedly sent the Australian dollar down thirty-five points? Right now, we're worth about fifty U.S. cents.'

Clare heard Peter go over the progress in the case with the federal commissioner, picked up another of the files, and attempted to ignore the heated discussion to get on with her work. She opened up the first file and saw it belonged to a Captain Michael Marshall. The file gave his last known address as living with his mother, in the northern suburbs of Melbourne.

'138 Bell Street, Preston,' she mumbled as she copied the address. She found a phone number, but there was no answer when she dialled it. She knew that could've been for a myriad of reasons. Marshall might have fled the city, like so many other people had, or he and his mother might simply not be home, for any one of a hundred everyday excursions. Clare had a bad feeling in the pit of her stomach that that wasn't the reason and she feared there was a much more sinister explanation.

The next file she looked at was for August Richers, he was a former corporal and SAS soldier, trained under Murphy. According to the file, he'd faced charges for assault on several occasions, due to involving himself in a number of bar brawls whilst on leave. He was also charged for insubordination to his superior officers, prior to receiving a dishonourable discharge. He seemed the type of man who could look after himself. It appeared he'd requested to serve under Murphy in Afghanistan. She wondered why he would ask to serve under a particular officer and what they could possibly have in common. The late colonel, it seemed, had come from a wealthy background with a tradition of service to the armed forces that went back three generations. Richers, on the other hand, seemed like white trash, growing up with the barest of education in a working class neighbourhood of Melbourne. She would have to ask him herself, if she got the chance.

Clare next opened up the file of Sergeant Chris Knight. He was the only one of the group who was still actively engaged in military service. His current assignment was at Watsonia army barracks, serving as a training officer for the signals division, specialising in ground-based communications for the infantry.

'He's a fucking glorified radio operator,' she said to herself with a laugh. 'Oh, well, I suppose somebody's got to do it.'

Clare dialled the number for the barracks, explained who she was and asked to speak to the sergeant. A woman at the switchboard asked her to told hold on for a moment and said she'd connect her. Clare continued looking at the files, with the hold music playing in the background on the telephone loudspeaker, trying to discern any further useful facts, which might come in handy. Finally, she heard click and another voice say hello.

'Hello,' said Clare. 'Is this Sergeant Chris Knight?'

'Yes,' replied the deep male voice, 'this is he, how can I help you?'

Clare explained she was a sergeant with the major crime squad and asked if Chris would be available to answer some questions in relation to a matter she was currently investigating.

'What's it all about?' Chris asked, his voice taking on a shade of anxiety.

'I'm sorry,' said Clare, 'but I'm not at liberty to discuss this over the phone. I could come to the barracks or you could come here. It's your choice.'

'I'll come to you,' said the sergeant. 'I don't want my men to think that there's anything untoward going on with me, having the police crawling around the barracks. It doesn't set a good example.'

'How do you know it's even got anything to do with you?' Clare asked him. 'It could be about somebody else.'

'I don't think so,' replied the soldier. 'Mike Marshall and August Richers are both friends of mine. We meet once a week, like clockwork, for drinks. They didn't show up yesterday and I haven't been able to contact either of them. I think I know what you're going to ask me about and I'll tell you everything I know. To tell you the truth, it'll be a relief to get it off my chest, after all these years.'

'All right,' said Clare, 'if you're going to be coming in here, I want to make sure you do under escort for your own protection. Can you connect me to the commanding officer? I'll need to talk to him and arrange transport. For the moment, stay inside your office and don't put yourself anywhere you'd be vulnerable to attack, is that understood?

'Sure,' said the sergeant, 'I got it.'

'What's the commanding officer's name?'

'It's Major Jeffrey Taylor. I just saw him go into his office a little while ago, so he should still be there.'

'Can you put me straight through to him, or do you need to send me back to the switchboard?'

'No, you'll need to go back to the switchboard,' said Chris, 'and then ask for the major's office. Okay, hang on and I'll dial you back. If you get disconnected, just call the barracks again, and ask for Major Taylor's office.'

'Will do,' said Clare. 'See you in a while.'

Chris hit some buttons on the phone and a moment later, Clare found herself talking to the woman who'd originally connected her to Chris. 'Can I speak to Major Taylor, please?'

'Certainly,' replied the operator, 'please hold the line.'

A moment later, the repetitive sound of a calling phone echoed down the line and then another woman answered. 'Major Taylor's office, how can I help you?'

'I'd like to speak to the major,' said Clare.

'I'll just put you through,' said the woman. 'Who should I say is calling?'

Clare explained who she was and waited another few seconds as the call was put through to the major's office and picked up by a man with a distinguished, cultured sounding voice, 'Taylor here.'

'Hello,' said Clare. 'My name's Sergeant Clare Carbone, I'm a detective with the Victoria Police, Major Crime Squad. I'd like to talk to you about one of your men, if you have a minute.'

'Certainly,' replied the major, 'always got time for the constabulary. What can I do for you?'

Clare went into detail explaining the situation to the major in regards to Chris Knight and the need for secrecy. 'We need to get him in here in one piece for questioning. I know it's asking a lot, but would it be possible to send him in under armed guard, if you have a couple of military police to spare?'

'Of course,' said the major. 'Do you really think he was in involved, in the rape, I mean? He's one of my best men, always a fellow of exceptional character and behaviour, in my experience and I've been here for five years. You really couldn't get a better man, anywhere.'

'I'm sorry to say it, major, but I do. I think he was actively involved and he's already told me as much. I think he's keen to spill his guts once he gets in here. If he provides us with a confession, as I suspect he will, I'll charge him with aggravated sexual assault. I honestly don't know who holds jurisdiction over the matter. He may end up at The Hague if this incident is characterised a war crime, I don't know. I intend to seek remand for his physical safety. I think keeping this man safe and getting what info we can from him is the absolute priority right now.'

'Of course, I agree with you,' said the major. 'I'll arrange to bring him to my office straight away and then for him to receive armed escort to you as soon as humanly possible. He might be a good man, but in the end, we've all got to pay the piper for our sins.'

'Yes, we do,' said Clare. 'Thank you for your cooperation.'

'My pleasure,' said the major. 'I'll put you back to my secretary and if you could provide her with the details of where Knight is to be taken, I'll get him over here, right now. Will he require a lawyer, at this stage?'

'I wouldn't mention that to him, just yet,' said Clare in an almost a whisper, as if involving the officer in a low-level conspiracy, trying to speak between the lines, without directly asking the major not to provide the sergeant with such information, 'but if he asks for one, we'll provide counsel for him.'

'I understand,' said the major. 'Very well, it's been good talking to you, sergeant. If you could please keep me updated, it would be appreciated.'

'Sure,' said Clare. 'I'll let you know as soon as we do.'

'Very good,' said the major as he pressed the transfer buttons on his phone, 'carry on.'

Clare gave the details to the secretary, providing the city address for Knight's transportation and then hung up the phone.

She cocked an ear and heard the lowered tones of the three men in the next room, which seemed to have decreased in volume whilst she'd been on the phone. She got out of her chair and stretched, amazed by how overly exerted she'd come to feel over the past few days. She decided she needed coffee and made her way to the break room, two doors down and in the opposite direction to the commissioner's office. She made herself a Styrofoam cup of strong, black coffee, then sneaked past the commissioner's office, and strolled down to the stairwell at the far end of the building. She pushed open the exit, and placed a wedge of paper under the fire escape door to prevent it from closing and locking her out.

She sat down on the stairs and sipped her coffee before searching her jacket for the packet of cigarettes she'd purchased on her way there, much to Ray's surprise. She knew she didn't have a lot of time and was well aware that the other team would be waiting for her call.

'Fuck it,' she said, 'they can wait for a minute.'

Clare lit up the cigarette and breathed in the smoke, letting it trail away from her in the still air, rising upwards, out of sight. She thought about what Rob had said to her about meeting someone and the conversation rebounded in her mind. She'd lied to him about the last time she'd been in a relationship, and didn't want to go into details about the awful time she'd had. There were just some things she considered too private to talk about and that bastard was one of them. His name was Harry and he was a cop. They had met at the academy and she'd loved him deeply, but after three years of dating and seven years of living together, things had gone sour in the worst possible way. He started drinking with his friends on the force after every shift and developed a problem. Along with the alcohol came a level of violence she hadn't expected. He would drink at the police club after nightshift and stagger home, pissed out of his skull, and try to make it with her. She would refuse, and then they'd fight until he'd find another bottle in the fridge and drink until he passed out on the sofa.

One night, after a particularly bad row, he'd started smashing the place up and threatened her, until she felt forced to pull out her gun and point it at him. 'Don't point that thing at me, unless you're prepared to use it,' he had snarled at her.

'Harry,' she'd replied coldly, 'if you don't walk out that door in the next few seconds, I'm going to kill you where you stand.'

'Fuck you,' he said as a parting remark and slammed the door after him, 'you fucking bitch!'

Clare packed up all of her belongings and used his absence as an opportunity to get the hell out of there. She hadn't seen him since, but heard that he'd managed to get sober, and was now a senior sergeant in charge of a station somewhere out in the western suburbs. She'd vowed after, not to become involved with another police officer and so far, she'd managed to keep her promise. That was five years ago and, although, she didn't hurt like she once did, there was still a part of her that wanted a good, healthy relationship, but that man, whoever he would be, would need to go so excruciatingly slow she didn't think anybody could possibly be up to the task.

She finished her cigarette, dipped the butt into the last of her coffee, came back into the building through the exit, and disposed of the butt in a bin on the way back to her office. She passed the commissioner's office and heard the three men still talking, but at least they were still being civilised about it. She washed her mug and went back to her desk.

Once inside her office, she picked up the notes she had taken from the files, grabbed the phone, and dialled Russell's mobile. She informed him she'd managed to track down Chris Knight and that she, Ray, and Peter would be spending some time back at the office, questioning him, and seeing if he had any viable information. She gave him Michael Marshall's home address and told him there'd been no answer when she had called.

'August Richers lives at 24 Nadine Street, Whittlesea. Get whoever you've decided on for the other team to head out there, and like Ray said, for God's sake, be careful.'

'Okay,' said Russell. 'We're just on our way back to technical, as we speak. We had a great Chinese meal, too bad you missed it.'

'Another time,' said Clare.

'I'll take you up on that.'

'You got a date,' said Clare almost before she realised the words had come from her mouth.

'Okay,' said Russell with a laugh. 'We'll gear up and head out as soon as we get back. I'll let you know what we find.'

'All right,' said Clare. 'I've had a justice of the peace waiting in her office, so that she can issue warrants of entry for the properties. I've prepared them and just need to get her to approve and sign them. The grounds of the warrant state that we have significant proof that both

Marshall and Richers committed an aggravated rape in Afghanistan, based on what Chris Knight has told us.'

'But you haven't spoken to Knight yet, have you?'

'A mere detail,' replied Clare. 'He'll spill his guts as soon as he gets here. I'd bet my job on it.'

'You already have,' said Russell.

'The warrant will be on the fax at technical before you leave. Make sure you take them. You might not even have to execute them, but I wouldn't bet anything on that.'

CHAPTER TWENTY-SEVEN

Russell put the phone down and turned to Rob in the passenger seat. 'She's quite a woman, that Clare.'

'Yeah, I think so,' said Rob, looking out the window to stop from laughing.

Russell pulled the car up into the driveway, got out, and lit up a cigarette while he waited for the others to arrive on foot. He offered one to Rob, who took it, lit it up, breathed in the smoke, and then watched it float away on a gentle breeze.

'I do love a smoke after a meal,' he said. 'I gave up for a whole year, when I was in Tibet. I had my first one on the day I decided to leave. Old habits die hard.'

Russell went to the back of the car. He opened the trunk, grabbed out three Kevlar vests, and handed one to Rob. 'I know you won't be doing any initial entries in either of the residences, but I want you to wear this. The bastards of things are bloody uncomfortable, but in the end, it might save your life. They'll stop a round from a handgun, but probably not from a high-powered rifle, at mid to close range.'

'Then I'll try to avoid high-powered rifles at mid to close range,' said Rob as he began to strap on the vest.

'As will we all,' said Russell with a chuckle.

A short while later, the rest of the team arrived. Larry let them into the building, where they geared up and checked their firearms.

'Okay,' said Russell, 'like Peter said, it's probably best if we divide up into teams. The two teams will consists of Josie, Le Mar, and June for the first and for the second, it will be Marcus, Annie, and I. We need to find two men who were involved in the rapes of FOTS' mother in Afghanistan. Clare's been lucky enough to track down the third and we all know what happened to the colonel. Josie, I want you and your team to head out to Preston and check out Michael Marshall's house. Clare said he's listed as living with his mother. If he's not there, see if you can get any info from the old dear. That might just be his mailing address. He may have somewhere else that he actually lives. I can't warn you enough about how dangerous FOTS is. If anything inside or outside the house looks in the least bit suspicious, make sure you call the bomb squad. In fact, now that I think about it, it might even be better to call them and have them check out the place, before anyone goes in. If there's no answer at the door, then get the squad to check things out, both on the exterior and inside before you go in.'

'No worries,' said Josie. 'Where are you going?'

'We'll be heading to Bundoora to check out the residence of one Mr. August Richers, who was also involved in the rape.'

'Okay,' said Josie, 'I guess there's not much else to be said, let's get going.'

'Hang on,' said Russell, rushing to the rear of the lab. He looked in the fax machine and found some papers, which he divided into two piles as he returned. 'These are the warrants we'll need to use to gain entry inside the properties, just so everything is nice and legal.'

Josie took possession of one pile of papers and then she and her team headed out the door.

CHAPTER TWENTY-EIGHT

August Richers sat at the bar of the Bundoora Hotel talking to a striking blonde woman, buying drinks for friends who sat in a far corner of the room. 'Looks like you're out celebrating tonight?'

'Yeah,' replied the woman, 'it's my twenty-fifth birthday.'

'Well, let me buy you a drink, too. It's the least I can do.'

'Why, thank you,' said the woman, exposing a toothy smile, 'that'd be nice. Why don't you come over and join us?'

'Yeah, thanks,' said August. 'Let me just pay my tab here at the bar and I'll be right over. I'm August,' he said extending his hand.'

The woman laughed. 'I'm April,' she said taking his hand in hers. 'I guess we're both months of the year.'

'Miss April,' said August with a good natured chuckle, 'you sound like a pinup girl from Playboy and let me tell you, you pretty much look like one, too. I mean that in a good way, so don't take offence.'

'I'm sure you do, and I don't take offence at all,' said April giving him an approving smile. 'I'll see you soon.'

He paid his tab and headed over to the table to join the women. He found out they were all old college friends who'd attended La Trobe University in their younger days, which was located not far from the hotel and it had become something of a tradition for them to return here, when any of them had birthdays or other significant events occurred in their lives.

August waited until all four of them had consumed enough alcohol to impress them with his adventures as an

SAS soldier and about his time in Afghanistan. He told them a constant barrage of lies about his exploits as a hero and about the friends he'd lost in ferocious imaginary battles that had gone on for days, and then as his crowning glory, showed them his tattoo of the SAS insignia, which he'd had inked into his shoulder while on leave in Thailand.

At nine o'clock, he leaned over, whispered into April's ear, that he had a significant amount of amphetamine in his pocket, and wanted to share it with her, but not with her friends, because he felt she was special. She looked at him in a way that told him his whisper had been successful, grabbed him by the hand and then two of them said goodbye to the other women, who hooted about the great sex they were going to have as August and his conquest left the hotel.

Once out in the street, August suggested they go to her place, as his was a pigsty and he didn't want to expose her to his soldier-like environment. 'You're far too nice,' he added as he kissed her on the mouth, causing her to respond with equal enthusiasm.

'Okay,' said April as she pulled away from him and hailed a taxi in front of the hotel.

Mark, who'd been sitting half a block away in his Volvo, started the car and followed the taxi, watching the two of them make out through the back window of the cab and smiled. 'Enjoy it, while you can, August,' he said, 'because it's not going to last.'

The taxi headed through the city, even more deserted in the darkness that it was in the daytime. It reminded him of a ghost town, or some science fiction novel where the entire human race had been wiped out due to a rapidly spreading pandemic. He'd seen a movie like that recently, in which there was only one man left alive in the whole of New York City, along with his dog, a German shepherd, and victims of the disease, who'd become mindless killing machines, but could only go out at the night. He remembered that the star of the movie was Will Smith, but the title much to his annoyance, eluded him. He remembered though it was a remake of a Charlton Heston movie called The Omega Man, which in his opinion had been a much higher quality film, even though it lacked the computer graphics and special effects of the latter.

He passed over Bourke Street, which intersected with Little Collins Street, the site of the stock exchange bombing, still cordoned off by crime scene tape, which ran across the entire street, guarded by uniformed police. He wished that he could've got a better view of the damage he'd caused, but doing anything other than passing by was more of a risk than he was prepared to take. There'd been enough footage on the television over the last day to satisfy his curiosity, but of course, it was nothing like the real thing, with the smell of death lingering in the air, while bits and pieces of debris continued to fall from the wrecked building, making loud crunching sounds as they hit the pavement. Watching the police and forensics team trying to fit all the pieces together and gather up clues and evidence would have been a real kick, but alas, it was just not to be.

The taxi crossed over the Westgate Bridge, took a few turns into suburbia, and stopped outside a cream-coloured weatherboard house in Footscray.

Mark stopped the car, turned off the lights and watched as both August and April exited the cab, and headed into the house. He hated looking at this Richers fellow from a distance, with his ruggedly handsome face, long greying hair pulled back in a ponytail and toned body and just wished he could jump out of the car and kill him in the street, but knew that would attract too much attention. He saw the scenario in his mind. He would shoot Richers, the woman would scream before he could get a bullet into her brain, curtains in the adjacent houses would be pulled back to see what was going on and, inevitably, the police would be called. They would arrive in force, because he'd used a gun and then he'd have to make a quick escape and the odds would be distinctly against him.

He hated it when the odds were against him. He was a planner and not one to go with the emotion of a moment, although he did pride himself on his adaptability and sense of improvisation. One had to be flexible when undertaking such nefarious tasks and if he was anything, it was adaptable.

Mark waited until the two of them went inside the house and saw the living room light come on. He got out of the car and stole up the street, opened the front gate and walked up to the window. He saw the pair of them snorting some sort of white powder off a coffee table adjacent to the sofa. He stood away from the window and pondered the situation. He figured that the powder was either meth or cocaine, something to enhance and prolong the sexual experience. Heroin wouldn't have that effect. It would only send them off to sleep. It also posed another problem. He wanted to enter the house when they were both asleep and use the element of surprise to his advantage, but with the stimulants in their bloodstream that wouldn't happen for quite a while. He'd have to rethink things and possibly come back early in the morning, after the two of them were spent and exhausted. He looked at his watch and saw it was almost ten. He would need to get back to the embassy, so he could deal with Best and Bakas. Once he'd accomplished that, he'd work on destroying the embassy itself and then return. It seemed like the most logical plan.

There was also Chris Knight to consider and he'd yet to think of a way of getting to him through the army security that surrounded the barracks in Watsonia. The current atmosphere of terrorism in the city had seen a tightening in security, so no one got in or out of the campus without a pass. He'd already tried keeping watch for him outside, but the man never seemed to leave the place and it was no wonder; the uniform depot supplied his clothes, there was a pub on the campus and a mess hall, where he could go to eat. The place was virtually a self-contained little world and the sergeant had little reason to leave, given the place catered to all of his needs. It was something he would need to think about, but he was sure, in the end, he could do it. No one's untouchable. All he needed to do was surmount the obstacles in his path in order to get to the goal.

Mark left the house, strolled causally back to his car, started the engine, moved the gearshift, and took off for the city. He made good time due to the lack of traffic on the road and passed through the city at ten-thirty. It took him another few minutes to get to his place of work and soon he was entering the embassy through the automated gates at the front, using the remote control and his personal PIN provided to all embassy attaches.

He parked the Volvo out of sight, in the underground car park, went to the back of the car, and removed a cooler from the trunk. He used the remote again to release the elevator and rode it to the second floor, where he placed the cooler in the bathroom of his office. He looked at his watch and saw that it was almost quarter to eleven.

'Good,' he said as he inspected the interior of the cooler, making sure there was adequate ice inside, 'plenty of time.'

He then went from room to room in the embassy, starting at the reception area on the ground floor and moving toward the back of the building, seeking out the remote controls for the spilt system air conditioners dotted around the place, and setting them at sixteen degrees Celsius, which was the lowest setting on the controls.

At five minutes to eleven, he took the elevator back to the second floor, took a seat in his office, and waited for the phone call that would hail the arrival of the law enforcement officers.

At two minutes past eleven, the phone rang. He smiled to himself as he picked it up and said hello into the receiver. 'It's Leigh Best and Eddie Bakas here. We had an arrangement to pick up some information from Mr. Andersson.'

'Yes, that's me,' said Mark. 'Hang on and I'll open the gate and meet you out front to bring you in.'

'Thanks,' said Leigh and then hung up the phone.

Mark went to the front entrance of the embassy and used his remote to open the gate. He smiled as the car pulled up out front and Leigh and Eddie got out. 'So, how'd you go with the info?' Eddie asked as the three of them walked inside.

'Very well,' replied Mark. 'I think what I have will blow you away. I even have a fair idea of who the man you are looking for might be. Please, follow me to my office and we can get started.'

'That's great,' said Leigh. 'The commissioner's going to be chuffed. We'll make sure you get all the credit, too.'

'Thanks,' said Mark trying not to laugh, 'I'm just glad I could help to further the cause of justice.'

The three men walked to Mark's office. 'Please take a seat,' he said, 'I have the info right here,' he said as opened a desk drawer, pulled out a Beretta pistol, equipped with silencer and shot Leigh in the forehead, causing him to slump forward in his chair. Eddie went for his gun, but Mark held the pistol pointed straight at him. 'Don't even think about it,' he said. 'Get out your gun, slowly and slide it onto the desk over towards me.'

Eddie did as ordered, taking the .38 from his shoulder holster and sliding it across the desk. Mark picked it up and threw it down on the floor behind him. 'Now, get Mr. Best's gun and do the same. Don't try anything. I'll kill you before you have a chance to put a round in the chamber.'

'All right,' said Eddie as he removed the gun and repeated the process. 'So, it's you, is it? You're the Fire of the Son.'

'Yes,' replied Mark with a laugh. 'I told you I had the information you wanted. I even told you I had an idea about who the Fire of the Son is. Don't you think that's funny?'

'Yeah, I get the irony,' said Eddie, 'but I can't say I'm amused.'

'One last thing,' said Mark. 'Get out both Leigh's and your identification and put them on the desk.'

Eddie removed Leigh's federal identification and his own police badge and ID and placed them in front of him.

'Now, say goodbye,' said Mark as he shot Eddie in the front of the head and killed him, causing him to slump to the floor.

'Okay, lots to do,' said Mark as he stepped out from behind the desk and removed the car keys from Leigh's pocket and placed them in his own. He dragged both men into his bathroom and left their bodies lying on the floor, their lifeless eyes staring up at the ceiling. 'Thank you both, you've been of a great service, to both me and The Prophet.'

Mark took the cooler from the bathroom and left it outside his office. Then went from room to room and turned on all of the air conditioning units, so that the place would be cold by the time he arrived back. He stopped for a cigarette and calmed himself, asking himself if there was anything, he could possibly have forgotten. When nothing came to mind, he rode the elevator to the ground floor and placed the cooler next to the reception desk. He felt the air around him and knew the compound would be stable. He opened the cooler and took out a small paintbrush and a litre tin of paint, which contained the clear liquid compound. He used the handle on the brush to open the lid and began by painting the back of the receptionist's computer and the inside doorhandle to the front entrance. He then put a coating over the elevator buttons, both inside and out, after pressing the button which would take him to the second floor. He first went to the ambassador's office and painted the space bar on his computer with a thick coat and then the back of the computer itself, so when he turned it on, he was certainly going to get the surprise of his life.

He moved steadily from the front to the back of the building, coating surfaces at random, knowing once the first explosion went off, it would set off the other unexploded coats of compound in a chain reaction that would move forward with every successive explosion until the building was demolished from front to back. Just for a laugh, he went to the break room and coated the exterior of all the staff mugs.

'Yeah, that coffee is going to have some kick to it, once you add the hot water.'

Mark could see it all happening in his mind. The staff would all arrive at work together and would wait for one of the attachés or the ambassador himself to open the door and then the receptionist would flick on her computer while she headed for the break room to make coffee. It would only take a minute for the rear of the computer to reach the required twenty-three degrees and then it would explode at just about the same time as the first mug in the break room went and then the elevators, and so on, and so forth.

Mark looked at his watch and saw it was almost two in the morning. He would take the federal police car Mr. Best and Mr. Bakas had so graciously provided and drive back to Footscray and take care of August and his girlfriend, so if he was pulled up for anything on the way, he could flash his ID and say that he was on police business. The ID was clean and it'd be a while before those in authority noticed Leigh and his colleague hadn't returned from their errand to the embassy. That was one of the stupid things about detectives, he thought to himself as he dumped the compound container in a rubbish bin and headed for the front door, they always worked such conventional hours.

CHAPTER TWENTY-NINE

Josie raised the binoculars from behind the car and looked at the door of the Preston House. 'There's a note on the front door, but it's folded over so I can't read whatever's written on it.'

'If I know anything about our man,' said Le Mar, 'I bet it says something clichéd like, 'Bang, you're dead!'

June laughed. 'I think we need to send in the bomb squad before we head inside. There's still no answer on the phone,' she added as she placed her mobile back into her jeans pocket.

Josie left her colleagues and walked over to the black van parked just down the street, outside of which, several men and women clothed in black body armour looked at what was happening with the house. 'We don't know for sure, but we think the note attached to the door might be soaked in that same explosive compound.'

'Okay,' replied Senior Sergeant Gary Allan, coordinator of the Victoria Police Bomb Squad, 'so we need to cool it down and it'll be harmless?'

'I'm no expert,' said Josie, 'but I can let you talk to one. Larry Batts from technical seems to know what he's talking about when it comes to this stuff. I'll get him on the phone.'

'Yeah, thanks, Josie,' said Gary, 'that'd be good. I've never dealt with this shit before, so a knowledgeable head would come in handy, right about now.'

Josie dialled Larry's number on her mobile phone, handed it over to Gary when it answered and walked back to talk to June and Le Mar. 'June could you call the local cops, so we can seal off the area? Le Mar and I will do a house-to-house for ten houses either side, as well the places directly opposite and move them all up the street. If this thing blows, no telling just how bad it's going to be. He might have others planted inside. Let's just be safe, rather than sorry.'

'Sure thing,' said June, removing her phone.

'Let's do the houses directly next door first,' suggested Le Mar, 'and then we'll do the others. I'll take the opposite side. You take the other.'

'Yes, sir,' joked Josie, teasing her colleague. 'How very assertive of you, Le Mar.'

'Hey, anytime I get a chance to tell you what to do, superwoman, I'm gonna take it, you can bet your sweet arse.'

Josie was about to enter the front yard of the house next door when Gary Allan called out to her. He jogged up and handed back her phone. 'I talked to Larry Batts and he confirmed what you said. He's on his way. I've sent one of my men up to the local service station to get a load of ice and we'll use a waste paper bin from the van to contain it. Larry said that the compound explodes at twenty-three degrees Celsius, or higher. The outside temperature right now is twenty. If it's treated, we're safe for the time being. Larry also said he's been in contact with the Israelis only a few minutes ago and has got some sort of spray that he can use and then shine UV light onto, to tell if the compound's present.'

'I tell you, I'm glad Larry's on our side,' said Josie with a laugh, 'he'd be a bad bastard if he was a crook.'

'Yeah, he would,' laughed Gary. 'While we're waiting for Larry to get here, I'll get my men to help you to clear the other houses and then we'll go and have a look-see about that note.'

'Thanks,' said Josie, moving off.

It took about twenty minutes to notify the nearby residents of the danger and get them to what the police considered a safe zone, about one hundred metres from the Marshall house. By which time, the uniformed police had arrived, thrown crime scene tape across the road and were keeping the citizens and the media who arrived not long after, out of the area.

About ten minutes later, Larry Batts pushed his way through the crowd, showed his police ID to the uniformed officers, and was then admitted to the crime scene. 'Hi,' Gary said with a smile as he walked up to the van. 'You must be Larry Batts.'

'Yeah, that's right,' replied the scientist, 'and I'm assuming you're Gary Allan.'

'Got it in one,' said the bomb squad coordinator. 'So, what have you got for us, Larry?'

'I just spoke to the head of Mossad. I left a message with him this morning, but due the time difference, he only just got my message.'

'Yeah, righto,' said Josie impatiently, 'so, what did he say?'

'I'm getting to that,' said Larry, as he reached inside his backpack and produced a can of fly spray, which he handed to Gary. 'If you spray this onto the paper and hold up a UV light, you should be able to see if the compound's present. It'll show up bright white under the ultraviolet. Once you get inside, spray the whole place, and then let the spray settle for a few minutes before you use the light. I've brought half a dozen cans and some extra battery-powered UV lights for your men.'

'That's great,' said Gary. 'We've only got a single UV light in the van. It'll save us a lot of time.'

'Hey, boss,' called out one member of the bomb squad, 'we're ready whenever you are. We managed to get a cooler from the fella at the servo to put the ice in.'

'That's good, Mick,' replied Gary. 'Could you accompany Mr. Batts back to his car and get a few things we're going to need for entry?'

'Sure,' said Mick as he and Larry took off towards his car, 'be back in a minute.'

Gary took the binoculars from Josie and raised them towards the porch of the house, where the veranda light shone from a dim bulb out into the darkness of the front yard. 'I wonder how long that note's been attached to the door. Either it's not been there for long at all, or it's not treated. It was thirty degrees today, so if it was hanging there, it should've exploded.'

'I see what you're saying,' said Larry, returning with the gear, 'but you're not taking into account the possible variables. There are a number of trees out the front of the house, which probably provided significant shade and may have kept the temperature lower than exposing the note to the direct sunlight, combined with any breeze passing the house, although all of this is a guess, at best.'

Gary laughed. 'Fucking nerds - destroy the world with 'em, but can't live without 'em.'

Once the bomb squad was ready, three of them led by Gary Allan, made their way through the front yard of the house and up onto the porch. Gary sprayed the note with fly spray and one of his colleagues used the UV light to see if the paper was compound treated. He turned around a few seconds later and gave the thumbs up sign, which Josie and the others interpreted as meaning that the note was clear. Gary grabbed the note from the front door, placed it into an evidence bag he'd brought along for just such an occurrence and walked it back out for Josie, Le Mar, and June to inspect. Typed out in capital letters was a note to Clare.

SORRY SARGEANT CARBONE, BUT YOU MISSED
THIS ONE.

Josie took her phone from her pocket and immediately phoned Clare. She told her about the note and the situation with the house. 'The bomb squad are going to spray the place and if we get the all-clear, we'll go in and see if there's anything in there worth salvaging as evidence.'

'Can you get the note to me straight away? Rob might be able to do his thing with it. It might lead us somewhere.'

'I'll do better,' said Josie. 'As soon as we're done here, I'll drive the note over to Rob, personally. Larry can take the others back to the taskforce building in his car.'

Clare laughed. 'No wonder they call you superwoman, you're not just a pretty face, are you?'

'Nope, and I've got a great arse, too,' said Josie with a chuckle.

'All right,' said Clare, 'Just let me know what's going on and get Rob to call if he sees anything important. I'm just about to interview Chris Knight and then I'm going to apply for his remand in custody, with the on-call magistrate, who's not going to be happy about being woken up at some ungodly hour, once I've done the interview.'

'Good luck,' said Josie.

'You too,' replied Clare. 'I'll call Russell and tell him what's going on, and be careful.'

'Yes, Mum,' said Josie as she laughed and hung up the phone.

Josie looked up and saw that Gary and the same two colleagues were entering the house for the second time, this time wearing masks, which she assumed were to protect them from the fly spray that would imminently be filling the inside.

'Officer,' called out one of the reporters from behind the police tape, 'would you like to make a comment?'

Josie turned her back to him and walked over to join June and Le Mar who stood watching the house, waiting for the bomb squad to return. 'I just called Clare. Once we're done here, Larry can take you back and I'm going to take the note over to Rob and see if there's anything he can see.'

Le Mar looked at her and his dark face turned cloudy as he frowned. 'No way, Josie, I'm coming with you.'

'Yeah, me too,' added June. 'You never know when things are going blow up and you need our help. They might call you superwoman, but you're not, really.'

'Yeah,' said Le Mar with a laugh, 'don't believe your own publicity.'

'Well, I guess that's settled,' said Josie. 'Look,' she added directing her gaze back at the house, 'they're coming out.'

Gary walked over to the trio and removed his mask and helmet. 'It looks as though it's all clear. I'd give it a minute for the fly spray to settle down properly before you go in. The place is going to smell like a chemical plant. We emptied three full cans inside the place. No flies will be able to inhabit the place for the next hundred years. You three want a coffee before we head off? I've got a full thermos in the van.'

'Yeah, sounds good,' replied June.

'I'll have a double,' said Josie.

'Make that two,' said Le Mar as the four of them made their way to the back of the van.

The detectives drank their coffees and watched as the bomb squad packed up their gear. Russell got permission from Larry to borrow some of the lights and to take the fly spray to the next crime scene in Bundoora, and the van left the scene.

Josie went back to the car, opened the glove compartment, and retrieved a box of surgical gloves. She took out four pairs and handed one pair each to the detectives and another to Larry. 'Okay, are we right to head on in?'

'After you,' said Le Mar, gesturing towards the house with a wave of his hand.

Josie led the way into the residence. Once inside, they decided to take a room each and look for anything that may add up to evidence or some sort of clue.

June took the living room and saw that there was an address book lying beside the phone. She picked it up and looked through it and opened it to the pages with names starting with the initial M, and saw Michael's phone number. She took out her mobile phone and rang the taskforce office, asking them to trace the phone number and put an address to it. One of the taskforce detectives told her it was an unlisted number to Michael Marshall and the address belonged in Whittlesea, on a property located on the outskirts of Melbourne. June wrote down the address, thanked the officer, and hung up the phone. She dialled the number, but an automated voice informed her it was currently out of order. Using her phone again, June through the directory service, managed to connect to the Whittlesea police station, and asked to speak to the office in charge. She spoke to a Sergeant David Anthony, gave him her ID number, which he looked up on the COPS database to confirm, and then asked what he could for her.

June explained the situation to the sergeant, who listened intently. She asked if somebody could go straight out to the Marshall property and see to the man's safety.

'I'm afraid you're too late,' said the sergeant. 'There was an explosion out there, yesterday. We just assumed it was an accident. Marshall had a reputation for drinking too much, too often, and doing stupid things. I, personally, arrested him a few times and threw him into the tank so he could sleep off the grog. There were two bodies found at the scene, or actually, the little of what was left of two bodies. The coroner thought they were a man and a woman, although he wasn't known for having a woman, and was a bit of a loner.'

'I'd say the woman was his mother,' said June, 'and I think they were both murdered by the Fire of the Son.'

'Thanks,' said the sergeant, 'I'll let the coroner know, right away. Jesus, that bastard must really be filling up the drawers in the morgue by now.'

'Sadly, to overflowing, we need to catch him, soon. We think he's got worse planned.'

'Are you getting close?'

'Yeah,' replied June, 'but not as close as we'd like to be.'

'Good luck,' said the sergeant.

'Thanks,' said June as she hung up the phone.

The other detectives, who'd stopped working and listened to the phone call, all walked into the living room.

'So, the note was right,' said Josie. 'I don't hold out much hope for August Richers at this stage.'

'I'll phone it into Clare,' said June.

'No worries,' said Josie, 'we'll keep looking and see if there's anything else we can find. I suggest we wait until the forensics techs arrive to go over the place and then head over to Rob with the note.'

'Sounds like a plan,' said Le Mar.

CHAPTER THIRTY

Russell used the binoculars to look at the house up the street from where he sat parked. There didn't seem to be anything that stuck out as being particularly suspicious about the dwelling. There was no note on the door, although anything could've been hidden in the jungle at the front of the property, which a mower hadn't seen for some time, judging by the length of the grass that was over a foot high in places. The living room light as on, but he didn't see any shadows of movement behind the curtains, nor was there any noise emanating from the place, which he noticed the lack of when he did a casual walk-by a few minutes after arriving.

He breathed a sigh of relief when he looked in the rear-view mirror and saw Gary Allan and his crew from the bomb squad come driving down the road, followed by a convoy of marked police cars from the Bundoora station.

Russell, Marcus, Annie, and Rob got out of the car and met the van as it pulled up. He asked the uniformed officers to start evacuating the houses on either side of the street and to set up a perimeter around the house, with crime scene tape to keep everyone back.

'Could we get some lights put on the house? I don't like the way the grass hides everything up to the front door.'

'Sure,' replied a female senior constable, 'I'll arrange for that, right away.'

'There's going to be media here, soon, you can bet,' said Gary as he started to attire himself in his protective gear. 'They were at the other house, too.'

'Fucking vultures,' said Russell. 'You can bet FOTS will be watching it, too. I don't know how they hear about these things so bloody quickly.'

'The public informs them, especially where we're concerned. There've been far too many bombs going off in this city of late. Wherever we go, the media is sure to follow. It's almost eleven, too, so there's probably not a whole lot going down around the city. If we can get this job out the way before they get here, there won't be much to report on.'

'Agreed,' said Russell. 'Are you just about ready to go? It looks like the uniforms have everyone back behind the tape.'

'Okay,' said Gary to his team as he armed himself with the UV lights, a can of fly spray and placed his mask over his face, 'let's go. I want to get home soon. My missus cooked a roast a few hours ago and I don't want it to go to waste. Besides, my wife's temper makes any bomb we're ever going to come across look like a firecracker.'

'You and your bloody roasts,' laughed another of the officers from behind his mask. 'You need to lose weight, anyway, you fat slob.'

'Come on,' said Gary leading the way to the front door.

Russell watched the three officers as they entered the property and couldn't help but to have great admiration for their bravery. They willingly entered a place where they knew there was fair chance of getting themselves killed, or having body parts blown off them at any moment, leaving them permanently disabled. He speculated that they must get some sort of amazing adrenalin rush from the experience, but it wasn't a career choice he'd even considered when entering the force. Busting drug dealers and going undercover was dangerous enough, but what these men and women did was, in his opinion, almost downright crazy, but admittedly, as brave as all hell.

'You couldn't pay me enough to do that,' he said aloud without realising the thoughts had left his mouth.

'Yeah,' said Rob, 'it'd be one tough job, you'd have to have nerves like bloody steel.'

Russell turned around, startled by the reply to his words. 'Shit, you scared me,' he said and out of reflex placed a hand on Rob's shoulder, and for a moment, Rob got a glimpse of Clare sitting up in a hospital bed, looking completely exhausted, having just given birth to a child and saw the two of them looking down, smiling at the baby in her arms. Just as quickly as the vision appeared, it was gone and Rob found himself standing again outside the house of August Richers.

A few minutes later, Gary, and the other two bomb squad cops came out of the front door and gave the all-clear signal to the rest of the team.

Russell gave a visible sigh of relief and thanked Gary and his team for their assistance. 'You can go home now and have that roast your missus made. You've certainly earned it.'

'Thanks,' said Gary. 'There's no sign of a body, from what I could tell.'

'That's good,' said Russell, 'it could even mean he's still alive and out somewhere. From what Clare said about him, he's a bit of a larrikin with an eye for the women. It seems he got into a few dust ups as a result of his liking for the opposite sex.'

'Well, good luck with everything,' said Gary as he got into the rear of the van and prepared to leave the scene.

'Thanks,' replied Russell, 'I think we're going to need it.'

Just as the bomb squad van was about to leave, they all looked over and saw the television news media arrive. One of the reporters knocked on the door of the van as it passed through the crowd to try to get some sort of comment, but whoever was behind the wheel ignored the woman and drove on.

'Okay, we need to get inside the house and out as soon as possible,' said Russell, handing out pairs of surgical gloves. He then went over to the unformed cops guarding the crowd and asked them to tell the people they would soon be able return to their homes.

The detectives, followed by Rob, walked into the house and immediately noticed the smell. 'Christ,' said Annie, 'it stinks worse than if somebody did die in here.'

'That'd be the takeaway food,' said Marcus, pointing to the leftover containers strewn all over the place. 'What a bloody pig.'

'You say this guy used to be in the army?' Annie asked as she dabbed vapour rub under her nose and passed on the jar. 'Aren't they neat freaks?'

'Yeah,' replied Russell, 'the SAS, actually and, yeah, they are neat freaks, but apparently, not our August.'

'How many rooms are there?' Annie asked. 'I want to get out of this dump as soon as possible.'

'There are two bedrooms and the living room, plus the bathroom, and toilet,' replied Russell. 'I can't wait to see the condition of those.'

'Yeah, well, you're on your own,' said Annie, heading for one of the bedrooms with Marcus trailing behind with a grin.

'That's why you get paid the big dollars, Russ,' he added with a laugh before disappearing.

Rob and Russell looked around the living room and aside from a bit of pot, which August had left unsmoked, there was nothing suspicious. 'Not you'd notice if there had been a struggle, in all this mess,' said Russell.

'What about this?' Rob asked holding up a photo that had fallen face down on the mantel. 'It looks like it might have been taken not too long ago.'

Russell took the photo and examined it. It showed two men fishing, beers in hand, holding up a couple of large trout beside a river. 'Yeah, we'll keep that to identify him. Good work, Rob.'

'No worries,' said Rob feeling as if he'd just accomplished his first actual police work.

'You guys find anything?' Russell sang out to the others.

'No, nothing that'd qualify as evidence,' replied Annie, returning to the living room. 'A bit of drug paraphernalia, but that's about all.'

'Yeah, same here,' said Russell, pointing to the pot. 'We found what looks to be a recent photo of him, but fuck all else we can use. All right, we need to try another tactic. Let's split up, and go and see if we can gather any info from the neighbours about Richers' habits. We might come up with something that way.'

'Good idea,' said Annie. 'Anything to get out of this cesspit.'

Marcus and Annie made their ways to the next-door neighbours, while Rob and Russell went across the road and knocked on the door of the house opposite. 'Aside from the neighbours, houses in this spot are often the ones that see the most of all. You'd be surprised how many reports we get from houses opposite to drug dealers, as opposed to next door. They also make the best spots for surveillance, for obvious reasons. What time is it?'

Rob looked at his watch. 'It's after one.'

'Shit,' whispered Russell.

'Who's there? I've got a gun in here,' said a woman's voice from behind the door.

'It's the police,' replied Russell. 'I know it's late, but we were wondering if you could spare a few minutes to answer some questions about the man who lives opposite.'

'How do I know you're the police?'

'We have ID,' replied Russell. 'If you'd just open the main door, you can leave the wire door locked and we can show you who we are.'

There was silence for about thirty seconds and then the door opened enough for a pair of eyes to peer out at them. 'Show me your identification, please.'

Russell and Rob both produced their police ID and placed them flush against the wire door.

'You don't look like a copper. Copper's don't usually have beards,' said the woman.

'I know,' said Russell, 'I usually work undercover for the drug squad, see, like it says on my ID'

The door opened wider and an old woman, dressed in a robe, with long grey hair tied to the top of her head in some sort of sleeping arrangement, looked closer at the detective's identification. 'All right,' she said, 'I believe you, but you can't come in.'

'Fair enough,' said Russell. 'We just wanted to ask you some questions about the man who lives opposite you, his name's August Richers.'

'Yes, I know August. He's always been nice to me. He's an awful drunk, always coming home and singing at the top of his voice in the early hours of the morning, but as I say, he's always been nice to me. He helps me out of my cab when I get back with my shopping if he happens to be out on his porch, smoking a cigarette and sees me.'

'Sounds like a real nice fellow,' said Russell. 'Do you happen to know where he drinks?'

'As a matter of fact, I do,' replied the old woman. 'My husband, Kerry, gone now three and a half years, God bless his soul, used to have a drink or two with August down at the Bundoora hotel. Kerry said he was always in the bar till closing, most nights.'

'Are there any chances of getting directions to the hotel?'

'Sure,' said the old woman, opening the wire door and stepping out onto the porch, apparently, without thinking. 'If you go straight down Plenty Road for about a couple of kilometres, then turn left at Station Street and drive for about another half a kilometre, you'll see it on your left, you can't miss it.'

'Thank you very much,' said Russell, 'and I do hate to be a bother, but could I possibly get your name for the records?'

'It's Jacinta… Jacinta Fowler, but my friends call me Jazzy.'

'You've been a big help,' said Rob. 'We'll let you get back to bed.'

'Thanks,' said Jazzy as she headed back inside and closed the door after her.

'Come on,' said Russell, 'we need to get straight down to the Bundoora.'

The two men walked across the road and met by Josie and the others as they entered the street, gaining entry when they flashed their identifications at the police who had now moved the tape to the front of the Richers residence.

'He drinks down at the Bundoora Hotel, most nights,' said Russell.

'One of the other neighbours told us the same thing,' said Marcus. 'Apparently, there's a nightclub there, open til two.'

'June, could you stay with Rob? There's no sense in taking him to a place where FOTS might be.'

'Not a problem,' replied June.

'Rob, you do your thing with the note and the rest of you can come with me. I know it's a long shot, but we might be able to catch Richers if he's still at the hotel. I have the photo, so we can ID him. Call me on my mobile phone if the note provides anything.'

'Sure,' said June, 'good luck. I think we'll go look for somewhere local we can get a coffee and have a sit down on a decent chair.'

'Okay,' said Russell looking at his watch, 'it's almost half past one. The nightclub's only open for another half hour, so we need to get down there, pronto.'

Rob and June took the note from Josie and headed for the car in which June and the others arrived, while Russell and the other detectives took off at speed in his car. A minute later, the street was almost silent, interrupted only by the quiet whisper of the two uniformed police officers standing guard in front of the Richers' place, smoking cigarettes in the dark.

June started the car, drove up to the cops, and wound down her window. She handed one of them a card with her name and mobile phone number on it. 'Give me a call straight away, if Richers happens to show up.'

'Sure thing,' said the smiling young man, taking the card and putting it into the breast pocket of his uniform jacket. 'I sure hope you get this prick,' he added.

'Me too,' said June as she wound up her window and moved off out of the street.

CHAPTER THIRTY-ONE

Clare looked at the man sitting opposite. He was nervous and she couldn't blame him. Outwardly, he was trying to convey the picture of a calm and collected individual, but little things only an experienced detective would know, gave him away; like the tiny beads of sweat on his forehead that glistened on his skin whenever he moved his head to a certain angle under the light. He blinked like he was nervous, too, a subconscious trait resulting from agitation she'd seen a hundred times. She waited for Ray to return with the coffees they'd ordered prior to starting the interview. She was glad he'd accepted Ray's offer of coffee, because Ray would be sure to make it extra strong, keeping Knight wired and talking.

'Okay, here we go,' said Ray as he came through the door followed by Peter, who held a third cup that he placed on the table and left the room. The senior sergeant placed the large mugs down, and pushed one towards Chris Knight, who grabbed his cup with both hands and brought it up to his mouth.

'Thanks,' he said. 'You make a good cup.'

'My pleasure,' said Ray. 'Now, we need to attend to the business at hand. Before we do that, though, we need to issue you with a cautioning, informing you of your rights.'

'Sure,' said Chris, 'I understand.'

'Clare, would you do the honours?' Ray asked as he leaned over and switched on the recording machine to the side of the table.

Clare waited for a moment for the recording to begin, not wanting to miss anything. 'This interview with Mr. Christopher Knight is being conducted by myself, Sergeant Clare Carbone from the major crime squad, officer number 244186 at the Fire of the Son Taskforces office at one-fifteen a.m. on Saturday, 3rd February, 2010.

'In attendance also, is Senior Sergeant Raymond Owen, from the major crime squad,' said Ray. 'Officer number 488090.'

'Christopher Knight,' said Clare, 'you're attending here this morning in order to answer a series of questions in regards to a case of aggravated rape that occurred in Afghanistan sometime between March and April of 1995. Do you understand that?'

'Yes,' replied Knight, taking another sip of his coffee.

'You have the right to remain silent, but anything you do say, may be taken down and used in evidence at later proceedings. Do you understand this right?'

'Yes, I do,' said Knight. 'To tell you the truth, I'll be glad to get it off my chest.'

'You may seek to have legal counsel present during this interview, at which time the interview will be suspended until such counsel arrives. Do you understand that?'

'Yes,' replied Knight, 'I do. I'm not asking for a lawyer, right now. I'll probably need one later for court, but right now, I just want to get it all off my chest. It's been playing on my conscience for fifteen years and it's about time that poor woman got justice for what the four of us did. It was a despicable act and whatever the court does to me isn't going to be half as bad as the way I've been beating myself up over it for the last decade and a half.'

'So, you do understand all of your rights?' Clare asked again, just to be sure and for the benefit of the tape.

'Yep, loud and clear,' replied Knight.

'Good,' said Clare taking a sip of her coffee. 'I'll now ask you a series of questions in regards to the incident.'

'Fire away,' replied the sergeant.

'Can you tell me who was actually involved in the sexual assault?'

'Yeah, there was Major Murphy, Captain Mike Marshall, and Corporal August Richers, and me. That was all, just the command staff, none of the grunts.'

'So tell me about the rape.'

'Well, it's a bit of a long story, actually.'

'That's okay,' said Clare taking a sip of her coffee and wishing she'd gone out for a cigarette before the interview started, 'we're not going anywhere and I've got plenty of time.'

'Before I do that,' asked the sergeant, 'I'd be interested to know how you found out about it. It's not like any of them other fuckers would've confessed.'

Clare grabbed a manila folder, which she'd set down the table prior to the commencement of the interview. She opened it and took out a set of three photos, which she slid across the table, one at a time. For the benefit of the recording, she said aloud that she was showing Knight three photos of Daniel Murphy, taken post-mortem, at the crime scene.

'The first photo is of Colonel Murphy slumped over in his chair, his confession stabbed into the back of his neck, which the coroner believes happened after he was killed. The second photo is a close-up of his face. Do you want to know how he died? He had his penis and his testicles cut off and shoved down his throat and a gag placed over his mouth. The coroner is unsure at this stage, as to whether he choked or bled to death. The third photo is a close-up of the confession, which details the rape that took place in the desert. There, are you satisfied?'

'Yeah… yeah, I am,' replied Knight as his face turned almost completely white. 'Who the fuck did this?'

'It was the son of the woman you and your buddies raped,' replied Clare, trying hard not to sound too sarcastic, but feeling as if she was failing in the attempt.

'This was done by the Fire of the Son,' chimed in Ray.

'Are you telling me that the kid who was there, is the same maniac who's been blowing up everything around the city, to get back at us, for the rape?' Knight asked incredulously as tears began to fall from his eyes, when the realisation of the enormity of what he'd done came crashing down upon him.

'Yeah, that's just what I'm telling you,' replied Clare. 'Now, we need to get back to you telling us about the rape.'

Knight blew his nose on a tissue from a box on the table and began to tell the story. He let his mind drift back to the desert, to the night he remembered as if it was yesterday. 'We'd destroyed a village in the middle of the desert after hearing some of the terrorists that had ambushed us a few days before might be hiding there. We fucked off all the villagers and sent them on their way. One of the troopers accidentally killed some bloke, who was the husband of the woman we assaulted and the father of the boy. They were both pretty upset, as you might imagine, and the major told us not to let them bury the man and to just shove his body into the rubble of the village. Once all the villagers were gone, we set up camp and kept an eye on the place, just to make sure no one came back and to see if any of the terrorists showed up, perhaps looking for weapon caches hidden around the place.

'Richers received the order to keep a lookout for anyone entering the village throughout the night. At about midnight, he saw two people enter the ruins, informed me, and then the captain and the major were alerted. He was pissed off about having to wake from a deep sleep and ordered both Richers and I to enter the village and to take the trespassers alive, if possible, for interrogation. Once we'd done that, we were to radio back and the colonel and the captain would attend and interrogate the suspects to find out about the weapons. We set off into the darkness, equipped with night vision glasses, body armour and our guns. When we got there, we saw that it was the wife and the kid of the man killed earlier on that day. They had dragged the body of the man from the rubble and had dug a hole to bury him. We captured them without much of a fuss, coming in both behind and in front of them. They weren't armed and surrendered like a couple of frightened sheep.

'When the colonel arrived, he was livid and vowed to teach them both a lesson. He beat the boy to within an inch of his life and left him lying in the dirt. He then ripped the clothes off the woman and raped her, there and then, right in front of us. Richers and Marshall got off on the whole thing, cheering for the colonel while he did the deed. When he'd finished with her, they both gladly took turns raping her in the sand. When those two animals were finished, the colonel told me I had to do it, too, because if I didn't, it would put them all at risk and if I didn't, he'd kill me and make up some story about a struggle between me and the woman for my gun and that I got shot and killed. To tell you the truth, I couldn't get it up and frankly, I didn't want to. I found the whole thing more than a little distasteful, but couldn't do anything about it, without losing my own life. I lay down on top of the woman and pretended I was fucking her, but I didn't actually penetrate her, just kind of pumped away with my pants down around my ankles, and acted the part. I remember looking at her face and seeing the tears flowing down her cheeks and I never in my entire life, or since, have felt like such a louse, such a human scumbag. She seemed to know what I was doing and kind of smiled sadly, looking at me with such compassion. I'll never forget it.'

'What happened after that?' Clare asked as she took notes.

'Richers and Marshall wanted to kill them both, but the major didn't want shots going off that might bring the rest of the company down to the village. He told me and Richers to take them in the jeep he had driven down, out into the deep desert, a couple of hours away and leave them there. He said they'd die of thirst before the end of that day. I remember him saying that it'd save ammunition, too. He was a cold bastard.'

'Did you take them?'

'Yeah, we took them, all right. I didn't have much of a choice. We left them in the desert just before sunup, but when Richers wasn't looking, I dropped my canteen, which was about half-full of water, off the side of the jeep and left it in the sand, where I hoped they'd see it. I guess they must have, if they lived.'

'So, why didn't you report all of this when you got back from Afghanistan?'

'I honestly don't know,' replied Knight, shrugging. 'I guess maybe it was out of some sort of distorted loyalty for those guys, perhaps the fellows who'd died and I guess I didn't want to tarnish the name of the army. It's been good to me all my life. It's all I've ever known as a job and I'm pretty good at it.'

Clare shook her head and breathed a deep sigh. 'Look, Chris, I guess I have some sympathy for you and you pretty much had me, up until the point where you said you said you had some sort of loyalty towards those bastards, and they were bastards for what they did. I don't know if they deserved the deaths they got, but it was despicable act and to force a kid to watch, well, I don't even know what to say about that.'

'Yeah, you're right. I should have reported it, I wish I had, now.'

'Chris,' said Ray, 'I'm now informing you that you will be formally charged with aggravated sexual assault, conspiracy to attempted murder, and accessory to attempted murder, which was when you left the two of them in the desert, knowing that there was a good chance they'd probably die of thirst. Even with your half-full canteen, they may have still perished, had not luck been on their side, however that happened.'

'We'll be applying for you to be remanded in custody for the time being,' said Clare, 'both to reduce your risk of flight from justice and to protect you from the Fire of the Son, who it seems, would very much like to get hold of you.'

'Sure,' said Chris, 'I understand.'

'One more important thing I didn't ask you before,' said Clare, 'is did you know the names of the woman and the boy?'

'I remember the name of the boy, because his mother cried out his name when the major was beating him. It was Arkmed and her name was Ishtar, I think.'

'What about their surname?'

'Haziz, or Hazeil, something like that, I'm not real sure.'

'Thank you, I think that pretty much covers everything, for now,' said Clare scribbling down the name.

'For the benefit of the tape,' said Ray, 'this interview is now concluded at two-fifteen a.m. Mr. Knight will be taken to processing, where formal charges will be laid and he will then be taken before the on-call magistrate, where an application for remand will be made.' Ray turned off the tape, gave Clare a surreptitious look, knowing he didn't want to hear what was about to be said between Clare and Knight and left the room to join Peter.

Once the door closed, Clare leaned over to Chris. 'Look, Chris, I'm not telling you what do, but it seems you're person of good character, you have a place to live, excellent references, and no priors. There's a good chance that if brought before a magistrate, you'll get bail. If that happens, then there's also a good chance that the Fire of the

Son is going to get you. We can't look out for you every moment of the day, but if you're in custody, then at least you'll have a fighting chance. If you were to say something that perhaps gave the magistrate the impression you might take flight, then he or she would have little choice but to keep you locked up until your next court appearance. Like I say, I'm not telling you what do.'

'So, what happens to me from here?'

'I'll have some uniformed cops take you down to the city watchhouse and you'll be formally charged, and then the on-call magistrate will attend and decide if you're eligible for bail, or whether to remand you to custody. Somebody from the crown prosecutor's office will also attend and argue vigorously for remand in this case. There's quite a lot to figure out, given the offence occurred on foreign soil, committed by Australian citizens and about who has jurisdiction in the case. Just wait here and somebody will be in to get you soon.'

'Okay,' said Chris, 'and thanks for all your help, Sergeant Carbone. It feels like a weight's been lifted off my shoulders, being able to tell somebody about it, after all these years.'

'No worries,' said Clare as she made for the door. 'See you later.'

'Yeah, I'm sure you will,' said Chris.

Clare left the interview room, walked two doors up, and entered another room, which was full of both federal and state taskforce members who stopped watching the closed circuit television as she walked in the door.

'Good job,' said Peter, patting her on the back. 'At least we know what happened to start all this off and have the Fire of the Son's real name.'

'Yeah, Arkmed,' said Clare.

'Yeah,' said Peter, 'and we know, too, that he's a Swedish citizen, or has spent time there, thanks to Rob. We're getting close, Clare, I can feel it. That reminds me, has anyone seen Leigh Best and Eddie Bakas? They were supposed to go and get that list of names from the Swedish Embassy at eleven.'

There was a consensus in the room that no one had seen them.

'Can someone call Leigh on his mobile?'

'Yeah, I will,' said one of the other federal officers, who pulled out his phone, went through the contact numbers, and dialled Leigh's phone. He waited until the ring went to voicemail and then left a message asking that Leigh call him. 'No answer,' he said as he hung up the phone.

'I have a bad feeling about this,' said Peter as he left the room and went to Leigh's desk, followed closely behind by Clare. He opened up the appointment book on top of the desk and then the blood drained from his face. We need to get some people over to the embassy as soon as possible.'

'Why?' Clare asked. 'What's wrong?'

'The name of the senior attaché that was supposed to supply the list of Swedish citizens in Victoria is named Mark. It all makes sense. He's a Swedish citizen and the attachés drive Volvos, it's their national car, and the name... Mark... I bet that's what he uses instead of Arkmed.'

CHAPTER THIRTY-TWO

Rob watched as the blonde man with the intense blue eyes, scribbled out the note on a wooden dining table. He turned when he heard the soft sobbing of a woman from behind him and saw an elderly woman, sitting in her nightclothes on the floor, looking petrified.

'Okay, so that's what you really look like without the disguises,' he said as he moved closer to the man.

The blonde-haired man looked at his creation, laughed and then turned and slapped the woman across the face, telling her to be quiet. He then cut the cords from the blinds in the living room, bound her hands behind her back, and used a dishtowel from the kitchen sink to gag her mouth.

'We're going to go for a little ride,' he said to her, 'and visit your son, Michael. Won't that be pleasant? It was so good of you to offer his address to me, thanks for that.'

The woman sobbed behind the gag, her eyes wide with fright.

The blonde man pulled a knife from out of his jacket and placed the point of it at the old woman's throat, digging it in slightly so that a drop of blood slid down her neck. 'I'm going to get the car ready and if you're not in this exact spot when I get back, then there will be severe consequences, do you understand? Please nod if you do.'

The old woman nodded, conveying her understanding.

Rob watched through a crack in the living room blinds as the blonde man left the house, leaving the door slightly ajar, went out to the front, and proceeded to back a Volvo sedan up the driveway and around to the back of the house, leaving it opposite the garage and adjacent to the rear door of the property. Rob looked out through the kitchen windows and saw him pop the trunk and leave it open as he headed back.

Once inside, he grabbed the old woman by the hands and stood her up to her feet. 'Don't make a sound when we get outside,' he said, 'or you won't make it to the car.'

Rob watched as he walked the old woman outside in the darkness, bundled her into the trunk, and closed the lid. He returned to the house, folded the note, stuck it onto the grate on the security door out front, and locked the front door and the rear door as he went. He jumped into the car, removed a set of gloves he'd been wearing and placed them into the console beside him, started the engine, and moved off.

He memorised the numberplate to the car, which seemed to be sort of unusual, like diplomatic plates. He thought about trying to get into the car, but decided against it. He needed to get back and tell the others what this fellow looked like, so the police could issue an alert. Besides which, he had fair idea about what had happened to both Michael Marshall and his mother and didn't need to see what had occurred in between them arriving and the explosion, which had destroyed the house. Rob closed his eyes, concentrated, and found himself sitting again in the all-night café that he and June had gone to in order to get coffee and keep themselves awake. He blinked at the brightness of the overhead fluorescent lights and tried to compose himself.

'I know what he looks like and I've got the numberplate to his car.'

'Great work,' said June, grabbing her phone. 'We need to let Clare know straight away.'

'Okay,' said Rob. 'You do that and I'll order another coffee and go to the loo. Give me your notepad and I'll write the number down.'

June handed over her notepad and Rob scribbled down the car's numberplate and then went off to the bathroom, ordering a coffee from the fellow behind the counter as he went. He closed the door to the bathroom behind him and looked in the mirror. He'd never seen himself look so completely haggard. The strain of the investigation was beginning to show on every inch of his face. He just wished it was all over and they'd already caught the bastard. He thought that death, in the end, might actually come as something of a relief and although he didn't know exactly where it was going to come from, he could feel the end of his life inching its way inexorably forward, as though it was twilight and night must soon fall. 'I guess that's just the way of things,' he said to his reflection, which smiled sadly back at him.

Rob returned to the table and spoke to June. 'Clare told me they know who FOTS is. He's some senior attaché at the Swedish Embassy, goes by the name of Mark Andersson. The ambassador's on his way there now, as well as half a dozen members of the taskforce. He's going to provide us with an address, so we can do a raid on his place before morning. Hopefully, he won't be aware of us coming and might have the nuke there.'

'That'd be great,' said Rob, feeling uneasy about the news, 'but it just seems a bit too easy.'

'Let's hope not,' said June. 'Come on, we need to get out of here. I told Clare we'd meet her at the embassy.'

CHAPTER THIRTY-THREE

While the other detectives spread out and looked around the crowded nightclub, hoping to spot August Richers, Russell went to the bar and waved to get the barman's attention.

'Hang on a minute, I've got customers who were here before you,' replied the barman, who looked like an old bikie, covered in tattoos, wearing a leather vest without anything underneath.

Russell banged loud and repeatedly on the bar and the barman turned around, seeming at first angry, but quickly settled down when he saw the police identification in the detective's hand. Several other patrons saw it at the same time and moved away, leaving a space at the bar where the two of them could talk.

'Have you seen this man?' Russell asked, producing the photograph and handing it over to the barman.

'Yeah, that's August, the no good bum. What trouble has he got himself into this time?'

'Plenty,' replied the detective. 'Has he been in tonight?'

'Nah, he doesn't usually come into the nightclub. He mostly haunts the public bar until closing and then makes his way elsewhere.'

'Was he in the public bar tonight?'

'I dunno,' answered the barman, picking up some glasses from the bar and drying them with a dirty dishtowel. 'I only work in here from ten onwards. Terry's the man you want to talk to, but he goes home after the bar closes at ten.'

'Have you got a contact number for Terry?'

'Yeah, hang on a minute and I'll get it. He sometimes relives me here, so we got a relievers' book, with all the names in it.'

'Thanks,' said Russell as he looked around the bar. Apparently, the word had spread that he was a cop and several people avoided eye contact with him as he scanned the place. *Going to have to do a drug bust here, sometime.*

The barman returned a short time later with Terry's number scribbled on a napkin, which he handed over the bar. 'There you go,' he said. 'Anything else I can do you for?'

'No, that's plenty,' replied Russell as he took the napkin.

'Good,' said the barman. 'If you wouldn't mind making yourself scarce, I'd appreciate it. Having cops around is bad for business and the customers don't like it.'

Russell smiled. 'Yeah, no worries, I'm outta here,' he said as he headed for the door, tailed by the other detectives, who blended into the crowd as they usually did in similar situations, when working a bust for the drug squad.

Outside, Russell dialled the number. It took a few rings before a tired sounding voice answered the phone. 'Who the fuck is this? You know what time it is?'

'Sorry to wake you,' said Russell, 'and I wouldn't have unless it was urgent.' He went on to explain who he was and asked about August and if he'd been in the public bar earlier on that night.

'Yeah, he was there,' said Terry with a yawn. 'He managed to sleaze onto some chick and left the place with her about nine, or half-past, thereabouts.'

'She wasn't a regular, too, was she?'

'Semi-regular,' replied Terry. 'I've seen her and her mates there a few times, but I wasn't on first name terms with them or anything. I think they were all old Latrobe

Uni students, who meet back there for birthdays. I saw the chick he took off with, though. She wasn't bad.'

'I don't suppose you know where they went?'

'No, no idea, sorry, mate.'

'Okay,' said Russell feeling somewhat disappointed at the outcome of the call. 'Thanks for your help and sorry for waking you.'

'Yeah, not a problem,' said Terry as he hung up the phone.

'It looks like August managed to pick up in the bar,' Russell told the other detectives. 'Hopefully, he's all right.'

CHAPTER THIRTY-FOUR

August Richers woke to the feeling of water splashed onto his face. He blinked his eyes, wiped his face with the back of his hand, and looked up at the man who had the knife to his throat and placed the empty glass down beside the bed.

'I suppose you're the boyfriend, are you? I can explain...'

Mark laughed and looked over at the woman in the bed, causing August to cast a glance to his left. He saw April, struggling for breath and clutching desperately at her throat, as the carotid artery in her neck bled out, spraying the dresser next to the bed with her blood, which spurted out in a long stream, along with each successive beat of her heart. The two of them watched her, one with fascination and the other with horror, until the blood stopped and she lay still.

'What sort of fucking maniac, are you?'

'You're going to find out, soon enough,' replied Mark as he brought the handle of the knife hard down on August's head and knocked him unconscious with one swift, heavy blow.

When August next opened his eyes, he shivered in the early morning cold, looked around, and saw that he was in a field of some sort. He tried to move his arms and legs but found he'd been pegged to the ground on his back, naked, his arms, and legs held firmly in place by ropes attached to wooden stakes that had been hammered into the ground.

'What in Christ's name is this?' he called out. 'Okay, look, I screwed your girlfriend, but it's not a bloody capital offence.'

Mark laughed from behind him. 'I wouldn't know that stupid little slut if I tripped over her in the street,' he said.

'Then what in fuck's name is this about? Did I rip you off for some money? Did I forget to pay my credit on some meth bill or something? I'm sure we can work it out.'

Mark laughed again, 'No, nothing so tiresome or mundane. I'm here to repay a debt to you, one you accumulated in Afghanistan, about fifteen years ago.'

'You want to tell what this is about? Because I'm pretty well fed up with trying to frigging guess.'

'Okay,' said Mark as he kicked August hard in the ribcage, feeling his ribs splinter under his shoe, 'let me just jog your memory. About fifteen years ago, you and your major, a captain, and a sergeant, raped a woman who only wanted to bury her husband, after one of your men destroyed our home and killed him. There was a young boy there, only thirteen years old, who the major almost beat to death and forced him to watch, as you and the others defiled his mother. Does that ring any bells?'

'Oh, shit,' said August as the blood drained from his face, 'that was you, the kid? I thought you died out in the desert?'

'Yes that was me, I'm the son, the Fire of the Son.'

'You're the fuckin' bomber?'

'I am, and after I'm done with you, I'm going to set off a nuclear explosion in the middle of the city. I'm going to kill the prime minister of Australia, half his cabinet and turn inner city Melbourne into a wasteland. You want to know something funny? I'm probably going to get away with it. You Australians are such idiots. You couldn't find your own backsides with a compass, a map, and a road sign thrown in.'

'Oh, no,' gasped August struggling with the ropes, 'this can't be happening. You're supposed to be fucking dead.'

'Yes, that's right,' said Mark. 'Because you left me and my mother for dead, and believe me, you're going to pay for it.'

'What in fuck's name are you going to do to me, leave me for dead here, to rot into the ground?

'No, I'm afraid that'd be too easy a punishment for what you did, the way you destroyed my life and my family. Let me explain,' he said as he moved towards August and towered over him, holding something in his hand. 'Behind you, there's a nest belonging to a colony of Mexican fire ants. I've covered over the nest with a Perspex box, so that none of them can escape. It will also make them very angry and want to attack upon their release. They're not native to Australia, you know. They emigrated here, probably on some tanker, which stopped in Mexico, or came out of there in the first place. They've been a big problem for this country. They kill the native ants and their bite is just like their name, akin to being set on fire. Absolutely agonising, from what I've heard. It took me a great deal of effort to find such a colony. I had to scour the countryside for months. I found a few other colonies, but they just weren't big enough, for what I needed, but here, there's a colony, undisturbed for a few years. I'd estimate them to be at least a hundred thousand strong. The thing about Mexican fire ants is that they're territorial. You get on their turf, they attack you in force, and of course, the more you struggle against them, the harder they attack, because they think you're attacking back. After a few hundred thousand bites and a couple of hours, you'll be dead and I promise you, you're going to go insane first and scream all the way to the grave, August. The other thing about Mexican fire ants is that like most ants, they're attracted to sweet things that contain sugar.'

'You're not really going to do this,' screamed August. 'Please, just shoot me and get it over with.'

'There'd be no fun in that,' said Mark as he turned over a jar and began to pour a thin trail off honey over August, beginning on his chest, and down onto his genitals and then trailed it over to the upturned box. When he'd finished with the jar, he threw it to one side and lifted up the gag around August's neck, placing it over his mouth and tightening it from the back, so that passersby wouldn't hear his screams. 'Goodbye, August,' he said as he walked over and kicked the Perspex box, letting the colony loose to attack, and then walked back to his car.

He lit up a cigarette and watched, leaning against the body of the police car and saw the angry colony race out of the nest and up onto August's body. He smiled as August started to twitch and spasm with agony, when the ants began to sting him and to increase in their ferocity as he reacted to the bites.

He listened for a little while to the music of August's agonised muffled screams from under the gag and took a mental picture of the scene in his mind, as he got into the police car, started the engine and drove off, enjoying the early morning breeze as it blew through the window and ruffled his hair.

'Now, for the grand finale,' he said as he headed back to the city.

CHAPTER THIRTY-FIVE

Clare was in her car with Peter and Ray, on their way to the Swedish Embassy, when she got the call from the taskforce office to say that the place had exploded and six police and the Swedish ambassador were all inside at the time of the blast.

'Apparently the whole embassy just caved in,' said the federal officer over the loudspeaker. 'They didn't stand a chance.'

'Shit,' Clare screamed at the top of her voice and began smashing her fist on the steering wheel. 'I'm going to put a bullet into that fucker's head myself, if it's the last thing I ever fucking do! We should have known he'd do something like this to cover his tracks!'

'Pull over, Clare,' said Ray, 'that's an order, I'll drive.'

Clare pulled the Commodore to the side of the road and got out. She started banging her fist on the hood of the car as tears streamed down her face. Ray took her in his arms and held her while she sobbed into his chest, feeling hardly able to control his own tears.

'It's not your fault, Clare. It's his, that son of a bitch. We're going to catch him, real soon, you wait and see.'

'Why didn't they send the bomb squad in first?'

'I don't know,' replied Ray. 'I guess they thought their colleagues were in danger and went in all gung-ho, without thinking.'

It took Clare a few minutes and a cigarette to compose herself, then the two of them got back into the car, and Ray insisted on driving. 'Nothing against you, really,' he said, 'but I know how angry you can get, Clare and I'm just looking out for everybody else on the road. It's that Latin temper of yours.'

'Yeah, and fuck you, Owen,' she retorted and looked out the window, feeling ashamed that a smile could find its way onto her face.

The three of them rode the rest of the way to the Swedish embassy in silence. They listened to the early news reports that filtered out over the car radio, which told them next to nothing, except that there had been an explosion at the embassy, that the damage had been severe and several police and one high-ranking diplomat were included amongst the casualties.

As Clare pulled up, she saw a row of body bags lined the street behind the crime scene tape. Emergency crews were still going through the wreckage, but held out little hope of finding any survivors from the building, which was almost levelled.

'Hi, Clare,' said a familiar voice from behind her. When she turned around, she saw Rob standing there, along with June. 'We just got here.'

'Yeah, me too,' said Clare looking down at the body bags and sighing. 'Rob, isn't there anything you can do to help us find this lunatic? This is just going to keep happening until FOTS is either dead, or he sets off the nuke. We have to find that nuke in the next twenty-four hours, or we'll be forced to evacuate the city and if he sees that happening, he's likely to set it off earlier.'

'I need something of his, like a hair, or something he uses a lot,' replied Rob. 'If I can get that, I can follow his psychic trail, but without it, I can only see what his victims see up until they die.'

The two of them just stood on the curb away from the embassy, transfixed by the wreckage of the building, watching as more bodies collected on the sidewalk, losing all track of time. They went for a walk, grabbed a coffee from a local Seven-Eleven, and returned about an hour later, after hardly having spoken a word between them and just stood there again, watching the sun come up over the building and seeing the devastating scene in the cold light of day.

'This like some sort of nightmare,' said Clare.

'Yeah, just it's so surreal,' agreed Rob, 'I can hardly believe what I'm seeing.'

Peter walked over to join them. 'I've just been on the phone to immigration. They do a police-check on all foreign nationals entering the country, diplomatic status, or not. It seems that Mr. Andersson has an apartment in Carlton and not far from here. They're sending a photo of him to the taskforce office as well.'

Ray heard the news from where he was standing. 'I want the bomb squad contacted and given the address. We're not going to make the same mistake, twice. I want that apartment scanned from roof to fucking floor before anyone sets foot in it.'

'Okay,' said June, 'I'll phone the taskforce office and get them to contact Gary and his crew.'

Clare looked at the rubble and again at the line of body bags. She knew Eddie Bakas was among them and she hated Chris Knight and his soldier comrades for what they'd done. Eddie had twins, about six or seven years old and he'd been a devoted father and husband. Somebody was going to have to tell his wife about what'd happened and how he'd lost his life. She thought it'd best be coming from Ray and Peter as the ranking officers in the case. She was lost in thought when her phone rang. Ray tapped her gently on the shoulder and brought the noise to her attention.

'Oh,' she sighed as she grabbed the phone from the pocket of her jacket and raised it to her ear. 'Hello, Clare Carbone here.'

'Hi, Clare, it's Joey Martell from homicide. 'I've just read the alert put out by the taskforce, looking for a girl and a guy who were at the Bundoora Hotel last night. We have a DOA here, in Footscray, with her throat cut, by the name of April Osborne. Her friend came to pick her up for a workout this morning. Figured she was a bit hungover and used her spare key to get in. She found her lying in her bed, bled out. It seems that she left the hotel with August Richers, who's our main suspect at this stage.'

'No, it wasn't Richers. FOTS must have followed them from the hotel. He probably has Richers somewhere as we speak, torturing him in some unique and colourful way. We can expect Richers' body will show up somewhere later and he won't be a pretty sight. I'm going to come over and look at the scene with some of the other members of the taskforce. Have forensics arrived yet?'

'Yeah, they've been here for a while. It doesn't look like they're about to wrap up anytime soon.'

'Okay,' said Clare, 'give me half and hour and I'll be there. Don't let the coroner remove the body. I want to try something unusual. Could you give me the address?' she asked as she grabbed her notepad and pencil from the inside pocket of her jacket and jotted down the street and house number.

'Okay,' said Joey, 'see you when you get here.'

Clare dialled Russell's phone and found he was back at the taskforce office. 'We came back here, when we had no luck with August Richers. I let the others catch up on a bit of sleep and put out an alert, asking to contact either me or you if any information came to hand.'

'Yeah, I just got a call from homicide. It seems they found the woman who left the Bundoora with Richers.'

'Dead, I suppose,' said Russell sipping on a coffee.

'As a doornail,' replied Clare. 'I was just going to head over there with Rob and see if he can pick up on anything. I was hoping maybe you'd care to join us. I think I'm getting a bit used to having you around.'

Russell laughed. 'I do grow on people... like fungus. I suppose you're at the Swedish Embassy?'

'Yeah, it's a fucking disaster. Those poor people inside didn't even have a chance to get out.'

'How are you doing, Clare?'

'Don't ask,' she replied feeling tears begin to well in her eyes. 'I've sure started the day in a lot better ways. I feel angry. If I could murder this person, I think I'd do it, without the slightest hesitation.'

'Yeah, me too,' said Russell, looking at his watch. 'It's almost seven now, how about we meet at the house at say, eight?'

'Sounds good,' said Clare, 'I need to stop and get another big cappuccino to get me through the rest of the day. The sun's only just come up and I'm feeling exhausted already.'

'Well, let somebody else do the driving, then,' suggested Russell, 'you don't want to go falling asleep at the wheel.'

'Jesus, not you, too,' said Clare as she hung up the phone and sought Ray amongst the crowd of people, ambulances, and police cars at the scene. She told him about the murder in Footscray and that she was taking Rob and heading over there, and would be meeting Russell at the crime scene.

'Take June with you, too,' said Ray, 'and that's not a request.'

'Me?' asked June, who was standing nearby. 'Where are we going?'

'I'll tell you on the way,' replied Clare. 'Could you go and get Rob and the three of us will take off.'

'Once you've finished over there,' said Ray, 'give me a call and we'll meet at Andersson's apartment. It's probably going to take a while before the bomb squad clear the place. Give me a call, too, if anything unusual pops up at the scene over there.'

'No worries,' said Clare. 'I'm probably going to stop by my place, too, and take a quick shower and get a change of clothes. I smell like a feral dog.'

'Okay, talk to you later,' said Ray, who pulled his phone from his pocket and began to make a call.

Clare, Rob, and June left the scene and headed to Clare's apartment in East Brunswick. She let June drive after giving her directions and took the opportunity to call the taskforce office. She spoke to one of the state police officers, Mandy Crompton, and asked that someone get the dead officers' addresses and next of kin, so that Ray and Peter could go and visit with their families to inform them of the terrible and tragic turn of events.

'Sure,' said Mandy, 'I'm on it. At least we know the name of the arsehole we're after. Immigration just sent over his photo and I have to tell you, he really does look like an evil bastard.'

'What does he look like? Can you give me a description?'

'Yeah,' said Mandy, shuffling papers on her desk to retrieve her copy of the photo. 'He's got blond hair and the most intense blue eyes you ever saw.'

'Thanks,' said Clare. 'Just give that info to Ray or Peter when they get back to the office, will you?'

'Not a problem,' replied Mandy. 'Anything else I can do for you, while I'm here?'

'No, nothing else I can think of,' replied Clare. 'I'll talk to you later.'

'Bye,' said Mandy as she hung up the phone.

Clare looked out the window at the passing houses, and people in the street. There was something in the back of her mind she just couldn't quite put her finger on. As the car pulled up at a set of traffic lights, she saw a blind man and a golden retriever cross the road. She looked at the eyes of the dog as it passed in front of the car and, suddenly, the thought she wanted came to the forefront of her mind. She turned to look at Rob sitting in the back of the car.

'Rob, didn't you say that this Arkmed fella had brown eyes when he collected the bomb from off the tanker?'

'Yeah, that's right,' replied Rob. 'I remember distinctly that he had brown eyes, dark hair, and a beard, but I remember having the feeling he was pretending to be something that he wasn't.'

'I just got the description from the taskforce and Mark Andersson has blue eyes and blonde hair. So, now we know for sure that he uses disguises to make himself look different.'

'Isn't that going to make him harder to catch?' June asked as the car pulled up outside Clare's apartment block.

'Probably,' replied Clare, 'but at least we're getting more information on him as we go and you know what they say, knowledge is power.'

They left the car in Clare's security parking space underneath the building, which Clare accessed using a swipe card from her wallet and then took the stairs up to her place. Clare held her breath as she opened the door and sighed with relief.

'Good, the cleaning lady's been. The place was a bit of a mess when I left. Come in, you two, I'm just going to take a quick shower and change and then we can be on our way. Rob, there's a card on the phone table next to the sofa, could you ring up and order me a large, extra-strong cappuccino and get whatever you two want. We can pick them up on the way through.'

'Sounds good,' said Rob as he let himself fall onto the sofa and grabbed the card and cordless phone from the nearby table.

'You're not worried about FOTS watching the place?' June called out to her from the living room.

'He can't be everywhere at once,' replied Clare, sorting out clothes from a chest of drawers. 'I suspect he's probably off enjoying himself while he tortures August Richers to death right about now.'

'Okay,' said Rob hanging up the phone, 'the coffees will be waiting when we get there. I've put them under your name.'

'That's good,' said Clare, heading for the bathroom with a pile of clothes, dressed in her nightgown. 'I feel like I haven't had a good coffee for bloody days.'

Clare walked into the bathroom, turned on the shower, which always took a while to heat up and placed her clothes on the bathroom bench. She looked at herself briefly in the mirror and then applied make up remover to clean her face. When the bathroom started to fog up, she walked over to open the window and saw that the condensation had gathered on the outside of the shower and the word SWIFT spelled in large, capital letters. She realised in that moment that FOTS had been there, entered her private domain and how badly he wanted both her and Rob dead and out of his way.

'Fuck,' Clare yelled as she came barrelling out of the bathroom. 'We've got to get out of here, now! He's been here!'

Rob and June took about one second to comprehend what Clare was saying and together, the three of them ran out of the apartment, almost stumbling over each other in their rush to avoid what they knew was going to happen any second. They made it to the stairwell when the compound exploded, ripping the front door of the apartment off its hinges, and sending it over the balcony, crashing to ground below, where it managed to avoid causing any casualties. Clare looked cautiously around the corner of the stairwell, and saw that the apartment was well and truly on fire. 'Christ, that was close,' she said as she leaned back against the wall and breathed a sigh of relief.

'Yeah, too close,' said June.

'I guess the cleaning lady wasn't the only one to do a job on your place,' said Rob.

'No, I guess not. June, grab your phone,' said Clare. 'Call the fire brigade and then get Ray on the line.

CHAPTER THIRTY-SIX

It was six in the morning when Mark heard on the car radio that the Swedish embassy had exploded. 'Shit,' he said to himself, knowing that soon or maybe even already, the police would know exactly who he was.

He pulled into the apartment block and parked the police car in a vacant space close to the building. He took out his keys as he headed for the stairwell, dismissing the elevator as a waste of time. He puffed as he took the stairs two and three at a time and finally made it to the landing on the third floor, where he stopped for a moment to catch his breath. He headed for his apartment and opened the door with his key. He decided to put the kettle on and have a quick coffee, knowing it would take them a little while to get his address, now that the embassy was in ruins. He wasn't a registered car-owner and the lease on the apartment was private. They could, perhaps, gather his details from immigration, dating back to when he had to sign the criminal check forms before entering the country, or from the Swedish ministry of foreign affairs, who had the details of all embassy staff on file. That would take a while, though, due to the time differences between Australia and Europe.

While the kettle was boiling, Mark went to the bedroom and removed the silver suitcase, which contained the nuclear device from behind the back of his wardrobe, and placed it on the bed. He then took another case, which he had already prepared, just in case of a situation developing, like the one in which he found himself and placed that onto the bed as well.

He knew it was stupid thing to do, leaving the nuke there, and he should have left it at the hotel, but he couldn't help it. The urge to just drag it out sometimes and open it, imagining the power and force of the detonation, the fate of thousands held in his hands, was just too great to resist and so he'd elected to leave it in his apartment. He berated himself for his lack of judgement, but now he just had to cope with the situation, like it or not.

He used the key, which he wore around his neck to open the case and looked inside at the device. Every time he inspected it, he couldn't help but to marvel at the elegance of it, the sheer wonder of its design. He leaned over and kissed the digital readout panel, as if kissing a lover.

'You are beautiful,' he whispered to it and then closed the lid and locked it. Mark took the two cases into the kitchen, made a coffee, and watched the television for a while, amused by the destruction of the embassy. He was pleased to find the ambassador had perished in the explosions as well as another attaché and, of course, the police he'd killed.

He thought about the portion of unused compound in the refrigerator as he reached for the milk, but decided not to use it. It had become too predicable a method and besides, if he knew anything about police methodology, they would assume he'd coated the place with it, anyway, and it would take them quite some time to check it out before they came inside. He wondered if Clare Carbone's residence was still intact and if she'd yet taken her last shower. She was a smart woman. Too damn smart for his liking and killing her would be something of which he could be proud. Most of the idiots he'd managed to dispose of, he felt, were beneath him, mere imbeciles, but Clare, and Rob Swift, for that matter, would be kills he could wear with pride and something he could brag about upon his return to Afghanistan.

Mark finished his coffee and decided to leave the television on, just to confuse matters when the police arrived. He took the two suitcases out into the lobby of the apartment block and locked both the main door and the security door behind him and then took the elevator to the ground floor, and placed the suitcases into the trunk of the unmarked police car. He took one last look at the apartment above him. He'd liked living there. It'd been both comfortable and functional.

He drove over to Ringwood and went to his room via the back stairs of the Lotus Garden Hotel. He took the silver case up, returned for the other, and parked the car at the rear of the car park, shielded from the street. Once inside, he turned on the air conditioner, which rattled and hummed as it blew cool air into the room and lay down on the bed. He could afford to rest for a little while, for tomorrow would be his big day, the time of the grand finale, the day when the name Mark Andersson would go down in the annals of history. He laughed as he rolled over, finding it exceedingly amusing that everyone in this country would hate Mark Andersson, that poor bastard, whose bones lay bleaching at that the bottom of the ocean. His only mistake had been to fit the profile needed for the Prophet to put his plan into action, and by doing so, help him to seek his own private revenge. Tomorrow would be the day, he thought to himself as he dozed off and dreamed dreams of death and destruction.

CHAPTER THIRTY-SEVEN

'Here you go,' said June, handing over the bags to Clare. 'I got you a pair of Levis, a t-shirt, a pair of sneakers, and some sports socks. I also got you a thin tracksuit top to cover your shoulder holster. I know it's rather informal, compared to what you usually wear, but it's the best I could on short notice.'

'That'll be fine,' replied Clare, taking the bag and heading towards the bathroom, still attired in her robe.

'Carbone,' called out a gruff voice just as she was about to enter the bathroom.

Clare turned and saw the commissioner standing in the corridor. 'Sir, I'm sorry about my dress,' she said feeling embarrassed.

'No need to apologise, I heard about what happened,' he said coming towards her, 'and I'm sorry. I know this bastard has it in for you and Swift. I just wanted you to know the department will compensate you for everything you've lost. It's only fair, and we'll set you up in another apartment as soon as possible. Until then, I insist that you stay at the Hilton... and keep up the good work. If he's trying to kill you, it means you've gotten under his skin and he sees you as a threat.'

'Yes, I suppose it does.'

The commissioner looked at her for another moment, as if he was about to say something else, but then seemed to change his mind. 'Carry on,' he said then turned around and headed back towards his office.

Clare went into the bathroom and changed her clothes. She borrowed eyeliner from June, applied it in the mirror, and then headed out back into the main taskforce office.

Ray started laughing as soon as he saw her.

'What's so funny, Owen?'

'I've just never seen you look so casual before. I'm so used to seeing you in your black skirt and jacket. It's just unusual, that's all. You look fine, though.'

'Glad to have your approval,' said Clare sarcastically as sat down at one of the desks. 'How's it going with Andersson's apartment? Has it been cleared to search yet?'

'Yep,' answered Ray. 'I just came in to tell you. I want you, Rob, and the rest of the team to get straight over there and search the place thoroughly. Oh, by the way, I got this for you, from technical,' he said holding out a shoulder holster, a Glock pistol, and a box of ammunition. 'I know you lost yours in the explosion and I don't want you going anywhere without being fully armed.'

'Thanks,' said Clare taking the gun, slipping out the magazine and loading it with bullets. 'Where are Russell and the others?'

'Right here,' said Russell from the doorway, trailed by Annie, Josie, Marcus, and Le Mar. 'Don't worry, Clare, we're never far away, especially after this morning. I'm going to stick to you both like frigging glue from now on.'

'Where's Rob?'

'He's in my office,' replied Ray. 'Poor chap, just isn't used to the rigours of police work. He dozed off while I was talking to him. It was actually very funny to see. Peter and I had a good laugh about it.'

'I've told him a few times,' said Clare with a smile as she made her way to Ray's office, 'that he'd never make a cop.'

'And I've told her, she'd never make a psychic,' said Rob, walking out of the office, blinking his eyes and yawning as if he'd just woken.

'We can go and look at Andersson's apartment now. It's been cleared by the bomb squad,' said Clare.

'Are you coming over, too, Ray?' Russell asked.

'No, I'm afraid Peter and I have the unenviable task of going to see the loved ones of the officers who were killed in the embassy this morning. It seems Andersson murdered Leigh and Eddie last night. Both of the bodies had bullet wounds to the head and were almost completely unrecognisable because of the burning. We still haven't been able to locate their car, but the emergency teams think there's a good possibility that it's under the rubble in the underground car park. We were able to identify them by their fingerprints. The state and federal commissioners are going to see their families, personally, to offer their condolences once we've broken the news.

'I don't want a word of what we've told you to leave this office, not even to other members of the force. The trauma these families are going to have to go through is bad enough, without having that knowledge, too. Is that understood?'

'I think I speak for us all,' said Clare, 'when I say we won't breathe a word. The best we thing can do is catch this prick, so we can honour them.'

'My sentiments, exactly,' said Russell. 'I couldn't have said it better myself.'

'Oh, by the way,' said Ray, 'there'll be a joint-memorial service to honour the dead from the stock exchange bombing and our officers, at St. Paul's Cathedral tomorrow morning, at ten. The prime minister himself had planned on attending, but given the level of risk he'd face with FOTS still on the loose, it's been decided that he'll attend the Sydney service instead and will do a video link up to the other churches involved.'

'Hang on a minute,' said Clare, 'how widely known is it that the PM won't be attending?'

'We've only just heard,' replied Peter. 'The PM's office has just released a memorandum to all relevant agencies.'

'So, do you think it's safe to assume that Andersson still thinks that the PM is going to be at St. Paul's, tomorrow?' Clare asked. 'He would've been informed that the he was going to be there, prior to the explosions at the Swedish embassy.'

'That's his target,' said Ray, 'that's where he's going to set off the nuke.'

'Christ,' said Russell, 'it's going to be like finding a fucking needle in a haystack. There's going to be thousands of people there. The streets will be jam-packed.'

'Especially if he's wearing some sort of disguise,' added June.

'All right, I think we need to start setting up straight away,' said Peter. 'I'm going to get some snipers onto the buildings opposite the cathedral. We need to circulate officers all through the crowd, each of them familiar with his likeness. We also need to have other officers within a wider perimeter. He doesn't need to get that close if he actually has a nuke, even a small yield bomb will destroy a half dozen blocks, at least. He just needs to get reasonably close to make sure he gets his target.'

'I've got another idea, as well,' said Clare.

'What's that?' Ray asked

'Rob,' replied Clare. 'We need to get over to this apartment and see if we can find something that'll help Rob to find Andersson's psychic pathway. We can track him by that. Isn't that right, Rob?'

'I can sure give it a go,' replied Rob shrugging, 'but I've told you before, all this psychic stuff is not an exact science.'

'Well, it's worth a try, in my book,' said Ray.

'Yeah, I agree,' said Peter. 'So, what are you doing, just standing there? Get out of here.'

'Okay,' said Clare. 'Peter, can you call Joey from homicide and tell him we won't be attending the crime scene in Footscray for obvious reasons and get that poor woman's body to the morgue?'

'Will do,' replied the commander, 'and good luck.'

CHAPTER THIRTY-EIGHT

Chris Knight woke at the sound of the siren. He slid off the top bunk, dressed in his green prison issue tracksuit pants and top, waited for the door to unlock, and then headed out of his cell for muster. He stood in line with the rest of the remanded prisoners and waited for the corrections officer to count him off. Once that was completed, he went back to his cell, collected his toiletries, and headed for the shower.

He didn't mind prison life that much. It was much the same as the army in many ways. A regimented life was, in the end, what he'd become used over the last twenty or so years. Of course, the people who populated the prison were vastly different from those soldiers in the army. Here, there was no honour and the man next to you would stab you in the back for a packet of cigarettes, so you had to watch out for yourself.

An old con in the prison van on the way over to the remand centre in Spencer Street, who could see that he was what they called a cleanskin, meaning he'd never served time before, informed him of the unofficial rules of prison life. The most important was to stand up for yourself, so if anybody had a go at you or tried to start a fight, be prepared to punch them to the ground and never back away, otherwise you'd be seen as weak, and an easy mark for anyone with a bit of muscle.

His first fight had occurred only a day after arriving, when some young punk had decided that he could take food off his plate in the dining room. Chris responded by smashing him in the head, then taking plastic plate, breaking it in two, and slicing open the man's face, so that it would leave a long and permanent scar. He then sat back down at the table and continued eating his food, as if nothing had happened. When the corrections officers rushed to the scene, the young fellow said he'd slipped and asked to be taken to the infirmary. After that, everybody pretty much left him alone.

Chris entered the shower room and stood underneath the water, letting it soak him and wake him up properly. He washed his hair and his body and was just about to leave when three very large men with huge, bulging muscles entered, and one of them pushed him back against a wall.

'So, you're a rapist, eh?'

'We don't like rapists,' added a second man leering over Chris' naked body.

'Get fucked,' said Chris. 'Mind your own business.'

All at once, all three men began throwing wild punches at him, sending him crashing to the floor, his arms held up in a futile effort to protect himself. He attempted to fight back, but found himself quickly overwhelmed by the trio, who threw him face down onto the floor and held him.

'Let me show you what we do to rapists in here,' said one of them as he penetrated Chris' anus with a soapy finger and then his penis, followed by the other two, who raped him until he bled from the rectum.

'Your death going to provide us with smokes, for a whole year,' said one of the men who grabbed Chris savagely by the head. 'By the way, Arkmed says hello,' he added as he snapped Chris' neck and left him dead on the floor of the shower, the water continuing to spray on his back and to wash away the blood and semen that leaked from his lifeless body.

CHAPTER THIRTY-NINE

Clare and Rob were the first to enter Andersson's flat. They looked around and although they trusted the bomb squad had cleared the place, including the five hundred millilitres of explosive compound found in the fridge, they both couldn't help but feel he'd left some nasty surprise for the two of them.

The apartment contained expensive, tasteful appointments, with a plush leather lounge suite and large LCD television in the living room, expensive cutlery, and even a few bottles of vintage wine stored in a rack in the kitchen. They both had to admit that he had damn good taste for a ruthless killer and psychotic lunatic.

'Jesus, the place is so neat,' said Rob.

'Yeah, it's too neat,' observed Clare, 'obsessively so, which is a sign of a highly organised mind, too.'

'I agree,' said Russell, looking through the only bedroom. 'It's a wonder he had any time to plant all those bombs. He must've spent hours upon hours, cleaning this place. Look, there's not one cobweb anywhere on the ceiling or in any of the corners in the whole apartment and there's not even a speck of dirt in the grout in the kitchen tiles.'

'Yeah,' said Annie, 'you might say that Mark and August were polar opposites in the way they kept their places.'

'It's fucking creepy, if you ask me,' said Josie. 'Let's just get this over with and get out of this fucking mortuary. It feels like a goddamn tomb.'

'Okay, come with me, Rob,' said Clare, 'and I'll show you something that, hopefully, this neat freak has forgotten.'

The two of them headed for the bathroom and Clare searched around until she found a hairbrush in the medicine cabinet above the sink. She looked close and smiled, noticing that there were several small blonde hairs at the base of the brush.

'Okay,' she said, extracting them with her gloved hands, 'I hope this is enough for you to do your thing.'

Rob pulled a glove off one of his hands and let Clare drop the hairs into his palm. He closed his fingers around them and suddenly, found himself standing in a room, not furnished in nearly the lavish style of the apartment, overlooking Andersson, who appeared to be sleeping on a single bed. Rob looked around and saw the silver case in a corner that Andersson had taken possession of, just prior to destroying the tanker down at the docks.

'Yes,' he said, 'now I've got you, you bastard.'

He looked around the room, suspecting it was some sort of cheap motel, probably attached to a pub, but there were no coasters or boxes of matches with the name on it to tell him where he was. He tried looking out the window, but Andersson had the blinds pulled down, so all he could see were glimpses of neighbouring houses, which gave no clue as to his location.

Rob tried to walk through the walls out into the corridor outside the room, but for some unexplainable reason, he couldn't leave the room. He figured it was because the hair was so minute it only provided him with a limited vision, as opposed to touching someone in the flesh. He remembered a similar thing had occurred when had touched some of Tony Green's blood and his consciousness transported to the site of his torture.

Rob gave up and decided to return to the apartment. He closed his eyes, concentrated, and was soon standing face to face with Clare again.

'So, did you see him? Can you track him?'

'Yeah, I saw him all right,' replied Rob. 'He's asleep in some shitty hotel room. I tried looking out the window, but the blinds stopped me. I can't open them physically to see what's outside and there was nothing inside with an address on it. I couldn't leave the room, either. I think it's because the hairs are so small a part of him. At least, though, we know the hair works, at least, partially. I can go back again and give you progress reports about what he's doing.'

'That's bloody fantastic,' said Clare. 'How often do you think you can go back?'

'I honestly don't know. Let's try every half hour and see how we go. It takes a bit out of me every time I do it and I'm already suffering from a lack of sleep now.'

'Did you say he was sleeping?' Russell asked from the hallway where all the detectives had gathered to watch Rob use his abilities.

'Yeah, he was sound asleep when I saw him.'

'Then maybe you need to do the same thing for a while. He doesn't sound as if he's about to do anything right away. It might be a good chance for you to catch up on some sleep, too, and recharge your psychic batteries.'

'I agree,' said Clare, taking an evidence bag from her pocket and holding her breath, while carefully depositing the hairs out of Rob's hand inside the plastic, and sealing it. 'We don't want to lose these,' she said, 'they're our only link to Andersson and the nuke.'

'All right,' said Russell, 'I think we all might as well head back to the Hilton. If you're going to sleep, Rob, you might as well do it in style.'

'Can we order room service, while we're there?' Josie asked. 'I'm bloody starving. All this running on adrenalin is great, but a girl's gotta eat.'

'Don't see why not,' said Russell. 'You got to celebrate the little victories on the way, and Rob being able to see this bombing bastard, is in my view, a victory, of sorts.'

'I might invite Larry up for a bite to eat,' said Annie with a smile, 'he has, after all, been a big help to us. He probably saved our lives.'

Josie laughed. 'Have you put that application in with the Mountie's, yet?'

'Nope,' replied Annie with a chuckle, 'but I sure got my man.'

CHAPTER FORTY

The detectives went back to the taskforce offices and discussed what Rob had seen of Andersson in the hotel, briefing the rest of the taskforce and swearing them to secrecy, as far as Rob's abilities were concerned. He tried several more times with the hairs to see where Andersson was, but he remained asleep on each occasion.

Rob, Clare, and the rest of the protection team didn't reach the Hilton until seven that night and ordered dinner, which consisted of a variety of meals from a Chinese banquet, to a thick porterhouse steak. Each of them ate with enthusiasm, talking and conversing with hope for the first time in what seemed an age.

Ray and Peter joined them later on, looking for some cheerful company, having been the bringers of terrible news to the families of the slain police officers at the Swedish embassy and were buoyed by the news Clare gave them about Rob being able to see FOTS and report on his movements. They commended Clare on her resourceful thinking and even allowed for a couple of bottles of wine to be brought up the suite to be shared between the lot of them, so that they were still alert and sober enough to perform their duty, should they be called upon.

Rob ate some fried rice and went to sleep in one of the bedrooms, feeling exhausted. Clare promised to wake him in a couple of hours and, although he didn't look forward to going back and spending more time with Andersson, or Haziz, or whatever his name was, he was motivated by the fact that it was a noble enterprise and would in the end, save a lot of lives, even if it took his.

Rob fell into the dream, almost as if he was slipping underwater and the sensation wasn't in the least unpleasant. He found himself in a familiar desert, sitting around a campfire with a group of Aboriginal people he'd met before, when he'd come there awaiting judgement in what they had called the Blackfella Court.

'Hello, Rob,' said Cameron, looking at him with his compassionate brown eyes, 'we've been waiting for you.'

'Hi,' replied Rob, looking at each of them in turn and feeling the warmth of their unique magic flowing through him, giving him new energy. 'Why have I been brought here?'

'We didn't bring you here,' said Emu, 'you brought us here. You have a powerful magic, Rob, which reaches far, even into the next plane of existence. When you call us, we come. It is simple as that.'

'Why would I do that?' Rob asked them. 'I don't remember calling you.'

'Because you need us,' replied Snake. 'It was not you exactly that called us, but your spirit.'

'Aren't I my spirit?' Rob asked them feeling somewhat confused by the conversation.

Hoppy laughed in his child-like way. 'Ah, whitefella,' he said, 'you're pretty dumb, aren't you?'

'Yeah, I guess so,' replied Rob who also started laughing. 'I can't even fix cars.'

'Remember last when you were in the desert,' said the boy, 'and you gave a bit of your spirit to the Mother in exchange for some of hers?'

'Yeah, I remember that like it was yesterday. She was beautiful, a secret lake in the middle of the desert, and she spoke to me.'

'Well, the time has come for you to retrieve that piece of your spirit,' said Cameron, 'and to give back to Mother what rightfully belongs to her. You'll also need that piece of spirit to pass into the next world, when it's your time to go.'

'Are you telling me that I'm going to die, too? I seem to have been getting that message from a few places, lately.'

'You must go,' said Cameron pointing off into the desert, 'time is growing short, and soon you must wake from your sleep.'

'You're not telling me I have to walk across the desert again, are you? I remember that walk and it bloody near killed me.'

Deuce, the one member of the group who'd remained quiet, stood. 'You're in a dream, Rob, you can fly with me,' he said as he jumped up into the air, transformed into a majestic eagle, and took off into the sky.

'Go,' said Cameron, 'fly with him.'

Rob imagined himself to be flying, and as soon as the thought entered his head, he lifted up off the ground, and rose up into the air, where he remained hovering over the campfire and the little group of dark-skinned people.

'Go,' said Hoppy, pointing his finger at the quickly departing eagle, 'you can do it, whitefella.'

Rob looked at the eagle, which was rapidly disappearing into the distance and thought about moving in that direction. He started to move and gather speed. He thought about going faster and soon he was soaring through the desert as though he'd been strapped to a rocket. He quickly caught up to Deuce and slowed down so the two of them could fly abreast.

'This is good, isn't it?' Deuce asked him, although his beak didn't seem to utter any actual words.

'How are you talking to me?' Rob asked. 'I didn't see your mouth move at all.'

Deuce laughed. 'This is a dream, Rob. Anything is possible. Imagine you're talking to me and I'll hear your thoughts and you, mine.'

Rob looked down at the magnificent expanse of the desert below him, with its yellows, its reds, which all seemed to blend, separated by the green of the grasses and the vegetation, like some profound painting no artist could ever really convey.

'I forgot how beautiful it is out here. I don't know how I could have.'

'We simply see the world we live in,' said the eagle, 'and right now, you live in another world. I don't think you ever really forget, it's just that the memories become dimmer when you move away from the experience.'

'Yeah, I guess you're right,' said Rob as he swooped down closer to the ground and watched the desert go by, trying to take in every detail as it passed by.

'We need to stop here,' said Deuce, pointing with his wing to a set of large orange boulders, which signified the entrance to the Mother. 'We must dance first, to show our respect before we go to see her. It's the done thing.'

The two of them glided down to the ground and Deuce resumed his human form. 'Wait here,' he said as he gathered a couple of sticks from the base of a desert oak and returned. 'Follow my steps.'

'I remember doing this, when I was here before.'

'Follow my steps,' repeated Deuce as he began to sing a song in a language that Rob didn't understand. He then began tapping the sticks and performing series of intricate steps.

Rob followed, but this time, it seemed easier than when he'd performed the dance in the desert all that time ago and soon he was moving in unison with Deuce, letting his body flow with the song and enjoying himself immensely. Just when it seemed that he had the hang of the dance, the singing stopped and Deuce handed him one of the sticks.

'Do you remember how the ceremony finishes?'

'Of course,' replied Rob, 'we snap the sticks together so that they can't be used again for the same dance.'

'That's right. So, on my count of three, we'll break them.' Deuce counted and then the two of them broke the sticks over their knees and threw them out into the desert. Deuce smiled. 'You've done well.'

The pair walked around to the back of one of the boulders and descended for about five minutes until they reached the Mother. Rob looked out at the enormous lake before him, which seemed even larger than when he'd last visited.

'Is she bigger? She seems larger than when I was here last.'

'No,' replied Deuce. 'Perhaps, it's the memory of her that has grown dim in your mind, so that she seems bigger now. She's the same size and will always remain who she is.'

Rob moved over to the edge of the water and dipped his hand into the cool liquid. 'Hello, Mother,' he said in greeting. He felt the slight electrical charge run up his arm and found it exhilarating and felt her speak to him, offering a greeting through their touch.

'You need to swim in her,' said Deuce, 'and hurry, because your dream is almost done.'

He began to undress, but was stopped by Deuce. 'Rob, you're in a dream, remember, you can just think your clothes off.'

Rob imagined himself naked and in an instant saw his clothes gathered in a pile on the ground beside him. He took a running jump and splashed down into the lake, going deep underwater at first and then with a few easy strokes, breaking the surface. He laughed aloud when he felt the electricity of the Mother surge all around his body and felt her talk to him through the water.

'So, you have come to reclaim the part of your spirit you gave to me. Your time in this plane is soon to end.'

'Yes,' said Rob. 'I can feel it coming toward me and to tell you the truth, I'm a bit scared of dying, even though it doesn't seem that bad.'

'Death is a matter of perspective,' said the Mother. 'I was once a being like you, but I've transformed into what I am now.'

'You mean you reincarnated into a lake?'

The Mother laughed and Rob felt it through his body, reverberating through the pores of his skin, touching his nerves like a shiver. 'Not quite, but you might say I died, that all of my people died and our knowledge was transferred into this water. I don't expect you to understand, it is a complex concept.'

'No, I don't understand completely,' said Rob, 'but I think I can see what you're getting at. You're saying that death is transference, from one thing to another.'

'That's close enough,' said the Mother. 'I am giving you back the part of yourself that you left with me and taking back that part of me that was put into you. You'll need this part of you to complete the task you have to undertake. That part of your spirit has been energised here, in this water, and it will help you to find the power you need.'

'Thanks. I could sure use some more energy, about now. I've been feeling pretty exhausted of late.'

'I know,' said the Mother, 'that is why you called out, to find the missing part of yourself.'

Rob began to feel a build up of electricity in the water, and then saw a bright light appear at the far side of the lake. It approached him, circled around him a few times and then flew up into the air and hovered above him, like a miniature sun. At the same time, he felt something leave him and swim off into the dark water, which he assumed was the part of the Mother that'd left this place with him so long ago.

As he watched, the light began to grow in intensity, until he had to turn his eyes away for fear of damaging his sight. Suddenly, it made a loud screeching sound and hit him fair in the chest, causing Rob to call out and fall back into the water for a few moments.

'It is done,' said the Mother. 'You are whole again.'

'I... feel... so... I can't even begin to describe it,' said Rob, almost delirious as he made his way to the bank of the lake. 'Thank you, Mother.'

'It is my pleasure, Rob,' replied the lake. 'We will not meet again on this plane, so I will say goodbye to you. It was good to know you and to have been a part of you. I will cherish the memory.'

'Yeah, so will I,' said Rob as he dragged himself out of the water and sat for while, looking at the glistening lake below him, trying to embed the scene into his mind, like a photo he could remember forever. He stood, wished himself dry and dressed, and found himself fully clothed in an instant. He turned to Deuce and smiled. 'Thank you for bringing me here, again.'

'It was you who brought me here,' replied Deuce. 'Thank you, Rob.'

'So, what do I do now?'

'Come on,' said Deuce, 'we need to get you back to your world and to do that, we need to go outside.'

The two of them began the climb to the top of the cavern and were soon standing out in the desert under the heat of the sun. 'Go now,' said Deuce. 'You need to return to where you came from.'

Rob offered his hand and the Aboriginal man took it in a firm grip and then the two of them embraced. 'Goodbye, my friend, you are a good man, Rob.'

'Rob... Rob... Rob,' repeated another voice, almost an echo of the voice, which came from Deuce. 'It's time to wake up,' said Clare.

Rob opened his eyes and could hardly believe the energy contained in his body so soon after waking. He sat bolt upright and faced the detective. 'Okay,' he said with a smile, 'let's see what that bastard's up to.'

Clare produced the evidence bag, broke the seal at the top, and emptied the hairs onto Rob's palm.

Rob closed his hand around them and found himself again in the hotel room of Mark Andersson. He stood in the corner of the room and watched him sleep as the soft sound of a television came blurred through the walls, emanating from the room next door. He looked around again, hoping to see something he might have missed on his previous visits, which might tell him where he was, but the outcome of the effort was be exactly the same. There was nothing in the room that gave the slightest indication as to the location or address of the hotel. 'Damn,' he said to himself as he sat down on a chair, close to the bed.

He watched as Mark stirred and woke. He ran his hand through his hair and looked at his watch to see it was nine in the evening. He stood up off the bed, opened a suitcase that seemed to contain all manner of personal belongings, and retrieved a clock radio, which he plugged in and set to the correct time, synchronising it with his watch. He set the alarm on the clock for seven the next morning and placed it on the chair in which Rob sat, passing it through his ghostly form as if he wasn't there and then went back to sleep, a slight smile upon his lips.

He willed himself back to his own hotel room at the Hilton, looking up at Clare who waited for his return, sitting on the edge of the bed and talking on her phone. She hung up when she heard Rob stir and turned to face him, her face full of expectation and questions.

'I don't think anything's going to happen until at least seven in the morning,' said Rob sitting up. 'I saw him set a clock radio and then go back to sleep.'

'I guess it's the quiet before the storm,' said Clare. 'At least we can all get some sleep tonight, to be ready for tomorrow. I think it's going to be a big day, one way or another.'

'Yeah, the biggest,' said Rob in agreement. 'I can't say I'm looking forward to it, but at the same time, I wish it was already over.'

'I know exactly what you mean,' said Clare.

'Any of that food left over?' Rob asked her. 'I feel, suddenly, very hungry.'

'I think there's still some food in the fridge. You can nuke it with the microwave, out in the kitchen.

'Great,' said Rob as he jumped off the bed and left the room.

Clare watched him go and had the strangest feeling Rob was somehow different, in a way she couldn't quite explain. She shrugged and stood, thinking the idea of food wasn't a bad one and headed out to the kitchen as well.

CHAPTER FORTY-ONE

At quarter to seven, Clare woke Rob on the lounge room sofa, where he'd dozed off while watching an old Humphrey Bogart movie. 'I love Casablanca,' he'd told her enthusiastically, 'it's a bit of a favourite.'

Russell, who was sleeping next to Rob, stirred and opened his eyes. 'Is it time?'

'Yeah,' replied Clare,'

'All right,' said Rob sitting up on the sofa and rubbing his eyes, 'let's get this over with.'

Clare handed him the hairs from the evidence bag and Rob again travelled to Andersson's room. He sat beside the bed, watching the digital readout on the clock and the minutes pass for something to do. He looked down at Mark, sleeping peacefully on his back, the whisper of a snore coming from his mouth and wondered just what went on his mind. It was strange, he thought, that when people slept, they didn't seem the least bit harmful and the expression on his face was one of peace and tranquillity.

At seven o'clock, the alarm buzzed next to the bed and Mark stuck an arm out, pressed the snooze button, and went back to sleep for another agonising ten minutes, while Rob continued to wait to see what would eventuate and for some sign to tell him where he was.

At last, the alarm sounded again and this time, Mark sat up, stretched his arms, and yawned. He got out of bed and made himself a strong black coffee, using the cup and jug, which must have come with the room and complimentary condiments, contained in a dirty little bar fridge that stood against the far wall.

He sat back down on the bed, switched the clock over to the radio setting, and drank his coffee while he listened to the morning news. He turned up the volume listening intently to a story about the morning's memorial service that was to take place at St. Paul's Cathedral. The broadcaster informed that the police killed in the Swedish embassy blast were also to receive a eulogy from the prime minister for their bravery, along with the Swedish ambassador who'd also lost his life.

Mark laughed. 'It will be your last official duty, Mr. Prime Minister,' he whispered to the radio. After finishing his coffee, he left the cup on the chair beside the bed, turned down the volume on the radio, stood, and retrieved his pants from hanger behind the door. He reached into the pocket and pulled out a disposable mobile phone, which he switched on and dialled a number. He waited for a moment and then spoke to another person on the end of the line.

'Is Knight done?'

Rob couldn't hear the reply, but knew as soon as Mark smiled that Chris Knight was dead. 'Shit,' he said, 'this bastard has connections everywhere.' He'd have to remember to tell Clare about the phone, and the number Mark had called, so a trace could be organised and the people responsible for Knight's death, arrested for what they'd done. Mark listened for a while longer and laughed at whatever the other person told him and then hung up the phone, looking very pleased with what had happened.

Andersson put the phone back into his pants pocket and laughed. 'Just what he deserved,' he said to himself, which Rob presumed was about the manner in which Chris Knight had met his demise.

Rob watched as Mark went to the other side of the room and used a key from around his neck to open the silver case. He lifted the case up onto the bed and put the key into a socket somewhere inside and turned it, so that a number of bright red digital readouts lit up, registering all zeros across them. He reached up into the lid of the case and pulled off an envelope taped to the roof, which he opened and pulled out a single piece of paper, on which

Rob, looking over his shoulder, saw three lines atop of each other each containing a series of numbers.

Mark proceeded to enter the numbers into the digital readouts, one at a time, and then set the timer for two hours and forty-five minutes.

'Oh, shit,' said Rob, feeling almost sick with panic, 'he's armed the nuke. I have to get back and tell Clare and the others. He looked at the clock, saw that it was seven thirty-two, and knew that it was set to go off for ten-fifteen, a quarter of an hour after the beginning of the memorial service.

When he was finished, Mark closed the case, dressed in a robe, which he brought out of his clothes case, grabbed a toiletries bag, and strolled down the hallway to the bathroom, whistling a tune as he went.

Rob followed him and looked around, but could see nothing on the inside of the hallway or in the bathroom that contained the name of the hotel. He swore and decided to go back to Clare while Mark was busy in the bathroom. When he arrived back at the Hilton, his panic was such he could hardly get the words out. It took him a few moments to slow his breathing as he collapsed onto the sofa and gratefully accepted a drink of water brought to him by Annie, which he gulped down.

'He's armed the device,' said Rob. 'It's set to go off at ten-fifteen.'

'Fuck,' said Russell. 'Clare, phone Ray and let him and Peter Bell know what's going on. We're going to have to do something to evacuate the cathedral and the surrounding areas.'

'We'll never be able to do it,' said Clare. 'Look,' she added as she turned on the television and saw the crowds already gathered in the city centre. 'There's a hundred thousand people there now and more coming in all the time. Most of them have taken public transport, so they can't get out of the city quickly, and if we warn them, there's going to be a panic that's going to kill thousands in the rush, and it might force Andersson to set it off sooner. We'll never have enough people or transport to move them all in time, not even a fraction of them. We have to find him, before he gets to the cathedral, or better still, the city centre.'

'He's got a key he wears around his neck,' said Rob, 'to turn it on, and there's a piece of paper with the arming codes written down. If we can get them before he detonates it, we might have a chance to shut it down.'

'Could you tell where he was?' Russell asked.

'No,' replied Rob despondently, 'I'm sorry, but I can go back, at least a few more times, while my strength holds out.'

'Okay,' said Clare, 'have a rest for a little while, Rob. We don't want to use you up too soon. We'll wait another half hour and then you can go back and see what he's doing. I suspect that he'll wait until the last minute to make his approach to the city, so there'll be no time to stop the detonation, but if we can get him on his way...'

'That's right,' said Russell, 'once he leaves the hotel, Rob can go with him and let us know the streets he's passing.'

'Jesus,' said Clare, already feeling herself beginning to perspire despite the air conditioner running in the suite, 'this is going to be close.'

'Too fucking close,' said Russell. 'Way too fucking close.'

CHAPTER FORTY-TWO

Mark left the bathroom after showering, feeling good about himself and about what he was about to do. He returned to his room and changed his clothes, putting on a shirt and tie and then his pants that were hanging on the back of the door. He searched the bottom of his suitcase and found one of his many passports, which he took out and placed on the bed. He then dug back into the case and found a razor sharp scalpel, which he put next to the bed, along with tube of superglue.

He then searched his jacket, found Leigh Best's federal police identification, and placed it beside the passport. With practiced hands, he removed the photo from the ID using the scalpel and then the photo from his passport. He thought he could probably have passed for Mr. Best in a pinch, late at night with a surrounding darkness, to the eyes of a tired officer, but in the cold light of day, he knew it just wouldn't do.

He managed to remove the plastic covering from the photo by carefully slitting open the top of the plastic and then putting his own photo inside, easing it down with his fingers so it didn't crease. He used a thin line of superglue to stick the plastic back to the main ID, wiped the excess off with a tissue, and then left it to dry for a few minutes. Once inside the plastic covering, it would pass at a glance and that was all he needed.

While he was waiting, he went back to his suitcase and removed a set of contact lenses, and went to the mirror beside the bed and inserted them so that his eyes were now a light shade of green and used an eyeliner pencil to colour his brows back to their original brown. He looked at himself and smiled.

'Hello, Mr. Best,' he said to his reflection. Mark grabbed a towel, placed it over his shirt, grabbed a set of electrical clippers from his case, and shaved his head. He then lathered it up, using shaving soap and used a disposable razor to remove any tuffs of remaining hair, so it seemed as if he was completely bald. He wiped of the last of the soap off with his towel and then looked at himself once more. 'Good job,' he said.

Once he was done, he packed up all of his belongings back into the case and put the superglue and the covered scalpel into the pocket of his pants to use later on. He put on his shoulder holster and Leigh's gun, which he took from out of the lid compartment of the case, making sure the firearm was fully loaded, then placed his jacket over the top of his clothes, and made ready to leave.

He took the silver suitcase out to the car park, placed it in the trunk, and at the same time removed the two Kevlar vests and a shotgun, which he placed on the back seat, covering the gun with the vests. He returned to his room, took the second suitcase down to the car, and placed that into the trunk as well. He got into the car and started the engine, leaving the hotel behind and driving to a shopping mall, two suburbs down in Box Hill, arriving just on eight-forty five, thinking he'd made good time. He left the car in the underground car park and walked inside, feeling the coolness of the air conditioning as he entered and sighing.

He went straight to his intended destination and purchased a large, blue cloth wheelie-case, big enough to cover the silver case, from a backpacker store. He paid the woman, who noticed his gun under his jacket and smiled as he produced his police identification.

'Yeah, I'm off on a conference,' he lied to her as he accepted a receipt for his cash payment, which he threw into the first bin he passed on his way back to the car.

He put the case onto the backseat and drove the car to a local park, stopped and reached over and retrieved one the vests, which he placed onto the passenger seat and then removed the scalpel and superglue from his pocket. With great care, he cut around the large yellow lettering that said POLICE on the front, and threw the rest of the vest onto the floor of the car. He then jumped out of the car for a moment and removed the wheelie-case, which he put onto the front passenger seat and then went back to the driver's side.

Mark opened the tube of superglue, trailed it along the back of the POLICE patch, and then held it firmly against the front of the wheelie case until it adhered tightly to the cloth. He put the tube and the scalpel into the ashtray and waited, lighting up and finishing a cigarette before he got out of the car, opened the trunk, and placed the silver case inside the wheelie-case. He stopped the car at a bin prior to leaving the park, threw away the used vest, the scalpel, and the tube of superglue, and looked at his watch. It was nine-thirty and about time to make his move. He put the car into gear and headed for the city.

CHAPTER FORTY-THREE

'Okay,' said Clare, 'are you about ready to go again?'

'Yeah,' replied Rob finishing the last of his coffee. 'No time like the present.'

Clare placed the hairs back into Rob's palm. He closed his fingers around them and noticed it took a while before he found himself outside the hotel in the car park and saw that Andersson was just about to drive off in a white Commodore. He rushed for the car and dove through the metal into the backseat, where he saw two police vests and a shotgun.

Without warning, Rob was all of a sudden back in the hotel suite, looking at the detectives who sat close to him on the sofa. 'What happened? Why are you back so soon?' Clare asked.

'I don't know,' replied Rob feeling confused and disoriented. He looked down at his hand and noticed that the hairs had slipped from his palm.

'Shit,' said Clare looking down at the floor, 'where are they?

'Don't move,' said Russell, 'everybody keep perfectly still. Russell leaned over Rob and tried to see if he could spot them, but they were gone, swallowed by the lightly coloured carpet on the floor. 'I can't see them anywhere,' he said getting down onto his hands and knees.

'Me either,' said Clare who got down to join him.

'I'm so sorry,' said Rob who leaned down to see if he could spot them, but to no avail. 'I feel really bad about this.'

'Oh, well,' said Clare, 'I guess it can't be helped, you were in a trance, but did you see anything before you came back?'

'Yeah, I did,' replied Rob who went onto tell them about landing on the police vests in the back of the white Commodore. 'I think he looked different, too, as if his head was shaved, but I only saw the back of him.'

Russell looked at Rob curiously. 'Did you say a white Commodore?'

'Yeah, that's right. I remember it distinctly.'

'I bet he's got Leigh Best's federal police car,' said Russell, 'and maybe he has his ID as well.'

'That makes sense,' said Clare. 'It hasn't yet been confirmed the car was crushed under the embassy and both Leigh's and Eddie's bodies were badly burned, along with their clothes, so nobody would've checked for their identification if there was nothing to check for.'

'We need to get to the cathedral,' said Russell, 'right bloody now.'

All of the detectives and Rob rushed to the door of the suite and took the staircase downstairs, instead of using the lifts. Clare used her mobile as she ran and called Ray and told him what was going on.

'We think Andersson's got Leigh Best's car and probably his or Eddie's ID. Can you put an alert out straight away? He's probably headed for the city as we speak, but make sure no one tries to arrest him, he might destroy the arming codes and the key if he thinks he's been caught, that is, if he even has them on him.'

'Okay,' replied Ray, 'not a problem. What does Rob say?'

'We can't rely on Rob's visions anymore to find him,' replied Clare as she pushed open the door to the ground level and stopped for a moment catch her breath. 'It's a long story, but we're on our own.'

'All right, whatever you say, Clare, whatever you need.'

Russell pulled up to her with a screech of tyres. 'Jump in,' he called out. Clare bolted for the car and jumped into the backseat, alongside Rob and Annie. Josie sat in front passenger seat, both checking her gun and talking on her phone simultaneously. 'Okay, Marcus, June and Le Mar will meet us a block away from the cathedral. I think it'd be better if we go there on foot, instead of going in all gung-ho, sirens blaring and all that. We don't want him to know we're onto him.'

'My thoughts, exactly,' said Clare as she reached for the seatbelt and then began checking her weapon.

'Hold on,' said Russell, 'this is going to be on hell of a ride.'

'Punch it, Russell,' Clare yelled. 'We have to get there before him.'

Josie reached out and slammed the portable blue light onto the roof and hit the siren. At the same time, Russell pressed down hard on the accelerator of the car, sending the Commodore rocketing forward, leaving a trail of smoke behind in its wake.

The police cars took the three levels of the underground car park at speed, drifting and squealing the tyres in the turns as they made for the entry gate. Once there, they pulled up briefly and the attendant asked for their entry ticket.

'We're the fucking police!' Russell yelled at him.

Josie leaned over Russell and pointed her Glock at the attendant. 'Open the fucking gate now, or I'll kill you!'

The attendant looked down and saw Clare, Annie, and Josie all pointing guns directly at him, dived into the office, and hit the open button for the boom gate.

Russell pulled the car to the end of the driveway, slowed briefly, and when the oncoming traffic stopped to let him through, he floored the accelerator again and went speeding off into the city followed by June at the wheel of the other car.

CHAPTER FORTY-FOUR

Mark took the freeway to the city, knowing at this time of day, after peak hour, the traffic would be much simpler to navigate. Besides which, just about everybody who was going to the city was already there, thinking they were attending a memorial service, but really they were just waiting to die, although none of them knew that. He smiled at the thought of the looks on their surprised faces when the bomb detonated and they were all vaporised in the blink of an eye, not even long enough to say, Oh, shit!

He glided up onto the Box Hill on-ramp and switched on the radio as he hit the open road. He looked at the clock in the dash and saw that it was just nine thirty-five, and estimated that it would take him fifteen minutes to get to Hoddle Street in Clifton Hill and another ten minutes to get to the cathedral, leaving him about fifteen minutes to plant the bomb and get the hell out of there. He listened to the news and shook his head in embarrassment to learn that another suicide bomber had killed himself in Iraq, blowing apart a café and some innocent men and women. *What an idiot*, thought Mark. That man just wasted his life for a few measly peasants.

'There wasn't notable victim among them and now, he's dead. I'm completely different. I'm going to blow the hell out of the prime minister and his senior cabinet members and I'm going to get away with it and do it all over again, someday. When I get back to Afghanistan, they'll hail me as a hero. I might even kill that fucker of a

Prophet and take his place. Why isn't he here doing this instead of me? Lazy piece of shit.'

He switched the station and found some classical music. He liked the classics; they reminded him of Petra and her superb ability to play the violin, long ago in Sweden. That was before she became a radical and put the violin down, to learn how to make bombs instead of music.

He pulled the car over to the left side of the freeway and took the Clifton Hill Street off-ramp. He turned left and headed up Hoddle Street, passing the railway station and stopped at a set of lights. He looked ahead, saw the traffic had come to a standstill, and wondered why. As he got further down the road, he realised there was a checkpoint and that all the car incoming cars to the city were being stopped and the drivers questioned. He hoped his false identification would be enough to get him through without any hassles and felt that it was so close enough to perfect that it would take a close examination to see through it.

As he approached the checkpoint, he felt as if something was wrong. It was as if the police knew his car or that something wasn't quite right. They moved him through the checkpoint almost without a second glance, too easily accepting his identification and explanation that he was part of the anti-terrorist contingent of the federal police and headed to the city to undertake security of the memorial service. However, when he looked into the rear-view mirror he saw several of the police went straight to their radios as he passed them, as if they were reporting on his progress towards the city and the direction he was taking. Mark looked at his watch and swore. He was behind time. It was almost five minutes to ten.

He pulled up at a second set of lights, looked casually into the rear-view mirror and saw several police cars farther down the line of traffic behind him, trying to keep him in sight without actually arresting him. Why would they do that? he wondered and then he thought they must think he had some way of turning off the device, but couldn't figure out how they knew about him driving this car or assuming Leigh Best's identity. The embassy was still in ruins and the cars beneath it were still buried under tonnes of rubble and Leigh's body would have had the clothes burned from off it and the ID, too. No one would have, or could have checked to see if it was missing. It was then that it suddenly hit him.

'Rob fucking Swift,' he said, banging on the steering wheel of the car. 'That fucking prick got hold of something of mine in the apartment! I wonder how long he's been watching me. Are you here, now, Swift? If you are, well, you can just go fuck yourself.'

Mark jerked the wheel to the right and sped out into oncoming traffic, dodging through cars and trucks coming toward him. He looked behind and saw the police cars that'd been tailing him, also pull out, their lights on and sirens blaring as they raced after him.

Mark hit the lights and siren inside the car and took off up the wrong side of Station Street, towards the cathedral. He skidded left into Swanston Street, passing the Royal Melbourne Institute of Technology, almost knocking over a group of students casually walking across the street, but managed to jump out of his way at the last moment. He veered to the correct side of the road again and ran up onto the footpath, passing a set of lights that would've slowed him down and knocking over some vacant tables at a café. He slammed the car back down onto the road and hit a bunch of pedestrians waiting at a tram stop, driving straight over them, mangling their bodies and killing several of them in the process.

Mark looked up and saw the cathedral only a few hundred feet away. He began to laugh manically and pressed his foot down harder onto the accelerator. 'I guess there's no getting out of this, now,' he said as he brought the car to a grinding halt in Flinders Street, opposite the entrance to the magnificent church. He looked at the clock on the dashboard and saw that it was after ten already and revved the engine of the car. 'Funny how time flies when you're having fun,' he said and began laughing at his own sarcasm.

Ahead of him, he saw Clare Carbone and several other detectives step out from behind a parked car and point their pistols directly at him. 'Fucking bitch,' he said to himself. 'I should have taken you, instead of that weakling, Green.'

'Give it up, Andersson,' shouted Clare, 'we've got you.'

Mark revved the engine of the car again, making it sound like some sort of angry beast, but remained where he was. It was as if he and Clare were the bull and matador, each of them readying themselves for the final charge. Mark raised his gun and aimed it at Clare through the side window of the car and fired, causing the detectives to take cover, but the bullet went wide, due to the angle of the shot.

Mark revved the engine again and looked at his watch. There were only eight minutes to go, anybody in the near vicinity was going to die, and there was nothing anybody could do about that. He spun the wheels on the car and caused a thick cloud of smoke to envelope him, in order to provide cover and then put the car into gear and headed straight for the entrance to the cathedral, intent on ramming through the front doors and getting himself inside.

'Look out,' Russell yelled as the car came careening out of the smoke, jumped up onto the sidewalk and smacked straight into the entrance of the cathedral, causing the wooden doors to splinter and explode and a tonne of bricks and mortar to fall from the foundations, creating a thick choking smoke that enveloped everything and made it almost impossible to see.

Clare and Russell approached the car on opposite sides with their guns drawn. 'Get out of the car... now!'

Russell shouted to the driver's side. 'With your hands above your head.'

'Sorry, Detective,' said a man's voice from further inside the deserted cathedral, 'but I'm afraid nobody's home in there. You're going to have to come up here to see me... you see, I've moved.'

The two detectives moved further inside and hid behind the pews in the last row of the church, just inside the entrance, while Josie, Annie, and Rob waited near the car. June and Marcus went to the back of the church.

'Tick, tick, tick,' said Mark. 'Time is slipping away.'

'Give it up, Haziz,' shouted Clare. 'You're not going to kill the prime minister. In fact, you never did have a chance. He was never going to be here.'

Mark fired a shot in their direction, but with the smoke still clinging to the air, he had no chance of finding his mark, anymore than Clare or Russell did of returning fire.

'Well, that's a shame,' said Andersson, 'because I was so looking forward to killing him. I guess I'm just going to have to settle for destroying the city, instead. I see you know my real name, too. You're a smart girl, Clare.'

'Smarter than you, you dumb fuck,' replied Clare, distracting Andersson while Russell moved to the side of the church and up a few more pews toward where Mark was situated.

'Hey, Haziz,' said Russell, 'how about you put down your gun and we talk about all of this, like civilised human beings?'

'That's a good idea,' replied Mark with a laugh. 'You put yours down first and then I'll do the same.'

Clare moved to the opposite far wall of the church and further inside, covering the sound of her footsteps with Mark's voice as he spoke.

'I can't do that,' replied Russell. 'I'm afraid I wouldn't be covered by workers compensation if I put down my gun and then you shot me. They'd say it was my fault for getting shot in the first place.'

'Very smart... what did you say your name was?'

'I didn't, but just for the record, it's Russell.'

'So, where's your friend, Clare, the marvellous Rob Swift? I thought he'd be with you.'

'I'm here,' said Rob, ducking into the back row of the church pews and taking Clare's original position. He took out his gun, and although he didn't think he could do much good with it, it at least made him feel a little secure.

'Keep him talking,' whispered Annie, falling in beside Rob, followed by Josie, 'we're going to follow Clare and Russell.'

'So, you know me, do you?' Rob asked through the cloud of smoke.

'Of course,' replied Mark with a laugh. 'Tony Green was very complimentary towards you when I tortured him.'

'I guess it's good to have fans,' said Rob watching Annie and Josie disappear into the smoke.

'Oh, yes, I'm a big fan,' said Mark, 'and I'll remain so for the three minutes, or so. After that, though, I'm afraid all bets are off.'

A sudden shot rang out of the smoke, followed quickly by another. 'Stay right where you are,' said Clare, 'because it wouldn't take much for me to kill you, right now.'

'Okay, come on up,' said Russell's voice through the smoke, 'we've got him.'

Rob found the centre aisle and walked up to the front of the church, followed by Ray and Peter who'd been waiting at the front door to make a move inside. The two of them ran ahead of Rob and up to the top of the church, where the shaven headed Arkmed Haziz also known as

Mark Andersson was lying on the floor, bleeding from a stomach wound.

He laughed at the lot of them. 'What have we got left, about two minutes?'

'Where are the disarming codes?' Ray asked as he rammed the barrel of his gun into Andersson's forehead. 'Tell me, now, or I'll fucking shoot you.'

'Why don't you ask your pet psychic, Rob Swift?' Andersson spat back.

'Tell me where the fucking codes and the key are, now,' Clare said as she raised her gun and pointed it at his knee.

'Fuck you, slut,' replied Mark.

Clare pulled the trigger on her gun and shot him in the left knee, causing Andersson to cry out with pain, and then pointed it at the other knee. 'We don't have time for this. Tell me where they are!'

'They're gone,' replied Andersson wincing with pain. 'I flushed them down the toilet and threw the key into the rubbish. I'm afraid we're all going to go up in a big fireball in about ninety seconds.'

'Well, I'm afraid you're not going to see the fireworks,' Clare said as she raised her gun and shot Andersson twice in the head.

Russell grabbed Clare and kissed her passionately on the mouth. 'I've wanted to do that since I first met you,' he said as he held her in his arms, 'and I'm glad it's going to be the last thing I probably ever do.'

'I don't know about you lot,' said Ray, 'but I'm going to make a run for the train station across the road, it seems like a better idea than just standing here waiting for it to come.'

'I'm with you,' said Peter.

'Me too,' said Josie

'Sounds like plan,' agreed Annie, 'a doomed plan, but a plan, nonetheless.'

'Same with me,' said Marcus who came running from the rear of the church and was the first down the aisle, followed by June.

Russell took Clare's hand. 'Come on,' he said.

The detectives started running from the church, when Clare looked back and saw Rob still standing there. 'Come on,' she urged him.

'You go,' said Rob. 'I've got an idea. If the place hasn't blown up in the next two minutes, come back and see if it's worked.'

'I'm not leaving you,' said Clare. 'What's the idea?'

'Ah, fuck it,' said Russell, 'I guess I'm staying, too.'

Rob undid the zipper of the wheelie-case and pulled out the device. He opened it up and saw that there were twenty seconds remaining on the digital readout. 'I hope this works,' he said to the others as he sat down beside the bomb, closed his eyes and concentrated for all that he was worth.

Clare and Russell watched in utter amazement as an electrical sphere, about six feet in diameter slowly developed around the outside of the case. It sparked blue, red, and orange in different places and seemed to pulsate with a heartbeat as if it was alive. Their jaws dropped in further astonishment as the time for the detonation came and went and there was no explosion.

Clare looked inside the sphere and saw that the digital readout had stopped at two seconds. 'What did you do, Rob?'

Rob opened his eyes and immediately, both Clare and Russell could see the strain on his face in having to maintain the energy of the sphere. 'It's something I learned while I was in Tibet. Time inside the sphere is suspended, but I can't hold it off forever, it's very draining. We need to get a chopper in here and drop this in the ocean, or somewhere it can't do any harm.'

'Hurry,' said Russell, 'go and get Ray.'

At the sound of Russell's urging, she turned and ran, screaming out Ray's name at the top of her voice.

'You and Clare make a great couple,' said Rob smiling and closing his eyes as he focussed his energies.

'She's an amazing woman,' said Russell, 'I should ever be so lucky.'

'Look after her,' said Rob with a sad smile. 'Maybe, name one your kids after me, when I'm gone.'

'You're not going anywhere, Rob.'

'Yeah, I'm gonna to die today. I have to make a choice soon and I know what it is now. I need you to explain to Clare why I did what I did. I had to.'

'Explain what?' Russell asked him.

'You'll see when it happens,' replied Rob. 'You might also want to take off Andersson's handcuffs and put his gun back in his hand. There might be come awkward questions asked if he's found the way he is now.'

'Good idea,' said the detective retrieving the terrorist's gun, removing his handcuffs, and placing the pistol near his hand. 'Who said you'd never make a cop?'

About two minutes later, Ray and the others ran back into the cathedral and stopped in their tracks, completely awestruck by the sight of the sphere. 'Jesus,' said Ray, 'I've never seen anything like it in my life.'

'Me either,' said Peter, 'it's bloody incredible.'

'What about the chopper?' Russell asked them.

'On its way,' replied Ray. 'It should be here in a couple of minutes, compliments of the commissioner. We need to get Rob and this … thing, out front.'

Rob opened his eyes and stood. He lifted his hand, palm upwards, and said the word, 'up,' to the sphere. The sphere lifted off the floor and hovered in midair, about four feet off the ground. Rob turned his palm and told the sphere to move and the great ball of energy began to travel in front of him as he directed it towards the entrance of the cathedral. The detectives followed behind in almost complete silence, mesmerised by the sight of the sphere, which seemed to exert an almost hypnotic hold over them and afraid any noise they made would disturb Rob's concentration.

Josie grabbed her phone and quietly snapped several pictures of the sphere. She whispered to Annie it was strange that the sphere didn't come out in any of the pictures, although the case inside it did.

'That's because it's spiritual energy,' said Rob. 'It can only be captured by the eyes and in your heart. Machines don't have the capacity to understand or observe it.'

When they reached the front entrance of the cathedral, they saw that police had blocked off both Flinders and Swanston Street, with police cars at each of the corners, so that the intersection was completely clear of traffic. Overhead, they heard the steady thump of the chopper blades as it made its way to the church.

Rob walked the sphere to the centre of the intersection amid the gasps and astonishment from the nearby crowds of people, who were completely unaware just how close they'd all coming to dying, or even what was inside the great ball of crackling light.

The helicopter landed in the centre of the intersection, the pilot got out, and spoke to Ray, who explained about the sphere, and told him that the plan was to drop it in the ocean, far enough away, so the radiation wouldn't affect the coastline.

'Got you,' said the pilot,' but I think it's going to be too big to fit inside.'

'That's okay,' said Rob, 'it'll travel on its own, outside the chopper. It just needs to be within about one hundred feet of where I am.'

'All right, you're the boss,' said the pilot. 'Let's go.'

Rob boarded the chopper and sat on the floor, his legs crossed and his eyes closed as though he were meditating. Clare, Russell, and Ray followed him, each taking seats and putting on headsets provided by the pilot, so they could talk between them.

Clare looked across at Rob and was worried. He seemed to be shrinking into himself right before her eyes, growing older with every passing minute, as if the energy it took to keep the case from exploding was draining his very life essence.

'Hurry,' she shouted out to the pilot, 'I don't think we have long.'

The helicopter took to the air and Russell watched out of the window in amazement as the sphere, too, lifted off the ground and began to shadow their every move, as though magnetized to the bottom of the chopper.

'Yep, it's coming with us,' he said as he took Clare's hand in his own.

The chopper flew above the city, passing over the great skyscrapers that made up the business district and the Melbourne Arts Centre, with its long, white pointed roof that reminded of Clare of those times as a child when she'd accidentally dropped a cookie in her milk and it splashed upwards.

Rob opened his eyes and, without speaking, looked down at the passing city, knowing this would probably be the last time he'd ever view it with the eyes of a living being. He tried to take in every detail, every passing car, every traffic light, and every ant-like person he could lay his eyes on. His only regret was he didn't get a chance to say goodbye to Michelle, his sister, and his nephew and niece, but at least, they'd know he gave his life in the service of others and hoped one day they'd be proud of him. He closed his eyes again and continued to focus what energy he had left.

'I'm going to head out to international waters,' said the pilot, 'to the continental shelf, where the water's deep.'

'Okay,' said Ray. 'What's our ETA?'

'About fifteen minutes, give or take a few minutes. How's he holding up?'

Ray looked at Rob and saw that he seemed to be deteriorating. His skin had turned a grey colour and dark patches had developed under his eyes, which weren't there a few moments ago. 'Not so good,' he said.

Clare unbuckled her seatbelt and moved over to where Rob sat and whispered in his ear. 'Is there anything we can do to help you, Rob?'

Rob opened his eyes and looked at her. They were bloodshot and it seemed to Clare that he was dying right in front of her. 'Yes,' he said. 'If you all join hands and then you take my hand, I can use some of your energy.'

'Did you hear that?' Clare asked the other two men over the headset.

Ray and Russell were already unbuckling their belts and moving forwards as she asked the question. The three of them took each other's hands and then Clare grabbed Rob's and held it tightly in her own.

'Jesus Christ,' Russell exclaimed as he felt the drain of energy that hit all three of them like a fist. 'I don't know how he got this far on his own.'

'Because he's special,' replied Clare as a tear fell from her eye.

'Hold on,' said Rob, using the contact to speak to each of their minds, 'it won't be long now.'

The three of them did as Rob asked and gave everything they could for the next fifteen minutes, until at last, the pilot informed that they'd reached the continental shelf.

Rob let go of Clare's hand and the three detectives collapsed to the ground, completely exhausted. 'Thank you,' he said as he rose and opened the door of the chopper, to see the sphere still intact and suspended about ten feet below where the chopper hovered. 'I have a choice to make. If I let the sphere go, I'll only be able to keep it intact for about a hundred feet and then it'll explode and destroy the chopper and kill you all, so my choice is simple: I need to go.'

'But we can get closer to the water,' protested Clare.

'I'm sorry,' said Rob with a sad smile. 'Be well,' he added and then jumped from the chopper and landed face down on the sphere. He heard Clare scream, but didn't look back, not wanting to see her in tears, preferring to remember the way he'd always known her; a tough and resilient woman, with the same sense of duty and responsibility he possessed. In time, she'd understand what he'd done and why he did it

Rob took a deep breath and let go of his hold on the sphere, sending it plummeting in a freefall towards the ocean. He felt it hit the water with a tremendous splash and then heard the chopper increase the power in its engines and make its escape from the area before it was too late.

As the sphere began to sink beneath the waves, he began to breathe deeply, saturating his lungs with oxygen and then just before he went under, he took one huge breath and held it. He used his fast depleting energies to increase the speed of the sphere, sending it down towards the bottom of the ocean. He looked backwards once and saw the sun, sparkling on the surface and then pressed his cheek into the body of the sphere. He felt the pressure of the water increase, as he got deeper, pushing down on his body with ever-increasing force and wished he had the energy to construct some sort of protective bubble for himself, but all of his ability was focussed on keeping the sphere together. He just needed to hold on for a little while longer, to let the chopper get as far away as it could before he finally gave up, let the bomb tick down, and detonate.

As the sphere travelled deeper, he found himself in complete darkness, feeling the pressure begin to press on him like a bone crushing vice, and knew that he must soon black out. He thought about Aroha and her beautiful smile, trying to keep himself awake. He thought about Clare, Russell and their child, his sister, his nephew, his baby niece and when finally, the weight of the ocean became too much for him to bear, and the pressure forced the air from his lungs, he gave up and breathed in the surrounding water. He felt himself lose his grip on the sphere and saw the digital readout reach zero and then there was a blinding, white flash …

CHAPTER FORTY-FIVE

Rob opened his eyes and saw that he was lying in a field. He sat up, looked around, and could hardly believe the beauty of the place. He watched the wind as it swirled listlessly through the grass, stirring each individual blade in just the slightest manner, the movement barely perceptible to the eye. From there, it moved upwards, touching the uppermost leaves on the trees in front of him, causing them to whisper in a language he couldn't discern.

Then it was quiet. It haunted him, the almost deafening sound of weighty stillness that surrounded him, covered him like a blanket, enveloping him. In that silent moment, it seemed as if the whole world was still, unmoving, stuck in an insurmountable void from which it could not escape. He held his breath fearing the utterance of inhalation would disturb the statue-like atmosphere of the moment and he would without knowing it commit a sin of unforgiveable imagining.

Then, in a sudden flurry of movement, the wind appeared again and he felt as if the world had returned to life. It moved the colourful flowers in a nearby field and rocked a branch on the tree above him, causing it to creak, as it moved back and forward, trying to relay to him a hidden code, which he was unable to ascertain. He listened to the wind and closed his eyes to gain the full effect of the sound, the gentle ethereal whisper, and flinched as it caressed his face, as if touched by the silken fingertips of an angel.

He looked up when he heard a voice and saw Aroha standing on a hill in the distance. He got up, started to walk towards her, and found he was capable of moving at incomprehensible speed, and was with her in less than a second. He took her in his arms and kissed her. 'I am dead, aren't I?

Aroha laughed and pulled him to her. 'Dead,' she said, 'is a state of mind. I prefer to say that you now exist on an alternative plane.'

'What is this place?'

'It's whatever you make it,' replied Aroha, smiling. 'Just try turning it into something else. I don't know... try the universe.'

Rob called up a picture in his mind from long ago of a photo he'd seen taken by the Hubble telescope. In the blink of any eye, the field disappeared and it seemed as if the whole universe was in front of him. He could see galaxies, comets, and stars that were burning out and others that were in the process of being born.

'Wow, that's amazing,' he said.

'You haven't seen anything yet,' said Aroha taking his hand. 'We can explore the whole universe together, and the good thing is that it's expanding at a rapid rate, so there's always something else to see, some new thing that has just developed. It goes on forever, Rob and we've got forever to explore it.'

'Can I see my parents and Tammy here, too? I want to do that before I take off anywhere.'

'Of course,' replied Aroha, 'but before you do that, there's something I have to show you, something you have to do.'

'What's that?'

'Come with me,' replied the beautiful Maori girl, taking his hand in her own, 'it won't take that long...'

EPILOGUE

Clare sat in the little chapel and listened to the preacher and the procession of people who stood behind the podium talk about Rob's life and the gift he'd given the people of Melbourne. Particularly moving was the eulogy, given by the prime minister who'd travelled from Canberra to be there. He spoke about Rob's bravery and his sense of self-sacrifice and announced that he was to receive the highest posthumous civilian bravery award for saving millions of lives. He presented the award to Michelle, his sister, who broke down in tears as she took it and held it to her chest, close to her heart.

The Victorian Police Commissioner, Ron Rouse, not be outdone, also praised Rob for what he'd done and told the gathered congregation Rob would also receive a posthumous award for outstanding bravery in the course of his police duties, and that there was a plan for a plaque to be erected in his honour at the newly refurbished St. Kilda Police station.

Clare herself had little to say, and told the crowd that she considered Rob to be a friend and that he thought it'd be the greatest honour to be simply known as a good bloke.

Later, the congregation gathered at Michelle's house for an informal wake.

Clare glanced at the elaborate food laid out and catered for by the prime minister's department and just didn't feel hungry at all. She looked around at the people who stood around chatting and could see their mouths moving, but she just couldn't hear their words. She kept picturing those last moments of Rob's life, the tremendous explosion and the water that shot hundreds feet up into the air and took his life, while she, Russell, and Ray made it away in the helicopter and looked on from a safe distance. Her guilt had been eating her up for days and she found it hard to forgive herself for not stoping him jump from the chopper, even though she knew he had no choice and had made up his mind to do it, even before he'd left the cathedral.

'Are you Clare?' asked Scott, Rob's nephew, as he took hold of her hand.

'Yes, that's right, I'm Clare, and you're Scott, aren't you?'

'Yep, that's me, all right,' said the little boy, smiling and pointing at his chest. 'Can you come with me?' he asked her and began tugging at her hand.

'Sure,' said Clare with a laugh. 'Where are we going?'

'Uncle Rob wants to talk to you out in the backyard.'

Clare was shocked when the words came out of the little boy's mouth. 'What did you say?'

'Go with him,' said Michelle, walking up and placing her hands on Scott's shoulders. 'He has Rob's gift. If he says Rob's out there, then he is. Go with him.'

Clare let the little boy lead her out into the backyard and into the shade of a large gum tree at the far side of the yard. 'There he is,' said Scott pointing to the base of the tree. 'I told you I'd bring her out here, Uncle Rob. Uncle Rob wants me to say something to you for him. He can't talk to you, because he's dead, you know.'

'Yeah, I know that,' replied Clare, who couldn't believe what she was hearing. 'What does he want to say?'

The little boy listened for a moment and then turned to Clare. 'He says you don't have to feel bad and it wasn't your fault. He did what he had to do.'

'I see,' said Clare. 'Is there anything else he wants to say?'

'He wants you to know that he's happy and he's back with Aroha, that's all.'

'Can you tell him that I said thank you?'

Scott laughed. 'He can hear you, silly, he just can't talk back, because he's dead, you know.'

Clare started to laugh. 'Yeah, you said that.'

'Uncle Rob said to say you're welcome,' said Scott, who turned and began walking back inside. 'He's gone now, and I want some more ice cream.'

Clare turned toward the back door, saw Russell standing there, and smiled. She still found it hard to get used to him not having a beard anymore, even though it'd been a couple of weeks since he'd shaved it off. She walked up to him and kissed him gently on the lips. He took her hand without saying a word and Clare was unsure whether he'd been privy to the conversation with Rob outside or not. She turned go back inside and out of the corner of her eye, she thought for a brief moment that she saw the faces of two people standing under the tree, but when she looked, she saw nothing and in the back of her mind somewhere, like a gentle breeze, she thought she heard the words, 'Be well.'

THE END

About R.B. Clague:

R.B. Clague was born and raised in Melbourne, Victoria. He attended Heidelberg Technical School and studied social sciences at Monash University. R.B's employment in a variety of fields throughout his career has included health care, child protection, forensic psychiatry, juvenile justice, community outreach, and youth residential work with several non-government agencies.

R.B. spent seven years, employed in various states and Territories around Australia as a probation and parole officer, including three years in Central Australia, where he worked with Aboriginal people on remote desert communities.

Other writing credits include: "Whitefella dreaming" "Desert of the Mind" "Sigh of the Wind" "Daisy" and "Twenty Twisted Tales". R.B. currently resides on the north coast of New South Wales, where he writes full-time. He always has several projects underway.

Social Media Links:

Website: www.rbclaguebooks.com

Facebook: https://www.facebook.com/RB-Clague-159705757406912/?ref=bookmarks

Instagram: https://www.instagram.com/r.b.clague/

Twitter: https://mobile.twitter.com/rbclague @RBClague

If you enjoyed this story, check out the other Solstice Publishing books by R.B. Clague:

Whitefella Dreaming (Rob Swift Book 1)

Just an average guy, Rob Swift has a great life - he works with Michael, his best friend, in a job he enjoys, and the love of his life, Aroha, lives just downstairs. On the way to work one morning, an Aboriginal man runs out in front of their car and is killed in a horrific accident. The accident also kills Michael and leaves Aroha in a coma. His life shattered, Rob can only hope Aroha will awaken. When her sleeping form is possessed, and she rises to declare her soul will remain in spiritual prison until Rob pays for his actions, it sends this average guy on an electrifying journey into the unknown, leaving him forever a changed man as he battles to save the woman he loves.

http://bookgoodies.com/a/B00YPWC8PE

Desert of the Mind (Rob Swift Book 2)

Rob Swift has just got his life together again after a life-altering journey through the wilds of central Australia. He has the woman of his dreams, a successful career, and a network of newfound friends.

The thing that sets Rob apart is his innate capacity to see the past, the future, and his ability to move almost effortlessly through the deserts of his mind. En route to a business conference in Melbourne, he is called on once again by the sorcerer to undertake a mysterious task: find one of his people, in the city, who has fallen into trouble.

Later, while using his gifts to help the police, Rob inadvertently stumbles into the mind of a psychopath, and is soon engaged in a deadly game of cat and mouse, with an adversary who possesses skills akin to his own.

Desert of the Mind is the second of four novels in the Rob Swift series.

http://bookgoodies.com/a/B0142ZNXQ6

Sigh of the Wind (Rob Swift Book 3)

After suffering a terrible tragedy, Rob Swift travels to a Tibetan monastery in order to train his psychic talents. Once there, he discovers his gifts have summoned him to this place of spiritual learning, along with others of similar ability. When Kenny, one of of the trainees becomes lost in his own psyche, it's up to Rob and Kate Cameron, another of the initiates, to enter his mind and bring him back - a feat only ever attempted once before by the Dalai Lama himself. The two of them must also race against time before they're pulled away from the real world and become lost in the illusion of a false reality.

http://bookgoodies.com/a/B01BYT68XI

Now I Lay Me Down To Sleep 10 Supernatural Bedtime Stories

Volume I is an exciting, scary, and sometimes funny collection of supernatural stories best read at night. Ten Solstice Publishing authors have written short stories about things that go bump in the night.

http://bookgoodies.com/a/B0155N5T9I